THE SWAN BOOK

OTHER BOOKS BY ALEXIS WRIGHT

Plains of Promise
Grog War
Croire En L'incroyable
Le pacte du serpent: arc-en-ciel
Take Power (as editor)
Carpentaria

THE SWAN BOOK

A NOVEL

ALEXIS WRIGHT

ATRIA BOOKS

NEW YORK LONDON TORONTO SYDNEY NEW DELHI

Wright

ATRIA BOOKS

An Imprint of Simon & Schuster, Inc.
1230 Avenue of the Americas
New York, NY 10020

Copyright © 2013 by Alexis Wright
Originally published in Australia in 2013 by the Giramondo Publishing Company
Previously published in Great Britain in 2015 by Constable

First Atria Books hardcover edition June 2016

ATRIA B O O K S and colophon are trademarks of Simon & Schuster, Inc.

For information about special discounts for bulk purchases,
please contact Simon & Schuster Special Sales at 1-866-506-1949
or business@simonandschuster.com.

The Simon & Schuster Speakers Bureau can bring authors
to your live event. For more information or to book an event
contact the Simon & Schuster Speakers Bureau at 1-866-248-3049
or visit our website at www.simonspeakers.com.

Interior design by Esther Paradelo

Manufactured in the United States of America

10   9   8   7   6   5   4   3   2   1

Library of Congress Cataloging-in-Publication Data
Names: Wright, Alexis, 1950– author.
Title: The swan book : a novel / Alexis Wright.
Description: First Atria Books hardcover edition. | New York : Atria Books, 2016.
Identifiers: LCCN 2016000291 | ISBN 9781501124785 (hardcover)
Subjects: LCSH: Indigenous peoples—Australia—Fiction. | BISAC:
    FICTION / Literary. | FICTION / General. | GSAFD: Dystopias.
Classification: LCC PR9619.3.W67 S93 2016 | DDC 823/.914—dc23
    LC record available at http://lccn.loc.gov/2016000291

ISBN 978-1-5011-2478-5
ISBN 978-1-5011-2480-8 (ebook)

FOR TOLY

All those traveling black swans
Gone to desert lagoons after big rains
In the Todd River next to Schultz Crossing
And thirty flying north along Larapinta Drive
in Alice Springs on the 14 January 2010

And in memory of Yari Tjampitjinpa
(Kumantjayi Zimran)

A wild black swan in a cage
Puts all of heaven in a rage

—Robert Adamson, "After William Blake"

CONTENTS

PRELUDE: IGNIS FATUUS

Upstairs in my brain, there lives this kind of cut snake virus in its doll's house. Little stars shining over the moonscape garden twinkle endlessly in a crisp sky. The crazy virus just sits there on the couch and keeps a good old *qui vive* out the window for intruders. It ignores all of the eviction notices stacked on the door. The virus thinks it is the only pure full-blood virus left in the land. Everything else is just half-caste. Worth nothing! Not even a property owner. Hell yes! it thinks, worse than the swarms of rednecks hanging around the neighborhood. Hard to believe a brain could get sucked into vomiting bad history over the beautiful sunburnt plains.

Inside the doll's house the virus manufactures really dangerous ideas as arsenal, and if it sees a white flag unfurling, it fires missiles from a bazooka through the window into the flat, space, field or whatever else you want to call life. The really worrying thing about missile-launching fenestrae is what will be left standing in the end, and which splattering of truths running around in my head about a story about a swan with a bone will last on this ground.

So my brain is as stuffed as some old broken-down Commodore you see left dumped in the bush. But I manage. I stumble around through the rubble. See! There I go—zigzagging like a snake over hot tarmac through the endless traffic. Here I am—ducking for cover from screeching helicopters flying around the massive fire-plume storms. And then, I recognize a voice droning from far away, and coming closer.

Oblivia! The old swan woman's ghost voice jumps right out of the ground in front of me, even though she has been dead for years. White woman still yelling out that name! *Where's that little Aboriginal kid I found?* No name. Mudunyi? Oblivion Ethyl(ene) officially. She asks: *What are you doing girl? I never taught you to go around looking like that.* Her hard eyes look me up and down. The skin and bone. My hair cut clean to the scalp with a knife. I am burnt the same color as the ground. She takes in the view of the burnt earth, and says, *I never expected you to come back here.* The ghost says she still recognizes the child she had once pulled from the bowels of an old eucalyptus tree that had looked as though it could have been a thousand years old. But this is no place for ghosts that don't belong here, and the virus barks continuously, as though he were some kind of watchdog barking, *Oooba, booblah, booblah!* The old woman's ghost is as spooked as a frightened cat in flight by the virus's sick laughter carrying across the charred landscape. It frightens the living daylights out of her, although she still manages to say, *I know who you are,* before swiftly backing off across the landscape until she disappears over the horizon.

If you want to extract a virus like this from your head—you can't come to the door of its little old-fashioned prairie house with passé kinds of thinking, because the little king will not answer someone knocking, will not come out of the door to glare into the sunlight, won't talk about anything in level terms, or jump around to appease you like some Chubby Checker impersonator bent over backwards under a limbo stick. Nor will it offer any hospitality—swart summers or not—no matter how much knocking, trick-or-treating, ceremonial presents, or tantrums about why the door was kept closed.

I can prove that I have this virus. I have kept the bit of crumpled-up paper, the proper results of medical tests completed by top doctors of the scientific world. They claimed I had a remarkable brain. Bush doctors, some of the best in the world, said this kind of virus wasn't any miracle; it was just one of those poor lost assimilated spirits that thought about things that had originated somewhere else on the planet and got bogged in my brain. Just like assimilation of the grog or flagon, or just any *kamukamu*, which was not theirs to cure.

The virus was nostalgia for foreign things, they said, or what the French say, *nostalgie de la boue*; a sickness developed from channeling every scrap of energy towards an imaginary, ideal world with songs of solidarity, like "We Shall Overcome." My virus sings with a special slow drawling voice, like an Australian with *closed-door syndrome*—just singing its heart out about cricket or football without a piece of thought, like Harry Belafonte's "Day-O (The Banana Boat Song)"—*Day-o, day-o! Daylight come and me wan' go home,* etc. Well! There was nothing wrong with that. It could sing its homesick head off to the universe of viruses living in the polluted microscopic cities of the backwater swamp etched in my brain.

The extreme loser, not happy with having trapped itself in my brain, was acting like it had driven a brand-new Ferrari into the biggest slum of a *dirty* desert in one of the loneliest places in the world, and there had to fit high culture into a hovel. The doctors said it was a remarkable thing, an absolute miracle that nobody else had ended up with a virus like this freak lost in my head, after testing thousands of fundamentalists of one kind or another. They called medical testing a waste of public money and drank polluted swamp water to prove it.

Having learnt how to escape the reality about this place, I have created illusionary ancient homelands to encroach on and destroy the wide-open vista of the virus's real estate. The prairie house is now surrounded with mountainous foreign countries that dwarf the plains and flatlands in their shadows, and between the mountains, there are deserts where a million thirsty people have traveled, and to the coastlines, seas that are stirred by King Kong waves that are like monsters roaring at the front door. Without meeting any resistance whatsoever, I have become a gypsy, addicted to journeys into these distant illusionary homelands, to try to lure the virus hidden somewhere in its own crowded globe to open the door. This is where it begins as far as I am concerned. This is the quest to regain sovereignty over my own brain.

• • • •

So I lie in the brochures that I send the virus, saying I must come and visit, saying that I have blood ties in homelands to die for in the continents across the world of my imagination, and a family tree growing in dreams of distant lands. The fact, I say, is that my homeland has grown into such a big spread that it has become a nightmare of constant journeying further and further out. I am like Santa Claus riding the skies in one single *mungamba* night to reach umpteen addresses, and why? Just to deliver the good of myself, whether the receiver wants it or not. The virus was quite interested in my idea of belonging everywhere, and asked why I took these journeys that bring in more places to crowd up its little world. I say that I begin locally, navigating yellow-watered floods that grow into even greater inland sea-crossings, to reach a rich alluvial plain that feeds shaded gardens, where the people who live there say they do not know me and ask why have I come. Always, I move on.

And so I travel, fired up with the fuel of inquiry about what it means to have a homeland, to travel further into strange and unknown lands covered with holy dust and orchards of precious small, sun-ripened fruit that are sometimes half destroyed by war, and at other times, slapped hard in the face by famine. But still, even when I bring gifts to their door, the local people, although hungry and tired, find the courage to reject a person from their paradise no matter how far they have traveled, simply for not belonging.

I tell the virus that I have felt more at home with the cool air flowing on my face from a wild Whistling Swan's easy wings sweeping over snowcapped mountains in its grand migration across continents, than in those vast ghostly terrains of indescribable beauty that have given me no joy. I must continue on, to reach that one last place in a tinder-dry nimbus where I once felt a sense of belonging.

The virus thinks I want what it wants—to hide in a dark corner of its lolly-pink bed, where it dreams, in my diseased mind.

DUST CYCLE

And I hear the clang of their leader crying.
To a lagging mate in the rearward flying . . .

When the world changed, people were different. Towns closed, cities were boarded up, communities abandoned, their governments collapsed. They seemed to have no qualms that were obvious to you or me about walking away from what they called a useless pile of rubbish, and never looking back.

Mother Nature? Hah! Who knows how many hearts she could rip out? She never got tired of it. Who knows where on earth you would find your heart again? People on the road called her the Mother Catastrophe of flood, fire, drought and blizzard. These were the four seasons, which she threw around the world whenever she liked.

In every neck of the woods people walked in the imagination of doomsayers and talked the language of extinction.

They talked about surviving a continuous dust storm under the old rain shadow, or they talked about living out the best part of their lives with floods lapping around their bellies; or they talked about tsunamis and dealing with nuclear fallout on their shores and fields forever. Elsewhere on the planet, people didn't talk much at all while crawling through blizzards to save themselves from being buried alive in snow. You could bet your life on it—they hardly talked, while all around the world governments fell as quickly as they rose in one extinction event after another. You be the judge. Believe it or not.

Ignis Fatuus = Foolish Fire. That's you, Oblivion! You're just like that old Rip Van Winkle fella of the fairy-tale time. They were always calling out to him: "Wake up coma man." That man who slept like a log, more than an old dog, and kept on sleeping for so many years that when he woke up and went home, his house was gone—just scrub there, and nobody knew who he was anymore. He was empty—like a mystery man. Nobody remembered him. He could have been anyone. They kept poking him in his bony ribs wanting to know "Who do you reckon you are?" and what his name was and why he kept saying that his house had disappeared and all that. It is very hard to lose a house. Why would anyone want to do that? So bloody good job. Serves him right. You should always know where to find your home.

"It was here! It was here!" That was what the Rip Van Winkle man kept saying. He was just like you for making up stories like that, Oblivion. Nobody liked him either.

Some say that there was an accident before the drought. A little girl was lost. She had fallen into the deep underground bowel of a giant eucalyptus tree. In a silent world, the girl slept for a very long time among the tree's huge woven roots. Everyone had forgotten that she even existed—although, apparently, that did not take long.

Locked in the world of sleep, only the little girl's fingers were constantly moving, in slow swirls like music. She was writing stanzas in ancient symbols wherever she could touch—on the palms of her hands, and all over the tree root's dust-covered surfaces. Whatever she was writing, dredged from the soup of primordial memory in these ancient lands, it was either the oldest language coming to birth again instinctively, or through some strange coincidence, the fingers of the unconscious child forming words that resembled the twittering of birdsong speaking about the daylight: but the little girl could not understand the old ghost language of warbling and chortling remembered by the ancient river gum.

Her fingers traced the movements of the ghost language to write about the dead trees scattered through the swamp, where *dikili* ghost gums old as the hills once grew next to a deepwater lake fed by an old spring-spirit relative, until they had all slowly died. This happened during the massive sandstorms that cursed the place after the arrival of the strangers from the sea. Their voices were heard arching across the heavy waves in the middle of the night. All their shouting ended up on ribbons of salt mist that went idling from the sea along an ancient breezeway—traveling with sand flies and tumbling bats through kilometers of inlet, along a serpentine track, dumped where it could dig into the resting place of the old story that lived inside the ancestral people of the lake.

The beetles blanketing the lake shook the night in a millisecond that shattered its surface, like precious old venetian glass crashing onto a pavement. The roar of those harsh-sounding voices from the sea startled the ghosts that rose from beneath the lake's water—from hearing those men calling out—*half past midnight, half past two,* echoing from inside several brackets of reeds.

Sleepy children from the little dwellings around the lake heard voices speaking from large leafy fields of water lilies. They felt words chasing after them, surrounding their feet like rope trying to pull them back as they ran away. Anyone daring to look back into the lake's echoes heard voices like dogs barking out of the mouths of fish skimming across the surface as they chased after the hordes of mosquitoes—*around four o'clock.*

Those echoes of voices, which originated far out at sea, were coming from the Armed Forces men involved in a large-scale sweep-up of the ocean's salty junk, floating about, bobbing and buoyant across the horizon.

The men from the Army were taunting these haunts of ghosts and' outlaws to surrender themselves by dawn because they shouted: *Grab your liberation! Freedom! Called ghosts, you what?* It was a tragic demand to abandoned steel, planks of timber, brass lanterns and fittings, whose ghost sailors were unable to respond to military voices. But surprisingly, the empty wreckage obeyed. Vessel after vessel crawling out from behind the waves gleamed with the light of the stars dancing with the moonlight.

A parade of tugs towing the collected ruins churned across the breakers and headed towards land, and while the voices giving orders rose and fell, the flotilla began motoring through the deepwater channel towards the vast lake where the caretakers lived—the Aboriginal people who were responsible for this land. Whatever the men from the Army had been saying to each other on that night of bringing the junk to the lake was quickly forgotten, since around here, the words of strangers meant nothing.

Up to that point in time, the people of the lake had felt secluded in their isolation, even invisible to the outside world. They were more interested in singing in praise to the ancient spirits for the seasons lived alongside eels, freshwater mussels, turtles and other aquatic life. Now they were truly startled by voices that resembled angry animals fighting over a few scraps of food.

It was freakish, yet they were frightened for no reason except instinct, from having their invisibility exposed by a simple little thing—lit up in the night as though it was the middle of the day by the beams from the Army's high-powered searchlights swiveling on the tugboats—eyeballing along the shoreline for witnesses.

Their instinct for invisibility caused the entire population to slink away from their homes and slip into the bush, but in this inglorious fleeing for safety, something more sensational was noticed by one of these so-called nouveau journalists of the event.

Somebody had eyewitnessed the lake bubbling from tugboats mix-mastering the water with their propellers, whisking it like a spritzer and putrefying all the dead ancient things rising to the surface, spraying it around like the smell of eternity. No wonder the local people, the traditional owners and all that, were too frightened to go back to the lake anymore. They had heard stories—bad stories about what happened to anyone who went back there.

Oblivia's fingers kept on writing the swirl language over the dust that fell on what the tree had witnessed in its lifetime, and the history of the stories that continued to be told by the locals about the years of fighting like a bunch of battle-axes—for umpteen friggen decades, without success, to get back what was theirs in the first place, and of years later again before these old families quit their tourism of other peoples' lands by saying they had had enough of wandering around homelessly for years worse than a pack of overseas gypsies, and returned to their rightful place of belonging, their ancestral domain.

Then, to top it off, they had no sooner set foot on the place, when they were told that Australians now recognized the law of Native Title after two plus centuries of illegal occupation, but unfortunately, on the day that they had left their land, their Native Title had been lost irredeemably and disappeared from the face of the planet.

The first thing they saw on their arrival at the lake that no longer belonged to them was the audacity of the floating junk. Even the tugboats had been left there to rot unfettered and untethered. Undeterred, the traditional owners ignored the view, and acted as though the lake was still the same tranquil place that it had always been from time *immemorial,* before the day that their people had been frightened away.

They took up their lives with the eyesore view of rust amongst the lilies, and very soon, everyone felt as though they had never left. But, it was strange what a view can do to how people think. The rotting junk clung to its secrets and, in turn, the local people who did not really know what they were staring at or why the junk was staring back at them, also became secretive.

They wished and dreamed for this emotional eyesore to be removed and gone from their lands forever. It was foreign history sinking there that could not be allowed to rot into the sacredness of the ground. Their conscience flatly refused to have junk buried among the ancestral spirits.

These were really stubborn people sticking to the earth of the ancestors, even though they knew well enough that the contaminated lake caused bellyaches, having to eye each cup of tainted water they drank from the lake, but drinking it anyway.

There was not much choice about pure and pristine anymore. It was no good thinking about contaminated water leading to deformity in their culture for an eternity.

These people were hardened to the legendary stuff of fortune and ill fortune. They saw many children being born without any evidence of contamination. All children in living memory of the lake people's history, and regardless of the Army intervening in their parenthood, were deeply loved by their families, until this girl came along who was so different to any child ever born in their world, it made everyone think about why Oblivia had been born at all after this dumb girl was dragged out of the eucalyptus tree by old Bella Donna after years—a decade of being missing—and who disowned her people by acting as though she had bypassed human history, by being directly descended from their ancestral tree. Time would tell if this was true or false. Who was anyone to judge anything?

The junk on the lake was used as regular target practice for bombs falling from the warplanes that appeared unpredictably, flying low across the water from time to time throughout the year. Surprised at first, the local owners soon realized that their homeland was really a secret locality for Defense Force–scheduled training maneuvers. What a blast was that? Things getting blown up, up and down, in the isolated northern part of the nation.

Only heaven knows, there were millions of people throughout the world who either offered pigs as sacrifices to their Gods, or flowers, or the first grain of the new season's crop. There were even others who offered their own people to the Gods. Now the day had come when modern man had become the new face of God, and simply sacrificed the whole earth. The swamp locals were not experiencing any terrific friendship with this new God. It was hell to pay to be living the warfare of modernity like dogs fighting over the lineage of progress against their own quiet whorls of time. Well! That just about summed up the lake people, sitting for all times in one place.

These were anti-halcyon times for the lake people, where the same old festering drains and degraded lands were struck hard and fast by a string of bad luck, which all in all, amounts to the same thing happening with the surprise of being struck once, or twice, or a hundred more times as though it were a chosen place.

Sandstorms continued pouring over the lake and turned it into a swamp. The sand flew about in this freak weather until it banked up into a mountain with a pointy peak reaching into the sky. The mountain blocked the channel leading from the sea to the swamp.

Then an elder, a healer for the country arrived to examine the devastation, which he called *a total ugly bitch of an annihilation*. He turned up like a bogeyman. A *kadawala. Dadarrba-barri nyulu jalwa-kudulu*. He claimed that he was feeling pain in his heavy heart. Turns up from nowhere like an airplane. *Bala-kanyi nyulu*. He just flies where he wants to. This old *wululuku* was an Aboriginal man with an Asian heritage, the kind of person all sorts of people liked to call a half-caste, yellow fella, or *mixed-blood urban* Aboriginal. Half-caste. Thinking! Thinking! Mixture. Mixed up. Not straight this or that. Extract! Lost purity. Not purely trustworthy. Exactly! No matter! He liked to call people a lot of names too, but he called himself the Harbor Master. He favored calling himself by his own *worldly acquired* bona fides: a bony man with sun-darkened brown skin and sunglasses, a slack shaver with stubbly growth on his face—someone who resembled Mick Jagger. Someone with special healing powers who traveled anywhere he was needed, just by thinking himself into a sick person's mind. His was *wanami*, like fuel, and *wakubaji*—goes like anything. He started to live like a *persona non grata* sitting up there like a motionless exile on the sand mountain's summit. Japanese typo. Something *sage-guru-expert* turnout. He became simple, like a snail-eating dune hermit. Somebody short on detail about what else he was going to feed himself with, and no tap water either to boot. Still, only kings live above everyone else, watching everybody else like this. So, maybe, he was a bit of a king too.

Oblivia remembered thinking that dust had a way of displacing destiny the first time she saw a swan. A red ghost was rolling in the sky when a lone, gray-black swan suddenly appeared at lunchtime over the riparian rook of this northern world. General swamp people sitting around as slack as you please, were shoveling freshly sautéed fish fillets into their mouths when they heard the strange song of the swan. The whole place went silent. Nobody said a word. Everyone stopped eating. Half-raised forks froze midstream above the dinner plates. The dinner went cold while everyone stared at the first swan ever seen on this country. Only their thoughts wild with noise were asking why this strange bird stilted the heat of the day with song where there was no song for swans. The locals asked the storming almighty red dust spirit relation, *What's that bro?*

In all of this vast quietness where the summer sun was warming the dust spirit's mind, the swan looked like a paragon of anxious premonitions, rather than the arrival of a miracle for saving the world. Seeing the huge bird flying through the common dusty day like this, disturbed whatever peace of mind the sticklike Oblivia possessed. Everyone watched a swan's feather float down from the sky and land on her head. Oblivia's skin instantly turned to a darker shade of red-brown. What about her frizzy hair then? Well! There was no change in that. It was always sprayed out in fright. *Ngirriki!* Messy! Always looking like tossed winter straw that needed rope to tie it down. She was *psychological. Warraku.* Mad. Even madder than ever. That was the most noticeable change. She did what was expected. She nose-dived like a pitchfork into the unbearable, through broiling dust vats, to countless flashbacks of what was over-the-top and dangerous. Everything in her mind became mucked-up. This is the kind of harm the accumulated experience of an exile will do to you, to anyone who believes that they had slept away half their life in the bowel of a eucalyptus tree. Well! Utopian dreaming was either too much or too little, but at least she recognized that the swan was an exile too.

Suddenly, the swan dropped down from the sky, flew low over the swamp, almost touching the water, just slow enough to have a closer look at the girl. The sight of the swan's cold eye staring straight into hers, made the girl feel exposed, hunted and found, while all those who had suddenly stopped eating fish, watched this big black thing look straight at the only person that nobody had ever bothered having a close look at. Her breathing went AWOL while her mind stitched row after row of fretting to strangle her breath: *What are they thinking about me now? What did the swan have to single me out for and not anyone else standing around? What kind of premonition is this?* Heart-thump thinking was really tricky for her. She feasted on a plague of *outsidedness*. It was always better never to have to think about what other people thought of her.

It was through this narrow prism of viewing something strange and unfamiliar that the girl decided the swan wasn't an ordinary swan and had not been waylaid from its determined path. She knew as a fact that the swan had been banished from wherever it should be singing its stories and was searching for its soul in her.

The black swan continued traveling low, then flew upwards with its long neck stretched taut, as though it was being pulled away by invisible strings as fine as a spider's web held in its beak. She saw a troupe of frost-face monkeys holding the strings at the other end of the world. They were riding on a herd of reindeer crushing through ice particles in those faraway skies. Those taut strands of string twanged the chords of swan music called the *Hansdhwani* that the old gypsy woman Bella Donna would play on her swan-bone flute while you could watch the blood flowing to the pulse of the music through the old white lady's translucent skin. It was the swan raga the girl heard now coming down from the sky, the music of migratory traveling cycles, of unraveling and intensifying, of flying over the highest snowcapped mountains, along the rivers of Gods and Goddesses, crossing seas with spanned wings pulsing to the rhythm of relaxed heartbeats.

This was when the girl realized that she could hear the winnowing wings from other swans coming from far away. Their murmurings to one another were like angels whispering from the heavens. She wondered where they were coming from as they entered her dreams in this country, this first time she saw a swan. She could not have known anything of how long it had taken the huge black birds to make the migratory flight from so far away, to where they had no story line for taking them back.

The swans had become gypsies, searching the deserts for vast sheets of storm water soaking the centuries-old dried lakes when their own habitats had dried from prolonged drought. They had become nomads, migratory like the white swans of the northern world, with their established seasonal routes taking them back and forth, but unlike them, the black swans were following the rainwaters of cyclones deeper and deeper into the continent.

Bevies of swans crossed the man-made catchments and cubby dams on pastoral lands, and flew down to the tailing dams of mines, and the sewerage ponds of inland towns, where story after story was laid in the earth again before the dust rose, and on they went, forging into territory that had been previously unknown to these southern birds except, perhaps, for their ancestors of long ago, when great flocks might have traveled their law stories over the land through many parts of the continent. The local people thought, *They must have become the old gypsy woman's swans!*

So it was really true. The old *badibadi* woman had always said she could call swans, but it was a white swan she wanted most of all, not these black ones. Bella Donna and the girl that she had adopted after years of searching for her and pulling her out of a hollow in the trunk of a tree, lived together on one of the old rusty hulks stuck out there in the middle of the swamp where the black swan was flying. The girl remembered how the old woman was always talking about how she owed her life to a swan. Telling Oblivia about how much she missed seeing the swans from her world. It was a foreigner's *Dreaming* she had.

She came beginning of dust time, some of the old dust-covered people claimed, remembering the drought and the turtles that had lived there for thousands of years crawling away into the bush to die. They had studied her bones that could be clearly seen under her thin translucent skin. This they claimed was caused from eating too much fish from her life at sea, and said that Bella Donna was a very good example of how other people were always fiddling around with their laws. These were people old enough to still remember things about the rest of the world, whereas most of the younger generations with a gutful of their own wars to fight were not interested in thinking any further afield than to the boundary of the swamp. All of these big law people thought tribal people across the world would be doing the same, and much like themselves, could also tell you about the consequences of breaking the laws of nature by trespassing on other people's land. They were very big on the law stories about the natural world.

The girl was full of the old woman's stories about swans before she had seen one, and even if words did not pass through her lips, she would imitate Bella Donna's old European accent in her mind: *I have seen swans all my life. I have watched them in many different countries myself. Some of them have big wings like the Trumpeter Swan of North America, and when the dust smudges the fresh breath of these guardian angels, they navigate through the never-ending dust storms by correcting their bearings and flying higher in the sky, from where they glide like Whistling Swans whistling softly to each other, then beating their wings the harder they fly away. I know because I am the storyteller of the swans.*

Where I came from, whole herds of deer were left standing like statues of yellow ice while blizzards stormed. Mute Swans sheltered in ice-covered reeds. The rich people were flying off in armadas of planes like packs of migratory birds. The poverty people like myself had to walk herdlike, cursed from one border to another through foreign lands and seas.

You know girl? I owe the fact that I am alive today to a swan. But anyhow, my story of luck is only a part of the concinnity of dead stories tossed by the sides of roads and gathering dust. In time, the mutterings of millions will be heard in the dirt . . . I am only telling you my story about swans.

Could an ancient hand be responsible for this? The parched paper country looking as though the continent's weather systems had been rolled like an ancient scroll from its top and bottom ends, and *ping*, sprung shut over the Tropic of Capricorn. The weather then flipped sides, swapping southern weather with that of the north, and this unique event of unrolling the climate upside down, left the entire continent covered in dust. When the weather patterns began leveling out after some years, both ends of the country looked as though normal weather was being generated from the previously dry center of Australia. With the heart of the country locked into a tempestuous affair, hot and sticky, what was once the south's cool temperate climate mixed with the north's tropical humidity until the whole country was shrouded in days of dust—*Jundurr! Jundurr!*—or, all the time in heavy cyclonic rain.

Its journey took the black swan over the place where hungry *warrki* dingoes, foxes and *dara kurrijbi buju* wild dogs had dug out shelters away from the dust, and lay in overcrowded burrows in the soil; and in the grasses, up in the rooftops, in the forests of dead trees, all the fine and fancy birds that had once lived in stories of marsh country, migrating swallows and plains-dancing brolgas, were busy shelving the passing years into a lacy webbed labyrinth of mud-caked stickling nests brimmed by knickknacks, and waves of flimsy old plastic threads dancing the wind's crazy dance with their faded partners of silvery-white lolly cellophane, that crowded the shores of the overused swamp.

Up you too, Oblivia snarls under her breath after being reminded of the people she suspected were keeping an eye on her, after they saw the swan looking at her.

The swan had swung into shock-locked wings when human voices interrupted its nostalgia, but still it kept flying over the dust-covered landscape. This child! The swan could not take its eyes away from the little girl far down on the red earth. The music broke as if the strings had been broken, and the swan fell earthward through the air for several moments. Maybe, it was in those moments of falling, that the big bird placed itself within the stories of this country, before it restored the rhythm of its flapping wings, and continued on its flight.

Oblivia gave the swan no greater thought after it had disappeared, other than to think that it was heading in the right direction—towards water, to reach the sea, the place that she knew existed from stories she had heard of what was beyond the northern horizon. She thinks people are talking about her and glares unkindly towards the multitude of residential shacks jammed cheek to jowl like a sleeping snake ringing the swamp: a multicolored spectacle in the bright glare of sunlight, of overcrowding and overuse, confusion in love, happiness, sorrow and rage, in this slice of humanity living the life of the overcome. All about, birds squabbled noisily, chasing one another over the rooftops for space in air thick with the high cost of living for a view of a dead lake.

These people keep looking at me. The girl mouths the words—*read my lips*, centimeters from Bella Donna's face. No sound comes out of her mouth since she had decided not to speak, that it was not worth speaking. She would rather be silent since the last word she had spoken when scared out of her wits, the day when her tongue had screeched to a halt with dust flying everywhere, and was left screaming *Ahhhhhh!* throughout the bushland, when she fell down the hollow of the tree.

Bella Donna felt invaded by Oblivia's hot breath striking her face. In an instant, her sense of privacy diminishes into the spoils of war flattened over the barren field of herself, even though she recognizes the girl's clumsy attempts to communicate with her. That the girl has never recovered from being raped. But feeling and knowing are two different things: she retaliates all the same, and like any other long-standing conflict around the world, one act of violation becomes a story of another. *Remember who it was who rescued you with her bare hands. Did you see anyone else digging you out of that tree? Out there in the heat? Sun pouring down on my head in the middle of the day? Did you hear anyone else calling out for someone to come and help me to pull you out before you died out there? No! There was nobody else coming along and helping an old woman. Nobody else spent years looking for you. It was only me who was walking and walking in the bush and calling you girlie—you remember that. Even your own parents had forgotten who you were. Dead! They thought you were dead. It was only me who looked for you.*

Try as she might to rectify the problem of the speechless child, Bella Donna knew that the girl would manage to make only certain sounds that did not even closely resemble vowels. It seemed as though the child's last spoken word had been left orbiting unfinished, astray, irredeemable and forsaken. The only sounds she heard emanating from the girl's mouth were of such low frequency that the old woman strained to distinguish what usually fell within the range of bushland humming, such as leaves caught up in gusts of wind, or the rustling of the *wiyarr* spinifex grasses in the surrounding landscape as the wind flew over them, or sometimes the flattened whine of distant birdsong, or a raging bushfire crackling and hissing from *jujuu jungku bayungu*, a long way off, which the old woman heard coming out of Oblivia's angry mouth.

The girl did not actually care whether the old gypsy lady from the land of floribunda roses was listening or not, nor did she care that the old woman kept saying she was in charge of caring for her until she was covered with dirt in her grave, and even from the grave itself, she would still rise to cook, and wash and what not, because she was a saint who took on responsibilities like this. *I told you these people keep looking at me.*

What for girl? My sweet Lord, they only see what they want to see. They are blind, not stupid. They see, but they are blind, the old voice did not feel like answering the girl—never understanding the speechlessness, making it up as she talked.

Oblivia! The startled old woman, believing she understood whatever the girl was saying or thinking, having cracked the code of the language of windstorms or wind gusts, spoke in a pitched tone of voice that implied she held a high status in this poor community. She had given the girl a fancy name and everything. Oblivia, short for Oblivion Ethyl(ene), was her unconsciously inspired, synonymously paralleling sentiment for a girl perhaps best suited dead, instead of returning like a bad smell from the grave. She continued with pride in hearing herself saying the name again, *Oblivia! You have become a very cynical person for someone of your age.*

The old woman was trying to make good use of her burden, whose aim in life was to get the girl to act normal: behave and sit up straight at the table and use a knife and fork properly, learn table manners, talk nicely, walk as a butterfly flies, dress like a normal person, learn something marvelous on a daily basis, and show some resilience. Over and over, Oblivia sings in her head: *Nah! Sporadically all the time. Be full of useful facilities.* And, this: *Treat people decent.*

It seemed as though Oblivia had learnt nothing in years of living with the old woman except how to stay bent and rake thin, but not even she could prevent the force of nature. She could not go around in a perpetual state of warring with the obvious, by forever imagining herself to be like a piece of rotten fruit peel curled up inside the tree. Bones straightened out. She grew taller, and her skin darkened from the nondescript amber honey of a tree's heartwood, to radiant antique gold—darkened, like a tarnished red-yellow ocher pit blazing in the sun after rain.

In this world of the swamp, people had good ears for picking up every word that went skimming across the surface of the water, and vice versa, from the old lady's hull and back. You could almost reach out and grab each word with your hand. They were listening to what was considered to be some general crap coming out of the old lady's kitchen. The girl copycats those nicely spoken words, but prefers the tempo of the local dialect, to interpret like a local, and with her tongue tapping around behind closed lips, echoes soundlessly the homilies of her home life: *Toughen up. Get out there. Make a difference. Don't be like the rest of the people around here. And have a good day.*

The old lady's speech was considered quite charming but inspired nothing in the local Indigenous people's summation, where it was generally thought to be, *Very good English for sure, and would go far for the language betterment of Australia, but not here.* Naturally! Out on the swamp where life was lived on the breeze, her tongue was considered to be too soft, like a cat's purr. It could not adapt to the common old rough way in the normal state of affairs, *cross-cultural-naturally*, where all English language was spoken for political use only. Whatever was decent about English speech in the way she spoke it, was better for chatting a long way away, in its homeland. Maybe, while taking a leisurely walk with ladies and gentlemen through the environs of a finely constructed English garden, with those whose day delighted in the sight of every fresh rose, or were surprised by a squirrel scampering across the path with a plump autumn acorn in its teeth.

Swamp people were not ignorant of white people who, after all, had not turned up yesterday. Having lived it all, they claimed to have at least ten, or possibly more generations of knowledge, packed up tight in their mentality about white people doing good for them. Seasonal crop farmers, harvesters of potatoes, cabbages, fields of beans, yellow pears, wheat for whiskey, wine grapes, dairy cattle or pigs, truffles and olives, death feuds, imprisonment, domination, the differences be- tween rich and poor, slaves, war and terror—whatever celebrated their faraway ancestral districts. Still! Why worry about the old woman's voice going—*Blah! Blah!* Or jumping—*Ting! Thang! Thing! Ting! Thang! What!*—it was only the needle of her compass spinning back to the north from any radius of her wanderings of the earth. Opera! It was only opera. This was how the local population living packed up and down in the great distance around the swamp described her kind of talk.

The old woman spoke loudly to the girl while feeding flocks of black swans gathering around the hull. She was fed up. She had always gotten on well with people everywhere in her life before being rudely treated by a child. *Not just from this swamp. Yes,* she said, *I have used my opportunities for influencing people across the world. You must use the voice.* The girl thought that she should be silent if words were just a geographical device to be transplanted anywhere on earth. Then if that was possible: *Was it possible for her voice to be heard by imaginary people too?*

Wanymarri white woman was from one of those nationalities on Earth lost to climate change wars. The new gypsies of the world, but swamp people said that as far as they were concerned, even though she was a white lady, they were luckier than her. They had a home. Yes, that was true enough. Black people like themselves had somewhere, whereas everywhere else, probably millions of white people were drift- ing among the other countless stateless millions of sea gypsies looking for somewhere to live.

Bella Donna of the Champions claimed that she was the descendant of a listener of Hoffmeister's Quartet in F. This music was cherished throughout the whole world she boasted: *But not here.* That was true enough! The swamp people had never heard of such music. She said on the other hand, whilst living happily enough among the Aborigines of Australia now, she was from many other countries equally and felt *not really here and not really there.* When you had traveled so far and wide in a lifetime as she had, of course you would be heard anywhere on earth if you had left your tongue everywhere. She had often told the girl that all of humanity's past and present had locations stored in her head. *That was what the head was for—storing knowledge about the world that you might want to use one day.*

Right! As if!

As all stories begin with once upon a time, so the old woman always began her story, while looking into the levitating crystal balls she juggled, as though all stories that ever existed originated from these objects. Anything was possible when her snowy hair seemed charged with electricity and flew about wildly in the wind. All about her tall lean frame, the faded red hibiscus flowers of her old dress billowed as if caught in a cyclone. Her hundred-year-old face creased into a hundred more wrinkles. White lines of fog filled the fractured lines in one ball. Red dust swarmed inside the other.

With eyes the color of the oceans, she continued staring absent-mindedly, perhaps from habits formed on journeys over listless seas, but the scary thing was this gave the impression that she was releasing the words she spoke from inside the mesmerizing glass, struck golden by the sun. So transfixing was the power of these objects, it did not occur to anyone that she might be fiddling with their minds, cursing them perhaps with overseas magic. Her trick made people stare straight into each spinning ball as it hung in midair like a miracle, the pivot reached before each slow ascension, while haphazardly heaping into their brains whatever they liked to remember about her story.

For all anyone in the swamp knew, she might have been Aine, the sun goddess of Ireland. An old woman, mortified from having been dredged out of her lake in haste, and then, having to suffer the indignities of being dragged around the world in stinking boats. The swamp had become the place for reincarnation for all sorts living around the place. For sure, she was grand enough, enticing people, tricking their dreams, and juggling things around the edges of their minds. A goddess who had dragged herself out of the ocean then become an ordinary old woman.

Her country of origin, Bella Donna had claimed, was where people of the modern world once lived happily by doing more or less nothing, other than looking after themselves from one day to the next to fuel the stories of their life, but they were *finished now*. Always she returned to the memory of a single white swan feather resting on the spiderweb outside a window of her childhood home next to a forest where deer lived. She would recite a line from a poet from Hungary, *Snow, fog, fingerprints sprouting swans' feathers on the windowpanes . . . It was just a childhood memory,* she always snapped abruptly on reaching this point of her story, as if her most treasured melancholy thought was not fit enough for *this* place.

She claimed that one day, some devil, not a person, but a freak of nature, went to war on her people. *Old woman what kind of freak was that?* Well! Swamp people wanted to know. Had a right to know. She looked startled, as though she had been asked to describe the inexplicable, of what happened to people affected by the climate changing in wild weather storms, or the culmination of years of droughts, high temperature and winds in some countries, or in others, the freezing depths of prolonged winters. *Peace,* she said, it was called peace by the governments that called on their people to fight land wars. She had seen its kind rampaging across the gentle lands of her country, destroying everything in its path, and leaving those who survived with a terrible story to tell.

Listen to what I say: cities, towns, homes, land, as well as animals and crops, were flattened and could be no more. It was bad weather that made fanatics like this. Her voice thrilled as though her tongue was on fire while she listed her foes: *Dictators! Bandits! People bashers!* She could spend all day listing the world's villains who had destroyed her people's land. Those willing to push the world into an unstoppable catastrophic slide of destruction and hatred with nuclear fallout, she shouted, as though swamp people were deaf to the sound of the outside world. *Everybody looking twice at his neighbor's property. One land-grabbing country fighting another land-grabbing country, and on it went with any people excess to requirement killed, or they left on their own accord by throwing themselves into the ocean.* Her voice fell into ladylike pretty-garden reminiscences now, quavering with the memory of a lifetime enmeshed with sea waves in a volatile shifting world that was irreconcilably changed. *With their country completely destroyed and radioactive, who could return? Which millennium, this one or next? What would her people be then?* Her words were caustic and frightening, but beguiling too in the minds of the overwhelmed swamp people trying to imagine this ghost country where nobody goes.

Then, without country, imagine that? Imagining! Can't imagine. For country never leaves its people. This was what the swamp people claimed while seeing some sort of country in her, and dragging it out of her by listening, like scavenging rubbish out of a bin, rubbish lying everywhere—hard to imagine where it all came from. She asked them to think about the people of her nation as they joined a trail of misery forged by those who were walking before them.

What about them? These people owned nothing but the clothes they wore and whatever could be carried away on their backs, handy things like: *televisions, computers, mobile phones?* Whoosh! Splat! Bang! They were the sounds you heard all day long when technology was being thrown over the side of mountains in the search for food and water. The story of her people, she claimed, was like the chapters in a nightmarish book. What would come next? The people of the swamp knew about stories. Stories had value. Could buy trust. Could buy lots of things. Even silence. This story was new cash among people full of suspicion of one another.

Helter skelter, running away, fleeing people became refugees marching onward just like deer would through winter steppes to nowhere. Hunger was constant. Waves of vermin, rats disguised as men, drove the moving chains of humanity into traps. The killing of people was without reason, fruitless and endless. This was Bella Donna's life when her people were being forced off their land. Eventually, beyond breaking point, there in the mountains under some spirit-charged rowan trees that were thousands of years old, they reached another summit of hopelessness. Bewildered, and staring down from above the clouds clinging to the sides of the mountains, they tried to locate holes in the scrims of mist to the fells, to see if the face of so much inhumanity was resting somewhere among the rivers and forests with smoke pluming from campfires, but eventually, even those who had survived to this point resigned themselves to a fate of total annihilation.

So be it! Miserably, but almost bizarrely joyous too for such a final realization that they were at the gates of their Maker, Bella Donna said those who were standing on the mountaintop ready to die, now turned their fragile gaze upwards to heaven. If there was a bigger picture than the landscape, they were acknowledging the existence of a much mightier hand inflicting this enormous punishment on their depravity, even though they had once felt that their lives were normal enough. Then, as they knelt on the frozen ground to pray silently for the end to come quickly, something very unusual happened.

They heard God approaching in the fog. Music, so sweet as though nature was singing, it was just like hearing *Spiegel im Spiegel* played lightly on a cello. A single white swan flew by: its wings beating with music. *The bell-beat of wings above our heads,* the old lady whispered, a line that an Irish bard had once crafted with ink on paper to sweeten the world. They saw a Mute Swan, one of the biggest of the eight known types of swans in the world. It circled above, and then flew down and landed among them. It whispered a greeting of good day and good fortune. Its hot breath formed a little cloud in the cold air.

Listen closely: *Our thoughts were not brave. Should this fat bird, the only one seen for days, appearing like an angel in response to our final prayers to Heaven, be eaten? Should angels ever be eaten, even one, by so many hungry people?*

The swan had dirty feathers, ingrained with the ash spread through blackened snow on the burnt plains of lowlands where it had walked under the clouds. It did not stay long. Swanlike, it ran heavily, carrying away the past, present and future on its webbed feet, slapping along the sodden, mossy, alpine swamp until it was treading water then air in its wake.

But unlike a wild creature, the swan returned. It flew in swooping circles around the people gathered on the mountain, forcing them to get up off the cold ground they had been kneeling on, and move. The freezing temperature, already sourer than a hoar wind, threatened to turn them into statues of ice. Several thousand people began walking in circles through biting wind and rain, their spirits lifting in the talk circulating about a swan that had once landed at the feet of a saint. The sinking into the well of memory about swans on that day was remarkable. Back! Back! And even further back, remembering how this very creature was descended from a Knight Swan, which of course convinced them of their own relationships to the swan's *descendancy*. Someone yelled to the swan flying above—*Lohengrin*. A chorus, re-membering Wagner's opera, replied—*The knight Lohengrin arrived in a boat drawn by a swan*. History! Swan history! Quicker! Quicker! Remembering this, and remembering that; and there it was, the swans loved and hated through the ages in stories laid bare by this huddling melee of the doomed trying to find warmth on frozen moss. They grabbed a trillion swans in their imagination, dragged them back from the suppressed backwoods of the mind. *So! God help us,* Bella Donna said, they all sang—*live and let live,* until the throng sang for their life to keep warm, then decided to head back down the mountain.

They followed the swan quickly, breathlessly, and down they went, becoming strong again simply from believing there was goodness left in the world. From remembering God and words, and lines of poetry, *Upon the brimming water among the stones, are nine and fifty swans*. The old woman looked as though she was back on the mountain that day years before, reciting lines they sang, quicker and more quickly, as their feet hit the stony path. *And scatter wheeling in great broken rings, upon their clamorous wings.*

Through the swan, they had put their faith back in life as routinely as though they had been watching a favorite weekly television pro-gram. They knew without reason that the swan would always be there on the land, would always return, and always be remembered. They were like their ancestors of the Dark Ages who once followed swans up and down imaginary paths with the single-mindedness of saving themselves—from what? *A similar misfortune?* The swan flew above the gushing bluish-white torrents coursing down the mountains. *We followed the idea of living,* she said, believing that this swan was a guide that had reached out from our past.

The swan flew on and on while every man, woman and child followed, tumbling in their own stream down rocky slopes and slippery moss to take up their flight, until finally before nightfall, the big white bird flew over the coastline through wild winds out to a gray sea, guiding Bella Donna's people to safety from wars.

Severely deluded into believing that they could be saved from whatever calamity chased them, the people went clambering after the swan even though the winds butting against their faces tried to push them back from the sea. But in the terror of having nowhere else to go, somehow the miracle of the white swan continued urging them onward. They stumbled through the darkness, and they ran along a river covered with solid ice until they reached the shore. They ran straight on into the freezing water, towards the abandoned, unseaworthy fishing boats still bobbing in the bay.

They set sail: following the swan's own long migratory flight out of the country, heading towards the moon squatting on the horizon. Bella Donna lamented to the swamp people, the swan disappearing across the sea was like the myth of Icarus whose wings fell off for not heeding the warning of his father. But, people running away do not always remember precisely what was in any old text locked away in the library. Instead! *Let's sail.* She sighed, and nodding her head, looked as though she was back on that same rough sea crashing on to the foreshore and revisiting the scrambling scene of their chaotic departure. She claimed it was an angel with swan wings pushing them out to sea that night; hands of the angel holding the masthead, covering the sails that should have been torn apart in the wind.

Gladdened to be nestling under moonlight and safely afloat, Bella Donna of the Champions said, *We wanted to relinquish our lands, their memories and stories, and after a little reflection and the buoyancy from being so far out on the water, we said we wanted to be exonerated from history.* Soon, indeed on the morning of the following day and every day afterwards as they headed further out across the ocean, only the inconsequentiality of the day before lingered in the memory of their new identity as boat people. They believed they had become mythical oarsmen with gilded paddles rowing sedately to beating drums, in time to the rolling wave of a chanter waving outstretched batons, with long white horsehair flying in sea wind. It was as though they were on a flying swan the size of a ship flying smoothly over the tops of waves. *We imagined ourselves sailing on the magnificently crafted Subanahongsa swan barge. Our swan's feathers shining like gold and precious jewels in the sunlight, and the pearl that hung from its neck, the size of a huge ball, shining in the moonlight.* And so she claimed: *We called ourselves the people who could call swans.*

Aunty Bella Donna of the Champions traveled the seas as wretchedly as any other among the banished people of the world, but as luck would have it, she came to live out her last days among the poorest people in a rich land. A hidden place. Another Eden. A place where hunger and death were commonplace to its elders, the landowners who knew that they were a social-science experiment with a very big cemetery. A small place where sometimes things got so bad when the swamp's little gang of brain-damaged, toxic-fume-sniffing addicted kids ruled, that parents asked only for one moment of peace. Where any silence was considered heaven-sent. People were gambling the cards and playing like ghosts. They were gambling about the Messiah. Made bets to see who was the luckiest. Well! Song sung true! Messiahs come and go, usually in the form of academic researchers, or a few chosen blacks and one-hit wonders pretending to speak for Aboriginal people and sucking-dry government money bureaucrats. They were the only Messiahs sent with answers. You got to practice what you preach. Pray God, waste not.

It was unimaginably miserable to be languishing at sea, moving from one ghost ship to another as the last living soul of the armadas, when finally, by simply saying enough was enough, this old woman invaded Australia. She saw the Australian beach lined with pandanus, smelt bush fires, caught the dust in the breeze laden with the aroma of overripe mangoes, *gidgee-kadawala* woodlands and bloodwood *Corymbia capricornia*, and she would listen no more to the law of breaking waves slapping against the shores of a forbidden land. She gathered up into a bag her old swan flute, a pile of books about swans, and those crystal balls. Then she walked straight across the Australian coastline and headed into the bush.

Anyone there? she called.

A bullfrog sitting in the *janja*, the mud, a lone tiny creature guarding the closed-gap entrance to the security fence of government transparency erected by the Army around the entire swamp answered, *baji*—maybe. It was happy enough to grant her asylum when she asked for a look.

She turned up on an Indigenous doorstep, and the children called out: *A Viking! A Viking! An old, raggedy Viking!*

All covered with dirt, grass and sticks, she looked as though she had forgotten how to walk or comb her hair and had swum through the scrub. Two laws, one in the head, the other worthless on paper in the swamp, said she was an invader. But! What could you do? Poor Bella Donna of the Champions! The sight of her made you cry. She was like a big angel, who called herself the patroness of World Rejection. She wasn't some renegade redneck from Camooweal or Canberra. This was the place for rejection: there was no hotter topic in the mind than rejection in this swamp, so to prove that they were not assimilated into the Australian way of life, the ancient laws of good manners about welcoming strangers were bestowed—Here! Stay! Have a go! We don't mind.

The old woman was terrified that she would be taken back down to the beach and thrown into the sea, and struggled to explain her lengthy and extraordinary ordeal. The crystal balls, her swan books and swan-bone flute in a canvas bag were all that she possessed, and these she tried to bargain for her life by pushing them into the hands of the elders. No one would touch them. Everyone backed away, fearing contamination from what were plainly the sacred objects that locked in her story. In quick gulps, she mentioned secrets—an important message about how she had been saved to tell the tale.

She was quizzed by the old people with the ancient wisdom. They asked if her secrets were in their national interest, by which they only implied their own big swamp of a nation, not the shebangs of anybody else's business. Well! Those hearts almost jumped straight from their chests from seeing so much horror in her eyes as she levitated the crystal balls, which created another illusion altogether, as though her world had once been like these balls, momentarily able to float in space.

All of this kind of thing happening out of the blue like that was not the message from a messiah that the Government in Canberra had told the swamp people to expect, but still, none could deny that she had been a sort of answer to prayers, even though she looked more like the local soil covering the roots of trees. She answered their inquiry by saying that her stories were of the utmost interest to the world. Well! they thought, why not. Our nation was small. Our boundaries not very large. It was very nice land. A bit flat. A bit hot. What they liked best, the kinsmen told her, was that they had nothing to do with the rest of Australia. They thought that they might like to have a bit of a holiday from some ancient responsibilities, and told her: *So stay. Have the floor old one. Tell stories.*

The maddest person on Earth told her stories of exile endlessly, but who listened? The swamp people were not interested in being conquered by other peoples' stories. Aunty Bella Donna of the Champions knew times when no one listened to the inconsequential stories she sung to herself: when hungry people feed themselves fat on voices droning from the radio, and repeat what they hear, they are like canaries. The girl replaced any dream of a big audience. But Oblivia stared into space, not listening. It was just music. Wave after wave of it rippling through the swamp. The score of a long concerto in gibberish and old principles cemented in language that ears had never heard before in that swamp.

First off! There was fright. Hell's people were naturally jumping around with Bella Donna's prolonged talking in this silent place of worship. She liked talking about surviving, intervention, closing the gap, moving forward as the way to become re-empowered, learning "lifestyle," of aesthetically pleasing houses and gardens. This confused the swamp. They thought she was really a local-bred redneck after all. The old people asked her: *Weren't you supposed to be some kind of a holy orator who remembered each epoch-making episode and emotional upheaval of the planet's nomadic boat people?* Heads spun with all the fires and violins endured in oceans as barren as a desert when she got back to the facts. She told it all: Feast and famine. Flutes of bewilderment. Drowning cellos. The voices of lovers. Crying births. Storms screaming. Wailing loss, abandonment, silence. Rejection. Bombing. Prayers. Theft. Beseeching. War. Puzzlement. Starvation. Staring at death. Organs from all over the world were playing in the swamp now. Thieving pirates. Robbers. Bandits. Murderers. And, somehow, more survival until: glory of migrating swan birds filling the skies.

Her poetry was about the grind. A treadmill recalling unlaureled bravery. Notes for those dead at sea. Men, women and children captured forever in the ghost nets of zero geography. She floated on the calm of swamp brine like the halcyon bird that sung the myths of wind and waves for the polyglotic nations of the sea. The uncharted floating countries of condemned humanity. Twenty-first-century castouts plowing the wilderness of oceans. But that was long ago she said. When the years passed and the floating worlds of refugees had grown white-haired, become weak and old of heart from waiting for any welcoming country on earth that was either big or small enough to let them in, all but one of those tens of thousands of obsolete people, the rejected of the world, had died.

The swamp people said her stories were lies. The sovereign facts lying on their table said that there was nothing worth hearing about from anywhere else on earth that was like her stories. Their sun hissed down and crackled on tin roofs. They did not need more heroes. Their own healer of country was already sitting up on top of the sand mountain trying to figure out what to do with it. And they knew what it meant to be sweltering in the heat, and dirt-poor. Politely, they asked the sick *wambu wanymarri* white lady to speak elsewhere about the snow, frost and chill. They had never seen any of that. *Go tell China! Africa! Bunda-berg! Istanbul! Don't come here with stories sounding like some kind of doomsaying prophet. We need our own practical measures to safeguard our culture. It is after all factual that terribly, terribly dry stories that flip, flop seven times in one hour straight are dangerous to the health of the mind.* No worries. What if times were blind and tight? *We were dead in the water in a dirty world,* she claimed while wiggling her fingers at the locals. Forget the raving. Forget the ranting. *We will not give away our rich prov-enance to the rest of the world, just to be like madamba—joined together like friends, no way,* the local broadcasters replied in song sung blue, and weeping like a willow.

Lesson over and another begins. *Oblivia! You must always remember eyes and ears are everywhere.* The old woman still spoke from a mind that lived elsewhere, with her speech that ran off to thoughts of hearing twinkling bells like the sound of a swan flying away. Oblivia listened to Bella Donna from a corner of the kitchen in the hull where she usually sat on the floor, without saying a word, imagining no one could see her. The old lady was retelling for the millionth time, the story of spend-ing years in a rowboat far out in the sea with only a ghost swan sitting beside her for company, while passing old houses and dead trees stuck out from the water. *I called out to see if anyone was there,* she said, *but only seagulls answered—laughing. Yes! Fancy that! Laughing at me. And kicking rats around the water for fun.*

Every now and then, every day in fact, the Harbor Master would come down from the sand mountain and row across the swamp, passing the rotting hulls, all the swans now living on the swamp that he called the wildlife, and anything else—decaying plastic, unwanted clothes, rot-ting vegetable matter or slime that bobbed, *wanami* diesel slick—on his way to visit the old woman who was looking after the girl he called The Human Rat. The stupid thing that got under his skin, who he was convinced was too lazy to speak, and was always sitting on the floor like a dog in the corner where she thought nobody could see her. Why did a thing like this land on her feet? Big question. This very thing made him wild enough to want to kill her because he thought she should be sitting up on a chair properly, if she was lucky enough to have one. He knew plenty of people who wished they had a chair to sit on. Why he even thought of himself, and he did not own a chair. If the white lady sat on a chair then the girl ought to be made to sit on a chair too, instead of acting like a white woman's black dog by sitting around on the floor, and the old woman beaming, *Oh! That's Oblivia for you.* These visits usually caused his mind to spew a bag of dead peace doves as soon as his eyes caught sight of Oblivia, and the more he saw her, and dwelled on all of her not-talking pretentiousness, and watched the old white lady struggling to teach the thing to talk, he was convinced that he had the girl pegged. *Git up off the floor and show some backbone like the rest of our people*, he snapped quick smart out of the corner of his mouth whenever he had the opportunity, behind Bella Donna's back, and added for good measure, *You make me sick.* Usually Oblivia ignored him, or else she shot him one of her several nasty expressions—eyes down, eyes blaring, screwed up or blanked face looking blacker than black, or more generally she spat on the floor between them, and with a bit of spit dividing their mutual disgust of one another, quite frankly, that's where the matter rested.

But Oblivia watched the Harbor Master who she thought ought to be doing something more about the sand mountain—unblocking the swamp for instance—he was taking long enough, and he should be more involved in fixing and healing like a real healer, instead of swooning about like some stupid cringing dog after Bella Donna. He splattered his soul that was fat with complaints all over the kitchen table for the old woman to see what the world had come to, of how difficult it was to heal anything these days in a place controlled by the Army like the swamp was. He was not superman was he? How could he take the love of Aboriginal children the Army men had stolen from parents and return it to them? And more so, he thought that instead of Bella Donna wasting her time on the useless girl, she should be consoling him and giving him some excellent full-bodied strength platitudes about how everything would work itself out for the best in the end.

The Harbor Master could not help himself, even though he sincerely believed Bella Donna was really a spy working for the Army and telling them lies about the swamp people. Why did he believe this? He told himself it was because he believed that he could spot a spy from a mile off, and he had. He could spot spies anywhere, and they were everywhere, even ones as small as an ant racing about and minding other people's business, or somebody obviously white and conspicuous like Bella Donna, although she just about knocked his socks off.

Like! Like! Oblivia overheard his whispering, and her guts had groaned and moaned while her stomach muscles tried to shove a jumble of dog-vomit words up her windpipe, although always in the nick of time, any of those screaming words that made it up to her mouth, crashed like rocks landing on enamel at the back of her clenched teeth. So, by remaining silent, saying nothing and stewing with hate and spitefulness in her guts, she reminded herself with a shiver down her spine that she would rather be dead than waste her breath speaking to an idiot.

The Harbor Master was oblivious to that tongueless thing Oblivia's attempts to communicate through a piece of spit and continued on with what he had come for—his total intoxication with the blissful Bella Donna who he claimed was on par with a saint, even if she was a spy and a traitor of the Aboriginal people. She was too much in his heart, so he kept telling himself, *Don't chase her away. Balyanga Jakajba. She's staying here. Jungku nyulu nayi.* She became his soul mate. She made his heart beat faster. Why ignore somebody who could wind his motor up? He was intrigued with Bella Donna's mission to kill off any strength and sign of leadership in the Aboriginal world by running straight to the Army with tales of Black insurgents, Black uprisings, Black takeovers etcetera around the swamp to keep his people in control, under the thumb and weak, but at the same time, needing with every ounce of her being to nurture a sickly, damaged and most obvious to everyone else, crazy, *warraku* Aboriginal child who would never be cured no matter how much the old white lady tried to change the girl's attitude by showering her with compassion, do-gooding, savioring and so forth. A complete useless waste of time. But, he thought, what was the use of him being a fan belt spinning around, that was always intervening and arguing with Bella Donna about her spying for the Army against any sign of Aboriginal strength, while mothering Aboriginal weakness, if that was the whole idea of racism. No! the Harbor Master reasoned. Who on earth was he to think that he could intervene in a white lady's prerogative to think the thoughts of racial fanaticism? A plain man like himself only had simple thoughts on offer. He was not the anti-racist God almighty, and he almost drooled down both sides of his mouth while listening to each of her nicely spoken well-rounded vowels as she gave a total list of her acts of compassion as though it was her penance for having sinned, for having survived the horrendous boat journey of her life. Whatever she spoke of, he believed that he could easily have listened to her talking all day long, if he did not have to be constantly busy minding the sand.

The Harbor Master was missing his monkey friend, who lived in an overseas country and who he claimed was a genius of world politics. He was always sorry about leaving the monkey eating grapevines, or where wolves hide out in forests of chestnut, or conifers, or larch trees that he claimed were like Bella Donna's rowan trees, a thousand years old. He missed not being on the scenery of world politics and speaking the monkey's language, and often complained, *I should be looking after all of my responsibilities instead of being caught up here having to guard the sand.*

But the joy of his predawn *gloriosus* rowing, was to glide among the dumped military ships and vessels that had once been used by commandos, militants, militia, pirates, people sellers, cults, refugees and what have you: everything dumped there by the Army and a very good place for a spy to hide.

This particular huge dark hull where he climbed up the rusty steel steps to come on board was the home of the old woman and the girl. He was their only visitor because he and the old woman had comparable memories of times when the countries in the world were different and, once he got Oblivia stirred up enough to spit on the floor, he got on with the job of reminiscing with Bella Donna about the world's geographies and analyzing the old maps they carried around in their heads. Some countries they remembered had even disappeared. They enjoyed a lamenting conversation of, *Oh! How I wonder what happened to that country! No. Did that little country disappear? Nobody lives there anymore. It just does not exist. You really mean that old place no longer exists, it can't be true but I guess it must have disappeared by sea rising, or wars. Had to happen.* Talk like that. Lead-poison-brains kind of talk. Conversations that meant nothing to overwhelmed swamp people who had always been told to forget the past by anyone thinking that they were born conquerors. They already knew what it was like to lose Country. Still, it did not pay to fret about the world when you were imprisoned. They were already the overcrowded kind of people living in the world's most unknown detention camp right in Australia that still liked to call itself a first-world country. The traditional owners of the land locked up forever. Key thrown away. They were sick to death of those two going on about what it was like having—*Been there!* And, *Been there too.* And, *You should have been there before the whole place turned to nothing.*

I wonder why you never see a white swan landing on the swamp? The old woman was always asking the famous Harbor Master this question, ignoring many large flocks of black swans that now already lived on the swamp, and he in turn was always singing and talking about the Rolling Stones songs that his genius of a pet monkey once sang. Yes, for sure, he missed the monkey he called Rigoletto. Sorry he had abandoned it after the monkey kept making a nuisance of itself by predicting colossal wars that started to frighten the life out of everyone. Sorry he thought the monkey was mad. *How does this swan look in your dreams?* He seemed to have been waiting for the swan to arrive too. No! She had never seen it in her dreams. These two had traveled to so many places in the world, surely, one of them had seen it somewhere, from viewing the land in a boat of banishment.

They looked for her lost white swan down in the chasms of gullies and valleys wrinkling the world, tramped through mill ponds, listened to the Mute Swans ringing the food bell in a Somerset moat, gone along the flaggy shore of County Clare and searched among the Liffey swans dipping for weed. It was like a giant séance for gathering the thoughts of at least half a million swans from Europe to Central Asia.

Bella Donna talked of having walked the stony shores among the Iceland Whooper Swans of Lake Myvatn to Reykjavík, of having skated alongside swans taking off on a frozen lake surrounded by icicle trees in Sweden, of having lived among migrating swans rushing to fly from snow on the mountains in Russia. She spoke to the *oo-hakucho* wintering in Japan's Akkesi-Ko, descendants of the great Kugui flocks that came from the olden times of the *Nihon shoki* in the eighth century and now sleeping on ice in the mist of Lake Kussharo. She had slid across the ice on Estonia's Matsalu Bay among sleeping Bewick's swans, still like statues, escaping wolves on their long migration. In her imagination, she had flown among the thousands of black-beaked Whistling Swans lifting into the Alaskan skies and in flight to the Samish Flats of the State of Washington, and far off, she had heard the bugling of the royal swans owned for centuries by monarchs, gliding along the Thames. Did she look around China for her swan? She had sat silently in a small boat under a Chinese moon where the Shao Hao people's winter angels live among kelp swishing in the sea of Yandun Jiao Bay. Long were the distances traveled, and all lonely! And all of them slow from too much hope in the heart, expectation, and the yearning to return.

The two old people's stories fly on through storming specks of ice, where the air had frozen into crystals that danced around the swan as it struggled to fly over the peaks of Himalayan mountains. They searched every abandoned, broken-down and flattened nest in the eastern kingdom on the Mongolian nurs, and then hiked, wet and wretched across grassy plains, while a migratory procession of white Whooper Swans flew over Hulun Nur, to Cheng Shanwei's Swan Lake. On lonely roads the old woman ransacked the nesting material of sweet swans running away from her over the ice on Dalinor Lake.

The old man and woman daydreamed themselves into every swan image on earth, and off they went again. *There they go—la, la, la,* the wild girl Oblivia whinged under her breath, excluded from entering their world of knowledge. So fair enough to travel in talk, about what it was like being among a pandemonium of snakes while wading barefoot and broke into old desert ponds covered with tumbleweed, to find a black-beak Whistling Swan with its head curled under its wing asleep, frozen to death. In the end it was always the same. No swan. Not the one she was expecting. Flat broke from renting hire cars, driving them until they become rust buckets. Finally! Their journey ended at the river where a poet carried a black-necked swan in his arms that was too weak to breathe. *Yes, ode indeed, lost swan.* Then the old woman and the Harbor Master each crawled back into their own separate, quiet dry caves dug somewhere deep in their minds. A silent place where each had their own swan blessed with flowers and fruit carved into granite gray brains.

He has the best intuition, the old woman said. Bella Donna was often full of her own gloating and fandangoing about geography and reminded the girl that she and the Harbor Master were very much alike. They were peas in the same pod. Exactly similar! Both had fled countries. Identical. He had always known the time to go too, uncanny, just like swans. *Which goes to show that Aboriginal people who put their minds to it, can track anywhere.* She could not praise him enough. She even continued rejoicing about the Harbor Master in her sleep, high praising the likes of him for his natural intuition about migratory routes, immigrating cycles and so on. It was for these reasons she had found a friend to talk to out here in a swamp that was in the middle of nowhere. *This is why he is very famous. He's the full packet, you betcha.* And all that . . .

Well! Nothing much comes marching in on thin air, even though the old woman was relentless in her belief that somewhere over the vast oceans lying between her and the old world, the grandest white bird of all labored in flight to reach her. But what did its continued absence mean? She could not understand it. Or why she was being denied her only wish. The only legacy she had left. Had she lost the ability to call her dead country's swan? Bella Donna offered the only possible explanation: *Because it was dead too.* The Harbor Master had to agree: *Died on its way. Fallen from the sky.*

Like a proper English-speaking child, the voiceless Oblivia learnt to sit straight-backed at the dinner table and chew fish, while contemplating the adult world talking themselves silly with their stories. In her mind she mused, *Brain rust rent-a-car mouths. Car dead. Brain dead. Aren't there enough black swans here, all nesting in rusted car bodies dumped amongst the reeds? And together they go: Toot! Toot!*

It took her no trouble to imagine the bird falling from the sky. She could see its body floating in any stretch of ocean that lay beyond the horizon—even though she had never seen the sea herself. She skipped a heartbeat. Any thought of distance did that. Her heart almost stopped beating every time she had to listen to their talk about traveling overseas to see swans. She was more comfortable with closer geography, with what lay in front of the horizon, as far as the top of the sand mountain, and into the ocean of the Harbor Master's stomach. She smiled at the gargoyle with a small white down feather sticking out from the corner of his mouth.

Bella Donna's world of exhausted journeying continued to shrink until it became so small, there was only space left for her one lost white swan. It loomed ever larger in her mind, until finally, her mind contained nothing else but the swan. She would not believe it was dead. How could anything so special, that was celebrated by hemispheric legends on both sides of the equator, be dead? She gifted the swan with eternal life. She quoted Hans Christian Andersen. Hadn't he written about a swan sitting on a nest of fledglings that perpetually flew off to populate the world with poetry inspired by their own beauty? Now her swan was the Denmark swan, and she wanted to know why it had not come to the swamp to create poetry. *Well! Why not?* How could a resurrecting swan, with the strongest pair of wings for flying halfway around the world, be lost? Perhaps it was always shot dead on arrival? Fallen in sediment. Its poetry condemned. Evading its final splash down in front of her eyes.

Oblivia thought about the invisible swan whose stories occupied every centimeter of their hull. Was it real? Sure! Acts of *descendancy* were important ideas in the swamp; and even, whether it was right to think about stories of birds like a white swan in the swamp.

One day Bella Donna's old storytelling voice told the girl: *A black swan flies slowly across the country, holding a small slither of bone in its beak.*

But then she hesitated, perhaps realizing she was deviating from the white swan she had been longing for. Her voice stalled, tapered off into whispers that even the girl, now the perfect mimic of the old woman, could not understand. It was as though the old woman had become so old, she was unable to continue either to dither or to go thither in a fantastical story that began not at the beginning, nor at the end, but centrally, in ether. *What was it? Ah?* Was she unable to comprehend progress? Did she now doubt the white swan's ability to navigate its journey? Or perhaps, she just told stories the way swans fly.

Obediently, Oblivia listened. She had become more interested than ever in the old woman's stories, even though she thought old Aunty was just facing another storm, and this made it difficult for her to speak. Where was it this time? She wondered if it had always been like this for old *wanymarri* white woman Aunty. All beginnings, wherever begun, lost? Perhaps even, that the old woman was neither life, dreams, or stories. Just air. The girl looked away and whispered into the steel wall of the hull: *She was nothing.* It might have been so! *Fat plague of loss.* The girl accused the old woman of being a victim by telling the wall, *You dream like a refugee—of never being able to return. Being lost all the time. That's all you think about. Think about that.* The girl had turned examiner of other people's consciences. But what would you expect? She knew old Bella Donna like her own thumb, knew exactly what it was like to be unable to realize one single idea without falling over a multitude of anxieties. In numerous conversations with the wall, she explained the crux of the matter *The old woman was a victim of her own mathematics.* She had become lost in senseless tangles. An eternity of trying to calculate the exact weight of a swan traveling from so far away through such a long period of time. How long would it take to reach its destination? *There are endless, infinite possibilities, you know.* When she thought more kindly, the girl softened her image of the old woman flying around in *etherland. Might be as good a place as any to be with her swan.*

You could see that the old woman had become a little bit *day-dreamy,* but she often tried to impress on the girl one single thing of importance: *A love story can be about swans, but the swan looks more like death with a bone in its beak. It could be a human bone, or a bone from another swan. Its mate, maybe.*

The old lady's fearful whisperings like this at night lulled the swamp people in their cradles, cocooning them like machinery rattling away, like swarming bees, and seagulls squalling for hours on end in the distance, or else remembering hawks piercing the hot air with their cries all day long. But it was different for birds. The seagulls and hawks flew around the swamp, absorbed in their own business of surviving in a peaceful and orderly manner. The birds disregarded the monologue of northern hemisphere *outsidedness* humming like the engine of a boat, trying to move their relevance to their native country further away in the fog.

When the girl whispered, the old woman interpreted—guessed what she wanted to know—and spoke for her, why *can't I see that swan with the bone if you can see it?* Something dropped into the water. Plop! Was this a fact that had slipped from her hypothetical love stories? The girl thought that she could hear ghost music. A string of musical notes gob-smacked in bubbles broke through the surface of the swamp. Even the old woman noticed the music, but she continued on her merry way with her story, regardless: *I have become an expert on music made from old bones, and I say it could be from swan bones, or bones of drowned people, or of drought-stricken cattle, imitating the scores of Mozart's fingers racing across the ivory.*

The greatest love story this country has ever known began somewhere around here, the old lady said while sniffling back at the bubbling water, speaking only to herself, or to somewhere way past the girl, that could have been the Harbor Master listening from the top of his hill.

A large flock of black swans whispering to each other in their rusted car-body bedrooms all over the swamp whistle, glide and bump over the waves driven along by the sudden arrival of gusty winds, while the old woman sings more: *I got to roll you over, roll over, rolling bones.*

Far into the night, the swamp music continued telling the old woman's love story through the girl's dreams where, in the underwater shadows, she looked like a cygnet transformed into two people entwining and unwinding back and forth in the bubbling swamp, in waves scattered by a relic dropped from the beak of the black swan imagined by the old woman.

Black swans kept arriving from nowhere, more and more of them, from the first one that had arrived unexpectedly and spoiled the swamp people's dinner.

After black swans came to the swamp something else happened . . . A soft yellow beam of light fell over the polluted swamp at night. It was the torchlight of armed men flying in the skies like Marvin Gaye's ghost looking about the place, to see what was going on. *Yes! Well! You tell me what was going on?* The Army men sent by the Government in Canberra to save babies from their parents said that they were guarding the sleep of little children now.

The swamp bristled.

This was the history of the swamp ever since the wave of conservative thinking began spreading like wildfire across the twenty-first century, when among the mix of political theories and arguments about how to preserve and care for the world's environment and people, the Army was being used in this country to intervene and control the will, mind and soul of the Aboriginal people. The military intervention was seen as such an overwhelming success in controlling the Aboriginal world it blinded awareness of the practical failures to make anyone's life better in the swamp. This "closed ear" dictatorial practice was extended over the decades to suit all shades of gray-colored politics far away in Canberra, and by tweaking it ever so little this way and that, the intervention of the Army never ended for the swamp people, and for other Aboriginal people like themselves who were sent to detention camps like the swamp to live in until the end of their lives. The internment excluded the swamp people from the United Nations' Universal Declaration of Human Rights, and the control proliferated until there was full traction over what these people believed and permeance over their ability to win back their souls and even to define what it meant to be human, without somebody else making that decision for them.

. . . .

Now the swamp people's voices were talking in the girl's dreams, telling her: *Your tree did not exist.* Screamed: *TELL HER. No strong tree like that ever existed here.* The girl panicked, would wake up in fright from not remembering anymore about how she came to be asleep in the tree. She started to believe what other people believed: *She was telling lies.*

The light quickly travels across water, twice over buildings, through the football oval, and along streets, then swirling around, the Army men on the boundaries go through the exit gates, before turning around, locking the gates, and the lights march off again.

The girl watched the other children. They play a game of pretending they are from another life—from the *space age,* living on Mars or some other planet, and run to be saved by the passing light.

When the old woman was not watching, Oblivia studied the running rays of light reflected on the surface of the swamp, unsettling a black swan that lifted, tail splashing, into garnishes of serendipity. There were bones rattling like loose change when the torchlight hit flocks of white cockatoos, causing them to screech from the rooftops where they sat roosting—*Sweet Lord.* A light ran again across the water saying, say again: *What's going on?*

Humpies! Hundreds sprung up all along the banks of the swamp like nobody's business now. Well! The dominant voices around the country and western bloc of the country's politics had not balked for a second about Aborigines when saying, "*Why not?*" This was what happens when you put the Army in charge of the swamp, long after it had become one of those Australian Government growth communities for corralling Aboriginal peoples into compounds. These were pastimes for kicking Aboriginal people around the head with more and more interventionist policies that were charmingly called *Closing the Gap.* But, so what? The very sight of the place was vilified up and down the country for being like dogs in the pound begging for food.

Well! So what if it was just another moment in a repetitious black-

and-white history repeated one more time for Aboriginal people from wherever about the place, after having their lives classified and reassigned yet again? Anybody's politics was a winner these days, so long as they were not blackfellas caring about their culture. So it was nothing for Australians to get excited about when Aboriginal people started being divided into lots and graded on whether anything could be done for them. Upper scale—if they could actually be educated. Lower scale—just needed some *dying pillow* place to die. Many Indigenous populations began to be separated regardless of family or regional ties. In growth centers like the swamp, thousands of Aboriginal people became common freight as they were consigned by the busload, then more conveniently, by the truckload. The swamp now renamed Swan Lake was nothing special. It was the same as dozens of fenced and locked Aboriginal detention centers.

Only starving skin-and-bone people with hollow-eye children who refused to speak came off those trucks and Army buses. Their clothes were stiffened with dried sweat and dirt from the journey. These strangers looked here and there initially, as though trying to avoid the heavy spirit of bad luck swooping down to sit on their backs. They got spite eyes from the local people. A little dull blue butterfly flew through one of the buses to have a look around and sat down on a young boy's head. He would commit suicide this poor little *juka*. Everyone knew. More boys and girls would die like this.

The swamp people, the big-time protesters, rocked to their foundations from three centuries of dealing with injustices already, will probably feel the same way in two centuries more—who's speculating on the likely projection of this tragedy? Now they were yelling and screaming, *Weren't we supposed to be the traditional owners? Doesn't that count for anything? Serious! Well!* They were right about that. So! *All right.* An Army general put in charge from the Government said they were the traditional owners of a convenient dumping ground for unwanted people now.

What were unwanted people? Well! They were little people who can't fight a big thing like the Army in charge of all the Aboriginal children—little pets owned by the Mothers of Government who claimed to love them more than their own "inhumane" families. *Disgraceful business?* So interracially intolerant Australia was still the same old, same old. Aunty Bella Donna, now old as the hills, said that she felt like a thief, even a kidnapper, and she went around the place like a madwoman trying to mop up any insinuating words she thought were generating from out of thin air—*I told you myself, that I found her . . . in a tree.* If she had saved the girl or not—what did it matter? The girl could answer anyone herself about what it was like to be saved if she thought about pillaging a few words from somewhere in her mind to speak. She could have said that she did not know who she was. Or that she was so damaged that she could not speak. She was under a spell. But she felt nothing about pain or joy, night or day. She thought no life was worth saving if it was no longer your own.

I think that girl caused all of this Army business coming here. Holy smoke why had the swamp people forgotten? The Army had come a long time ago. But this swamp was plaguing for revenge and pumped itself with so many compelling ideas of fear they were now far beyond the capacity to clean the floor off with a mop.

You should have left her where she was.

The cuckoos and cockatoos heard every single thing and, it might be, their nervous flinching and tapping of beaks on wood were imitating insecurities in the hearts of the children.

The light that came from the sky at night was relentless. It was the Army swinging around the searchlights. Where was the joy in this? Ungovernable thoughts unfurled into the atmosphere from the heads of people hiding beneath folded wings that might have belonged to the black swans that had died in the swamp. Yes, those grand old birds flying high into the greatness of life without paying a dollar for the flight could just be angels.

The swamp's murky water was littered with floating feathers, and it looked as though black angels had flown around in dreams of feeling something good about one another. *Well! Not around here when you were nobody, you don't feel like an angel,* Bella Donna said as though she read thoughts, but she was just passing traffic—generalizing about what was going on in the girl's brain. She had no idea of how the girl saw those wasted gray-black feathers.

Ah! All these feathers were just sweet decoration. Feathers floating on fading dreams, obscuring the address that was difficult enough to remember for transporting the girl back to the tree, where in her mind the route she chased while sinking away into slithers of thoughts slipped silently in and out of the old threads woven through the forest of mangled tree roots. When she runs in these dreams, her footsteps crush the delicate crisscrossing patterns of the worn stories, that reached deep into sacred text, the first text, in saying, *We are who we are*. Fancy words, scrolling back and forth in the girl's mind, float like the feathers that stop her escaping back to the tree.

Rubbish stackings, tied with yellow clay-stained stockings—too many of these human nests encasing the swamp. The sand bank that had grown to mountainous heights still separated the brackish water from the sea, while a fast-growing population of Aboriginal people from faraway places was settling, living the detention lifestyle right around the swamp.

The truck people kept on arriving. They were more like arriving cattle being segregated and locked up in "growth centers," now called National Aboriginal Relocation Policy by some mind-dead politicians claptrapping that they were dealing with rats. Suppose hard come, and easy go, for the traditional land of the swamp was snatched again. The real owners hidden in the throng could not count the number of times their land had been ripped from under their feet.

In this oasis of abandonment, home for thousands forcibly removed from other "more visible" parts of Australia by the Government, the swamp became a well-known compound for legally interning *whoever* needed to be secluded far away behind a high, razor-edged fence from the decent people of mainstream civilization.

It was just a contemporary painting—a pastoral scene, the old lady surmised in the early days, while her eyes swung along the ever-increasingly crowded shoreline.

It's really insanity here, she told the Harbor Master about the people living all about the place.

It's not like it used to be, honest, he replied, the magic lost from his voice. He was forgetting to sing his Mick Jagger songs. The girl sunk deeper into her thoughts: *So! What did I care? What about my story? Me! Different dollar please!*

Now while Bella Donna was carrying on like this, the population would peer out each day from package crates, donated cubbies from foreign aid, and rubbish that sprung up in the overcrowded slum now running around the entire shoreline. *What unimaginably difficult poverty-stricken circumstances,* Bella Donna cried, wiping up her tears with a bit of newspaper. She consoled herself with poetry, reciting lines like John Shaw Neilson's *I waded out to the swan's nest at night and heard them sing. . .*

The Harbor Master stayed on top of his mountain, too frightened to leave. He was just sitting like everyone else, and listening to all kinds of fruitless, high volume *megaphoning* protest from the minority landowners trying to reach inside the closed ears of the Army men protecting the swamp. *What do we want? We want you white bastards outta here.* Waste of breath. Their mantra was five or six words more or less, which meant the same thing: *Nobody asked us for permission, moron.* Every day, hours were put aside for protesting. It was like listening to a continuous earthquake of hate from a stadium built out of the swamp itself.

Can you tell me why those Aboriginal people had to be relocated here for—from across the country, Aunty? The girl sometimes imagines herself speaking politely, in a pretty voice, while mouthing off her soundless words.

God knows it was only a swamp, of what a storm gives, or easily takes away.

A low-pressure weather system was unpredictable and nobody knew whether it would bring more dry storms or blue skies sulking through another year. Still, a flood of mythical proportions would be required to drive the sand back into the sea. The ceremonies sang on and on for majestic ancestral spirits to turn up out of the blue, to stir up the atmospheric pressure with their breath, to turn the skies black with themselves, to create such a deluge to unplug the swamp, to take the sand mountain back to the sea. But more was said than done. The ancestral sand spirits flew like a desert storm and backed themselves even further up against the mountain. Silt gathering in the swamp lapped against the dwellings of the increasing population and crept further inwards as the swamp decreased in size. This was the new story written in scrolls of intricate lacework formed by the salt crystals that the drought left behind.

The swamp's natural sounds of protest were often mixed with lamenting ceremonies. Haunting chants rose and fell on the water like a beating drum, and sounds of clap sticks oriented thoughts, while the droning didgeridoos blended all sounds into the surreal experience of a background listening, which had become normal listening. Listen! That's what music sounds like! The woman once explained to the girl that the music of epic stories normally sounded like this.

This is the world itself, disassembling its thoughts.

It was just the new ceremony of swamp dreaming, the girl thought, for what she called, Nowhere Special. She thought it suited the wind-swept surroundings of the dead swamp, where children played with sovereign minds, just by standing out in the wind to fill their cups with dust given to them by their ancestors.

Dust covered the roads and nobody knew where they were anymore, and the old woman claimed that even the bitumen highways were disappearing. Soon, no one would have any idea about how to reach this part of the world.

If you leave here, you know what is going to happen don't you? People are going to stop and stare at you the very instant they see the color of your skin, and they will say: She is one of those wild Aboriginals from up North, a terrorist; they will say you are one of those faces kept in the Federal Government's *Book of Suspects*.

Bella Donna said that even though she had never seen this book for herself, she had heard that it had the Australian Government's embossed crest on the cover, and was kept at the post office where anyone could study it. What was a post office? The girl had listened.

This was the place where they kept faces plucked from the World Wide Web by Army intelligence looking at computers all day long, searching for brown- and black-colored criminals, un-assimilables, illegal immigrants, terrorists—all the undesirables; those kind of people.

Never ever leave the swamp, she said, adding that her own skin did not matter, but the girl was the color of a terrorist, and terrorism was against the law.

Bella Donna's home was camouflaged in the middle of the flotilla of junk littering what she called the vision splendid. The hull jutted out of the swamp like a war monument saluting in gray-colored steel. This joyless, rusting hull with a long war record of stalking oceans looked like a traitor imprisoned away from the sea, but it was not alone in this polluting junkyard choked up with so-called lost Army property. Its neighbors were the remains of all the *muwada*—cargo boats, trawlers, tugboats, fighter boats and rickety old fishing boats. These phantom vessels were either falling apart at the seams from decades of bobbing themselves into oblivion, or had become dilapidating wrecks.

While the hull was slowly sinking its huge belly in the yellow mud, the old foreign woman chopped carrots in the galley. She sang her premonitions as she chopped. *The hull was burying itself at its own funeral.* It was a kind of simple theory, as far as theories went. All kinds of conspiracies poured out of her old lips to the sound of the knife clipping the wood, chopping vegetables for another stew. *Was this going to be the unrecorded record of the world's longest suicide attempt?* The longest pause! You could feel the slide, slipping and dipping further into the mud, by a few millimeters a day.

The bounty the old white aunty business brought from overseas was about reading the signs of the unsaid and speaking about what was not obvious. Well! Why not listen? The resident Queen of the manufacturing and boat-building industry did reigning well. She knew what you needed to feel in your bones about nautical living, boat steel and planks of wood. Even her bones could feel how the hull was reorienting itself towards the fanfare of East Coast cities. She asked any passing spirit bystander she noticed hanging around her kitchen, *How else was the hull going to capture the glory from which it had been robbed?*

Sounds were destroying the memory of the girl who only wanted to be living in her tree again. She felt as though she was locked inside a suitcase that the old woman dragged along and pussyfooted about on noisy gravel. It was the *walk of life*, old Aunty claimed. How it felt to be living inside the steel of a battling war hero robbed of the hullabaloos, feeding off the fanfare of pomp and ceremony, had it not been dishonored. Sabotaged by traitorous telltale words, *Welcome Boat People*, which protesters had once sprawled in white paint across its side.

These words, decrypted many times by the old woman, had almost faded away from years of sitting in the swamp, just like the memory of most of those protesters of good causes, once they scrubbed up and rejoined their conservative Australian upbringings. The old woman said that she had often heard the hull moaning, crying out as though it had lost heart in the idea of achieving perfection through one last salute. Let there be Death! The girl walked around with the hull's colossal lament impaled in her heart. *What could I do?* she demanded. There was nothing she could do about glory.

So! Bad luck and so forth, Aunty said, because anyone could dream like fish on the other side of the sand mountain, where shifting winds were funneling the outgoing tide back to the sea.

The swamp people were really frightened of the flotilla. Some would not even look at the decaying boats. Some claimed that they could not see any dumped boats out there on their pristine swamp. *Ya only see what you want to see and that's that.* They did not go around looking for things outside of the *sanctum* of traditional knowledge. They said old scrap boats were dumped in the Congo, in real swamps, among the boa constrictors. Well! You learn a lot of things like that from looking at too many of those old movies.

Nor did it take much from a separatist-thinking swamp person to believe that Bella Donna was a real ghost even before she was dead, or that girl *whatsherface* too—for turning up years after she was supposed to be dead. Rah! Rah! Everything was vapor. There were plenty of people around who said that they would rather be dead than sniffing old fat hissing from a frypan where ghosts were frying up their fish. Exactly right! *Whitefella ghosts, seasonal plagues of gray rat ghosts, other vermin ghosts like swarming cockroaches, march flies and infestations of hornet nests.*

So floating junk, if seen in the light of having too many foreigners circulating in one's own spiritual world, could always be ignored for what it was—other people's useless business. Of course it was infuriating for all of the witnesses of the swamp world to see so much waste not being put to some proper use. After all, anyone could see that foreign ghosts were not particularly harmful if you got past the innocuous cunning way that they could steal a whole country, kill your people, and still not pay all those centuries' worth of rent. It was just that all those men, women and children in the detention camp living cheek to jowl in broken-down shacks, crates and cardboard boxes had no affinity with dead strangers. Cramp was better. So much preferable to being haunted when you did not feel like being frightened by other people's ghosts.

Only the old woman had decided to be radical by taking up a grandiose lifestyle on one of the flotilla's rust buckets, and in the end, when she had claimed responsibility for the girl, she had taken her out there on the water to live. She said that the hull was part of the Australian way of life. She was helping to make Australia a great country. *I am not a separatist from Australia*, she claimed.

The detention camp was now a settled population of traditional owners from kingdoms near and far, and swamped with a big philosophy about the meaning of home. Why do they do it? *They could also seek asylum and permanent Australian residency by living on navy junk,* the old woman claimed, referring to her hull as a solid piece of Australia that was immune to traditional landownership laws. She liked being part of mass Australia and owning her own home. It gave her a sense of authority when it suited her. *You think that they would want to grab the chance to become fully Australian. A chance to live like everyone else.*

• • • •

It was easy, and eerie, to see bleeding-heart, rust-staining yellow water. It gave you the shivers. If you looked closely at the flotilla for long enough you saw people at war. Saw military parades. Dead men marching up and down on the decks, and in your sleep you dreamt of people screaming and running for their lives from the explosions. The girl did not say much about that, or the ghosts screaming in her sleep about the wars they had never left.

The rotten and broken-down vessels were a jarring sight, but the old queen marveled over the slicks of pollution—the strange panorama of toxic waste swimming on the surface of the water. The water gleamed with blue and purple oxidizing colors, and if you were to look long enough at the sun hitting the swamp from 1400 to 1600 hours in the winter months, this polluted glare became even more dazzling— where the water was broken into trails of rainbows made by the movement of swimming swans.

Swamp people regarded this particular sight as something evil, created by devils, easy, easy now, and in this respect the swans coming to the swamp with no story for themselves generated a lot of talk. They were suspected of being contaminated with radioactivity leaking from some of the hulls. Of course it was mentioned, considered, even nurtured by the swamp dwellers' constituency, now permanently submerged and half drowning in open wounds, by asking forlornly any question that would not be answered such as, *Was this the silent killer then, the Army's final weapon of mass destruction?*

No more! It was easier for the swamp people to shift unanswered questions to somebody else—*Here! Chuck it over to him,* passing the buck, and end up blaming the old Harbor Master for the pollution. They complained of not seeing him remove one speck of sand, and that the situation had gotten worse, and whinged, *He was supposed to be a healer for the country. That's what he came here for when he could have just arrived in a dream and blasted the mountain like that, like an e-mail, and finished the job off like we asked him to do. Just get rid of the sand mountain, that's all we wanted, and he could have done that from anywhere, instead of ending up coming here personally. We can't look after him forever. Well! Pronto. We are waiting . . . and he should finish the job off straight away, not taking years to do something.*

The sand mountain that the Harbor Master lived on seemed to be growing even further towards the sky, while its shadow now rested over the swamp for a good part of the day. Anyone would have thought that the Harbor Master was actually shoveling the sand up to the sky himself. The shadow spread uncertainty as to where it would all end, as much as being a feast to be devoured by the swamp's full-time philosophers, soothsayers and fortune-tellers emerging at the crack of dawn from their homes of cardboard and similar stuff—like worms crawling out of holes, to look way up the mountain where they could see for themselves how it had grown a couple of centimeters higher during the night.

All the great holy and wise people of the swamp would come and stand around on the shoreline looking across the water towards the hull, and while deep in whispered conversation with each other, you could tell by their sour facial expressions that they were not happy at all about what was happening to their land. The girl thought that they were accusing the old woman of upsetting the Harbor Master and jumping in with the status quo. It was during this time that Oblivia began to understand that nobody noticed her on the hull. It was obvious that the locals acted as though she never existed, was too unimaginable, unable to be recognized and named.

Traitors! Bella Donna's voice rang like a big tower bell over the water to any assembly on the foreshore looking her way whom she accused of not being patriots to the Australian flag. She had good communication skills for throngs. The whole riled swamp now ate each other's venom for breakfast. They yelled at her: *Yea! That's your story.* Patriotism! *Ha! We'll show you what bloody patriotism means.* A blaze of color of Aboriginal flags unfurled in the wind, some intact, some tattered, or just bits of faded material, even paper colored black, yellow or red, were hoisted up on sticks of makeshift flagpoles in her face.

Boat person! Loser! Terrorist!

As the worldwide know-all of everything, the old woman claimed that most of the rotting boats dotting the lake had belonged to an army of textbook terrorists who invaded other countries. She had once chopped carrots for terrorists and claimed: *I am recognized in all the seas of the world.* She waved her stick at the sea wrecks bobbing up and down or stuck in mud, noting with sage-like authority which of the old boats had carried people she knew, which had run from wars in faraway countries and which had fled over dangerous seas trying to reach this unwelcoming land. She knew millions of people, shouting it around, *I knew all those people who didn't even make it. Those left behind to suffer the hand of fate. Those millions of refugees out there somewhere who were still dreaming of coming to your paradise,* she yelled.

Water levels went up and down, and during the winter months many wrecks were left squatting in the mud.

What became of their owners? The girl mouthed this question as many times as Bella Donna spoke the words for her, hoping to coach Oblivia to ask more about her sea journeys.

The earth buries the dead. Lovers to Lovers. Dust to Dust. Their families hate all of us, Bella Donna said, giving the same answer every time.

Far off behind the dwellings on the other side of the swamp, on the top of the sand dune mountain that blocked the channel between the swamp and the sea, now that the Army had taken over the Harbor Mastering responsibilities, the old Harbor Master had become even more reclusive. His mind felt strange. Useless. He felt unable to control what was happening anymore. He hardly ever scrambled down the sand ghost, or longed for the pleasure of brushing past the swans guarding the hulls in the middle of the night, and those old sailor spirits crying down in the mud, while rowing the stagnant waters to visit Bella Donna of the Champions.

His worries grew proportionally with the sand mountain steadily reaching towards its zenith, knowing undeniably it would eventually be vanquished by its own weight. He fretted about this final collapse. What would he do? This was the reason that he could hardly risk leaving the mountain, yet he had to see the old woman to tell her of his dreams.

He frequently dreamt that he would leave the swamp by clinging to a ghost flying like a huge Zeppelin of sand through the atmosphere, as the drought moved somewhere else. Culture was such a formidable thing to him now. He did not know how to hold on to such a thing anymore. This idea of the sand taking him away from his country was his constant concern—the thing he had to tell her—to be calmed. Only she knew how to look at him straight in the eye and tell him he was wrong, and when she smiled, it was as though she had looked through music—a pleasing melody, that had come out of his mouth.

Whatever she heard reflected through the filter of foreign musical manuscripts nestled in her brain of tonally lifeless melodies, he could have been playing a shakuhachi in Japan, or whistling like an Asian songster, or seducing the world through a bamboo flute. How would she hear him? She was still attached to the libraries and archives left behind in the western part of the world. It was as though she had never left.

Sorry! Really sorry! About the sand! We will both go together, he warned, turning away, and with a further thousand apologies, forced his rowboat through the league of hungry swans packed around the hull. Until finally, he ran back up the mountain to wait, too anxious of missing the moment when the ghost would decide to collapse and be gone with the wind.

The girl felt the anticipation of change creeping towards the swamp. She already saw the old man as streamers of sand blowing their own *espressivo andante* of an exodus song for homeland.

Him sand—every grain is sacred. The Harbor Master was desperate to inform others to be prepared to leave on the big journey, calling on the locals, even the alienated and stigmatized truck people from the cities, and whoever went up to the top of the mountain to ask him why he lived his lonely life, separate and unsociable and isolated in this out-station from the swamp's growth town.

Well! It was truly something strange to do, the old woman even thought that, although she was also living apart from the rest of the community. But unlike the Harbor Master, who everyone seemed to care about, nobody came over to the hull and asked her what her re-sponsibility was.

You should leave and the sand might follow you instead, she had suggested, and he laughed.

She told him that people were wishing on a falling star for bulldozers to come and destroy the sand mountain.

They say it was foreign people thinking in a pristine environment that was making this trouble etcetera! The sand got no mind himself. Nothing to do with it.

The Harbor Master was insulted to be called a foreign person who did not know his own culture. He stomped around on the mountain. Sand rolled through the air, teasing the whole swamp before flying off somewhere. He could not get the insult out of his head.

Old Aunty ignored it all. At times like this, she just played Hoffmeister type of music on her swan-bone flute to the swans.

Pythons and lizards, the fattest catfish from the swamp, bats and marsupials, were thrown like flower petals up the sand mountain as offerings. All of it landed with a thud. Taipan snakes shimmering about, danced among dead catfish with bodies coiled and heads raised off the ground.

Don't expect me to drive it away, the defunct Harbor Master called down to the gathered people below who thought he, an old man, just an old *malbu*, could have so much power in his body that he could snarl like some unidentifiable animal throwing poisonous snakes around in the sand and move a mountain away with his bare hands. But! He said his sand was welcome to stay regardless of all the inconveniences. *It will go away when it wants.* Well! Anyone could be a genius about drought saying something like that.

Bella Donna was sulking because the Harbor Master had become too tied up in matters that did not concern her and preoccupied with arguing with the community now doubting his powers as a healing man for their country. These days she even tended to ignore Oblivia, and the girl felt neglected, a bit miffed, and renewed her vow never to speak again. Who was she kidding? The truth of the matter was that Oblivia had long forgotten how to speak, and did not know she could speak, and had no confidence to speak. She was glad that the Harbor

Master had stopped coming to the hull. She was happy to hear him arguing with everyone thinking he was a fake, because he probably was as far as she was concerned. The reason she thought so was because she knew the Harbor Master only had a big mouth and that was not going to move the sand mountain. No. The Harbor Master was not even a big-shot character from one of the old woman's many treasured books. And certainly, Bella Donna had not incorporated him in the long self-edifying narratives about her journey to this, the concluding triumphant chapter of her life.

It particularly annoyed Oblivia that Bella Donna remained fascinated by her ugly-face ghost-man the Harbor Master and that the old woman had stopped telling her stories. In particular, one obscure and favorite story about a little *juka* who was called God's Gift. The old woman claimed she had seen the boy many times. She was always looking out for him and wondering when she would see him again. His home was the world itself because he was a special gift from God. She had heard about this boy people had been waiting for to care for their deer on the other side of the planet. His aura was seen standing among rays of sunlight shining through a dark misty forest next to snow-capped mountains where God lived. Or, she told of people having seen a vision of the boy living in the swamps throughout the world where swans lived, and also where God lived. She told stories of how the boy was thought to live in the houses of ancient cities where fig trees grew out of cracks in the walls and from the rooftops and, only rarely, could you get past the troupe of monkeys who were guarding him, to see him more closely. It seemed as though she had seen this boy all over the world, or wherever you found God.

The old woman often saw him visiting family along the swamp. He was always visiting she claimed. *Oh! You should meet him one day. He is a proper good boy. A boy the whole world would love.* The girl scanned all the shack houses around the shore of the swamp hoping to locate the ones where monkeys lived and where fig trees grew from the rooftops, among the din of ghetto blasters and loud television.

The old woman claimed that she had just seen him running around the swamp with his pet monkeys and even with a fox in his arms. God was here. *Did you see him too?* She thought anyone would have noticed somebody like that—a gift from God. Bella Donna would sigh and re-sign herself to failure, knowing that telling stories to the child was pure waste. The little girl had no imagination: *Never sees a thing.*

Look out! Taipan snakes dancing all over the ground.

It was impossible for Aunty Bella Donna of the Champions to con-duct herself like normal people, like those who did not call out for all manner of things to be brought to them—calling to the skies to bring her swans. In that *la la* voice of hers, she snorted about the swamp's negativity, *Why be like other people calling all these trillions and zillions of flies to come here, dragonflies, sandflies, march flies, blowflies to swim in their teacup?*

Believe it or not, everyone thought that the old white lady was one of those people who had invented climate change and that she really had brought the swans to the North to live on the swamp. The old black swans had heard her voice running along streams of dust floating in the breezes, that dropped in and out of the skies, and back and forth along telegraph wires, and through kilometers of pipelines, and on bitumen roads of state highways, until reaching the droughts in the South, where great colonies of swans normally lived. A flock of swans deranged by drought, then another, and another, labored the distance, flew the same path to the swamp when it stopped rain-ing, no *janja* for what seemed forever, when the wetlands dried up. No one cared for the swans coming to the swamp's detention camp. Nobody knew what it meant. The very presence of those swans living with Aunty Bella Donna of the Champions on a swamp that belonged to a few brolgas, linked them very firmly with what they called, *some other kind of madness.*

In yellow froth and feather waters covered by films of dust, the swans led mottled brown and gray cygnets to the old lady whenever she ap-peared on her raft. They whistled soft music while gliding alongside their swan caller's floating platform. Her raft, constructed of melaleuca paperbark trunks, was tied together with randomly found wire and rope, and that it floated at all was thanks to a little bit of starlight for luck. She looked awkward—juggernauting long poles that moved the platform. It was like looking at a brightly dressed, long-legged water-bird walking through the muddy water. All along the foreshore, the swamp dwellers watched through the permanent haze of insects at what was happening to their lot. The old loved weeping spring was now the stagnant water among sad old lilies and long wriggling serpents.

Those black swans would glide from all corners of the swamp to the old woman. They moved through the water with their long straight necks held high and their fine black-feathered heads slightly cocked to one side to listen to her stories about the world she had known. Drops of water would fall from their red beaks, with the signature white bar above the nostril, while they listened to her. The swans, continuously quavering, their beaks dipped slightly into the surface of the water, testing the level, sensing the evaporating moisture running away into the atmosphere. Suddenly, a swan would orate the reply by arching its neck towards the sky and trumpeting a long, mournful call. Soon all that could be heard for kilometers around were swan bugles heralded skyward in prayers for rain.

In those days of graceful gliding swans, swirling around in loops in settled softness, there was often a serene calmness that ran throughout the swamp. The swans stayed all seasons, even until the swamp almost dried up when the old loved spring did not flow. Sometimes, the whole mass would suddenly disappear in the middle of the night and the swamp would seem empty and silent—as though they had never been there—then unexpectedly, they returned, homing to the old woman. Perhaps it was her stories. Or, she really could call swans.

Among the miracles of overcrowding, conjuring more, praying for more—more swans arrived instead of rain on the swamp. Though they were previously unknown in this environment, the swamp people thought that the swans had returned to a home of ancient times, by following stories for country that had been always known to them. Swans had Law too. But now, the trouble was, nobody in the North re-membered the stories in the oldest Law scriptures of these big wetland birds.

The southern swans kept descending in never-ending ribbons from the sky, and some said it was because they had noticed their kinsfolk below, detained and locked up. Their migrating journeys to follow their people across the continent had already taken many months. The swans were gathering into flocks of thousands, crowded in the swamp in black clouds that the old woman poled her raft through as she fed them.

Throngs of people gathered on the shoreline to throw nets, to catch one or two fingerling fish—and watch Bella Donna. It gave them something to talk about. They laughed. It was fun to watch the floating contraption with pole sticks moving abruptly through the choppy waters where the swans swam idly up and down in the turbulence. But seriously, no one had ever hoped or prayed for swans to come into their lives. Why would they? Swan eggs. Cygnets. Good things. But not for eating in this place! These were Law birds with no custodians in their rightful place. No one was that far down on their luck.

And to see the swans swimming about was considered a bit of luck for softening the look of the polluted mess of the place, staring at persistent drought, or having an accidental bomb fall in your face on a regular basis from the Army, or your spiritual ancestors dug up by miners and turning spiteful on you, or Army surveillances protecting your little children as though they were the parents who loved them. Everything had its impact. And bugger it all, apart from the things that were supposed to happen to close the gap of disadvantage in all of those makeshift dwelling places, a swan lake had emerged in the chaos. So that was one good story for local folk to say: *Wasn't that lucky?*

Yet what was the real lexicon about swans in this swamp? The swamp people, tight-lipped though they were about the presence of swans, really feared any ancient business that was not easily translatable in the local environment. There was total agreement on that. Old wise folk were talking strongly about it too, saying: *We do have our own local birds. Can't you see them everywhere if you bothered to look? All kinds.* Of course they had. Currawongs abounded. Noisy miners ran through the place. Thousands of brolgas were standing around, *tall and proud,* and living happily with the swamp people for aeons, thank you very much. The gray-feathered cranes with long stick-legs were the emblematic bird of the local environs. Brolga! *Kudalku!* Brolga! A bird of a big dreaming; a bird with a bare red-skinned head sitting on top of a long skinny neck joining a large body covered in gray feathers.

These birds crowded the lake too. They were the guardian angels roosting on every rooftop of the shanty shacks to watch over families—all of their kinfolk living inside. These homeland brolgas casually walked into any house without fear, gently prancing off the ground with spread wings, and stealing food they plucked straight from the kitchen table in a casual leap. No one cared less about what brolgas did as creatures that belonged there, with every right to have a bit of food—and who would harm a brolga anyway?

The girl fed the swans. She ran through the water with the fledging cygnets. She started to believe that by helping them to survive on the polluted swamp, she might learn how to escape as freely as they had been able to take flight. She wanted to fly. Dreams of stick wings attached to her arms that possibly grew feathers filled her mind with flights to escape. A great space in her mind played with words— *disappearance*, and *invisible*. She never thought that escaping a life of living with Bella Donna of the Champions was impossible. She was often flying like a swan. She watched the old woman obsessively, and decided to learn how to talk to swans too. Yes, she would be fluent in swan talk. She could feel the miracle of leaving every time swans lifted themselves off the water, the lightness of being airborne, in watching them fly until they disappeared through the dusty haze, and leaving her to dream about all of those invisible places she had heard the old woman talking about, that lay outside the swamp.

She watched the swans growing fatter and heavier, each a little battleship, that could still run in a rush across the water to take off, and fly back in to grab food thrown into the air. They swarmed in packs of hundreds for the food that the old woman threw at them. Other people's food! Piles of it in plastic bags and buckets, dumped like daily offerings to spirits on her floating platform. Old Bella Donna even had the audacity to swan around, humpy to humpy, counseling the greedy, and then collecting all the food scraps that anyone could have eaten themselves. She took everything: a pile of finely chopped yellowing cabbage, egg shells, old bread, wilting lettuce leaves, potato peels, fish bones, orange skins, a shriveled apple core. She poured the lot onto the water and watched the frenzy of swans and brolgas devour every piece of scrap in moments. Then the swans drifted off, and resumed an endless activity of sifting waters stuffed with algal blooms, scum on the surface, and slime-covered waterweeds.

As time passed, the swamp people grew skinnier than any normal person sweating it out in the tropics, while the swans became fatter on their food. The old woman, ancient now, did not have a guilty thought in her head. She prowled about on moonless nights to steal food right from the arms of children. Little things sound asleep from the exhaustion of clinging to their own special watermelon, from watermelon day, army fruit, good fruit given to them to treasure by the protecting armed forces. Such hot summer nights. Very easy being dead to the world. Deaf to the feral cat jumping out of the way when the door creaked, the breeze tinkling chime bells, or a thousand things moving, banging and clapping, while the ghostly old woman with thieving household brolgas walked straight in to snatch food right out of their little fingers.

The girl followed the old woman wading among the swans floating on their fat bellies, their red beaks preening themselves right next to their old benefactor's bright floral-patterned dress billowing in the water. Silently, the girl was a shadow that listened to the stories and secrets whispered into swan ears, and whatever she remembered, it was mostly poetry for swans.

Swamp people said the swans were frightening them. They accused the swans of looking right into their souls and stealing the traditional culture. Bella Donna said she did not know why a swan would want to look into somebody's empty soul. Just an insult a minute. She had already looked inside their souls herself and said that she had found nothing there. *Just thin bits of weak weeds lying on the bottom of your guts trying to stay alive.* Perhaps swamp people had empty souls, but they did have pride. They jumped around a lot and told her, *Enough's enough now, don't you go talking like that.* Anyway, she retaliated: *What could there possibly be for a swan to see except these little bits of weeds lying on a tin plate in a tiny pile at the bottom of your soul?*

Guess there was no answer for *that*.

But red-ringed, black-eye swans dipping their beaks like fortune-tellers swilling and swirling old tea dregs around while swimming by the girl could create beautiful thoughts, staring straight into her eyes. The girl in turn thought she might read their fortunes in the language nature had written in the blackish-gray-tipped curled tail feathers scalloped across their backs. It was how swans read each other when choosing a mate. She was determined to solve the mystery of why they had left the most beautiful lakes in the country—a vision created in her head by the old woman's stories of other places. Her existence revolved around learning the route they took, how they had crossed the interior country, the old woman's geography of featureless sand dunes stretching to kingdom come, just to reach a North country polluted swamp. *It was the love stories,* the old woman chuckled to herself. She was amused at the girl's addiction to bolt holes. In the muddy waters the old woman went on feeding squads of cygnets volumes of a tangled, twisted love story about the gods only knew what, which they soaked up like pieces of wet bread.

All children wanted were answers to universal questions about how people should live, and strangely, the girl thought she would find these answers by tossing herself in the old woman's madness of singing to swans. Just as she believed there was a secret route back to the tree— she believed there had to be a secret route that had brought the swans up to the top of the country. The mysteries were running away from her. Her mind too tied up in a jungle of tracks to run. Another way. Hidden passages. Places to hide. Always running. She had to become Aunty Bella Donna of the Champions who knew how to call swans, and time became desperate. But Oblivia remained out of kilter with the old lady's shadow, never quite fitting the cast of the sun, while the old woman sung her stories slowly, moving more and more slowly those days.

This story that began across the ocean, in a faraway land of a country that had already lost its name. In this place people were often telling common stories about themselves as they looked out at the awfulness of their land. The stories were never about history, or science, or technology. They talked about a useless landscape that grew nothing and which most of them could not see anyhow because of their blindness. These people spent ages compar-ing better times before who can tell what happened, except saying: We were already late when the God of the world said Git.

Ice-covered lakes dried up where the swans once lived. Beautiful creatures of snow-white feathers with yellow beaks had flown half-dead, halfway around the globe to reach extraordinary destinations in faraway lands.

Here, dead clumps of grasses by the sea billowed until whisked from the earth and into highways of dry wind crossing the continent that went round the world and back again. Trees stopped measuring the season and died slowly in ground bone-dry several meters deep. Finches had been the first to swarm into jerking clouds hightailing it out of their hemisphere. In winter or summer, only the old-fashioned homely birds scratched the ground for moisture from long ago.

You could see the white eyes of the old fishermen watching the flowing rivers in their memories, listening to them go on and on, it was like listening to the poetry of a canary's song dancing in those minds to sweeten the drought . . .

Draw breath, Aunty. Frequently the girl would interrupt her by laying her hand on the old woman's arm. Life was short. The old woman spoke faster, and was short of breath. The girl was greedy to know exactly what the old woman had to say and nodded repeatedly at her, asking Bella Donna the questions about what makes the world go around. Oblivia needed explanations quickly, not blind fishermen. How do you fly solo? Which way should you run to escape this world? Where do the swans go? No one else knew how to tell her how to shuffle the cards, so what harm was there in believing a mad person?

The old woman finally leant forward and whispered into the girl's ear that the best journey she had taken in all of her travels in the world was with a swan in a sampan. The girl convinced herself that only the mad people in the world would tell you the truth when madness was the truth, when the truth itself was mad. Then the old woman began a new love story, *All rivers flow to the sea*, and its breath finished when Aunty Bella Donna of the Champions of the earth, who might have been an angel, died.

THE DUST ENDS

The night Bella Donna of the Champions died, boobooks called at her passing spirit, and when a swift wind swept through the distant woodlands of eucalypts, the rattling gumnuts could be heard as she traveled away. All night long, butcher-birds flew in circles and sung through the swamp. That was the parish! Traditional. Even first-class. The country, finishing off the dead woman's broken serenade to the swans while the humidity wrapped itself in a heavy haze over the swamp and caught all of the leaves falling from the trees.

Around the swamp, the air was charged up like an electrified cat, always stifling and crowded. Oblivia dreamt the old woman was in the kitchen talking about her life, but her voice was jumping simultaneously between stories about times and places in the world that no longer existed. *All dead, just like me now. Extinct. Uninhabitable.* She was breathless with excitement. It was as though the old woman still wanted to breathe life into the stories of all those people in her life that she had seen escaping from their lost countries, taken to sea by a swan.

But then, what of her life in the swamp? *Our life here,* the girl uttered in her sleep. And the reply came out of nowhere. *Existence!* Just a word echoed from far away by old Bella Donna—a woman who was too worldly, too immersed; too spread everywhere, and she cried to the girl, *I don't know what is happening to me.*

Only the girl felt the sadness of losing the old woman forever, whose voice became less afflicted the more distant she became, *Well! Can you believe this?* Old Bella Donna had just been to the cloud house of a white swan in a Zhongguo city glowing with stars shining like antique lanterns, where the swan was still writing about itself with a quill in its beak, the same poem of missing its home, that it had been writing many centuries ago.

I feel so light now. It was the feeling of sunlight falling through dark stormy clouds embracing the giant granite swans placed all about the Indonesian village of stone carvers. And off she goes again, but instantly returns and tells of falling down through the dusty rays of light that form a sea around the ceiling of an ancient temple. It was where the golden swan boat of an Indian goddess swings from waves stirred by thousands of chanting devotees.

Finally, the old woman's home was in sight, the country that was once covered with fir trees, where wild deer with bells in their antlers had run through fog snaking over the snow-covered floor of forests.

The white swans dipping for weeds in the river.

A crescent moon moved so low across the swamp that its reflection over rippling water looked like the wings of a magnificent white swan. It looked like the type of swan from other parts of the world where it might be called Hong, or Cigne, Kugui, Svane, Zwaan, Svanr, Svan, or Schwan. Its light glowed over the houses in the slum. Water lily leaves shone in the moonlight. The light rode silver saddles on the back of hundreds of black swans huddling around the hull with necks tucked under their wings, where they dream their own names, Goolyen, Connewerre, Kungorong, Muru-kutchi, Kuluin, Mulgoa, Kungari, Koonwaarra, Byahmul, and the recital continues, collecting all of the country's swans. Then water lily leaves were blown over the water. Swarming insects backed away.

While circling in the skies, the swans dived endlessly through invisible crevices to other worlds. They were still searching for the old lady, always catching sight of her spirit, not letting her go. It seemed that the entire flock would not stop mourning for her. Everywhere, all over the swamp, there were swans behaving strangely, continuously sifting the water with agitated beaks, as though they were trying to find a way to reach the old woman's spirit, sepulchred beneath.

Then one day their behavior changed. The entire population emerged from the reeds where they usually built their nests to join bevies of others swimming in from distant reaches of the swamp, until they eventually formed one massive flotilla that skirted around the floating dumps. The formation moved in a tight huddle with curled wing feathers that rose aggressively, an armada of thousands that floated slowly, around the swamp, to follow a threat that was visible only to their eyes.

Suddenly, on necks held high, and feathers vertically angled like black fins reaching for the sky, a sea of hissing red beaks pointed towards what threatened it from above the swamp. It was all action after that. In a spear-like dash across the water, the shadow was pursued until the long drawn-out choreography of swans finished with downward pointing beaks nestled into their necks. The flotilla often changed directions in this pursuit without the slightest hint of any confusion in its vast numbers. They turned as one living presence that shared the same vein of nervousness. At any moment, just like a sudden change in the direction of the wind, the mass would retreat then, just as rapidly, swing back across the water into another attack, always watching whatever was menacing the swamp through the single eye of the flotilla, gauging its movement, so that their mass would slow down, speed up, or turn sharply, to match the wings hovering above and create gusts of wind rippling across the swamp.

Oblivia slept so soundly, she missed the dawn spectacle: the sand went berserk and smothered the whole swamp before shifting, and flying off. The Harbor Master was about, saying his farewells. He said he was heading northeast, maybe riding on the cloud of sand somewhere out into the sea first, flying to where winds build ferociously. That was the story. Then, just like that, the mother of all sand mountains disappeared.

The official people of the local Aboriginal Government came and tore the hull apart. Books, papers, the lot were tossed all over the floor as though they did not want their hands contaminated by the devil, while the girl huddled in a corner. They were searching for the crystal balls because they might be worth something—you never know.

They had rolled away in the dust storm. She stared into the direction to where the sand mountain had flown.

The officials thought the girl was a liar—were convinced of it, but there was no point in arguing with her so they took the old woman's body away to be buried. Oblivia freaked, with the question burning in her mind: *What if they come back?* With the old woman's body gone, she felt unprotected and alone. She waited for something else to happen, something bad, expecting more people to barge into the hull at any moment. At nightfall, she felt as though her body had disappeared into the slate-gray wall of the hull and she was drowning, gasping for air under the surface, then she heard Bella Donna walking around in the hull and reciting poetry about a slate-gray lake lit by the earthed lightning of a flock of swans. . . . Oblivia felt her life slipping away with the words, as though the old woman was lulling her away. It would have been easy. But suddenly the mood changed to storm winds spun in the darkness, and Oblivia left so fast it was as though she had been picked up and thrown headfirst out of the hull, and was already rowing away from it. She ran off into the wasteland at the end of the swamp to search for the tree that she now doubted ever existed.

The swamp people watched her searching among the dead reeds from their homes. *Who's that down there?* They couldn't believe it. Don't look. *Can this madness ever end? I want to look.* She scratched the ground with her fingers, searching for some evidence that would prove the tree had once existed. She needed to confirm what was in her head, of having lived inside the darkened hollow. She was digging holes like a mad dog. *Don't look. I want to look.* There was nothing but dirt where she scratched more and more frantically, with her head screaming, over and over, *I want to know*, as though she was asking the ground to ask the people she knew were watching, but nobody went over to the park to tell the girl what had happened to the trees, whether the wood had been chopped up for firewood, or sawn for timber.

Nobody said: *See child, the timber of the trees was used in that house over there. Nobody said: Look here is a chiseled digging stick whittled from the last slither of wood of the trees that had grown here.* Either the tree never existed as far as anyone knew, or it was a sacred tree in a story only remembered through the ages by people who had earned the right to hold the story. Who speaks for the ancestors? Who speaks for a child wandering around alone? What was the problem?

There was a story about a sacred tree where all the stories of the swamp were stored like doctrines of Law left by the spiritual ancestors, of a place so sacred, it was unthinkable that it should be violated. Old people said that tree was like all of the holiest places in the world rolled into one for us, *no wonder she went straight to it.* Funny thing that. The tree watching everything, calling out to her when it saw some people had broken the Law. Something will happen to them. This ancestor was our oldest living relative for looking after the memories, so it had to take her. When the girl was found though, the tree was destroyed by the Army on the premise that this nexus of dangerous beliefs had to be broken, to close the gap between Aboriginal people and white people. Those stories scattered into the winds were still about, but where, that was the problem now. It made us strong and gave us hope that tree. The kinspeople of the tree had believed this since time immemorial. Really all that was left behind of the story were elders and their families whose ancestors had once cared for the old dried and withered, bushfire burnt-out trunk of a giant eucalyptus tree through the aeons of their existence. They were too speechless to talk about a loss that was so great, it made them feel unhinged from their own bodies, unmoored, vulnerable, separated from eternity. They had been cut off. They called themselves damned people who felt like strangers walking around on their country. The reciprocal bond of responsibility that existed between themselves and the ancestors had always strengthened them. This was what held all times together. Now we are sick of it. Sick of that girl bringing up that memory to make us feel bad. All these people could think about while watching Oblivia dig the bare earth that day, was being reminded of the tree exploding in front of their eyes and there was not a thing anyone could do about it. Nothing at all. Couldn't bring any of it back. That girl is doing this to keep reminding us. Something must be wrong in her head if she can't even think straight. Watching the girl was one thing. They could not go out there and explain to this child what it meant to lose that ancestral tree.

Nevermind! Nobody forgets. You sprog, the old woman had once explained, fell over the escarpment of an invisible plateau. Its geology was composed of stories much bigger than a little girl getting lost like you. Now the girl searched beneath the cracked parchments of clay where the dun beetles and ants lived, hoping to find a nest of termites feasting underground on the root system of the tree. The ants and skinks slink away. She leaves after a while, still wondering how termites could have devoured every scrap of evidence of the huge tree's existence.

Finally, the girl returns to the hull where the ghost of the old woman could still be heard talking to herself. The swamp people could never stay silent for long about her ghost either. Their voices swung bittersweet all over the swamp, and they were not just talking about each passing breath of their momentous lives. No! They were talking like the old woman. Her voice was triumphing over death. It made your blood run cold the way she returned like a witch inside of other people's voices. But what did she mean, swinging her mantra in some foreign antique language, the one the old sea explorers used when they saw a black swan for the first time, *Rara avis in terris nigroque simillima cygno.*

The girl listened while people around the swamp repeated the mantra to each other. She heard the same phrase sung every night because someone would start calling out the Latin words from a nightmare. Then, suddenly a very strange thing happened. Everyone spoke a few words of Latin in every conversation, and for a while after the old lady died and kept haunting the place, the swamp people started claiming that they were Latino Aboriginals.

It appeared that the old ghost had colonized the minds of the swamp people so completely with the laws of Latin, it terminated their ability to speak good English anymore, and to teach their children to speak English properly so that the gap could finally be closed between Aboriginal people and Australia. You could call it stupidity, naivety, logical, to allow oneself to become so integrated into the world of the old ghost woman, where all sorts were telling each other that speaking Latin made them feel holy. The swamp people, the eels, moths and butterflies, all wanted to go to Rome to live with the pope. Some people even claimed that the swamp was Rome.

In the eyes of the beholder, all the architecture around the swamp had become the *relics of the greatest city in the world.* Old swamp people were becoming the greatest Romans of all times, even greater than the Romans themselves. The swamp had become a colosseum.

How bold to mix the Dreamings. Those laws of the two sides of the local world were always clashing. She decided to ignore the old ghost woman sitting in the kitchen of the hull speaking in Latin all night. She would simply remember the living Aunty Bella Donna of the Champions claiming that she had not inherited myths from purists, and not believing that the black swan belonged to the night dreams of some of her ancestors. *The facts, girl. Here are the facts. It was the Feast of the Epiphany in 1697 when the crew of Willem de Vlamingh's Dutch ship claimed to have seen superstition come to life, when they saw alive, two black swans—a beautiful pair, swimming off the coast of Western Australia, and called it "the epiphany of the black swan"—a celebration for science, a fact stripped from myth.*

When the swans scattered, the sailors randomly ran down four swans, and once caught, they were taken on board the sailing ship. When they were taken out to sea, the swans became morose from their own stories being pulled away from them, but they were kept alive anyway, the birds of nightmare specimens in the hands of science, exhibits in Indonesia's old Batavia, where the devil swan feathers could be touched by anyone in order to defy their superstition.

The girl lived in a limbo world. The directions of its map spread out like a peacock's tail. Who created it? Well! There were these boys who once chased a little girl down. They kept roaming in her wilderness. Which little girl? What poor little girl? Talk is talk. Costs nothing. Oblivia hears it everywhere now: *You remember Aunty. She was one of those failure-to-thrive babies. Had FASD. Fetal alcohol spectrum disorder or something like that. You should not believe all the talk going around. You don't know if any of that is true or not. Aunty, it's true, as true as I am standing here. It's the truth of what you get with white government social engineering intervention mucking up more blackfella lives. She was a closing-the-gap baby. Us? Us left with the responsibility for looking after her.* Oblivia hears voices all the time, and thinks a lot about how stories are made, considering which words would be used down the centuries to describe herself, and representing what? Swanee! Like a devil's swan! The old woman had always claimed that she knew how to find the peculiar if she went looking for it. Destiny itself discovered the girl, and the old woman had explained: *You child, are really peculiar.* She once told Oblivia that she was joined with the *undoable.* It was the principle, she said, of the haphazard way sanity and madness were reaped from her having been gang-raped physically, emotionally, psychologically, statistically, randomly, historically, so fully in fact: *Your time stands still.*

Gang-raped. The girl hardly knew what these two words meant as she thought about herself in the sameness of passing time while sitting on the floor of the hull, pulling her head apart trying to remember what had happened to her, or perhaps whatever it was, it just happened to some other little girl that everyone was talking about and maybe it was not her either, or herself neither, but all girls. While trying to decide whether she was sane or mad like the girl she had heard about from listening to people telling their stories—whispering on and on about rape in a form of speechlessness, it was hard to hold everything back in her chest about the velocity of the things that she could not remember, about what those boys did to the girl she heard people talking about! Poor little girl! Which little girl? She did not know, and wished she had never been born. *It was not your fault.* Those were the old woman's final words on the matter, after explaining in general terms the cause and effect of an outrageous history that had created a destiny, to avoid speaking of a shame that was so overwhelmingly connected to the girl's experiences of life, and from her own shame of having to say to the girl that she had been raped by a group of boys, the plain raw truth of the matter being that this one boy, and that one over there walking about etcetera, were the ones who did it, and not speaking of what Oblivia could not remember from her childhood of something happening to her, where bits of truth were never enough while visiting her recurring nightmares, and not being able to speak of why she was waking up screaming and frightened of the darkness, and of being so petrified that she would be eternally connected to the age she had been just before she had been raped by holding on, and guarding that little girl before something bad happened to her, or even, explaining why she was found in the tree.

The girl continued to hear the hushed word *gang-raped* frequently, escaping through the cracks of the gossipy swamp—said without soul about an incident that had been forgotten, had to be forgotten, tucked away and hidden, but had returned. It was funny how some words can always be heard in whatever vicinity, no matter how softly they have been spoken. Just like eyesore words, standing out in normal conversations that attract everyone's attention by bringing back the memory of a little girl who had once disappeared from the face of the earth for a very long time.

A gang of boys who thought they were men were wracked out of their minds on fumes from an endless supply of petrol, glue, or whatever else they played with when they had chased the girl down. They were given a fresh start by a youth worker who coaxed them from the rooftops of the houses where they hung out, hiding under T-shirts pulled over their heads and sniffing petrol from Coca-Cola bottles. They were taken to an entertainment center where they could practice snooker and blackjack, and this was followed up with more largesse to close the gap of failed policies for Aboriginal advancement from the Government in Canberra.

A grand football oval, a state of the art stadium, was built by the Army so fast it was considered to be a miracle. This monument, a grand design in the landscape, overshadowed the slum, the shanty houses where those brain-damaged petrol sniffers ended up crawling around on the floor, along with whatever else was blown in by the wind. There was nothing wrong with grandness-emitting hyper rays of positivism to build muscle and brawn, sinew and bone, to breathe hot breath and punch the air. Life went on. Money well spent. Football carnival days were definitely the rage. Families cheered their boys. The floodlights poured gold on the big crowds.

The swamp people would not need to speak about anything else really except football, and they spoke it in ghost Latin that nobody else understood, when the swamp became Rome for a while, because the Army said, *Rome was not built in a day. So let the Government do all the talking, all the planning, and the thinking and the controlling,* and tell old *Jacky Jacky* what to do in Rome.

People tell stories all the time: the stories they want told, where any story could be changed or warped this way or that. You see, the people of the swamp always claimed that the girl in the hull was a little foundling child, not the one who went missing—who was once lost in the bush. Yes! She had run far, far away, they said, and they said it was no good doing something like that. It only made people worry all the time. They did not fancy that she had hid in a hollow at the base of any old *eucalypti* tree. Yes! Fancy that.

The police and army search went on for days when the little girl they knew had disappeared. A line of emotionally charged people searched through every dwelling—pulling everything apart, then beyond, thrashing through the dried-up bush for five kilometers, working clockwise out from the swamp.

The thrashers told stories to occupy themselves: tales upon tales not to be taken lightly about things like this. In the unearthing of those sad old stories they found no lost child. All they found were new tracks of possibilities for things that had once happened and should stay buried with the past. These new versions of old stories did not fit the ground, because you know, old Law forms its own footpaths. A very bad feeling had spread among the thrashers. Soon they were saying quite frankly, *Why can't she stay lost? All this searching and searching,* they claimed, *and the only thing discovered was shame.* It was decided to let sleeping dogs lie. The search was called off. The girl's own heartbroken father was *manngurru nyulu,* and being so ashamed he felt weak, *mayamayada,* and now thought others saw him as being *warrakujbu* or mad, failing to take notice of his child, and had made a sudden request to all the *lungkaji* policemen, asking them to give up hope.

That was the moment when someone decided to make a nuisance of themselves, when that old bat Aunty Bella Donna of the Champions had decided to step in, to plow the ground with her own eyes, and to be totally ignorant of the ins and outs of family histories—their ground. She went on searching for the lost girl, losing all sense of time, and oblivious of how she was riling up spite and hatred from people watching what they did not want to watch—someone searching for a needle in a haystack. *Hey! Old dear. What? What? What did you say? You got to give up that ting you are doing.* Those old ears of hers, delicate white with networks of red veins, that had no trouble hearing everything else, decided to be stone-deaf to all the sneering, the abuse yelling anonymously behind her back, the *ins* and *outs* of what people thought about what she was doing on their land: *Why can't she stay lost?* She went on raking the ground, and continued ignoring those who said she ought to mind her own business.

She boasted obviously, not just round the hull, nor just to the swans, and expected eternal gratefulness from the entire swamp for finding the missing girl. *The triumph of good eyesight.* Who would have thought to look into the hollow of a tree? Evidently, no one!

In fact months passed after she found the girl before the old woman had thought of telling the parents she had found the missing child. Her little *bujiji nyulu.* The orphan. She had taken herself ashore from the hull on the Harbor Master's advice—*you got to tell the parents, her nganja, her kin, ngada, murriba, haven't you heard of the stolen generations? Janyii ngawu ninya jawikajba, I am asking you with my own mouth* so she went over to the place where the parents lived, where she called out to them from the street, *I found that kid of yours.*

Now very old people with minds crippled by dementia, the bewildered parents were not interested in mysteries at that stage in their life, and were still fearful of welfare people like the Army coming back to plague them over their failure-to-thrive baby, and poking around with accusing fingers at their families' histories for evidence of grog harm on the little girl's brain—as if they didn't already know what happens to the inheritors of oppression and dispossession. It's not that shit happens as other people have said; it's the eternal reality of a legacy in brokenness that was the problem to them. They came out of their little shelter, fearful that people would start accusing them of being drinkers again when they had never touched grog, that *kamukamu-yaa*, and whispered to Bella Donna to *shut up. Budangku*. No. They had long since finished, *windijbi* with grieving after accepting a plausible inquest report and had never expected to see their missing daughter again. *Don't you know? Don't you remember?* It was a story that created a lot of sad havoc about the place. Word spread of Bella Donna troubling the old couple without anyone really believing a girl was found in a tree, and since nobody was missing a child, a consensus was reached. They said: *Tell her if she wants, she should keep that stray girl. Her business. Not ours.*

Why am I lucky? This was how the girl was lucky. Lucky, that the old woman had not found a skeleton. Lucky, the girl remembered being told by the old woman, when there were women and girls around the swamp who had gone missing forever, although some of them might call up eventually on the one pay phone, just to say that they were *somebody calling someone,* to let their families know they are doing fine, living somewhere else. *We have escaped you know.* But on the other hand, some don't bother to contact anyone, and as far as anyone knows, nobody knew whether those women and girls who went missing were dead or alive. Nobody knows. Nobody knows if their bodies, still dressed in their best going-away dresses, were laying out there in the bush somewhere, buried in sand, or whether their skeleton was standing up against a dead tree, or they were looking towards the road to heaven, or towards the way to go home, or were just waiting to be found. You might see some of them out there sometimes. Who knows anything about the truth? There were many homes waiting for the public telephone to ring with news, or hating to hear any news, or yelling over each other in the night when the lonely public pay phone rang, shouting for somebody to go out there and king hit the phone with an ax, or piss on it, or bowl the thing over, or fire a shotgun right into its guts. Lucky, that some people would say anything for silence. Lucky that Oblivia did not know why she was lucky. Lucky that she never told the old woman she was lucky.

The girl had a different version of the events that led to Aunty Bella Donna of the Champions finding her asleep in the tree. The old woman had always claimed it was in the nick of time: *Child! Minutes!*

Otherwise! Otherwise it would have been a disaster, what would normally be expected—*You would have been dead.*

Oblivia frequently dreamt of a child like herself running for the hole at the base of a tree—a little girl in so many different forests, timber lots, old stands of ancient trees, that now, it was difficult to re-member any sequences of geographies stored in her mind. There were dreams where the child flees through densely overgrown chestnut trees. Sometimes she runs away in forests that smelled of resin, walnut forests, olive groves, mountain bamboo forests and cherry blossom trees. She still felt the cold wind on her face in alpine valleys of bare limb larch trees while running beside deer being chased by wolves. It was geography that was constantly shifting, for sometimes she runs by huge sea turtles stranded high in the branches of trees of the tropics, where there had been floods.

Quite often, Oblivia remembered a child running in the middle of a bush fire, to where it had been deliberately lit at the base of a eucalypt and left smoldering over several months until a large, charred hollow had been created into which a girl would eventually fall. On her shoul-ders, the child always carried long thin burnt branches like wings, but she balked, pulled away before reaching the hole in the tree.

Yet no matter how hard the girl tried to stop before reaching the hole, she was pushed along until squeezed into the hollow, no matter how small it became in her mind, and it breaks her wings. Once inside, she would fall through heavy air, plunging into darkness and weightless-ness, as if she had been swallowed alive. The girl had seen many versions of this charred stomach, where the floor inside the tree was overgrown with large, sprawling gray roots that grew down the shaft and on the way down were covered here and there with the initials of previous visitors.

The child in the dream looked as though she was no older than eight or ten years old, maybe she was younger, five or six, and very different to the story the old woman had always maintained—that the girl she had found was much older. Maybe, life stands still in a Rip Van Winkle way of sleeping. The girl that had eventually come out of the bowel of the tree had no memory of the swamp. Did not recognize it. Had no memory of the past. Her memory was created by what the old woman had chosen to tell her. *People only heard the swans calling. Nobody heard you running away.*

Oh! Yes! And I worked my skin to the bone looking after you for a very long time until you woke up from a coma.

There were many lost girls. In the old woman's stories, the girl was re-created in many lost childhoods. The ancient lost child of a Mountain Ash forest. The lost girl who had spent days running through a forest path of fairies where swan lovers flew one after the other, while circling above the swan poet's lake. A little girl became lost while traveling old tracks through the marshes to hunt where swans built nests near underground rivers. *You choose,* the old woman had said.

It was difficult for Oblivia to believe that the old woman had been capable of looking after an unconscious child, feeding her stories for nourishment, more than food. She kept dreaming those stories like a child, even when she could see and feel the strangeness of an adult's face reflecting back at her from the mirrored stillness of swamp water. She once remembered the old woman saying it was possible to hibernate underground in the drought, like frogs and swamp turtles, but Bella Donna was adamant in her discussions with the Harbor Master that it was impossible for a human being to shut down like a burrowing frog with cold blood. He did not like to admit it, but agreed. She would not be able to sleep through the drought like a frog, or like a swamp turtle, by conserving energy from living on a single heartbeat for whatever time was necessary to survive through hibernation. And Bella Donna had smiled at Oblivia, sitting on the floor, while the Harbor Master's flashbulb eyes were burning at the girl with disgust: *You were different. You were in a coma.*

The tumultuous universe of lost girls could still be heard from old Bella Donna's voice speaking through the walls of the hull. She must have left her voice behind after she died. Well! It was best not to argue with steel walls Oblivia thought, since the swans were milling around the hull, still waiting to hear the old woman's stories. She had more to think about. The swans were hungrier than ever now.

In this winter the swans only produced one egg. This precious egg, their ode to the swamp, sat in a nest marvelously constructed with thousands of sticks, dried algae and leaves individually chosen and carefully placed. The two swans had worked for weeks in its construction before the egg was laid. It polarized other swans, glancing, idling the day at the nest, as though admiring the egg's possibilities. The swan lovers constantly uncovered, cradled, and re-hid the egg under the leaf litter of their perfect nest where snakes slept for warmth. As time passed, the brooding pair looked as though they would stay forever protecting the dead egg, wishing it would hatch. Then one day, a group of haughty swans swarmed over to the nest and forced them to give up. More halfhearted nests were built crooked with randomly placed sticks and old bits of plastic rubbish, then all too briefly, only admired as foolish work of swans unable to predict what height the water levels would become with the uncertainty of rain. Whatever vague ideas of procreation had been in the initial motivation, these were abandoned for a different kind of infatuation—a love affair with the northern skies.

When swans mourned, their long necks hung with their heads almost touching the ground. It seemed as though the swans were now glued to the shores of the swamp where they looked dolefully towards the hull, waiting for the old woman's world of stories to appear, hoping for the hot air of the mirage to be filled with a cooling sweetness.

Instead of the swans saving themselves from swamp people's dogs, they continued staring like statues at the broken forms of silver reflections, shimmering over the water. It was like watching suicide—witnessing, the swans' refusal to swim away. Black feathers lay scattered over the ground and were blown over the water. Seagulls flew in from the coast many kilometers away and joined the nightly attacks. The swan frenzy raged on and on with bloodstained dogs and seagulls, while bleeding swans mingled with the red haze of sunrise, still sitting on the ground, heads tucked under their wings.

The swans kept dying in their eerie pact, leaving Oblivia to crawl over dead birds, and having to bury them under piles of broken reeds. Swamp people watched. *Will you look at the girl out there? Why? What is she doing now? She's burying the swans.* Pause. *What for? Because they are dead stupid?* So, so on, *manija* and so forth.

White smoke rises quickly in a breeze. It created a haze over the swamp from the bonfires the girl lit for the pyre of dead swans, and pushing the raft into the water and using the long sticks to poke down into the mud below, she carefully maneuvered it back over to the hull to be closer to the stories from old Aunty's swan books.

She is reading through the old woman's collection of books about swans to find a way of bringing the swans back to the remaining waters in the swamp.

Swans swimming correctly and sedately in swanlike fashion, screamed in her head, *good news,* but the mud-caked flocks remained in sync with their perpetual north-south swaying, plodding through puddles, beaks sifting through mud searching for nonexistent food.

The girl read about the many lives of swans flying around mystical, mist-covered palaces of princes who also become white swans. Curly wing feathers of black swans became the black curly heads of warriors in epic hunts, in places where the fearless steps of the bravest of heroes stalking along the banks of a coal-black river to kill a swan prince, might just as easily end in the hunter's death, or a swan that became a prince, or dead princes lying beneath waters flowing with green-gray algae.

When the rains finally came, all of the *winngil,* big rain—the bush dripped from clouds sitting on the land, until finally, with so much water flowing over grasslands and running through gullies leading into the swamp, the old lake reappeared again. The swans safe now from the dogs, were cleansed by months of preening from rain pouring over their feathers. The breeding nests were full with half-grown cygnets. Their packs again swarmed through the water where constant winds flowing across sheets of floodwater rippled each pulse of the country's heartbeat. The air was electrified by the sun disappearing behind the *madarri,* clouds that packed the sky, and reappearing like a fiery pearl in the mouth of the creature formed by clouds that looked like an enormous swan.

THE NEWS FROM THE SEA

Somewhere else, far away by the headwaters of a wide river, where another arm of the same Indigenous Nation as the swamp people lived, that belongs to other people—*maninja nayi jamba*—there was a young boy, a *juka* becoming a man named Warren Finch. He also stared at the future. The boy had just finished reading an article from a local people's community newspaper that he had been carrying around forever, that he had read as soon as he had hurdled over the big national benchmark for Indigenous people, to be literate in English.

This newspaper article was his only possession, and he had read it so many times each word was etched in his brain. Long ago, he had stolen the newspaper from his family when they had tried to hide it from him, snatched it out of his hands in fact, after he had asked them to read the story to him. He had kept it folded neatly in a rusted Log Cabin tobacco tin. He believed he owned the story, which was about the rape of a young girl in an Aboriginal community by members of a gang of petrol-sniffing children.

His elders, the old grandfathers, had told the young boy the story about a very important little girl who was raped by boys. Promised one for their country. His promised one. They said a terrible thing had happened on their country, at that *poisonous no good place* they called

Swan Lake, which was polluted by all of the rubbish from the sea that had been carted into the place, turning good pristine water into rust. They described the journey they had taken to get to that place after the terrible incident to deal with the matter as the big bosses of country, a journey which along the way, had taken them over all the stories for this one, that one and other ancestral rivers, and a long way across from the old sleeping man range, and a long way from all that good porcupine spinifex flatland country, mulga spirit country, gidgee tree, black soil sacred country. They said, with fists thumping their hearts, that they had reached utter badness at the end of the journey, the only blight in all of their homelands, the place where the Harbor Master was looking after that sand mountain on the other side of their own Aboriginal nation's territory that spread through hundreds of square kilometers across all their old song-story country—mother country, father country, grandparents country, and so on through family close-ness and feelings towards all things on their land. They claimed that those people *over there* had been paying for what happened to the country they were responsible for long before that thing happened to the little girl. They told the story of having felt radioactivity running about in the air *in that place*, and saw with their own eyes the Army in charge of the place—bossing everyone around inside a big fence, say-ing they were looking after all of the children, so all of the poison was already charging around inside the head *from a long time ago and still going on*. They even had to stop *dangerous thoughts* from getting inside their own brain, like a cut letting in the poison, and trying to steal the controls, and steering them around to do bad things to each other. *Boys should not play rough with little girls*, they said very quietly. It was no good for their whole nation. *You will see in time what we are talking about.* Then they told him never to talk about it, *never mention it again.*

The story about what had happened to the girl who was found in a tree became common knowledge through this large tribal nation. The story became a wild story. Everyone had an idea of what really happened. Some people were saying firstly that the girl was taken, kidnapped by the tree from her people as punishment. Others said that she was really the tree itself. She had become the tree's knowledge. Or, possibly she was related to the tree through Law, and the tree took her away from her people.

These elders, seasoned orators with centuries of reading Australian racial politics behind them, the AM to PM news aficionados, and track masters in how to skin a cat, or kill off a lame duck, had partly decided that it would be a good idea for this boy Warren Finch, already the joy of his people, to be brought up their way—the old way—away from the hustle and bustle of intra- and extra-racial Australian politics, a tyranny that they claimed was like a lice infestation in the mind.

Everyone in Warren Finch's world was full of gusto for the child and wore their pride on the outside. They already expected this finely built boy who shone like the rising sun, and was already as fearless as their greatest ancestral spirits, would one day become the best man that ever breathed air on this planet. His education was to be under-taken in isolation, out bush away from everyone. The story of the girl who was found in a tree was so polluting, it could only be resolved by feelings of resentment at the swamp people's spite for allowing some-thing like this to happen when they knew that the destiny of the girl belonged elsewhere, to the clans-country on the other side of the hills, in the homeland of their boy, more wondrous than the air itself, like a bit of a sweetheart that sonny boy Warren Finch.

This whole thing about the girl would never do for the direct relatives of Warren Finch who saw themselves as the antithesis of those other people, their over the hills so called kinspeople in the swamp, mixed up, undone people and what have you, who had thrown too much around of their brains and were germinating seed all over the flat, so that they ended up having to be guarded night and day by the Army. People in other words, who were so unlike their good selves, it was any wonder that they were related to one another. You have to weigh up the price of principle, of what it was worth, that was what Warren Finch's people believed, who reckoned that they owed their success to historical savvy, inherited from a line of hard-nosed, hard-hitting bosses you might call idiosyncratic, even mavericks, but real go-getter people, with the good sense for standing up and saying "Yes sir," or, "No sir, madam (as the case may be, and conveniently so) Australian Government." They prided themselves as being the anti-brigade, take-what-you-want people, of having their own unexpected orthodoxies to what was expected of them. They even kept full-time cheer squads, everyone in fact speaking the anti-talk, to spruik the river of a special crawling language from their mouths at any professional white or black designer of black people's lives.

Warren Finch's people were good at it and taught the next and the next generation to behave accordingly. For instance, and it was only poking a twig at the tightfisted ball of their status quo, for whatever it took to deal with people from the outside world coming along with great ideas for fixing up the lives of Aboriginal people, or wanting to take something else from them, mostly in the form of traditional land and resources, they agreed by presenting themselves as being well and truly yes people who were against arguing the toss about Aboriginal rights. They could rock the gray matter—like a peloton riding in the slipstream of the agreeable—just like the majority of Australia, while at the same time be just like anyone else—as anti-culture, anti-sovereignty, anti-human rights, anti-black-armband-history for remembering the past, anti–United Nations or –Amnesty International, as much as being anti-pornography, anti-pedophiles, anti-grog, anti-dope, anti-littering, anti–having too many dogs and pussycats, anti–any kind of diseases or ill health, anti-welfare, anti-poverty, anti–anyone not living like a white person in their houses, anti–having their own people building their proper houses unless the white government says it's okay—they can do it for a bit of training money. They wanted to be good Black people, not seen as troublemakers, radicals, or people who made Australians feel uneasy, thinking Aboriginal people were useless, wasting Australian Government money, and if it meant being anti–all these things to prove that they loved their children, and could get on, and if this is what it meant to be reconciled—Well! So be it. What else? What else did they have to say to make things okay so that they could get on with everyone else? Well! They were also anti-truancy, anti-consultation, anti-others, and anti-urban, –city blacks, -mixbloods etcetera, just as much as they were anti-racists, anti-anyone black, white, or whatever and from wherever else speaking on their behalf, and anti–anyone who opposed their human and personal rights, or their land rights, or their native title, anti–never having enough heat in the weather, or anyone who got in the way of what they said was Aboriginal-defined self-determination, and they were just about anti–any dissenting hindrances from Federal government of what they wanted, or any hindrances to hindrances in themselves, and anti–whatever else was somebody else's reality, or what any other people said about black people no matter if it was right or wrong, and they were anti about whatever there was to be anti about if white people say so, and even if they seemed to be just a bunch of negative people, or Uncle Toms, or coconuts, the upshot was that their highly successful and self-defined Aboriginal Nation Government was designed from such, and was as much.

A whirlwind blew the bit of newspaper out of young Warren Finch's hand. It landed in the river. That question, the young boy thought of what people thought of what happened to that little girl, as he watched the paper floating away, would now be carried off to the ocean. He was not sure who would answer the question. But somewhere, as the paper floats out to sea, he sees that a small group of hermit crabs have turned it into a raft. They are riding on the floating paper, and working to keep it afloat until eventually he imagines, after riding ten thousand waves, their little ship would moor in a harbor. He dreams that as luck would have it, the raft paper arrives safely in the busy shipping port under the cover of night. By early morning, a local fisherman in his fishing boat has dragged the newspaper in with his grappling hook, or perhaps it was dropped at his feet from the full-bellied seagull that flew overhead.

This man, Warren believed, would carefully dry the paper with his hardened fisherman's hands, because he honored the sea that had given him this piece of news. What he read when the paper dried made him feel like crying, and he asked the sea why it had sent him such news. He made it his business to show the newspaper that fate had brought to him to all manner of people who lived there, because they

honored the sea too, and were interested in the news from other countries that the gods brought to them.

Warren Finch thought about the law of a whorl wind for a story
that wanted to go all over the world, and continued on his way. . . .

Warren Finch could grab another person's luck, and dream it into a
ghost story. He went back to his favorite fishing hole where there had
been a hatching of blue butterflies. Thousands were springing off the
paperbark trees, and spilling through the wind like a quivering evanes-
cent blue river flooding towards the sky. The river fell apart, and the
butterflies flew about the wild banana vines which grew rampantly
over and under old growth, before winding around and through the
bushland trees.

A hundred swallows hunting the insects flittered about, flying up
and down from the skies above Warren's head. He had thought the
girl in the story was weak, he had often dreamed about visiting her,
and always the dreams were about how he tried to incite her to come
out of her hiding place in the tree as though he was frog-marching an
insect out from the darkness and into the sunlight of his world. He was
a child, but his mind was already laden like a museum, where old and
new specimens, facts and figures, lived together as evidence of his own
personal history.

On this warm to meddling hot day, Warren Finch started to conjure
up the circus that had taken place in his life. He could remember how
it annoyed him so long ago, when everyone said that he was uncom-
monly wise for someone so young. Now, the same as back then, he
would throw his fishing line into the water, neither caring whether he
caught fish or not because he always caught fish, even while he was
planning the content of speeches he would be giving, or not giving later
in his life. He was flicking the line in the direction of the blue butterflies, staring at trees, and he stared straight though the country, to the
place he had carried around in his mind most of his life, until he finds
the little girl again inside the tree, where he speaks to her, asking her to
listen to the love song he has composed for her.

So! Hold on to your seat real tight, hold your breath, keep your eyes in your head, and go on, don't be frightened.

Please! Calmness! Peacefulness!

Silence costs nothing just as silence means nothing.

Cheer up like loud people and clap your hands and stomp your feet about this. Louder.

I don't think I can hear you.

Oh! Come on! Don't be a sooky baby.

You have to be better than that.

Your little mad girl's world is a bit shy you know.

You are frightened of what people will think of you.

You do not want people to think bad things about you.

But I got to tell you to come out.

I insist. I want you to.

You have a story to tell.

So, clap louder!

Quickly!

Tell everyone you have a few home truths to say to them.

And plans?

Yes! Yes! Really! Let's think. You will have plans.

You have to listen to your plans.

I'm part of it.

He could still feel the way she had always moved back, flinching at the warmth of his breath filling the dark space as he reached inside the tree to find what he already thought he possessed, as though he could reach across any space of time and distance in his thoughts. She was embarrassed and confronted by the way he traveled with his imaginary crowds of ancestral spirits that proudly followed him over the land, and who were watching, as he came down to where she was sleeping cradled in the spirit of the tree. The girl kept slinking further away from the strange boy who came through the darkness to talk to her about his frightening ideas, using words he had heard running out of the mouths of old men and women, and from families calling to one another from one scrap of dirt to the next, about people who trespassed on their native land.

Warren Finch's boy heart thumped like an animal mapping its own way down through the roads it ought to travel, like migrating birds reaching their destination before embarking on the journey. He was at his own concert and hoarse from screaming for a ghost to leave the tree.

Warren Finch was traveling on the flat ground above the river, leaving the butterflies, to go where the gray-feathered brolgas were dancing ahead. The tall slender birds were performing a legendary fight in the Dreamtime story—one that the old law had marked on them forever with a wattle of flaming red skin on the back of their heads. He was studying this brolga dance which was being performed with the accompaniment of a whirly haze of dust sprayed from the rusty wrecks of car bodies strewn over the flats behind them. A coy wind rushed by, picking up and blowing their soft gray chest feathers, and a fine yellow dust that closed him in the atmospheric stench, and drew him further into the brolgas' traditional, well-worn, and danced-about roosting ground.

His elders had come by earlier as they did regularly, to check on Warren, the boy who brought only joy, and who was commonly called, *the gift from God*. He lit up their hearts. Even though he was a half-caste. They said he was the incarnate miracle. He even lit heaven at night. They agreed wholeheartedly with the ancestors, and with any new gods if they cared to be about in the country of the traditional owners, and with all the insurmountable riffraff bothering them in modern times. *This boy pumps up our hearts with proper pride and it feels good. What we say again, and again, and again is this, isn't it a mighty proud day wouldn't you say to be seeing this boy of ours out here on country?*

You could say that Warren Finch was a pretty special child. He was living alone, in the crowded space of the breeding colony of the brolgas, as he had done for several years of his schooling, away from his parents' outstation where they were etching out a living with cattle and growing forests of wild plum trees for carbon trading. In this isolated place, it was clear that his schoolroom and teacher were the land itself.

He was watched over every night in his dream travels by the elders who brought him lessons. They could not have cared less, or given two hoots about the fact that in the wider circles of Australian opinion, his education was typically called "special treatment," or perhaps even wasteful, by *somebody* following them around like a big shadow in the many guises of omnipresent Australia.

A colonial omnipresence looked like the daggers sticking out of the heads of elders these days. All fired by Australia. All conveniently rolled up nice and personal into one person called *Official Observer.* That official *who thinks himself,* from the Capital of Australia, Canberra, to ask *a bloody squillion and a half* questions about education, by ram-rodding with his own valued opinions into the minds of Aboriginal people. The elders refused to answer anything. They offered only their big sighs of resignation. That that was good enough to give anybody who they thought was not their business, as these elders claimed with solemn faces: *We are doing our own business here.*

The boy could not have possibly known how scrutiny works, or that he was a special test case for the curriculum of education devised by his elders. These were ancient-looking men and women—six of them—keepers of Country, who kept on living as though they were immortals. They were the bosses of this Aboriginal Government. Boss! That's all they were called. No other name suited people who wholly belonged to the old Laws of Country. They were Country and they looked like it, and you don't argue with Country.

The Observer was always reminding the old people just how many Australians, whether they knew anything or not, and not to mention the big national media governing Aboriginal opinion in the country, just loved being judge of Aboriginal failure. The elders always replied with heads together—better than one: *Well! Doesn't inward darkness like to latch on to some other darkness?*

But how can birds in the bush educate him? He should be in school. The National Observer literally pulled out his hair to get this so-called Aboriginal Government to listen to him properly, and it was not unusual to see him storming off from the Brolga colony until somebody ran after him and persuaded the white man to *please Mister* come back, to try to be more reasonable in his understanding. He knew what they were doing but he was not going to say it. He was not going to sacrifice his career by mouthing off his theories about the kind of education Aboriginal Government was creating, but he knew the boy would be dangerous in the end. He just wanted to know how he was going to big note himself to his peers, the Australian Government, and to the United Nations watchdog about honoring the rights of Indigenous peoples.

This trial with the boy's education since early childhood was just a little periwinkle of an experiment, with a *let's see how it goes* attitude for a right to educate, begrudgingly gifted by Australia while maintaining the perception that Aboriginal self-determination was unworkable, and after two plus centuries of jumping up and down about this very thing being nonexistent by Indigenous peoples.

Weren't the Indigenous People's Rights embedded in that 2020 Constitutional Agreement thing that Australia signed, sealed and delivered to me here right into this hand of the old man? What was that about? The oldest local Indigenous man, a white-haired wise man regarded in the highest esteem by his people, had excused himself forever from answering any undermining question posed about an absolute. He had his right on a piece of paper and that was what mattered as far as he was concerned. Long time we been fight for that. What? Three hundred years maybe fighting over me being Black and you being White? Like mangy, maggoty dogfight. Can't fight properly. Always having to scratch for fleas. Rubbish tings like that. Always floating around. Always. Can't ever get rid of it. The old man was told to be quiet by the Observer who was sick of listening to him talk about politics and his rights. *Hold your tongue old man. You are talking too much politics. You are obsessed.*

So what was that treaty I signed? older man asked again, while endlessly rolling the treaty word around the roof of his mouth with his tongue, just to feel how satisfying it sounded in his head, and it still pleased him to hear the word which he would keep saying a million times more perhaps, before he died. He had the right to feel pleased.

He had forged the only treaty of its kind in Australia after three centuries of denial about original land theft that led to the creation of Australia. He had gone to the World Court as mad as a run-over dog to do that. This old man got his treaty between Australia and the traditional owners of this piece of Brolga country all right, and pinned the bloody thing up on the door of his house. The words on the paper were faded by the sun, but that did not matter because the old man could recite what had been written on it, word for hard-forged word—one for every man, woman and child of his kind. This treaty was for the rights of Indigenous people over the traditional country that Warren would one day inherit as one of its senior caretakers.

Traditional responsibility. That was what these elders were training him for with their educational system that prickled the nerves of the "official observer," who was a man who had been one of the masterminds behind decades of failed Australian government policies, but somehow, because of all of his experiences, Canberra had judged him worthy of this position. Yep! No trouble at all. He was still king of his patch.

Thank climate change and even the wars such a catastrophe created, and thank the millions of refugees around the world being sick and tired of how they were treated, that had cleaved the opportunity for this one nation of Indigenous people deemed worthy enough, to force Australia to sign a treaty by bringing the country to its illegal colonizing knees in the World Court.

But Brolga people had been opportunistic. They had made sure that they were in the right place at the right time. They blamed themselves and others like the swamp people for their troubles so that rich people would give them plenty of money. Luck was involved too with being anti-people, when they found themselves caught up in a mix of new thinking throughout the world about how to treat poor people, oppressed people, Indigenous people and whatnot! Things like that! Not normally done for have-nots. They had a long tradition of knowing how to say *yes, yes enough*, and that was fair enough too, while agreeing to a heartbreaking trade-off—only done they believed for the long-term survival of their nation—along with the shame they would carry forever, a perpetual sadness and melancholy of the heart starting with the old white-hair man, to have the swamp people's part of their traditional estate, the Army's property and dumping ground, deleted from the treaty.

Well! Canberra bosses wanted to see treaties given like Christmas presents—they really did, because they wanted to explore the better angels of their nature, to explore what ideas of fairness and justice for all meant—right down to the last child sitting in the dirt with nothing. Usually in this tiny era of history, it was common in the Brolga Country and right down to Canberra to see people sitting around all day long thinking about what was utopia and what was peace. And to question what could have been the most peaceful era known in the existence of the world. Where had it all gone wrong? Were they already experiencing the greatest era of peace in the world but could not recognize it? Questions raised up more questions for goggling around in the mind. Can angels strike others in violence? Can lightning strikes be equated to genocide?

Meanwhile overseas people flocked to talk to the frail old spiritual man of the Brolga Nation Government who had lived forever on nothing but his own sustainability, the ancient intelligence passed down the generations that he said was his religion. Easy words, but he just called it, looking after Country. He was proud that he had seen his people at last recognized as real people, not just a secondhand, shit-cheap humanity. He was happy now that this oldest culture on earth was recognized as being fit to govern itself through its own laws, and to live on its traditional land. And, this boy, Warren Finch. This was what made his heart feel good.

The Brolga nation was chosen by an international fact-finding delegation to be their showpiece of what a future humane world was all about. A UN sign was erected at the entrance to the Brolga nation. It read, *Peace and goodwill to all peoples.* This modern Brolga nation was just the kind of place that International Justice could promote to bring an end to the wars of homelessness across the world. This high law said it was the showpiece, the example for the future, the hope for kindness to reign over the world for the next marvelous century.

So, these elders, now traditional leaders of the modern world, who already knew that they were high class, were hailed for sitting on their land since the beginning of time, and for having fought very quietly for three centuries the war of oppression. They joined the ranks of other peaceful men in the world like Mahatma Gandhi, or the Dalai Lama. They were properly cashed up for Rights of Culture, Land, Government, Language, Law, Song, Dance, Story—everything. It was under these circumstances, necessary to explain, that they had handpicked their brightest child—a gift from God even though he was a half-caste—and had gone so far as to have bequeathed him to their vision of the new world.

This was how he became the chosen one, singled out from all the others in this Australian war zone of torn people, and was hailed in vows under the Brolga Country moon as the truest gift from ancestral heroes, and having a bit each way, not just from God, but any other gods on the planet too.

The education Warren received at his Aboriginal Government's authorized school was a mixed marriage of traditional and scientific knowledge. In a curriculum that the elders had personally composed with all of the reverence of their traditional law, they watched over his education like hawks. In fact, they were like hawks with all progeny, teaching the young to survive in tough new environments. *We are swapping Band-Aid education for brand-new education, sealing the cracks—all the holes in the broken-down fences of Australian education policy for Indigenous peoples.* Yes, they continued the *better education, we know what is best* rhetoric in their ongoing war with the *skeptic observer* whom they continually accused *was pass 'em this and not pass 'em that—always out to destroy Aboriginal people like a record still stuck in the same grove.* Anyway. Whatever. Agree or not. This was the hammer, even in officially recognized Aboriginal Government, pulping confidence. The hammer that knocked away the small gains through any slip of vigilance. The faulty hammer that created weak ladders to heaven.

So there it was. Warren had been taught, from the day he entered his people's Aboriginal Government School of Brolga Nation as their *sweetest* boy of six years of age, that he would fulfill a vision primed for their own survival, that above all else, he would connect Brolga values with the future of the world.

This was how Warren Finch had been able to live on his traditional land as a practicing pupil out on his Country. The official words about this education were described as being: *culturally holistic in all its philosophical, political and environmentally sustainable economic approaches for a school's curriculum which honored traditional law and the art of sustainability for culture and land.* A lot of thought and hard work had been put into a boy like Warren Finch to create *New Light*. But everybody in his world already thought he would inherit the world after he learnt how to make laws by studying the dance and life cycle of the brolga.

There was another time Warren Finch remembers from when he was still a boy learning how to be a man. He had stopped somewhere along the fisherman's track above the high reddish-gray earth bank of the river, and was listening to the silence of the middle of the day. He reflected on the pleasure of his thoughts about what the future held, where one day in another place and time, he would recall this time. And he wondered what he would feel then, as he danced to a fiddler's tune with the dragonflies above the river affectionately known as the Pearl—a traditional breeding place for local river turtles. He found it difficult to see through the large flat leaves and flowers along the way, but he was sure the river was not dry like it had been in the winter, when the lily bulbs lay dormant, hidden in the cool ground with the turtles, deep below the surface.

In the middle-of-the-day sun that showered the land with bright light, he walked further up the river in search of the black angel he had already seen flying low just meters above his head, the previous night, having been awakened from his dreams by droning wings far off, that he could not see. He had called out: *Who are you, flying there?* The thing he had seen flying close above his eyes looked like a very large woman. A twinkling bell-like voice had also awoken him from his sleep. Warren Finch lived in a world of bells, where birds like willie wagtail and magpies sang like bells even throughout the night, and beetles and geckos cried bell-like, and grazing cattle wore bells that rang in their night foraging over stubbly grasses. His elders often reminisced about the days when their people did everything to the sound of a bell on the Mission, rung by a white manager who ordered them about. *Ding! Dong! Ding! Dong! Bell! Or: Ding-a-ling. Or, did it sound like: Dang! Dang?* They inherited bell clanging, whatever the variance in sound. It was stitched in the brain.

A black angel cloud flying in a starry night and playing harp music should be easy enough to find. But the moonlight shining sporadically through cloud cover only returned fragments of his dream by just revealing slithers of a woman's naked body that looked enormous in the sky. She had come to him like a promise, from moving slow along the river that flowed as slowly as his blood. He felt her presence bonding with his own, slowly flowing like the river did, in his blood.

Again and again he tried to recapture the woman's shadow passing over his thighs under the light of the moon. She aroused a desire he had never known before, and with sudden urgency, he tried to force the images of the woman to return, but her fly-about hair, breasts, arms, legs slipped quicksilver through him, and in an instant, the memory of her had faded away into nothing. He was as before, always alone, and although he tried with great difficulty to recall this dream of dreams, others more mundane reminded him of the practical side of his life, where his responsibilities lay.

His frustrating efforts to bring her back revealed nothing, except confusion whenever the dream suddenly surrendered a small memory, bringing him a small victory of being millimeters apart from the dark skin of the woman's body above him, before it again became a cloud passing quickly across the landscape, traveling away through terrains he had never known. He was never sure when these images would reappear, or whether he even delighted in the idea of traveling further to find a glimpse of what had already died.

BROLGA AND SWAN

Vignettes of flying grass seeds spiraling into columns on colliding paths, though neither a girl who hibernates and is kept alive through dreams inside the trunk of a tree, nor a boy who grows on his dreams of looking down on the world, could understand how destiny works. This was so: the girl refusing to have visitors walk into her dreams; the boy trading reality for dreams where he thinks he is a savior. How children relegate fate as though it was a toy—something to pitch against their repulsion of each other while playing with a vague knowledge of the future they had watched in a dream. Their story was unfolding dangerously through the complex design of children growing up in untidy times. Of times inscribed in the warped, dull state of a publicly determined fate. Or Law that stretched back to the beginning of time.

Oh! helplessness of helplessness, there were pirates of high places rattling knitting needles with the skills of an idiot, and measuring the overload of historical repetitiveness, where children like leaves into the wind were seriously jeopardizing each other's existence.

In this breeding season, thousands upon thousands of brolgas of the crane genus *Grus rubicundus* congregated noisily across the plains. They hovered in the sky above Warren Finch. Masses of brolgas danced before the boy by mimicking his movements and endlessly paraded in the dry cracked claypan all along the horizon of yellow flattened grasses. As this supreme ceremony of Country continued there were many groups of hundreds of cranes lining up, to prance springlike off the ground, to bow long thin necks at each other, lift heads to the greatest height possible to toss sprigs of grass, and to stretch gray chests skyward, wings still arched, while other troupes bounced with light grace a meter high up into the air and landed just as lightly, as though their bodies were pieces of floating paper. The sky was turning gray as thousands lifted and flew high into the atmosphere, passing others descending on ribbons, each hovering, waiting to find space to land.

The boy went down to the river where the yellow water was flowing. He thought of himself as being a human raft while he floated through the shimmering haze at the hottest part of the day and stared upwards to the sky where the old brolgas, some said were at least eighty years old, were gliding in the thermals of hot air.

On this day, the tantalizing movements of the old brolgas were stealing his thoughts away, lifting his daydreams up a thousand meters, and floating them there, all his secret splendors of the night suspended in the sky, chanting *Swans beat their wings into the height.* Too bad! Serves him right. He should have been paying attention to what was happening right down around his own two feet.

His mind sailed on and on into the thermals until he was in a trance floating along the river, so captivated in his thoughts now, he was almost touching the flying woman he had seen in his dreams. He felt good. He was in amidst the teeming brolgas searching across the landscape for the distant music of the nighttime minstrels, those black wings whooshing through a dry breeze, and remembering how he had once heard a traveler, a traveling Indian woman's voice swaying like that through a slow Hindustani raga.

His head was high, lost in the vastness of the clear blue sky, when he saw in the corner of his eye a flash of black, of last night's dream, now downstream in the river. His thoughts crashed in one swift jolt into the water, and only the brolgas were spinning alone in the ghostly quiet of the thermals.

He let himself be carried down the river, half walking waist-deep, half swimming, not noticing the riverbank owls, *julujulu,* in the trees, because he was thinking that his dreams were starting to come true. He was very young. How could he understand that his dreams belonged to the future? Again, he glimpsed what he chased, a small object upstream that was still too far away. Curiously, the object did not appear to be moving, although it always maintained a safe distance from him. Once out of the water, he walked along the bank towards the small, insignificant dot until he reached a point, past the owls roosting in the canopy of paperbark trees reaching across the river, to where he could see a black swan, visible only whenever the sunlight found its way through cracks in the shadows.

Warren Finch, who had never seen a real live swan before, could hardly believe his eyes. He was impressed with the sight of this magnificent creature, a whispering swan, sunning itself on the river. He could not understand how the swan could be in his country, or why he was glorying in this creature of more temperate regions.

The swan was gliding away, more interested in its surroundings, a sea of lily pads in a garden of long-stemmed purple water lilies. Warren was already claiming the mysterious swan as his own, for it had appeared in his dream of the previous night. Could there be two realities? Bird of the daytime; woman of the night? He moved carefully towards the bird, but the riverbank felt unstable and he was unable to concentrate. He did not want to listen to reason from the old brolgas above, that the swan did not belong to him at all. He was whispering words he had heard, *sweetheart swan of sweethearts,* and hoping that if he could pacify the swan with the power of his voice, it would not fly away. He knew where it belonged. Its home was right across the country in the South, thousands of kilometers away. He thought it might die.

He moved to find the quickest way up the river, taking great care not to snap the twigs on the ground, and all the while, almost believing that he was flying. He was up in the skies. The rhythm of his breathing was like a tabla beating to crush the occasional alarm calls of those soaring old brolgas. There was no stopping his desire: he wanted to touch the swan. Some old excitable fool that lived dormant in his heart was up and about. A rogue spirit that had become as transfixed as the boy had of seeing a swan.

Quite possibly the bird was injured. Absolutely! Rogue spirit agreed. *Let's go. Let's get closer. Quick! Quick! I will race you there.* Warren could justify trying to aid an injured swan. It was an act of compassion, condoned. *Cause. Cause it's true.* Any human on earth would have thought so. But the swan seemed content to stay where it was so the boy could not be sure, and of course he thought, it would be best to capture it. There was nobody around except his rogue spirit to tell him to leave it alone. He forced his way through the brambles growing densely beside the river and up and down the river gums. He ignored the thorny vines lacerating his body which could have been the country trying to teach him to stay away—if he had been thinking about education. Finally, he reached the closest point of the bank to the swan, but still, the bird was far from his reach, idling about on the other side of the river.

His eyes rested on a levee, some floating monument of sticks higher than the bank itself, all of the *yimbirra* refuse that was slowly on the move from up the river. It groaned up to where he was standing. He could see the inflammation banking right back up the river until it was out of sight, and it surprised him that he had not noticed it before. He thought of the big woman's nest as he leaped straight onto the summit of sticks, branches and rubbish stacked no less whimsically than a million flimsy thoughts describing the nature of the world in his head at that particular moment. The old fool in his heart steered while the boy walked over the top to the edge and leaned over, arms stretched towards the swan.

Now he could see that there was something troubling the swan; its wings flapped frantically at the water while its feet ran on the spot, tangled in a bundle of fishing line knotted in the roots and tree branches. The sodden and limp swan now sensing its end was certain, was pulled helplessly through the waters.

A wall of floodwater exploded through the piles of sticks, branches, tree trunks, old tires and broken-down motorcars, that went flying through the air behind the boy, and you know what he had? *Only that old fool at a steering wheel.*

The swan was drowning for Warren Finch, and all the boy saw were pictures of Aboriginal spirits with halos of light, just like Van Gogh had painted. The boy had not known what struck him. He had been so excited about the swan that he had not heard the river shouting behind him.

TWENTY YEARS OF SWANS

It was more than twenty years since the day Warren Finch had nearly killed himself for a swan, when he arrived in the Army-run detention camp of the swamp in a flash car—a triumphant long-anticipated homecoming to his traditional homelands, with enough petrol for driving up and down the dusty streets for nothing.

Around he drove with his friends, down every street, the back roads and byroads, sizing up everybody who was a *Black* thank you—checking out the despair, mentally *adding up the figures and checking it twice*, and deciding like he was White—that it was *all* hopeless, nothing would help, and driving on.

He was sure going to miss the pride of the place. The swamp had become truly wondrous in the eyes of the benefactors. These locals, along with the other detained people from God knows where, all jelly-soft now from years of intergenerational interventionist Australian policies of domination, were true beholders of wonder and fervor-ridden with the beauty of home. They had no say about anything important in their lives. This had been an Army-controlled Aboriginal detention camp for decades. Whereas Warren Finch's Aboriginal Nation Government that was just down the road, had grown prosperous with flukes of luck here and there called mining, and saying yes, yes, yes to anything on offer—a bit of assimilation, a bit of integration, a bit of giving up your own sovereignty, a bit of closing the gap—and was always paraded as Australia's international showcase of human rights. The swamp people had seen life triumph. Hadn't they witnessed the growth of an enormous flock of swans on their country? The swans had thought it was okay to live there. Well! This, and the loveliness of their children and country, traditional or adopted, gushed like a permanent flowing river through their hearts. Hearts must have it sometimes, for after a lot of bureaucratic argy-bargy with Canberra for around two hundred years—but who's counting the cost of crime?—the community had been successful in giving the swamp the far perkier name of *Swan Lake*. It was the only thing they had ever achieved in a fight with Canberra. Their name received official status from Australia and that was a beautiful thing in the eyes of the locals.

But nope! Not Warren. He saw nothing for the sake of sentimentality. He drove right around the watery expanse for a bit of sightseeing, an excuse for intensifying and exercising his cynicism while describing what he was looking at to people he was *mobiling* back down *South*. Finally, he snapped the mobile phone shut in disgust and parked his dust-covered white government Commodore thing in the shade of the memorial. The twin, giant, concrete-gray, crossed boomerangs. He stepped out of the car, into the full force of a north country summer's day, and glanced at the block at the base of the boomerangs—the sign inscribing a dedication to all those who had fallen in the long Indigenous war against colonization with the State of Australia—*and continue to fall.*

Who knows if Warren Finch paid much attention to the memorial, but he would have agreed on one thing at least, that it was a pretty ingenious idea to erect this traditional icon, so symbolically embedded with psychological power. Nothing was going to beat clapping boomerangs calling the stories and songs—not even Warren Finch standing around the base tapping his song into the concrete, just to check that the whole darn thing was not crumbling from shonky trainee workmanship, and likely to collapse on his car.

He would not have known the local stories about what they

thought was pride. The boomerangs belonged to the old people. They had devised an image of themselves as super mythical beings—giants of the afterlife clapping these boomerangs all day long. These were their longed-for days. They said they would be better off dead. *More powerful.* They would telepathically stream their stories forever through any time of the day they said: *We will haunt Australia good and proper, just like the spirits of the Anzacs living in war monuments all around the country, and just like the ghosts of wars living in all of that rust dumped in the swamp away from white people because they thought they were too powerful.*

Warren Finch was not some *random* person, someone who had come to look at Aboriginal people for the day as part of their job so that they could make up stories about what they had seen, and even though he did not have much respect for the sacred monument, he was convinced that those two gray swellings of cultural pride illuminated at least one fact—*that nothing easily slid into oblivion.* He gazed beyond the monument and zeroed in on the polluting junk that lay around in the swampy lake.

The vista seemed to excite him, and he started muttering on about some of his important theories of colonial occupation, but whatever personal conversations he was having with himself, those who overheard him said they could not understand what he was talking about, and dreamingly claimed, *No! Nah, nah. Whatever!* Of course the junk in the swamp was not a glorious sight, and well may this be true, but this man's time was in no way infinite. Warren was very conscious about how much the world beckoned for its few important people. He strode about life in his natural state of beckoning overload—*one, two, three, that's all the time I've got for you.* These days he spared only a minute or two on most things that crossed his path, and this was what he did while spending sixty seconds flat intellectualizing the swamp full of war fossils. *Tis this sight alone,* he chanted in a flat, bored voice, almost as though he was still speaking on the mobile, *that justifies many thoughts I can't get out of my head about dumped people.*

It's a mighty slow crawl from ancient lineage. That's why you can't fast-track extinction, he claimed, murmuring to his fellow travelers, although to them—recognizing the fact of their being Black, and his being Black—it was hard to understand why he was talking like that about himself. They did not want to become extinct through assimilation, if that was what he meant, while assuming it was. But, just what else would a man see? Someone like Warren Finch who was touched by all of the cultures of the world was now seeing the poorer side of his own traditional estate for the first time.

In the swamp there was a long-held belief and everyone knew what it was. The whole place believed that one day prayers would be answered, and it would happen like this: there would be an archangel sent down from heaven to help them—a true gift from God. Not like all the previous rubbish stuff. Then so it was. It was heard through the grapevine that the gift had been delivered. This would have to be the boy genius that everyone had heard about from those other people of their vast homelands—the ones who were much better off than they were themselves. The ones they were not talking to. Those rich sell-out Aboriginal people with mining royalties and a treaty.

So when the archangel Warren Finch arrived, sure they were supposed to know because it was supposed to be a miraculous occasion. A gift from God was supposed to be incredulous. Perhaps there would be more stars in the sky. Or, perhaps, beams of sunlight shining from him would dazzle all over the swamp. They had always imagined what this occasion would be like, and most had even prophesied how the archangel would hover over the lake indefinitely so that everybody could get a chance to see him up there doing his business by spreading his protective wings over them, and all would be well after that. Not like all those other so-called miracles for assimilation that had been endured and considered God-given failures. However, Warren Finch deceived everybody. He really looked no different in appearance to anybody else living in the swamp.

For a few moments, the archangel glanced over the lake, and he thought naming the ugly swamp Swan Lake was a really stupid thing to do. He started to interpret the name in traditional languages, and then in the many foreign languages in which he had fluency. He said the name was common enough, but what's in a name? It was not going to save people from heading towards their own train wreck.

What was more, he thought the name was only a deceitful attempt to stretch the largesse of anyone's imagination. He would not be tempted to pity the place. Instead, he took pleasure in picturing the atlas of the world and dotting all of the places he knew that were named Swan Lake. So he had to ask himself: *What was one less Swan Lake on the face of the world?* He considered the possibility of having a quiet word with the world-leading astronomy center of which he was the patron, to see if they could rename a hole of some obscure outer-space nebulae *Swan Lake*. Yep! Why not? Once he was down the road which would not be long now, he would make a point of doing exactly that on his way back to Heaven.

This was the era of unflinching infallibility, claimed Warren, the postmodernist, deconstructionist champion, affirming from the bottom of his heart that any view of a glitch in the modern world could be reshaped and resolved. He laughed, saying that he felt like a foreigner standing on these shores that represented nothing more than the swamp of old government welfare policies. He looked like he knew exactly what to do. Someone who believed as most people believed of him, that he owned the key to the place where political visions for the entire world were being fashioned. *And where was that?* This was his question to himself, his concern, as he turned back for a second glance at the swamp, and his answer was also to himself: *Brains! In the brains of the men on top.*

The late-afternoon shadow of the monument ran like a dark road across the entire lake, and Warren Finch's eyes were led along it straight to the old Army hull in the center of the water, the largest vessel amongst all of the wrecks. He had only parked in the broadest part of the shadow next to the monument because across the road he could stroll over to what he called—*their "so-called" Aboriginal Government building.*

As he looked at the hull, he thought about how ideas of *flightlessness* occupying his recent dreams were mostly about his childhood, and for a moment he once again felt the gravitating seductiveness of the swan woman's shadow. He was flying with her towards the realization of the journey his dreams had always evaded. Then he looked straight past the vision, and all he saw was the sun reflecting the shadow of the flotilla's rust and wreckage on the watery expanse, before a whisper of wind dissolved into a nothingness the muted hues of rippling gold.

The girl thought old Aunty and the Harbor Master had returned and were outside, their spirits walking over the swamp. Whispering on the water. It made her blood run cold. She wanted it to be old Aunty and the Harbor Master talking about raising the evening mist together, and already mist was blanketing the water, covering it like a shield. The voices continued a whispering conversation, where old Aunty was saying that lingering reservations kept occurring in people's lives, and were always holding them back from what they should be doing. Harbor Master was more specific. More grounded. He said someone was tapping the concrete boomerangs up in the park and arguing with the old people. The Harbor Master said that person thought that he was living in a big ship populated by castaways—a bunch of scavengers, he claimed. *A big captain shouting orders from the decks of the destroyer that gave people berth—if they liked the way he was singlehandedly shipping and trading the world.* The Harbor Master said he just watched and was keeping his own particular mouth shut.

Up in the middle of the memorial park of Swan Lake, several swans had scattered from puddle to puddle under a sprinkler watering what remained of a lawn. A plague of grasshoppers, *jibaja*, bloated from eating everything green, chirruped, jumped up and down, and rose away in a wave when the swans scattered. But dozens of the town's thousands of pet brolgas with the quickest eyes around the place suddenly remembered something from the past. This was their old friend Warren from their former colony near his own community. These aging brolgas also regularly sat under the park's creaking set of sprinklers, while enjoying the spurting jets of water, falling into deep sleep as water rolled off their gray-feathered bodies. The brolgas went haywire and immediately leapt up from the mud to run over and greet their old friend from days gone by.

The old brolgas had led the flocks from the abandoned rookeries after the brolga boy had deserted his country. These brolgas had become *half urbans* from living at Swan Lake. They were flourishing in the rookeries that they had built all around the swamp. Nests stacked on the rooftops of houses. Look out in bits of backyard and you would see a gray throng sitting there in a daydream of devising methods to steal food from the township that they too thought was wondrous.

Earlier in the day, when Warren Finch was driving around, the old brolgas had been taking a majestic stroll up and down the streets to knock over the rubbish bins, and to squabble in D minor about all the useless rubbish they saw lying on the ground. Everything was going along fine until the flash car beeped the horn at them wherever they were spotted. They had retreated back to the lawn in the park, to continue examining the exposed roots of the lawn struggling to replace each green shaft of leaf repeatedly plucked clean and eaten by insects, until finally, they sank into their deep peaceful sleep.

Disturbed again. The bright red and featherless heads crowned with buzzing flies watched Warren stepping out of his car, and looked very puzzled. It took them some time to gather up a distant memory of a boy dancing their dance. But once they recognized him, their excited trumpeting called in more brolgas, dogs and people. The bugling went on and on, and the ballet of brolgas prancing lightly off the ground followed each other up, up, up and down while trampling the excuse of a lawn into a feculent pool of mud.

Warren smiled slightly, but he did not dance with the brolgas. These days he was far more excited about how the world danced for him from way up high, or in the couch-grass backyards of every Australian city, its towns, and right down to any buffel grass–infested corner of the country where people watched a battery-operated television in their rusty water-tank home, cardboard box, or packing crate, and looked out for fire, flood, or tempest coming up the track. All people liked to dance for a gift from God. The Warren Finch dance. He was the lost key. He was post-racial. Possibly even post-Indigenous. His sophistication had been far-flung and heaven-sent. Internationally Warren. Post-tyranny-politics kind of man. True thing! He was long gone from cardboard box and packing crate humpies in the remote forgotten worlds like this swamp.

Warren Finch's name was saturated in the hot and humid air of climate change. He had a solid, strong face to stare at the world, like a modern Moses—same color, but in an Italian suit, and with the same intent of saving the world from the destructive paths carved from its own history. His whole body bent from carrying the world on his shoulders, and from lurching forward on the staff of responsibility to reach too much of heaven.

But look! To be frank, Swan Lake did not have arms wide enough to catch the troubles of the world, so what was he now doing in a place like this? What would he find out about himself from coming back to his *so-called* roots? Why would he call on his lost people now that he was the Deputy President of the Government of Australia, and basking in the parliamentary system of a powerful political dynasty that was long skilled in the mechanisms for overturning any of the commonly understood rules of democracy? It was true that who spoke the loudest received the most justice, consensus, transparency—all that kind of talk about being decent. If you wanted to take a swipe, you could say that he only got as far as he had, not because he had clawed his way to the top, but because the color of his skin was like Moses's, and everybody wanted skin like that these days.

There was nobody around, Warren noticed. Nobody there to greet him! The whole place looked abandoned, except for some homeless loners watching the brolgas dance. He was not used to being ignored when he arrived somewhere. Shouldn't there be an official welcome? He was not just anybody. Even the lowest of the lowest politician should expect to be greeted in an Aboriginal community out of re-spect, and here he was with supposedly his own people ignoring his first (kind-of official) visit to his own traditional country. One of his minders mused, *You must have been jilted bro.*

Most of the swamp people (those approved by the Army to

watch television) were in front of a television, and watching a good documentary about Warren Finch. They always kept up with the news about Warren. This documentary explained why Australia needed an original inhabitant on top of the political ladder and they liked that. They liked the idea that Australia needed a blackfella to hide behind. Warren was no lame-duck party man of the old guard political parties that had dominated Australian politics forever.

Only remnant racism stopped him from taking his final place on the top of Paradise Hill. Even so, *Warren Finch*, the documentary on television explained, *held more power than the Right Honorable Mr. Horse Ryder. Was that so?* That piss-dog Ryder, as he was locally known, was just that old nationalistic politician who (even though the country had changed its constitutional governing powers) continued calling himself a prime minister, and who was from the big bush electorate that included half of Warren's traditional country. The man was cling-ing to power by the slenderest of straws, and said that he loved Warren Finch like a son.

Well! It turned out that politics was just the same old caliginous turnout it had always been, but everyone knew Warren Finch was wait-ing it out. He knew he would lead the country in the end because in fact, he already did. The swamp people finished watching the documen-tary and gave it their usual thumbs-up, before getting on with dinner with plenty of Canberra politics to talk about. And there was: you had to give it to Warren Finch for being a survivor of deadly times, sitting it out with a string of rat-faced men and women backstabbers ruling Aus-tralia who had knifed him in the back.

But Swan Lake? Why break the progress of the claw on its way to the top by being seen in a small place that had no power at all?

The unexpected news of Warren Finch turning up in their Army-run Aboriginal Government territory was not only as incomprehensible as divine intervention, it was just plain inconvenient. He was right in the middle of Friday night's fish dinner. It was *kamu*. Suppertime. There was a lot of swearing amid the sizzling and splattering fat fly-ing out of frying pans cooking fish too quickly, about a slapped-down dinner having to be gulped half raw like a pelican eating fish. And just because nobody had bothered telling somebody that there was a visitor who looked like Warren Finch—the bloody deputy president of Australia—waiting up at the boomerangs like a complete *Nigel* for someone to get their arse up to the office to greet him.

So then! Now the local hierarchy of the Aboriginal House Government for Swan Lake were smudging over the recent brolgas' tracks with their own footprints, hurrying on the way up to the office to meet this Warren Finch if it was really Warren Finch, and wanting to get to the bottom of this mystery of why no one had shown common courtesy by forewarning them about his visit, because for one thing, someone could have cooked him a supper. They blamed the Army men, and the white controller for being the racists that they were.

This journey of racism was long, and all the way, the conversations they shouted to each other across the dog tracks went like this: *Why do we have to be continually gutted by these people making their punitive raids on this community?*

The schoolchildren sitting at home with stomachs full of fish and chips were quickly told by departing parents who had just glimpsed him again on the 5 o'clock news, to watch something educational for closing the gap between black and white, like the serialized exploits of Warren Finch while they were gone. Adults were out of homes with departing words: *What is wrong with you children?* Their children had no shame. They had bailed up and decided that they would not go up to the office to welcome their hero and, good go! present him with some flowers or something. They announced, *we are staying home*, and seriously gloated that the reason why they were not going to the monument to see if it was him or not, was number one, because it was too cold outside.

The temperature had already plummeted from 44 to 33.5 degrees Celsius, and number two, they announced that they were sick of hearing about Warren Finch, the role model for how Aboriginal children could become good Australians. *Why was the whole country telling us to become another Warren Finch?* His life story was center stage of compulsory Indigenous education policies from Canberra where the saga of the Brolga boy becoming number one Australian hero was constantly drummed into their ears. They were sick of hearing how he rose out of Aboriginal disadvantage, and how the whole country wanted other Brolga boys to be just like him. Only that day, this new generation had learnt that Warren Finch was a cultural man of high degree. His first doctorate, although he had numerous doctorates, was the first to be achieved through a university of Aboriginal Government. They mocked him on the television series, saying, *Yep! That's right. We know those old Brolgas outside taught you how to knock 'em down rubbish bins.*

The race was on, with more officials of the Swan Lake Aboriginal Government leaving their homes as the news spread, and running towards their office with hearts banging flat chat against rib bones in the heat of *furthermores* and whatnot speculations of what had sent Finch like some maniac to their office on a Friday night of all days. And how could he have traveled so fast to get there?

They had just seen him on the television news and he was supposed to be somewhere else, with people who looked like polar bears— where it was snowing, on the other side of the world. How could he also be at Swan Lake when they had just seen him talking to more old *tribals* in a European village with one of those unpronounceable names, and Warren Finch actually speaking the same language as those people? They were all standing around in the snow and it looked cold. Maybe it was minus 20 or 40 degrees Celsius. Who knows? Nobody would know at Swan Lake. They had never been in snow like that. Not any snow.

He had been speaking like this on the television news for weeks in daily reports as he moved from one country to the next, each time with ancient law holders by his side in his role (one of many) as the special old-law rapporteur to the world's highest authority of elders for ancient laws, ancient scriptures, and modern Indigenous lawmaking. He was wearing yet another hat from his home hat, or his national hat, who knew these days. He had too many hats. They say he was leading the development of new laws for the world on the protection of the earth and its peoples, after centuries of destruction on the planet.

The little world of Swan Lake though, and many others like it, were speechless, glued to the television, to watch Warren's fingers running down the pages of centuries-old documents containing ancient laws, and they were convinced that one day he would actually find secret information in these documents about how to save the planet, just like he was saving just about everything else. They knew he lived on an Indigenous high plateau. But somehow, perhaps another miracle was needed to understand how it happened, but he had left his important work with these polar bear snow people, and traveled halfway around the world since doing the news, and driven hundreds of kilometers from an airport, to be at Swan Lake on a Friday night.

Warren Finch would find it hard to communicate with people such as those who were running to meet him, working their way up the winding tracks towards the Government building. Why didn't he know that they only wanted normal things on Friday evening, why wasn't Warren Finch at home in Canberra relaxing, or at the Casino in one of the cities of heaven, and having the time of his life?

What was he going to open his mouth to say? But! On the other hand, this man they were running to meet was one of the most important men in the world who knew the world's cultures backward. He was Warren Finch. He had come from their country. What could they say when they were introduced to all this embodied in one man who was really their own? The only news they had to tell him was how good their country's fish was, that they had just eaten for dinner.

What would you offer a world leader for dinner when something lavish like a lobster or a frozen chicken should have been carefully prepared, or even flown in especially with a chef from the city? If only they had known. So, while *Australian political hero* easily rolled over the tongue, and put brains on fire, Swan Lake-ian people could only run proudly and empty-handed to meet Warren Finch. They had no food to give him. Many cheered his government's election song—*We are not war makers and poor makers.* Now they—*the little people trying to climb the life of snakes and ladders*—were finally going to meet him at last, their true gift from God. They had voted for him in every election. They were the master race of politics in a thousand-kilometer homeland that had pushed and shoved him, like a rocket, all the way to the top.

The Swan Lake Government officers were exhausted from shifting about their thinking, and moving through their humid tracks, and yet they still had some way to walk their carbon-neutral pace through the shortcuts. Could you believe that this was Friday night? No one believed in using their own vehicles just to drive over to the office, and especially not when the world's foremost environmentalist was visiting—and if anyone needed to know, they had some of the world's true environmentalists living at Swan Lake. They could bet a million dollars that they were not using much of the world's resources. It was exciting to think that they would soon be on television surrounding Warren Finch. No one was to know that down at the war monument Warren did not have his media throng, even though he was still wearing his familiar gray suit seen on television that night, the style of suit that made him look 1950s quintessentially Australian.

Warren took deep breaths because he had to, had to find within himself a memory of home, but nothing sprung to mind. He only caught the faint aroma of eucalyptus oil, an old memory past its use-by date sprinkled for luck on his suit. The fetid smell of swamp and fried fish was truly awesome and off-putting, and all he could think about were better memories of his life, and having closer familiarity with other places buzzing nonstop in his head.

Very seriously though, he looked like a composed bouncer standing outside a Docklands nightclub, while the breathless local leaders clambered to introduce themselves. With a blank face, he lightly shook hands. An awkward silence followed. What had he to say to these people?

This first sighting of Warren was surprising for some. He was not really as handsome in the refined way they had expected from someone who lived in the city. He looked different on television. But all the same, they saw themselves in him, even though he wore a designer-labeled suit of the Menzies era, and they did not. Much was said: *Welcome! Welcome! Complete grovel! Voice of the nation! Face of Australia. Three cheers for Warren. Go Warren. Go Finchy. Go us.* They cheered him wholesomely, like they generally did for football heroes.

Quiet! Listen! He was signaling with his little left-hand finger, indicating: *Watch the brolgas dancing.* His gesture made the local crowd feel as though he was no different than anyone else. They were just ordinary people together.

The brolgas danced chapters of the story they had produced out of their life at Swan Lake. It was an unusually frenzied repertoire, perhaps connected to the frustration they felt at losing their leisurely evening walk from house to house to snatch the bits of fish they had to gobble instead in the excitement of meeting Warren.

He gave a little speech, although it was pointless trying to listen to him, when all eyes were on the transfixing sight of excited brolgas leaping madly, as though hallucinating to the smell of fried fish hanging in the air. Warren had to speak louder, until finally, he was speaking loudly enough that his voice was carried across the swamp and into the hull, where, *Oh! Dear,* Ethyl(ene) (Oblivia) Oblivion or whatever her name was, was still cooking fish in a frying pan hot with crackling oil. She was not listening to anyone, but she was the only person who heard every word he said.

Warren claimed to be one of those people who used the voice given to him by the spiritual ancestors of the land for its only useful purpose, to uplift Aboriginal thought to its rightful place of efficaciousness, to be fit in mind and body, and residing in thought and action alongside the land. A high-pitched cockatoo squawked: *Gone were the days where the Aboriginal people's culture was being strangled in the sewer of the white man's government.*

Nobody listened. Poor buggers in poor people's clothes were not the ideal crowd for the voice from heaven. Perhaps the brolgas' dance was more mesmerizing, or swamp people preferred to muddle through life in silence after eating fish. Perhaps it was the point of view.

Anyone else would have been a dead dog though, if anyone else had spoken like Warren, saying that he thought they were: *Unable to change. Unable to experience the depths of self-analysis. Hell was hell. No point sinking any lower than that.* This was a talking surgeon cutting with precision, but then, quickly stitching all of the infections back into the wounds, covered with a couple of Band-Aids: *You need to expand yourself beyond personal selfishness. Bite the bullet if you want to make a life for yourselves. Don't get stuck on your whacko solutions if you don't want to live in whacko land.*

Well! Bravo. Great lame-duck applause! *Arrr!* After an uncomfortable pause, then came the automatic practiced cheerful roaring that could be heard a kilometer away, like that usually roared all afternoon at local football matches.

Now, the brolgas' long performance, locally interpreted for Warren as being about the law of freedom and life, was finished, and the birds walked off, leaving the razzamatazz of political mindlessness to the dancing tongue of Warren Finch.

The fish-eating people literally bent over backward into a dancing, circling mob ingratiating themselves all over Warren Finch, to take it in turns to sing his praises, and in chorus thundering: *Oh! We just want to congratulate you because what you said just now made our hearts feel really good.* They embraced him as though he walked the same dirt roads as they did.

They sung more bird music. *This was really good that you have come here finally, so far out of the way, to speak to the littlest people of Australia. Oh! You are really the true way.*

In her hull home, Oblivia Ethylene was thinking about a group of butterflies with pretty wings that had flown around her in the moonlight once, when she had seen a wild boy from the ruby saltbush plains in the glow of a night lantern. He was singing nursery-rhyme speeches to the stars in a parliament house constructed of dry winds and decorated by dust storms.

THE YELLOW CHAT'S STORY

Whaay? *Whaay? Why? And early may?* A lone, brightly colored yellow chat whistled from the top of the Crossed Boomerang Memorial, its longing song about ancestral ties went wafting down into the ears of the poverty people standing around below, who looked as though the sky was about to fall on top of them.

In the crowd, little Aboriginal flags held up in the breeze danced to a nervous low whistling of "Stand by Me," while the shock-stricken, distant relatives of Warren Finch were busy among themselves, obsessing about all of their shared origins no matter how distant or close they were to *good boy*, who was once the child prodigy of their large sprawling Indigenous nation. *Shouldn't you tell him how you are related?* You could hear the warbling chat feeling sick with shame that nobody really knew the answer to that question, that they all shared the same genes—*Shouldn't he know how . . . Shouldn't he?* Although in reality, Warren Finch was honestly acting as though he was nothing more than a complete stranger.

He yawned and stretched with his arms wide-open. He was weary of listening to his own preachings and speeches, and what was more, totally oblivious of the yellow chat's song—a rant, a rave, pointless to him. Homeland? What did it mean anymore? After the experience of being cooped up in his Government car for endless hours of traveling across plain after treeless plain, he had reached—whatever the term meant, and what others called—*his people*. The world was in fact his home, homeland, place of abode, and where his people lived. There were no childhood memories in his mind. His nostalgia had been the pull of movement, but movement had drained life from him, and he was ashen-faced, like the gray feathers of the brolgas standing outside of the crowd replicating his every gesture, stretching their wings too.

Still his relatives were excited with the belief of finally quelling his restlessness, and where they were breathing the same exalted air as he exhaled, they could not help realizing too, that the taste of his breath was so much sweeter than theirs. Fine! They had lost their fish dinner. Didn't matter. This closeness to the *gift* was exciting. His relatives felt complete to be so close to his flesh and blood, and could breathe at last for having a precious belonging returned to the ordinariness of Country. But there was one cold hard fact, for in reality he did not resemble any of them at all.

Slowly, the crowd started to feel let down. They began to feel normal again. A natural suspicion snuck back into the picture of life, the larger landscape, what was painted in the framework of life. They began to think that he looked more like one of those outsiders—the complete strangers. Those Aboriginal people from other places the Army had trucked in and who were now tucked up in their lives through marriage, family, living under the one roof.

Even the *outsiders* resembled his people more in the flesh and blood than Warren Finch, where on this night of wasted fish, each enlightened revelation like this was just another kick in the head. With these thoughts in mind, poison from their hearts swept to their brains, which asked further questions: *How could he look like a gift from God at all?* He now looked like the devil. Just a half-caste! It was insulting that Warren Finch thought they were his relatives. Nobody was related to him. They had never seen this man singing to the birds in this country. *His skin is not permeated with the dust of our plains. Where is his language? Where is the salt of our swamps on this man?* Now he was a total stranger. Nobody knew him at all. A familiar question popped out about heritage: *Where was his family among any of them?* It was a bit déjà vu, reminiscent of those old Native Title stories that ended up as laws to include or exclude families.

A bit of analysis would reveal that the genesis of Warren Finch lay with the elders who authored his childhood. Hadn't they perceived the era of colonialism continuing longer than their lives? They created movement in him that was like the traveling ancestral spirits. Now in his early thirties, it was true that he had little attachment for people, least of all his barely surviving, flag-waving relatives who noticed the difference. They could see that Warren Finch's feelings were nothing more than weightless dust, particles of responsibility from their own Brolga plains he had scattered across the globe.

Warren Finch's life could be simplified in an instant, by sitting in the seat of an airplane soaring through the thermals over his own homelands, flying him off to those cities and towns located thousands of kilometers away from them. There was no point sulking about it. If he did not have it to be local, then he did not have any affinity to his own humanity, and he only thought of a moving world, which he epitomized by *imagine what you will?*

Perhaps, you could imagine that he swam in the ponds of an ultimate paradise, where continuous cool sea breezes kept on working to distil any traces left of the North from the face of the rough boy who had once lived among the brolgas.

Perhaps you might find him at home in a foreign place that could carve regal, fine-bone men   those who grow older with carefully smoothed gray-black hair from a brown forehead.

How could any of the swamp people explain this comfortable face they saw on television that held a universal magic capable of mirroring the faces of countless millions of ordinary people, who like themselves, had been duped by their own sense of community into recognizing some uncanny likeness and affinity between themselves and Warren Finch?

Warren had not traveled alone. The vehicle was packed with his entourage of three tall and well-dressed, sinewy-bodied men. His friends looked like Indigenous football stars—the ones seen advertising high-end fashion gear on city billboards. In those brown stubbled faces, each wore the fine chiseled lines of what was commonly termed by *neocolonists* who study race, as nice interracial breeding.

These men were Warren Finch's minders, or security men for the Night Lantern—his global name. They viewed everything casually, through sun-reflecting sunglasses, like justice men, free and tolerant, comfortable wearing handguns strapped to their chests, and being wired for constant communications with the central security headquarters back in Heaven. The general perspective in Warren's world was that these were good men—the best you could get, barely in their thirties, but tougher than most. For their trip to the north end of the country, they had exchanged their expensive southern city suits for slick Italian casual clothes.

After the speechmaking, they hastened Warren away from old crying relatives, talking to him about oblique kinship ties, and all those gray birds. The locals called the haste, *Manhattan finesse*. Enough time had been wasted, especially the overperforming Brolgas' homage that they agreed had taken longer than *Swan Lake* performed back-to-back by every ballet company of the world, and quoted Auden, *Lion, fish and swan / Act, and are gone / Upon Time's toppling wave*. The entourage moved towards the office of the Aboriginal House Government of Swan Lake.

The general swamp people stood back and gawked with pride. They rejoiced to see these smoothed, supple-muscled, dark-skinned men of action, their own people in fact, moving around as though they owned the place, although on the other hand, they took the trouble to reassure each other that only white people behaved like this. Even the atmosphere had turned excitable. Heavy clouds bearing an electrical storm were now overhead, but the swamp crowd hardly noticed that, and you could tell they were dying to call out to the poster guys that they were exactly what a black brother should look like.

Warren disappeared into the office, leaving most of the spectators to stroll home in the storm to eat cold fish.

• • • •

In the humidity of the hot, airless building, before all the members were present, Warren Finch opened the meeting of the Swan Lake Aboriginal Nation Government. He announced matter-of-factly: *I am looking for my wife.*

His *mangkarri!* His wife! Listen. *Manku!* He's speaking, making his *jangkurr* speech about something. *Jangkurr-kanyi nyulu ngambalangi.* Let him talk to us. Don't start a fire. *Balyangka ninji jadimbi-kanyi jangu.* Be silent. *Kudarrijbi.*

He might start getting cheeky like lightning making the ground explode, *dumijbi jamba, malba-malbaa kijibajii,* like dynamite-*waya,* maybe. *Kudarrijbi* now. *Kuujbu nyulu kiji-anyi.* He's looking for a fight. Because of his wife. *Mangkarri-wunyi.* We'll see if he talks straight. *Diindi jangkurr nyulu ngambalanya.*

In this building where *truth* was the motto, the Canberra-imposed controller of the Swan Lake Aboriginal House Government of Swan Lake turned Army-controlled asylum was a real *weisenheimer,* the name by which the *mandaki* white man was commonly known around the swamp. *Miyarrka-nangka mandaki.* Whiteman can't understand. He was supposed to implement white ways of loving children as being better than theirs. These people of the Aboriginal Government looked him over, and thought as they normally did, *We turned our back on him.* They had turned their backs on a lot of people. They had issues with showing tolerance for any outside government policy people especially. No! Of course they were not tolerant people. Tolerance was not their forte. They either liked something, or didn't like it. Simple! It was one or the other, and nothing in between. No maybes crippled up in the heart. Or this or that prolonging nothing thought in the head. You don't survive on gray areas. This was what having sovereign thinking meant in the time immemorial law of the land. That was how their people had survived the aeons. The controller chose not to hear what Warren Finch had said about looking for his wife. The assumption was that he never burdened anyone about his personal life, so why should he have his Friday evening disturbed by listening to someone else talk about what ought to be—*their own business.*

Mr. Weisenheimer looked around the room at *his people*—the

worst basket case he ever had to work with in a long, distinguished career in Aboriginal affairs. All he could see were the innocent faces of the Aboriginal Government representatives who were his charges, still arriving late and sitting down at the table whenever they were ready. They were doing what he had already assumed they would do—just sitting there and staring at the table and not saying a word. He knew this because he was an experienced career man of Aboriginal Affairs. He had seen this happen heaps of times.

Weisenheimer knew Aboriginal people better than they knew themselves, but that was okay. That was how he earned his bread and butter. He was a learned man about Aboriginal people. An academic. He had a national reputation that set the benchmark for Aboriginals to achieve results in Indigenous policy, which he had influenced in its development for numerous years with the Government in Canberra.

These people though? He believed that the people he looked at around the room were *had it*. Did not have what the policy required of them. Did not share the dream of Australianness. This was the reason why they had to be in servitude. It was the only hope if he was to shape the next generation on his human farm. And quite frankly, he thought it was hard work, almost impossible to save the children. He expected that they would continue to have nothing to say, and it would take several generations—more than his lifetime of assimilating them—even if it all started tomorrow, to eventually one day see a good, decent Australian citizen from any of these people.

While the entire meeting remained silent, Weisenheimer was expert enough to instantly fetch to the surface something from somewhere deep within himself—the whim-wham thing called the goodness in his heart. He prattled on about his programs—about how well everything was progressing (now that he was in charge). In doing so, he chose to adore Warren for being Aboriginal, by instantly ignoring the statement of marital intention that was no business of his, but all the same it confirmed in his mind that all Indigenous people were the same, since even the great Warren Finch could just come straight out and voice his personal business to all and sundry—to anyone at all.

· · · ·

Good old financial controller! He raised his gray eyebrows and re-membered he had visitors in the room, which prompted him to get back into the saddle of managing the social, political, economic and cultural life of these people. You could trust him on this. He averted the staring at hands and the silence in the room with the appearance of busy work, pulling out of his white plastic shopping bag the remote control for the overhead fans, which instantly from a flick of his finger, spun a cool breeze on sweat-dampened skins.

Looking for my wife! The assembling representatives of Swan Lake's Aboriginal Nation Government were very surprised by what Warren Finch had just said. But they waited until everyone had sat down at the table dedicated to the ancestors, after they had greeted each other in their own languages, and an ancestral anthem song had been sung to the mighty ones, plus an obligatory *Advance Australia Fair* to show some interest in closing the gap. A few words were said about what Warren wanted, then the oldest one they called No One at All—who would rather be speaking in his own language, but spoke in old time blackfella English to Warren Finch to affirm the controller's beliefs—simply said in a few reluctant grunts that no one had seen a woman arrive in that piece of rubbish car they saw Warren Finch cruising around in without even thinking of coming into his place to say *hello. Her spirit must be living inside his head, that's what I think. His wife's spirit was either controlling him, or he had lost her himself—must have, inside all of that rubbish overseas knowledge stuff he got cutting loose in his brains.*

The Aboriginal Government seemed to agree since they were being cordial; they were practiced people in governing too, just like the government in Canberra he was more used to dealing with. They commonly sat around this table being nice and eternally grateful, patting the table, or looking at it. It was the table of expectation, like an empty plate. They did what was expected with the expectation that, after he had delivered the berating that they usually received from politicians about their mismanagement, and the lack of transparency that was always how Australians regarded Indigenous people in remote places whom they could not see anyhow, Warren would announce some good news. It was to be expected, since no one important enough had ever traveled to the swamp, without giving them news of extra funding—a relief to save the little housing program once again, or a few biscuits to carry them over a few more weeks with essential services like fuel for the generator, or sewerage disposal.

What else could politicians do with the enormous, gigantic mess that they had created? *No One at All* explained, by concluding what he always needed to say, *We are all living in the age of anxiety here, Mr. Sir Whatever-your-name, what's your sustainability for us?*

Welcome to the dystopia of dysfunction. The controller Weisenheimer again reclaimed the meeting by dismissing, or not hearing this local speech by the most important and most senior man still alive at Swan Lake. He was keen to have the first word about the business that needed to be completed in this impromptu meeting. He needed to bring proceedings back to a professional standing, and he made his stand, by saying that he was not interested in *loose change from Canberra.* He deliberately spoke in terms that he thought Warren Finch would know exactly what he was talking about, while at the same time knowing that his words would be full of mystery to these uneducated, local people. It was his place to speak to Warren on behalf of the meeting, and he gave this address:

We have been waiting for a long time, Warren, for a bit of action. Isn't that right that we have been waiting for somebody to turn up here and tell us how we are going to fix this crisis? We need someone to tell us how to run the community store, the health center, get the bums on seats at the school; fix up all the violence, alcohol, petrol-sniffing, criminality, overhousing, maintenance; tell mothers how to have babies, healthy babies, pretty babies, clean babies, immunized babies, and to implement Canberra's policy to teach these people how to love their children, and while I am mentioning health, to rid the place of diabetes, heart disease, kidney disease, mental health, eye, ear, nose disease and dogs; not to mention training people for work, to go out and be useful to society, to drive a bulldozer, build houses, be electricians and plumbers, grow and cook their own food, feed it to the children, and then to lift a box and bury themselves in a box. To have a choice! We really need we-can-do people, that other old black man Barack Obama–type people who become presidents and leaders of some sort or other—of their people. Warren! We will need money to do that.

How do you do? When the controller stopped speaking, each of the councilors got up from his or her seat like sovereign kings and queens of the place, and went and shook Warren's hand, and his minders' hands, and returned to their seats.

My associates, Warren said briskly. *This is Dr. Snip Hart. Dr. Edgar Mail. And Dr. Bones Doom.* Then Warren paused, to check whether his audience was still listening, and continued slowly. *Dr. Hart here has a doctorate in hagiology, mythology and oneirology. Dr. Edgar Mail holds a PhD of paleontology, paleoecology and ontology. Dr. Doom has many doctorates too, of ornithology and oology. Mystagogy. Musicology. In other words, you might say between them, they are pulsatory omniscientific, very scientific! Scientists in the laws of two ways, in all of the things a black man needs to know about today's world in the bush up here, down in Heaven, or Paris whatnot, to make music.*

All hands gripped the tear-stained table, though not the skeptic Weisenheimer. Only his eyes had not glazed over from Warren's music about Black science, but it did not seem to matter for the whole room was experiencing bedazzlement. How it felt to feel grand. These people agreed that they felt close to God! *Real close actually.* They smiled to be amid so much omnipresence—the omelet of *ology* words floating gaily in the breeze of the noisy fans, and then dissipating featherlike, over and over in the ear en route to the brain cells.

Play something nice Edgar, Warren said quietly, when no one could break from the word net that had been thrown over their heads; and now even furthering the sense of amazement and pure wonderment, the one called Edgar it turned out, was a musician as well. The Swan Lake Government men and women looked like statues under the appraisal of those soft, pale brown eagle eyes of Warren Finch studying everyone in the room.

Sure, Boss, Edgar said. *I'd love to play.*

. . . .

Edgar was a tall and beautifully proportioned, strong-boned, golden-brown-skinned man with a face so flat and smooth, it made him look like the brother of an owl. He cradled an old wattlewood violin in his arms as though it was a spirit creature and then, the silence in the room was broken by a long melody. The music softened his smoothly shaven face, and the sounds floated away like moths flying off softly to clear away any residue of hardness in the room, and with their little hair-coated legs, to coax gentleness back on the faces of those gazing on the musician angel. The music flowed outside, past the boomerang monument clapping thunder and lightning, and over the swamp and into the hull where the girl and the circling swans outside were listening to the sounds from far away, like the murmurings of owls spreading across the distant range country of ancient cypress trees and coming up through the stillness of a freezing night.

This music of faraway places poured through the building and the call of owls seemed to come from every angle over the swamp. The swans swarmed into a giant serpent formation on the water. The brolgas rose in skittish, frenzied flights up into higher altitudes to escape the owl-like sounds floating below them. The music drowned the sounds of barking dogs, and inside homes there were small children imagining it was flowing from the pumpkin flowers on the rampant vines which interlaced the buildings and covered them with large green leaves. In the Swan Lake Government chambers, the men and women of the government saw themselves swimming in medicines with the thought of the three doctors. They had never had a real doctor visit before. Never had a real doctor stationed there.

The sweet violin music kept blurring the here and now, and more of the fantastical escaped from minds usually locked in despair, even bringing back memories of the Harbor Master whose responsibility he now chanted to all the black consciousnesses sitting around the table, telling them to continue keeping a watchful eye on the sewers of thought.

The heads of the old spirits popped up from the manholes in their minds to see the traveling music passing by the cornerstones of memory. Lights were switched on. The despaired room spun with too many thoughts! But only thoughts, after all, of oodles of money from Shangri-La! Fancy that! Fancy sending three doctors to the swamp on fish-and-chip night. Oh! Man! Hear the gratefulness rising. Thank you! Thank you! Now black consciousness could see fat cattle everywhere in the room. Who mentioned cattle? The feast of music stopped suddenly. Warren Finch's voice had a way of slamming the door on any more thoughts about poor health, and people needing to eat a bit of fat steak, and having doctors galore arriving way out here in the sticks to do some good. *Forget the cattle!*

I am looking for my wife, Warren said it once more in plain English, and since no one spoke, he sat back with a slight smile on his face and continued to sift the room with his eyes.

Warren knew he had shocked these simple people to the core, by talking about a wife when no one thought he had one. The noise from the fans now paralyzed anyone's ability to think in the room, but quite honestly, there was nobody in Swan Lake who would even resemble the wife of someone as important as Warren Finch. Swan Lake Government now thought outside of their own beloved homeland, something they rarely did, and tried to imagine Warren Finch's big life elsewhere—overseas, looking for his lost wife in a European café—at another Swan Lake in a Mozart setting in Austria, or a beautiful model wife in Paris swanning around as she should, because these were places they thought any wife of his would belong.

He kept checking his watch to quicken the thinking in the room about how to respond to his demand to find his wife. *Now think fast,* and forget the cattle. There will be no cattle for you.

The financial controller Weisenheimer was not easily intimidated. He did not care for Warren's attitude and asked several pointed questions.

Why would your wife be here? Where did she come from? You can see for yourself that this Swan Lake Government is highly managed, and we know all the people living here. After all, and as you know yourself, this is an isolated community controlled by the Army. Everyone knows who comes here. Don't you? Weisenheimer only expected nods from his people. He intended to keep the meeting from entering into the known nightmares of bad terrain and talk about cattle. He had had a gutful of Aboriginal whingeing and complaining.

But a discussion erupted. It turned into genuine interest about the lost wife. Everyone tried in vain to remember anyone who might be his wife—names of famous women, movie actresses she might look like, as well as trying to recall whoever had recently turned up. No! Not Really! There had been no ladies leaving or arriving for many, many months. *Only dead people leave. Only babies arriving. That's all, if we are lucky!*

Still! It is really hard to remember everyone who turned up on our doorstops, who was looking for someone else by running away from who they should be living with, and taking care of, like they are supposed to do. Or something. You know, my sir, said Mr. *No One at All,* as the delegated speaker of the Swan Lake House.

The discussion took a strange exploratory route, analyzing the blocked tributaries of Western matrimony, and being a distinct nation themselves and people of the longest surviving culture in the world, they had become world-wise at studying such marriages. They favored a cynical critique, where each member of the Swan Lake Government had their own peculiar but excellent firsthand knowledge about other people's relationships: the warring spouses, neighbors, or adult children, and numerous family dealings with bad marriages in countless Western soap operas. They presumed the right to ask questions. *When a husband comes looking for his wife, you have to think whether there is anything good in marriage?*

Was this the bloody butcher's shop? The abattoirs? Nobody hesitated or blinked an eye at the fact that Warren Finch wanted to collect a piece of meat. He hardly noticed the fakery in the cynicism in their inquiring about his personal affairs. *Mr. God Sir. Well! Who didn't suffer in marriage?* Mr. No One at All asked. If Warren worried about his wife, so what was the mystery in that? He could join the club of broken marriages in Swan Lake. There was a bad smell in the room circulating with the fans, as if a very fat rat had died in the ceiling. The smell reached down the nostrils and mixed with the fish dinner into a nauseating retch but the ministers for Government seemed unaffected, used to problems like that, and asked if the putrid smell was still there to avoid Warren Finch glaring at them. And someone, probably the controller, changed the subject by bluntly asking: *What wife?*

So what does your wife look like? It was insulting for the minders to hear anyone speaking to Warren Finch as though they were talking to a piece of scrap. The retorts came thick and fast. *What was wrong with you people? Don't you know who you are talking to? You are speaking to the deputy president of Australia here. This man is so highly respected abroad, they call him Deputy Right Excellency, Deputy Mr. President of Australia. Show a bit of respect!*

Warren held up a gracile hand in a gesture that was like a blessing given by a holy man. This was the hand frequently seen on television news from countries throughout the world. It was the very hand that had stopped atrocities and made peace among war-torn peoples. The hand was loved throughout the world. Here though, it simply meant, *enough was enough!* The ghostly Harbor Master panicked in his ethereal heaven somewhere up where the rat smelled in the ceiling, and stirred up extra doubt in the room: *Does he really stop destruction?*

The question about his wife was a difficult one to answer without resolving what residual similarities lay between him and the people of Swan Lake. They could only answer him by asking what old bridge still existed between them and this top Australian? Did it mean if they spoke plainly to him that they were Australian too? Or, were they really invisible in anyone's language no matter what they said, and would remain un-Australian for loving ancient beliefs of their traditional lands too much. All history had to be tested in these questions. Why? All history needed to be addressed in their answers. So what wife was he looking for?

A wife, a wife, in any case, might end up being a piece of meat. Someone who might have been called *Does It Matter*, then asked a simple question really, and very politely, *What's her name then—your wife?*

I sent you people a letter, Warren snapped, while checking the time once more on his watch, and blimey, he kicked his brain for wasting time.

Honestly, nobody remembered receiving a letter: *Can you tell us what was in the letter?* Weisenheimer asked.

It was explained in the letter. Warren Finch said—full stop. He was in no mood to explain what should have been read in a letter.

Was it that impossible to read a simple letter? He was clearly annoyed that these people were trying to force him into talking about what was really, after all, a delicate matter. His minders thought so too. A man of his position expected to have things organized properly. It happened that way everywhere else on the planet, so what was the trouble with this place? Why could one simple thing not be done right in this place of all places—his homeland? *You want to tell me if someone wants to play around with me here?* He suspected the financial controller was lying. *If you are running the show you must have seen the letter.*

The meeting waited while some clerk was called up to the office to find the letter. Meanwhile, Warren looked miserably around the building at paper piled and paper strewn, and then blankly at one of his minders who immediately left the building to make a call on his mobile phone to an office so far away from everything abysmally slack-assed that he could see in the dismal swamp, and cheerfully spoke to the real world of Heaven, where things happened with a single snap of one's fingers, where people could not run fast enough to do things properly. When he returned, the minder reported that the letter had been sent a long time ago and there had been no reply. The two-line, three-short-sentenced letter was now e-mailed to the mobile phone that was passed around the room, so everyone could read the contents of Warren's letter.

Well! Wasn't that just typical, just typical.

At this point the electricity suddenly stopped flowing from the malfunctioning power station down the road, and the fans rumbled to a halt. There was sweat in the room. The Army mechanic, who had gone away fishing for the weekend with "neglected" children, would not be able to fix the problem, Weisenheimer announced. He was un-contactable. Finch had now clearly had it up to his eyeballs. *What use was a mechanic if you can't even contact the bugger when you haven't got any power?*

Well! You tell me? Who is the boss? You, or the flaming mechanic? Finch glared at the controller. *Or who the parents are around here?* He was now counting the bad vibes, all falling like dominoes. All the ammunition! He was a master at pinpointing incompetence. Unlike beef cattle, this was what fed the belly of Canberra, the paradise hungry to shut down the Indigenous world. A bloody lost letter, and the lost wife, now the lost power, plus the smell of a dead rat in the ceiling, who could dream of what was coming next? The question of Warren's lost wife quickly became a lengthy *in camera* discussion in the full-blown humidity of the tropics in the closed room where swarming mosquitoes were playing noughts and crosses on exposed skin.

So it was in this inner sanctum of the swamp's Aboriginal Governmental Nation, which was trying to find a pleasing resolution, while Warren Finch was simply wondering if they were even worth saving at all. Then, the last-straw cold tea circulated to the meeting by a young girl—long after she had responded without much enthusiasm to repeated loud, clicking fingers by Weisenheimer, because she was too busy ear-dropping at the closed door and dreaming that *she* was Warren Finch's wife—blasted the lid off politeness. No tea tipped the balance.

She was a promised wife. *A promised wife? Ah! Now that was different. This is very different to what we were thinking. Sorry, but we didn't think about that, because we don't do that kind of thing here anymore. It died out years ago. Nobody wanted to continue with this old law.* The old elder said this straight out because he said he was nobody, and not just because everyone knew that a discussion of a highly contentious issue like this might end badly by the end of the night.

One of the older women said she had been a promised wife. Another woman said that she was more concerned about how the township kept moving by itself, and if this moving around of people kept going on, soon there would be so many of them, they would be living off their traditional country, and something needed to be done about this. The controller urged the meeting to think very carefully about what Mr. Finch was talking about. He too wanted to hear the truth about the lost letter that might explain the reason for such a highly prominent person in the Australian community behaving this way—like what the locals would gleefully think was a deranged hobgoblin sent by Canberra to personally annoy him, so of course he asked: *What age would this so-called promised wife be?* He wanted to know if Warren required a child. Was it a virgin? What hymn sheet were they to sing?

The Aboriginal Government men and women saw all kinds of awful ramifications for Swan Lake and stayed quiet. Actually, they knew the reality of his request, but Weisenheimer was on a roll, becoming emotional—nothing would stop him. Now he lost the plot by asking a lot of questions on behalf of his people's welfare:

Why did you come here like this, making these demands of us?

Why didn't you just come here with good intent?

What about those doctors? Why were doctors being wasted as bodyguards? We need doctors here to look after the sick people. We've got plenty of sick people here.

Yes, Warren Finch could have gone anywhere he liked while he was busy out saving the world, other than visiting the people who needed him most, his own people in Swan Lake. And! Gosh! A man like Warren Finch was too busy, he did not need a wife.

So why come here and bother the little people on a Friday evening when people needed to be home relaxing after a hard week and eating their dinner while it was hot?

Warren Finch had obviously thought the whole thing through—start to finish—beforehand. He had come to collect his wife and expected a wall of silence, but he knew he would push on through the night if he had to, and he was digging in. He was prepared to get no sleep for days to get a result, and knew the ramifications of naming his mission.

Dr. Hart, Dr. Doom and Dr. Mail, his longtime minders, who always thought that they knew everything there was to know about Warren as his closest confidantes, now exchanged questioning looks. Warren Finch already had all the women he could ever want. Didn't he have some sort of long-term relationship with somebody in Canberra?

What about Marcella of Milan? Wasn't he seeing a Maria in Warsaw? It was hard to keep track of the women in his life. Why would he want to do this? What kind of wife was he thinking of?

Names, names, names, Warren continued, clicking his fingers impatiently. It was only a simple name that a person needed. *This was a reciprocal agreement and it must be honored,* said one of the ex-boxer-type minders. His minders were quick to take up the thread of what was news to them, while not knowing how a promise wife fitted into Warren's grand plan, in which he had always been honest enough to admit that he had no time for wives. The painful issue was prolonged further by excuses from the Swan Lake Government suggesting it would be happy for *the promise* to be annulled. *It was time to go home. Time for bed.* But it was up to him to make the final decision since they knew the families involved in the first place were now deceased.

Weisenheimer pushed on.

Warren, I can guarantee you as real as I am sitting here that we do not have anyone around here who would even remember this promise-wife arrangement.

He encouraged others to say something to end the matter, and they did.

You do not have to go through with it, Mr. Your Highness. You should feel free to marry someone else and we give you our full blessing, our boy.

Yes. This is what people do now because the Army is in control here for the Australian Government punishing us people. We still live in punitive raid times. They do not worry about the promise. We just get married with the controller's permission.

No! No! No! The minder called Dr. Doom fired the shots in a deep operatic voice of the likes you would hear in the *Teatro La Fenice* in Venice; a soaring ghostly phoenix roaring, that as sure as hell did not belong in this swamp. The boom killed free speech in an instant. Meandering *talkathons* were pronounced dead. There were no other cards to play except Warren's, and he had placed those squarely on the table. Men like Doom made many people wonder whether there were other Aboriginal people coming up through the education system who could use their voices like that.

Still, what was pretty much the *vox populi* of wishes in Swan Lake became grist for eyeballs bouncing back and forth, where they looked up from the bottom of a Rio Grande chasm between one of these super humans and the next. Warren Finch's eyebrows rose, and he transformed himself into television Warren with legs stretched out under the table, but nobody copied his behavior. It did not matter to them how much Warren Finch was relaxing because it just felt like intimidation. They knew that feigning to be relaxed was one thing for the champion peacekeeper of the world, but this type of person does not travel out of his way, just to reach a swamp and settle for rejection, be bluffed by diversions, or just plain mucked around. His relaxed state only emphasized his intransigence and he casually restated what he wanted, with a smile: *the law is the law.* He simply wanted what was his to claim from an agreement made between families, of *Our nations,* he said.

It should not be that hard to understand.

But nobody told us, somebody nervously chanted.

But nobody told us? Warren's sauna-soaked minders whispered, in mocked shock. The pressure-cooker room was not to everyone's taste.

You had to give it to the bosses of this swamp for being true masters of their own game. They were not going to be duped by anyone walking in off the street so to speak, or more factually, coming in off the road like some unannounced hobo Black fellow, and aiming to rip the dirt from beneath their feet. They knew what people like this try to do. He was making a claim on their traditional land. They dug their heels in. Claimed no knowledge of the letter. Claimed there was no misunderstanding, and the reason being, they were always kept in the dark. Nobody could blame people who were kept ignorant to whatever was going on behind their backs. A few words on a mobile phone? *Blah! Meant nothing.* It was not a letter they received. *You can't receive letters on a telephone. Never heard of such a thing.* They accused the financial controller: Ask him! *He never spoke to any of us Aboriginal people.*

The fuming controller's many freckles looked like a nest of redback spiders about to burst as he shouted that if anyone wanted to make an appointment to get information about themselves, his office door was always open. *Wasn't that true?* He yelled at each of the people he pointed to around the table. In the end, a mumbler spoke into his chin and called the controller a rude man. The controller was uncontrollable. He had lost the letter, but it was plainly obvious that no harm had been intended, so the meeting agreed on the spot that such an agreement might have been cemented between two families, and the good news was that the misunderstanding could be put right. A likely name was whispered, that matched Warren's information about a family promise he received a long time ago at the bedside of his dying father.

The financial controller took Warren aside, outside the building, over on the lawn, far from the meeting, to be discreet. *The girl you are looking for is called Oblivion Ethyl(son), Ether(son), something or other like that.* The Aboriginal Government was betrayed by Weisenheimer who could not keep his mouth shut for a minute about anything. They always knew that she had been promised to Warren Finch so they had banned promised marriages. She lived down on the hull. And everyone knew why she was there.

Very unfortunate business they say. She was interfered with. (Sigh.) *But that happened a long time ago mind you. Long before I arrived here.*

I already know about that. Warren Finch snapped—his words slamming against each other. Back inside the office, he saw the flinching and twitching, but he smiled like he had hit the jackpot, and the meeting resumed admirably, with everyone getting on with polite letting bygones be bygones.

The financial controller finished the meeting by limply saying, *She shouldn't be down there all by herself anyway.*

You got our backing Warren. We vote for you all the time here. There was a line formed and everyone took their turn to clearly state their allegiance to Warren. Whatever he thought was good enough for them—anything would be okay—a few cattle? And just like that— they personally acquiesced as though the girl had never existed.

The brolgas outside wished to dance all day, but the day was gone and now they too were walking away into the night. The swans overhead sent a few peals of their toy trumpet calls through the dust, and continued flying down the swamp to the hull.

SWAN MAIDEN

The moon was hidden behind the cloud of swans swarming over the swampy lake, where in the darkness, thousands hissed as they dived at the water and stabbed their beaks around Warren Finch in a rowing boat heading towards the hull. Battalions of swans swooped at the boat. Warren Finch could feel the warmth of their soft bellies as he brushed through their barricade.

One thing leads to another, and before the girl could really understand how to think like an adult, a complete stranger had boarded the hull. The man said he was looking for her.

The girl was fearful of the oars moving through the water and the noisy ruckus from the swans. She thought it was the owls she had heard earlier calling across the water. Now her invisible life had been split apart by a strange man's presence in her home, and in that moment of visibility she felt ashamed of how she looked.

You must be the swan maiden. His voice teased. She met him with a knife in her hand. He was still excited about how he had been challenged by the swans. *How romantic!* It amused him to cast himself into the story found across the northern hemisphere of the hunter who captures a mythical swan maiden in a marsh. He removed the knife in an instant, simply by reaching out and taking it from her hand while she was still in shock. *Don't hesitate if you want to kill somebody,* he said. *You want to do it straight—Pow! Slam! Into the heart. Get it over and done with—just like that.*

She looked away, but remembered hearing a voice once that was similar, and tried to understand the circumstances of how she had heard it. She could not remember because a flood of stories, swollen and submerging under their own weight rolled into waves that pushed her further away from its memory, until finally, the whole heavy weight of remembering collapsed, and she felt as though she was suffocating in her own life.

In these images returned from the past, there was the face of a small girl urging her to run, to become once more the story of when she was alone, sleeping inside the tree. But Warren Finch's gaze was like ice. A wall of ice in the way of running! His eyes held its glare. She heard him saying that her solitary life on the hull had now finished—*a girl should not be living alone in this place.* She did not want to hear him. *It was not safe,* he said. He looked her up and down like a cattle buyer. *Not right.* She was running away through the path made in her thoughts to the tree that stood clear in her mind. But stories were switching themselves around like rope thrown out in a crisis, and in the midst of trying to grab a story to save herself, the reality of swans called from outside in the sea of blackness around the hull. They reminded her that the tree was destroyed, there was nowhere to run. The swans' clamorous trumpeting made her realize that nobody ran from Warren Finch. Already, he possessed her life.

He liked to view people like an X-ray machine—technical, and without emotion, as though this was the way to examine the function of an asset. *She looks deranged. Unhinged. She still acts like a child. But she must be about eighteen, nineteen, even twenty. What's wrong with her. She can't always be like this.* The girl felt sick in the stomach. She was like a lizard trying to disappear down a blocked bolt-hole. Was it worth opening her eyes to see if she had succeeded, if neither he nor she existed? Working quickly, she installed the spirit of Aunty Bella Donna of the Champions, but the loudmouthed Harbor Master returned too. He said she must be joking. He laughed: *How can her memory rescue you, girlie?* He warned her to get away from the past. The girl fought back by reciting, in Bella Donna's high-tilting voice, the many swan maiden fantasies that have vanquished men who hunt swans. She screamed the story of the hunter, that of a fisherman, another of the man in the woods—of their capturing swan women that always eventually escape. Stories she knew well about escaping. Screams these into Finch's face to cover the sound of his voice.

He was trying to put aside his thoughts, the reality telling him to walk away, his ego telling him everything would be fine. *She's fine. She's okay really. It is all this. This place. How would anyone feel? Nothing that can't be handled with a bit of care. It will be fine.*

He would make it so.

The thing about a levee is the way that it breaks apart with too much flooding. This was the type of thing that excited the Harbor Master about taking over the scene. He had to come into Oblivia's mind and see what was happening, to sort it out, and he burst in and asked the girl what the hell was going on. *What on earth are you thinking?* He was in full swing for musings, and told her to stop digging into the ground. *Your roots are piss-weak! Won't grow in this soil. It's got no seed. Can't grow it.* His voice invaded every crevice in her mind, from knowing the girl did not know anything about God or the spirits or the Holy Ghost, and knowing she was too exhausted to dig around for any more old stories.

What is his name? Warren asked about the swan hunter in the story she was trying to concentrate on. *She does not know, shit!* The Harbor Master was the boss and she was trying to hear what he was saying. Warren interjected constantly. Then he asked kindly: *Would the hunter ever return the swanskin?* The question puzzled her. She did not know if the swan wife would survive without her magical swan cloak in a place where her kind of story about swans belonged.

Either the girl escapes or not! The words jam in her head. Drumbeat to erase the existence of Warren Finch from her mind. But droning wings from clouds of swans drum fear louder, insisting that she *Get him out of the hull.* The breeze caught by their frenzied wings flowed along the soft-feathered breasts and bellies of these boats that glide in the sky until finally, the wind rushed inside the hull and whooshed the girl into its embrace.

Are you awake? he asks, speaking loudly. His fingers click—*Ethyl! Is your name Emily, or is it really Ethyl?* He casually walks around the hull home, still with the knife in his hand, while glancing at the shabby books stacked on top of each other, or lined up on shelves, others that lay open on the pages of treasured passages, in which he reads a few lines to discover something of the girl's intimacy with the swans. He flips pages with the knife and reads at whim wherever his finger rests on a page, and in the silent room, only the sound of flicking pages is heard as he moves to another passage.

He continued reading and the girl looked away. She was ashamed. Her head screamed for this invasion of privacy. There was a complete casualness in his approach as he moved on, *And they fade away in the darkness dying.* Chinese poetry of swans, Baudelaire's swan poem, and those on the floor in foreign languages he casually moved aside with his shoe. Then he looked at her as though she would tell him why these books were on the floor and why she had chosen others to read.

Finally, he looked at the messy room and saw that she conducted her daily life like a child. They exchanged looks as though each was vermin. She was a frizzy-haired, sticklike kid—ought to be a young woman, but dressed in a rainbow-colored T-shirt and baggy, gray shorts. The girl thought of escaping but under his gaze she was petrified, and incapable of lunging past him and out the door.

You are Em-i-ly Wake, or are you somebody else? he asked, looking at her again as though she could be of mild interest to him. She did not know the name. Never heard of it before. It occurred to her that this stranger could tell her who she was, the identity she had sought by searching through words written on a page. Em-i-owake. She tried to say that her name was Oblivia Ethylene Oblivion, although generally, she thought Em-u-awake was something someone had said to her once.

Go slow Warren, he said quietly to himself, while simultaneously checking the time on his watch. *Do you know who I am? My name is Warren Finch.* He asked if he could sit down, and sat down anyway on the only other chair, on Aunty Bella Donna of the Champions' side of the table. This surprised her. She never used the chair. It still held the essence of the old woman's authority. He told her to sit down too if she wanted. There was no warmth in his voice but the girl slid sideways onto her chair. Her gaze traveled over the floor and out the door to the swans calling and thrashing and rushing through the water. She did not hear a word he was saying.

The swans swarmed in their panicky flight around the hull—great wings flapping wildly, as when they were alarmed by predators on their territory, and the great white swan that had haunted the swamp for old Aunty's spirit.

Already she felt the swans becoming disconnected from her. They were marooned in flight, unable to break apart from their fear. She saw in their erratic and chaotic struggle their desperation to flee, and understood the very same nervousness running through her own body. They were trying to persuade her to leap from the hull and fly with them. No, they would not leave without her. She wanted to run but she faltered, kept hesitating, not fully comprehending the extent of the swans' electrified sense of danger, the sudden readiness to lift in one synthesized movement greater than that of their predator from the first sense of a deadly strike in the water. But the eagle was already in the hull, and ready to swoop.

I suppose you don't know who I am, do you? he asked again, his eyes steady, ignoring the upheaval around the hull.

Sit there. You and I have got some things to talk about. And bloody relax. I am not going to eat you.

This was the first time she had looked a person straight in the face. She recognized his clothes. They belonged to rich people like the ones Aunty Bella Donna of the Champions had described. The people she had chopped carrots for while they protested about the state of the world and all that. He caught her glance and his face softened momentarily, as though it amused him to catch the rat girl off guard. She looked away quickly.

• • • •

We are married already, equally cojoined through Country, Law, story. Our marriage marks a new epoch in our culture. Our challenge will be the lying reality. Something to overcome, Warren Finch told Ethyl(ene) (Em, ya, I, or u awake) Oblivion(a), soon to become Finch.

The girl did not think so. She leapt the plank he had laid with words and dived into the sea tide in her mind—that big deep sea, where she struggled to hold her head above the surface. Around her swarmed old Aunty's stories of thousands of drowning people blowing swan whistles, and the boys of long ago with their faces covered by white masks. They pushed her aside as they jostled in some kind of game, reaching up with their arms to snatch from the air a face, Warren's face, so that he became one of them. The memories splashed everywhere, suffocating the air in a jostle of whistles. She saw the boys laugh from the blank space of their mouths. She felt relieved by hands pushing her down into the bowels of the giant eucalyptus tree where it was just stillness.

Stupid to take nothing. Somehow, in his struggle to overpower any of her attempts to escape him, Warren Finch had gathered up many of the books in an old fishing net she used to scoop up tiny silver fish bait that swam beside the hull. Apart from books, the only other things she took from the hull as he forced her over the side of the vessel were those tangled memories that filled her mind.

The swans swam all around the dinghy, cooing to be pacified by her. When she did not speak to the quizzing eyes that needed to understand the stranger and her odd behavior, their gray-, black- and white-tipped wings flapped frantically and they lunged with their long necks into the boat and bit Warren's arms as he rowed.

She would hear the swans in the swamp for the last time from where she sat in the backseat as the car drove off, hemmed in between two of his minders. Swans ran along the water in the swamp, and flew in a cloud that looked like a black angel lit by lightning, but receded into the distance and their bugling faded into the thunder and the skies dark with midnight storms.

• • • •

You can take it away, and with that, Warren Finch switched off his mobile phone. There was no need to speak. There was the journey ahead. He had just ordered the total evacuation of Swan Lake. The Army would do it. The whole shebang would be bulldozed that night. He imagined total annihilation. The swamp dredged. The unpredictability of seasons passing, weaving the light as he fell asleep.

The girl watched from the road as the kilometers passed, noticed the vegetation changing from one geographical region to the next, while stacking objects in her mind. The woman's voice on the radio was singing . . . *Pick me up on my way back.* How would anyone sing the particularities of 3,003–4–5 cans, 51–2–3 abandoned car bodies, 600 road signs, 86 carcasses of dead animals where wedgetail eagles swooped down and soared upwards, 182 old car tires? There were lowland territories of emus, swarms of budgerigars, twisting green clouds over spinifex *kinkarra* plains, isolated groves of old eucalypts, river crossings with ghost gums *dikili*, solitary *murrinji* coolibah trees around dry dips in the landscape, salt pans, salt lakes, forest stands of gidgee in dry grass, lone bottle trees and fig trees growing out of rocky hills, salt plains, landscape blackened from bushfires, *kulangunya* blue-tongue lizards, or frog calls, diamond doves, runs of spinifex pigeons. She would remember it all, by repeating the list over and over again, as the number of sightings increased, until she succumbed to exhaustion and sleep.

In her dreams she struggled to find a lifeline to grip. No safe anchor in the exploding water, where the chaos was so terrifying, the girl jumped out of her sleep. The car was still traveling, and it startled her before she remembered where she was.

The headlights flashed over telegraph poles beside the road, an endless line running behind them, which in her mind began forming a swan map of the country. She could imagine the swans flying above the wires strung across the poles in their slow migration along the Dreaming track from another age, while heading the journey up to the swamp. Now, she began fretting for them. Occasionally, the lightning lit up a landscape wild with wind and she remembered how the swamp drummed with rain in nights of storm.

In the relentless movement of traveling through a rain that had captured the country, her world became shrunken, pieces of memory flew off, became eradicated, until even the polluted slicks running across the swamp had disappeared into nothingness. She sensed everything known to her had disappeared and blamed herself. Had she really negated her responsibility for the greater things in her care? She could not ask what had happened to the swans. Would not ask to be taken back just to see whether they were safe. Her stomach had no momentum for pushing words into her mouth so that she could speak to anybody. She would have no words sophisticated enough to say to high-up kind of people like these men. Outside the claustrophobic car, the never-ending rain was falling heavily, so even if she had spoken, nobody would have heard.

Warren Finch slept in the front seat. He had fallen asleep from the moment they started out, but the three bodyguards talked on through the journey. A thick haze of cigarette smoke danced around in the car, and they sat in this smoke like genies squashed in a lantern. The three men talked nonstop about how things happened a lot to them while working for Warren Finch, and listening to them, you would think that they had never known any other life. They had never been born. Never had a home. Never had a family.

The girl fought the sound of these voices that talked on and on about things she did not understand. It became more and more difficult to stay awake, to remember the road, to count the signposts, her only way of finding the way back. She lost track of her calculations—the categories slipped into lesser numbers, and were forgotten. Now, she thought she was becoming delirious from imagining devils monotonously speaking in the talk of the bodyguards.

In lightning strikes their faces looked freaky. Nobody looked real with their skin replaced by a watery substance trapped in opaque layers of silicon. The lightning convinced the girl that these silicon remnants of ancient waters must be spirit genies that had decided to dress like men and were now working for Warren Finch, and pleasing his every wish. The girl wondered whether he knew of their true identity. It was no wonder that his pugilist scholars could do all manner of tasks, far more than any normal men. This was why Warren Finch was not sitting up awake in the front seat wishing to be rich and powerful and a genius. He already had his three wishes.

Who uses up their three wishes? A wish for this and a wish for that in each puff of cigarette smoke filling the car! The girl thought the sleeping man was running out of wishes, and she tried to imagine where the genies would live after he set them free. When that happened she would get her wish too. She would steal the magic lantern car and drive it straight back to the swamp to calm the swans swimming aimlessly around the hull. She would arouse the paralyzed huddle on the foreshore with heads tucked under wings, waiting for death.

In her dream, a migrating swan moved rhythmically through the night as it passed across the changing landscape while following the lights of the car below. It glimpses Warren Finch sleeping in the front seat, and caught off guard hits the power lines and flips in flight. With wings faltering it ascends disoriented higher into the sky and spins off towards the stars while struggling to breathe. Oblivia was slowing down her own breathing too. Hardly breathes at all now, she is in a flight to death. She slips into unconsciousness while following the broken swan flying off through the darkness. Then the swan is pushed aside by the Harbor Master walking towards the car from a long way off and suddenly he is in the backseat of the car, where he squashes himself on top of the two men and the girl. Oblivia wakes up in fright, opening her mouth wide as the Harbor Master punches her hard in the chest. He is pushing air through her lungs, while squeezing the wrist of each of Warren Finch's men in turn, until they are in so much pain, they are forced to wind down the windows to let in some fresh air, allowing the rain to belt into the car. *Stupid girl*, he says, and he remains in the car throughout the journey, watching the rain and taking note of the country, making it almost impossible for anyone to move in the backseat, especially Oblivia, who remains calm. Warren Finch kept sleeping, but the genies felt spooked by a foreboding in the car, a heaviness that stopped the talk, and made them think seriously about why they had bothered taking this journey right now, at this time of year, the stupidity of the whole trip really, and why they were not somewhere else instead.

OWLS IN THE GRASS

The grass owl has always been regarded as one of Australia's scarcest owls, rarely seen and with only a handful of nest records, yet here was a concentration of birds, with evidence of multiple nesting.

The girl finally discovered where the three genies lived. After traveling many hours they reached a night world where men in singlets ruled lonely roads. Sweaty men yelling out over radio and satellite phones to each other to dig out the rulebook: *That one written in hell.* From then on it was hell on earth on this lonely single road, a highway stretching a thousand kilometers over the heart of the country.

This was the place where the mind of the nation practiced warfare and fought nightly for supremacy, by exercising its power over another people's land—the night world of the multinationals, the moneymakers and players of big business, the asserters of sovereignty, who governed the strip called *Desperado*; men with hands glued to the wheel charging through the dust in howling road trains packed with brown cattle with terrified eyes, mobile warehouses, fuel tankers, heavy haulage steel and chrome arsenals named *Bulk Haul, Outback, Down Under, Century, The*

Isa, The Curry, Tanami Lassie, metal workhorses for carrying a mountain of mining equipment and the country's ore.

A crescendo of dead—the carcasses of splattered or bloated bullocks and native animals lay over the sealed or unsealed corrugated roads, where the eyes of dingoes and curlews gleamed in the headlights.

The genies stopped frequently to check the roadkill. Hunger filled the car. The girl watched as they collected those still with a trace of life: small rodents, mangled rabbits, various marsupials, broken-back snakes, a bush turkey, a smashed echidna. All of these bloodied, broken creatures still warm, were thrown in the backseat of the car. Along the way, the Harbor Master decided he could no longer be bothered staying in a car loaded with roadkill, so he got out, and walked off somewhere out there on the open road.

You could only expect to arrive in the most isolated destinations like this after midnight, one of the genies murmured to the others in the car, after driving hour after hour through flat and wide country to reach a place where the winds collided and spun the soil into clouds of dust. Home at last. The genies walked off into the bush. They spoke to the country. Let the country know they had come home. Who the sleeping man and the girl were in the car.

The genies constructed a campsite on ground thick with rats, and smiled whenever they passed the terrified girl sitting in the car watching the earth move with their footsteps. *Child! Pretty rats. Ratus vilosissimus. Bush rats!* The air was dry and smelt of dust, rats and the heat of many days that had stayed in the ground. The rats scattered in rolling waves at every movement while scurrying in and away for all the fur and offal thrown to them by the genies preparing the roadkill for the fire. Doom, Mail and Hart could not put aside something that had been niggling them ever since they had arrived on their country with the girl. None of them knew the stories from her country. They did not know anything about her, nothing of what she held within her, or the spirits of the law stories that she now brought onto their own territory. How would they know how these stories connected both countries? What other questions should they be considering if her stories did not connect with their country, not even one story line connecting their lands together, if that was possible? They did not know. And the girl? She had not spoken a word and as far as they knew, she was not able to speak.

These questions started to haunt them, and it seemed as though the ancestors were already asking them to consider the consequences of trespassing spirits, and how they connected themselves to land and to her, and what knowledge they would turn to on this country. They were not senior story-men, nor in positions of authority as elders holding the law of the country on which they stood. Not like Warren, still asleep in the car, who was a senior lawman with much authority on his own country.

Well! It was pretty serious stuff to worry about, and they thought Warren was stupid for bringing her along in the first place with the excuse of using all of that promise-marriage stuff—where did that come from? And simply by glancing from the girl and at each other, they agreed being back on their country was going to be one hell of a sobering-up exercise for each of them.

Since they were already calculating the cost of having her on their country, each man instinctively understood how these things work; of being responsible for looking after the girl. It was pretty obvious to them that there was something different about her—not because of Warren, but her strangeness made them feel uneasy, and convinced them that she had spirits looking after her. This was the thing that they had felt in the car, and now the whole mess of not knowing what to do about her continually bothered them. It was because of their foreboding about what they did not know about her, that they were already thinking about leaving, and realizing if they continued thinking like this, it would get to the situation where it would be impossible to leave, because if not today or tomorrow, any one of them could suddenly be seized, and driven into that state of impossibility. Leaving would become a rock hanging around their necks. Leaving would become tied to a sense of foreboding, seen as being riddled with bad luck, where anything could go wrong with the whole situation of watching, caring, and thinking while they went about their scientific work on the environment—the annual task, the one small important thing that they had been asked to perform by their own nation. Now, instead of the work being a joy, with a sense of respect, and honoring their country, they would always be waiting . . . watching and waiting while nothing happened, until their own berserk, cartwheeling prophesying was fulfilled.

The dust rose like shadowy priests wandering through the darkness. A celestial haze stirred up by the cattle. The cattle called to one another in response to their leaders, collars swaying around their necks ringing their bells. The girl was too frightened to leave the car, but Doom ordered her to get out. *Don't be stupid. Nobody is going to hurt you.* Blood boils in her face as she stands back in the shadows, too afraid of becoming lost and disoriented as rats scurry in and out of the ghost bush, where *darraku* was everywhere, and feeling that *kundukundu* scrub devil reaching out with the wind, and she feels him scratch, *kurrijbi* all over her body, scratching along her arms and legs, he ensnarls her into the foliage.

The cattle bells roll, and remind her of Aunty Bella Donna of the Champions singing sacred texts to unlock the terrifying memories of her people. Again and again, by ringing the bells she brought them to life, legendary heroes that stretched right back through the ages to the time when wisdom singers like Wainamoinen of the *Kalevala* were walking their land, *swans came gliding from the marshes . . . came in myriads to listen . . .*

The same old oracle was everywhere, even in the dust of rats. This time, Bella Donna was quietly singing the poetry of Ludwig Rellstab's *In der Ferne—In the distance—of fleeing one's home broken-hearted*, from Franz Schubert's *Schwanengesang D.957*. Hovering! Somewhere up in the sky! Asking the breezes to send greetings to a time when women stitched those white and golden swans in treasured embroidery that became heirlooms, before they fled along broad rivers towards the sea where white soot-stained swans were nesting in the burnt marshes.

Warren Finch did not stay asleep for long. The genies were too full of enthusiasm, divined more song and talked of seeing so fine a starry night. *Hey! Girl, look at that*, they called Oblivia frequently, constantly checking to see where she was as she stood in the darkness. They kicked rats away, and their laughter swirled about with the wind. *Hey! Girl, did you see that?* The car produced bounty—food, cooking utensils and bedding, more than anyone could have imagined would fit in its boot. A campfire was lit. Meals were cooked. Aromas filled the air. Wine and water appeared as though they had been divined from the windy earth itself. *You will feel pretty good while you are on this country, boss,* they reassured him. He was on their land. *It fills you up with life. All the energy you need. You'll see.* The men exchange knowing looks. There is no need to speak. They all belong to the same game. They know what Warren Finch has to work out before they go back to the city.

Let's go, jila nungka, Finch said flatly to Oblivia, after he had eaten every piece of meat on his plate. She had not eaten, or as Warren guessed, refused to eat. He could see hatred in her eyes, and felt how tense she was, but he took her by the hand, pulled her to her feet from the ground where she had been sitting near the fire, and led her back to the car. In this moment of pulling her away from herself, she knew he would overpower her life. Even the sensation of his hand touching her had sent her back into the tree in her mind.

Once Warren had left with the girl, the genies chatted lightly about city women, international woman who called him up night and day. Now therein lay the mystery: She was not in the same league. They had seen enough of her on this journey to know that he must be regretting his mistake. She was just a kid. Well! She certainly looked and behaved like one. *What did he think was going to happen once they got back home?* Anyone could have told him not to go around picking up "damaged goods" girls from dysfunctional Army-controlled communities like the swamp. Main thing being that bloody place was her homeland. *The man's got enough troubles.* What was he thinking? The girl was overcome with shyness and here they were, a thousand kilometers away, and she would not even look at them, let alone speak. *What he went and done now is a wrong thing.* They knew how lightly he treated women, but thought he understood which women had any chance of standing up to him. Well! That was too late now. He had laid the idea of "worldliness" at the feet of a recluse. Who knew what was the matter with him? *He's gone too far.* They did not have to say what each of them already knew, that they could not fix this problem. It would not be like having a "small smart chat" to one of the city women he was tired of, who he wanted to go and get lost.

I am so tired, Warren told her, after he had driven a short distance from the camp the genies had made for themselves, and threw his swag on the dirt.

Come here and let's get some sleep, he said, pulling the trembling girl towards him, onto the swag, and into the blanket of dust swirling over them. The surrounding bush smelled of the rats that were rushing through the grass whining for food, which made her believe they would attack once she fell asleep. She felt nauseated by the closeness of this other person, but surveying the surrounding darkness, she saw that there was nowhere to escape in the dryness of the strange country that frightened her. Forced to lie together in the cold, locked for warmth like sheltering animals against a windbreak he had erected with the canvas of the swag against the car, his arms wrapped around her made her feel that she was in the grip of a snake. She listened closely to the dry grass and shadows of scrub being rustled by the wind, singing stories and laws that she would never know, and knowing this single thing about being its stranger was like having the weight of the world on her shoulders. This was the kind of weight she carried to stop her from sleeping in this country. Whenever she drifted off to sleep, she would instantly be reawakened; just by the simple fact of knowing she should not be there, and knowing that rats crept all over the ground searching for food. She felt the country's power. Knew it could kill her.

Every sound convinced her that his bodyguards, the genies, were in the bush waiting for her to run. She does not trust any of them. But how could they be lurking around, when from further away, she could hear them singing the country through the night, their voices resounding in the wind gusts, and echoing through the landscape, as though there were many others singing with them. Her instincts keep telling her to run, she cannot stand being near him, feels like death to her, but fearing he would kill her, she remains frozen, barely able to move.

Whenever she moved slightly, even to breathe deeply, his grip tightened. But he slept easily: the songs travel with him, and he carries the spirits of homelands inside him. It makes him strong: the hands of the ancestors are in his own, acting in unison.

She lay very still in the hope that he would stay sleeping even though she did not want to be left awake to listen to the sounds of the country. She hears the sharp cry from a rat and imagines that a snake is killing it, and this convinces her that she is sleeping on *miya-jamba*, snake ground. She imagines snakes are everywhere and hates the place, and is hot from panicking to be off the ground. The thought of rats and snakes infested through every centimeter of this piece of country makes her growing hatred for Warren Finch grate that little bit harder, and she is desperate to move, but just when she wishes to kill him and reaches around to find a rock to slam into his head, forgetting to fear she might touch a rat or a snake instead because she can't see a thing in the darkness, or that he will wake up and see what she is doing and kill her instead, something happens. She forgets to act—either to run off, or to kill him. She has changed her mind? No, that was not it. Her mind changes itself. It is at war with action. Fights decisions. She forgets to act when memories quickly regain control of her brain, and instead of fighting, she escapes with a flood of thoughts running back along the song lines to the swamp, and the language inside her goes bolting down the tree with all the swans in the swamp following her.

He knew her terror. It was the fear of a child that even the rats sensed and were scattering in frenzy. What was he to do with her world? This was when he realized that he would never be able to reach her. Hadn't he given her a fair go? He had built a dream as complex and ingrained as her own, but where he knew that his would keep pushing him out in the world, she would always dig a hole to hide in. She was still the girl in the tree. Untouchable. Rolled up in a tight ball like a frightened echidna. Yes, it was easy to decide not to touch her. Perhaps he never would. What did it matter? Nobody would accuse him of being a pedophile or a rapist. Number one rule of his forefathers. What could he do? He drifted off into half-sleep like he always did, while thinking about a mountain of crises in any country that sprung to his mind, and through the wee hours of the night, he would spin by the world's troubles, resolving crises one by one, intervening step-by-step in other people's fortunes or misfortunes, in his dreams.

When the wind dropped, all she could hear was his breathing resounding through the sounds of owl fights, and screaming rats. Above them, she thought she saw spiderwebs being spun on fine threads that ran down from the power lines and across to the low-growing mulga trees. These enormous webs were being woven thicker and thicker and spiders were flying through the air in search of places to anchor their threads, as though setting a trap to encase them during the night. She lay flat beside him as he slept, and drifted into sleep with the thought of touching the walls inside her tree, and dreamed of a struggling swan enclosed by Warren's icy body while old Bella Donna sang from afar— *A swan with a slither of bone in its beak.*

The dawn landscape was gray and solemn as it revealed a silent vista of mostly grass and sparsely scattered scrub, until the baying of cattle echoed in a chain reaction that sallied back and forth from the distant horizons. When the sun rose, the cattle had already broken through spiderwebs and gathered around the two sleeping figures. She was in a cathedral of Law where marriages were always honored but she would not honor hers. The morning air felt cold. So were her thoughts, vowing that nothing would spring from the dirt of this ground.

You will learn that you and I are going to stand for each other as the only ones we can trust, so never forget that I am your best friend, and only friend, Warren said, preparing to leave, and added—always serious— *You remember that, and that will be the main thing I will want from you as a wife.*

She looked at the landscape—a vista of sameness in every direction— and knew that this was why women went missing on journeys with their husbands. They were lost forever. This country would devour anyone walking in it that did not know it. Only local people would know how to move through it. A voice she recognized was surfacing: *Look around here.* She thought this wedding country was the home of stories about women

thrown overboard, cast out, abandoned, those bodies lost in *wiyarr* spinifex waves.

Isn't it a great country, Warren said, already flowing into the day
ahead, and pushing aside the troubling dreams that had come to him
during the night, where he had met himself as a dead man, disoriented,
weak, and his ghostly face full of disbelief, while being supported by
the genies through the streets of the city, and he had watched as they
walked on, to a grave he would be buried in.

Swans mate for life: that was what she thought. And if a swan loved
its mate, then what would make one kill its mate as she had seen once
in a sudden and vicious attack, alongside the hull? It was a silent death.
There was no such thing as the dying swan call. It died without sound.
She had no sound either, and knew what it was like to be without
sound. This country would never hear her voice, or the language she
spoke.

The genies' camp was a mess. Their smart clothes were abandoned
over the ground, their pots, pans and swags spread in a chaotic pal-
ette. Encircling it all, dead rats in their hundreds lined the periphery.
Swarms of blue *Lycaenidae* butterflies, unusually massing in one spot,
flew above the heads of Drs. Hart, Mail and Doom who were now
dressed in their oldest bush clothes, that might have been buried for
years under clumps of spinifex. The three men were busy with the fire,
creating breakfast, and totally oblivious to the blot they had created on
the landscape. *Welcome home,* smiled Mail. Oblivia looked around at
their camp. It looked as though they had not moved from their position around the fireplace from the previous night. They were listening
intently to a distant magpie, just *jarrburruru* absorbed in its song.

Hear it? A Thessalian maiden no doubt, Doom said. A slight smile of
appreciation spread across his face as he spoke to Warren Finch.

Warren nodded casually. He began poking the fire with a stick to
send up the flames. His mind was set on the black billycan steaming
with the aroma of tea and with pushing away the shock of seeing his
dead face in a dream, which was still clear in his mind. Oblivia noticed
Dr. Doom's face softening, the hardness of the day before had disap-

peared. He looked like a boy staring into the distance, locked into
studying the structure of the magpie's tune. After a while he stood up,
and faced the direction of the songster. He whistled the song perfectly.
The bird replied. A song war continued until the bird flew from twig
to twig across the ground to investigate, and seeing how it had been
tricked, flew off.

Would you like to have some owl's eggs? Snip Hart asked her. He had
been squatting beside the fire, stirring a large frypan amid the smoke,
but had come over and spoken quietly while handing her a plate of
food. She looked away in disgust. She was not eating owl eggs. *Eat it,*
Warren demanded in a voice that made her wince at the ferocity of it.
Her eyes rested on the wanderings of a rat daintily sniffing over each
corpse of its dead friends. It touched the tips of gray bloodied fur with
its nose as though it was searching for a faint breath of life or a ticking
heart, before moving on.

The girl could not understand what the genies thought the reason
was for spending most of the night killing rats. They told Warren that
these were plague rats, *were attracted to the light of the fire.* There was
blood on thick sticks of wood resting on the ground beside the fireplace, right next to the king-sized frying pan filled with bright yellow
scrambled eggs. She tried to guess how many owls' eggs had been
taken from their nests and looked at the landscape of spinifex *kinkarra*
and grasslands, where nothing much grew higher than a meter off the
ground. The girl tried to locate where owls would nest in those plains
where there were no significant trees, except mulga. She remembers
owls nesting in the ghost ships on the swamp and she gets up and feels
that she is starting to walk off towards home, which feels very close in
her mind, but Warren makes her sit on the ground. The plate of food is
placed in her lap. He repeats this exercise a number of times before she
realizes that she is not going anywhere.

*Well! So many rats, so many owls, and all night, "The tremulous sob
of the complaining owl . . ."* Bones remarked excitedly, his face covered
with gray dust. In an authoritative voice, he explained that they were
sitting in the best place in the world right now to see owls. *Man! We are*

right in the middle of a plague of rats that are multiplying in droves. Never seen anything like it before. He explained that the rats had migrated in strands of millions flowing inland through the desert. In their wake, large flocks of native grassy owls had followed them, and the *Tyto capensis grass owls,* he explained, were also quadrupling in numbers each time they bred. The food supply was so good—*different, unusual, changed weather patterns are causing it. Well! It was like sitting in the middle of a feast,* said Doom, speaking knowledgeably about the extraordinary phenomena—a million-to-one chance they were lucky to witness. He had been visiting places like this for years, waiting for this to happen.

Yep, Snip added, *don't forget the owls were attacking the moths attracted to the fire as well and I think—*

Yes, of course, Doom interjected with science talk. *But I don't think the fire was a consideration in the mind of swarming rats being chased by owls.*

My friend! Who knows the workings of a rat's mind, Snip replied.

I thought that was our expertise: to know a rat when we see one, Doom laughed, but Mail took a more serious analogy about predation in a natural feast or famine occurrence.

Vigilance! My friend. It was only sheer vigilance—the nature of our ancestors, that had saved us from a storm of vermin.

Snip said he agreed because he felt Mail really possessed the mind of a genius, and laughed. *In a way,* he said, *I really equate that brain of yours, Mail, with a high tech microscope. Someone, who could without hesitation, and with the least bit of prompting, easily cast his mind back through time in a matter of moments, to situate himself inside the brain of the first man and re-create his prophecy.*

And the reason? Ancestry. It all boils down to the connective tissue of heredity. A miracle that is not restricted to time. The brain is a marvelous organ.

You are one of a kind, brother, Mail laughed.

This whole thing was one of a kind.

One continuously ponders the puzzle of life, Warren said with a deep sigh.

Of course, genius is always hard to ignore, Snip said, with a wink.

Exactly. The reason why *Tyto capensis* and *Tyto alba* were nesting like flies around the spinifex.

The souls of women, Warren reminded them, and looked at the girl who was still staring at her plate, unwilling to eat strange food.

You had better eat. It will be another long day.

The return to the highway commenced with a greeting from a blue-eye crow. It was crying next to its squashed-in-half mate left in the middle of the road. Warren stopped the car. The bird tried to defend itself as Warren sought to befriend it. Quietly, he moved closer, holding out his arm, then the bird did a very strange thing. It leaped onto his out-stretched hand and onto his shoulder, while crying *aah-aah-aah,* and began chuckling its secrets into his ear. He asked questions, calling it a wise bird, for wise it was with age from the color of its eyes, and then, he consoled it for its loss. The bird responded well to his voice, for it did another strange thing to demonstrate its ability to communicate its feelings to human beings. It began to mimic lines from that famous old ABBA song—*Money, money, money, it's a rich man's world*—which its ancestors perhaps learnt from listening to a truckies' roadhouse juke-box where they had spent decades pilfering scraps, and which the bird now sung repeatedly in so many *aahs.* He sang, and the genies sang, and the bird was almost beside itself.

The girl wanted to keep this lonely bird. Warren saw her moment of vulnerability and in that instant, she received his first lesson about what he meant by friendship. He sent the raven back off to where it belonged, into the northerly wind.

The day was spent examining owls' nests. Their vehicle had been left beside the road covered with Army-issued camouflage netting. Warren and the genies took great care to ensure that the vehicle would remain undetected, and had walked back along their wheel tracks off the main dirt road to buff up the grass.

They traveled on foot, walking into the vastness of low vegetation plains surrounded by smooth, tussocky hills. The work was hard. Dust rose with each step, filled the air with each breath of wind, and fell to settle in their hair, over their skin and in their clothes. They looked as though they had crawled in it, but they had blended into the country, and were indistinguishable from it.

The task of locating the nests of the grass owl was not easy. The nests were concealed at the end of tunnels constructed through the thick *kinkarra* spinifex grasslands. The genies walked in circles between each nest. Warren trailed behind. Oblivia always felt that he was watching her, just in case she tried to escape. She was seething with anger. She hated being watched, of knowing he was staring into her back, getting into her mind. She thought of ways of killing him once she had the chance. His phone rang. He was always busy on what the girl learnt was a mobile phone, capable of making calls from where they were, in one of the remotest places on the planet. Each time it rang and abruptly broke the silence of the bush, he would fall further back, while he talked into it. *Sure! Not now. Speak to you later.* Warren Finch, important or not, was determined to have this time on Country. He silently indicated *five days tops* with a show of his open palm to the genies when they looked back at him speaking on the mobile. They smiled. Agreed. He continued talking. Somebody else. *You will have to cope. You can cope for a few days can't you?* A lot of hard talking had to be done to keep the world busy while he was away. How to finally topple that old goat Ryder once and for all? Take the reins as the new President? March right up to what the country needed. It was time. He was saying how he wanted time to think, to prepare, to be ready for what was coming. How was he going being married and all? He repeats the question each time it's asked. Fine! Right!

Keep hitting if it makes you happy, he said, whenever Oblivia decided to run back to take another slog at his face.

The genies always tried to mask the conversations Warren was having by talking about owls to the disinterested or disconnected girl—they could not decide which—by naming and describing the two hundred odd species in the world. It became an endless conversation between the three men about the twenty or so types that included different barn owls, fishing owls, burrowing owls, wood owls, little owls like the one Picasso had as his sad pet. They discussed the Latin family names like *Tyto, Megascaps, Bubo, Otus,* but only *Ninox and Tyto* represented the nine different owls found in Australia. She learnt that barn owls could be used by farmers to control plagues of rodents as these owls were now doing out in the desert country. *I am in rodent country,* she thought while she turned and spat towards Warren. The three genies talked a great deal about why the owls had come from the east. What this meant. The ecology of the country had changed. Was this the Law doing something to the country? Then something changed. Words trampling her into the ground could also pick her up. She looked surprised to be told that each family of owls consumed several thousand mice and rats in a breeding season. *Yep!* Bones Doom commented, as though speaking for the girl's silences. She glared at him. She did not want to know these things. *These fellas will keep on breeding out here until they have consumed all the rodents, and then their own numbers will decrease, because most owls will not live more than a couple of years.*

Such a large bird, very unlike the sulphur-crested cockatoo which might live for eighty or ninety years, explained the gentle Bones.

There was no owl's nest passed before it received a thorough examination. The men never tired of their interest in how an owl had constructed its nest. With each clutch of eggs discovered, the find was welcomed by the genies as though a miracle had taken place, and chorusing, *Doom, how do you do it man, you are a fucking genius. How many is that now? 12,001? 12,002?*

The eggs were examined for number and weight, and each egg created serious discussion to judge its particular shape and age, held up like a diamond against the sun to examine the embryo forming inside, and then finally, enthusiastic thought was given to how each egg felt as though it was the first marvelous thing they had ever held in the hand. Oblivia thought all the nests were the same. Whenever she was the first to see a nest she did not volunteer the information. What did it matter? She could not be bothered that each nest consisted of six or eight eggs with a displeased sitting owl. Who cared? She wanted to go home. The urge to bolt through the spinifex overpowered her. Only the swamp loomed large in her mind. A vision now contaminated with the ghostly sight of Warren walking like a dead man. A vision that would not leave his mind either.

The information about the owls' nests, including the level of anxiety to the disturbed owl, was recorded on pocket-sized computers. Doom was constantly reminded how painfully slow and tedious he was in his search to locate each nest in a fixed area, before the group could move on. *It's for science. Nobody knows anything about why these birds come to this place, or why the rats are driven here.* The girl was desperate to go. Warren catches up with her each time she walks away. She knows that she slows them down even further. The work becomes slower. Always Doom gives the same answer, while sometimes glancing conspiratorially at Warren, the man on top of the nation who has up to this point, always been in a hurry. Warren nods. *Sure! Who hasn't got time for science?*

We were doing this all last night, Edgar Mail told the girl in a voice that was like an echo from distant spinifex groves, but there were other words burning inside of her: *Stupid girls get into trouble.* It was Aunty Bella Donna of the Champions' voice. *Stupid girls deserve to get what is coming to them.* The Harbor Master was dancing across the plain, stopping every now and again to stare quizzically at the owl hunters whom he repeatedly called, *stupid people.* He and the old woman were both shouting over the distance to reach one another, reminiscing about the bad luck of the girls with weather-beaten bones that lay scattered in places exactly like this. The Harbor Master called it *kinkarra nayi.* The desert. Spinifex. *Wiyarr! Wiyarr!* Everywhere. What next?

They said their bones were like white chalk. *Odd, how these bones were scattered around the ground throughout the spinifex.* The girl's stomach nods, rolls, and nods again. She saw prowling dingoes with white bones in their mouths wherever the sun's glare struck the horizon. The dead lady's voice reminded her that all men wanted was sex, *so how do you like that? It happened on the refugee boats. It can happen in the mulga too.* The girl remembered there was an owl, a *julujulu* that once lived in the darkened hole in the roots of the tree. She had felt its soft feathers with her fingers. Now she was reminded of its softness.

Edgar Mail continued talking, *You should remember that anyone can be a habitual colonist perpetually in search of difference to demystify myths, always trying to create new myths to claim as their own.* The girl could hear the old woman and the Harbor Master chuckling somewhere in the air above them, telling her to forget about what that man was saying. *What would he know about the Feast of the Epiphany, the twelfth day of Christmas back in 1697 when a white man first saw your mythical black swan swimming about over there in Western Australia, who had always thought black swans were evil and never really existed? Did he stand back and not touch, believing he would be doomed on a shipwreck for taking a black swan?*

You know, most of these eggs will hatch but when the food runs out in the summer, the rats will perish, and so too will most of the owls, Edgar Mail said lamely, while looking at Snip, who looked at Doom. The girl began to think about how she was going to disappear into ghost country, just like the girls who never returned. She looked out over the ocean of gray-green grasses and thought of how Aunty Bella Donna of the Champions had spent years looking across oceans to stop herself from dying at sea. The Harbor Master reminded the girl that it was very difficult, impossible really, to survive if you never existed.

The genies kept talking about Oblivia's name.

Immya Wake. You are kidding me. Nobody has a name like that.

No. No way man.

You tell them, Warren laughed, while looking at her. The girl felt as though she had been stripped in broad daylight. She looked away while trying to decide where to run, but there was no place to run. The plains country was already a coffin for brides.

That's not a good joke comrade, Snip snapped.

Yes! You are right, Warren replied. *Swan girl, I know your name is Ethyl. Will always be Ethyl. I don't know who gave you that other name. But from now on it's going to be Ethyl, short they tell me for Ethylene Oblivion. A beautiful name really, Ethyl.*

The genies wanted to know where that name originated.

The girl stalked off, spitting all over the ground as she went.

Warren Finch liked her spirit. *She was a good hater.* He smiled as though he was pleased with his new possession. The girl did not go far before she realized that she wanted to live, and this dead face Warren Finch was bloody well it, so when Snip commanded, *Stop. Stay dead still until I come to you,* she froze on the spot. All she hears is Warren's voice, talking again on the mobile phone.

Snip Hart charmed snakes. *Snakes are my thing,* he laughed as he appeared without a sound beside her: *Not yours I can see.* He urged her to pick up the snake coiled on the ground directly beneath them. She remained glued to the spot, full of hate for the man's continual speaking, leaning back and forth, taunting the snake to lunge.

Come on. I am right here, he urged. The girl felt the serpent eyes staring right into her mind. She felt the sensation of its glare and the immediacy of her fear traveling back through its nervous system, pushing its strength down though the muscles of its body, and from there her fear sat like a spring in readiness, as the snake prepared to strike. Snip waited. *Shh!* he whispered. Perspiration ran from her forehead onto the snake's shiny head and over the black beads of its eyes. The snake lunged. Her blood raced to the spot where it would bite before Snip Hart swung the snake up off the ground and into the air by the tail. It hung from the top of his upstretched arm, struggling for freedom.

He smiled: *See how simple it is?* He gave her a pat on the shoulder as he walked past to show the others. Snip was an expert on desert snakes. It was his country. The girl thought that the snake had not seen him because he was invisible to it. He was already inside the snake. It had only concentrated on striking her. *Snakes were also numerous,* Edgar Mail explained to Oblivia as they walked, *because all the unusual climatic changes which were creating plagues of insects and rodents, also increased the numbers of species that fed on them.*

You just have to be quick, Snip claimed, as if snake-catching was an ordinary skill that people needed to know to be able to walk in a country like Australia. Oblivia continued watching him as he walked ahead while trying to discover whether he really was invisible to snakes. In the sun, she was soon hypnotized by thoughts of hands that moved from running down the body of a snake and examining owl eggs, to hands she pushed away at night.

Snip Hart was fast. He plunged his arm straight down a hole in the ground, or a spinifex tunnel, and grabbed a snake. He announced the measurements and weight in breaking news, while noisily tapping the results into his computer with one hand, and with the other holding the snake. Afterwards, when he finished with each snake, and before releasing the writhing creature, he stared into its eyes to speak lovingly to it in simple words describing its numerous points of beauty, its measurements, and stroking it, he successfully seduced the creature into limp submission in his hand. In its hypnotic trance, he said, it only dreamed of loving this land. How many sexual encounters he wondered, had this snake experienced. *Ten?* Edgar Mail guessed, fingering the length of stubble on his face while studying the size of the creature. *Twenty, by its size,* reasoned Snip. Then he laid the creature on the ground, where it stayed motionless, and walked away.

There is a lot to learn about owls, Mail claimed dreamily in camp at night. He was singing his curiosity to the country and asking the ancestors for their reasoning, as he built his thesis on the plague of rats. *Not the type of thing you could learn in one day in a place where samples of the biosphere in a vast stretch of the country were being carried through some of these creatures we were examining. How do you explain their special stories of origins and creation, return and renewal, which are as new as they are old?*

No! Don't tell them anything. Wait until I get back. Warren on the other hand, had spent most of his day ignoring the world of rats, owls and snakes, and was still answering and making calls on his mobile phone's secure link. He spoke to people across the world in their own languages. He chatted to all of the policy makers he was interested in, and lastly, told his men that there were people trying to find their location, and continued to speak calmly, while fetching Oblivia back from another attempt to walk off in a half-awake dream, or having to duck from her sudden outbursts of arms swinging to either punch or scratch him, or avoiding another round of airplane spitting. *Ah! Janybijbi nyulu julaki jabula! Naah!*

Well! People will be looking for you, Edgar Mail said, already knowing. It was always understood that Warren Finch's life was lived in danger. He was simply a wanted man. Everyone wanted a part of him. To put it mildly he was a savior, and we know what happens to saviors. Threats were continuously being made on his life. This time, the threats were so serious, he was advised to think about his future security by old untrustworthy, O.K. Corral Horse Ryder, if he wanted to stay alive. Yet Warren and his men believed that this was simply how he had to live. In their world, it was hard to know what was sound advice, or what contained a threat, or what was just someone crapping on in their mind. It could not have been any different, and Warren relished each challenge, where he would constantly be dealing with trouble, and outsmarting anyone in the world who wanted to take a shot at him. It was these threats to his life that became the reason, the *modus operandi* for Warren's elusiveness, where nobody really knew or understood where he was. He led people into believing what he wanted them to believe. So routinely exercised was this art of illusion in fact, in a puff of the genies' smoky haze, Warren Finch could will himself to be anywhere in the world, instantly in flight to another country, instantly appearing in another part of the continent, or regularly popping up on the television all over the place, while all the time, it was assumed that he was still living normally, like other people. His artfulness in disappearing and reappearing was so strange, that as the swamp people had believed he was somewhere else, he could still make you feel that you had never seen him—that he was never there at all. This was why they were out on the genies' country. A bushland so vast in its sameness, that only the traditional owner could read the subtle stories of its contours. This was where they always took Warren to work out strategies to fend off the latest round of would-be assassins.

Let them wait. I am having a break. Want a bit of time to think things through.

Warren kept a lot of the information he had received to himself. Business. Policy. His security. The seriousness of new threats to his life. It concerned him after all. He would deal with the waiting game for others to strike first. Keep punching—just like he had told the girl.

Stay as long as you want, Edgar agreed. You are in charge. But you better keep it in mind that the longer you are away, the more difficult it is going to be to take control when you get back.

Nothing to worry about, Warren said. *There is nothing they can do without me. I am not even back in the country as far as anyone knows.*

I am just saying there are things happening in the country right now, Mail warned. *Might do better with your presence, that's all.*

I know that, Warren said in a tone of voice that made it clear that he did not want to be reminded of having other responsibilities: *What we are doing here. Finding out what is going on in the country. This is more important right now.*

The genies smiled and continued relaxing on the ground next to the fire well into the night, drinking tea, their eyes upwards, searching the star world. Nothing Warren said was of any consequence to them. His fingers rang up and down the girl's hand while she froze for what felt like a dead man touching her, and he thought of his own death march to the grave. The onset of owls screeching aroused quiet academic discussion which grew into an argument about a single pitch once heard, the purest of sounds, and whether this was an owl signaling its territory, or something else altogether—a voice from the spirit country.

Edgar Mail took the violin out of its case. He tuned it slowly as his fingers worked on the yellow wood instrument shining from the light of the fire. It softly responded to his touch while he listened, until suddenly, he began playing the melancholy tune of owls calling through the stillness of night. The music created ripples in the rhythm of the owl calls as he replied to their sound with his own composition. Near and far, the owls replied. The music was theirs. Edgar was almost in a trance as he walked around the camp with his violin and drifted away into the darkness of the surrounding spinifex with rats parting in haste to create a path, and his music calling and responding to the instructions of the owls.

He was playing like the old powerful chants of bringing up the country. Law music. The music was unearthly, but belonged to this land in the same way as the chanting of ancient songs and the sound of clap sticks beating through the night. The music now contained joyfulness, sometimes dropping suddenly into a barely audible lullaby, then out of this calm, it would suddenly grow again in pitch and rhythm until another and another crescendo was reached. Finally and abruptly, Edgar stopped playing, too exhausted to continue. He would have to remember the music. He said what they had listened to was the beginning of the first movement of music to grass owls in D flat major.

The nights in this windy landscape were spent with the law spirits who were traveling the country to scrutinize the marriage of plagues—keeping the balance where insects, rodents, snakes and owls were breeding. Warren Finch wanted the ancestral world to create the balance in his marriage. He whispered into her ear that this was the way he wanted the land to see them. Oblivia moved away as though he was already a ghost. She saw the infestations of the day were still exactly the same at night. She was back in the tree in her mind. Safe there. Worse than ever: scribbling that silent language in the air. In truth, Warren was becoming convinced that for whatever reason he had taken the girl in the first place, it was not going to work. Even the act of consummating it seemed a waste of time. When he looked at her all he saw was a child. You can't have sex—make love with a kid. She was scared stiff of the sight of him. Terrified when he touched her. His face, to her, was contorted with death. That was how she dreamed at night beside him. He saw clearly that it was beyond his power to change her, but by morning he would see the day afresh as a challenge to be met to make his marriage work, just like he tried to make everything else work, whatever the challenge, because to him, that was what life was all about.

He kept reminding her that they would become friends. *In the end you will trust me.* That he should succeed in gaining her trust was important to him. The first goal he wanted to achieve. She was his last real link to a world he had severed, the attachment he had planned to keep. Sometimes she thought he was right. She would trust him.

During the day whatever else he thought, he kept his distance, walking behind, always speaking to someone on the mobile phone. He knew that she had overheard some of these conversations. He said that these were just people he loved. People that he trusted. He depended on them for their safety. *Yours too now,* he added.

Warren Finch did not sleep at night. In fact, the death dream returned the moment he dozed off on this country. He lay awake with their future—his future—weighing heavily on his mind. He had decisions to make, and he wondered whether it was worth taking the risk of continuing his political life. His death seemed to be the only future from it, and he kept revisiting the scene of being led to his grave.

Could he bring her into that world? He tossed the question over and over, although he knew that it was not a safe decision to take her any further. She would need a lot of looking after that was for sure. He tried to push aside any imagining of what his life would be like with her. Couldn't form a vision of it. Somehow, thinking about the future did not seem to make any sense as the night wore on. He was more familiar with having a rough ride in politics and doing it alone. Never thought about his own personal future before. Just the country's future. It was his specialty. The only dream he felt that he could make real. This was the best way he knew of dealing with his enemies. As though making enemies was his life. He looked at Oblivia pretending to be asleep. Wondered how much longer he could stay, but confirmed in his own mind, that until he knew where the new threats were coming from, he would keep stalling his return. There were government security people on to it. They kept updating him. Getting closer, he had been told. He only trusted his own bodyguards: Hart, Doom and Mail. They had been close for years. If they thought his life was in so much danger, so be it. They had agreed: *We will take as long as it takes to deal with it.*

Tomorrow they would be out of this death country, and it couldn't be quick enough. But what to do about her? It almost did not matter to him which way the wind blew. He was always ready to fall. Yet he knew she would not be able to take the blows, although she had given him a few, and continued to lie awake until dawn, knowing he would have to do something about it. She would struggle. For the first time in his life he had to admit that he really felt jinxed.

• • • •

The vehicle was left far behind covered with spinifex, where it melted into the landscape on the edge of the salt lake country through which they were traveling. The whole country could burn behind them if disaster struck, but the genies were not interested. They were born and raised on the land and they knew how to walk in it.

Don't look back, Edgar Mail said, surprising the girl as he whispered into her ear. *We wouldn't want to see you being turned into a pillar of salt.*

In the days that followed, they continued traveling further across the white sea. The defining landmarks of this salt lake country were small crags that jutted out here and there in the salt. These were the possession of spirit guardians traveling on a journey far away to important story places. The salt crust broke underneath them with each footstep. There was even more solitude in this place than in the spinifex country they had just left behind. They felt the presence of the enormous white glistening body that contained the quietness of a resting serpent spirit fellow who was listening deeply to hear even an insect perching on its skin, come there to recite its song. The landing of butterflies. The feet of a lizard pounding on crystals of salt.

There were battalions of stink beetles crawling over each other and the salt. Plague grasshoppers jumped away at the coming of strangers. Moth storms swept across the lake. Crimson and orange chats whistled from the heath of spinifex, pittosporums, mulga and eremophila scrubs growing along the sides of the lake. The girl saw green twisting clouds of budgerigars crossing their paths at various times throughout the day. Up high, harriers and kites cried out as they glided in the thermals. To look back was to see fine salt crystals dusting over their tracks as little storms of salty filaments gurgled about in the desert air.

That was during the day. The salt glowed at night, and the body of the lake moved differently when the ancestral winds lowered themselves from the skies and whistled eerily across its surface. The night spoke in dreams which took the wandering thinker far below the surface, to be jostled in a spirit sea populated with the salt-encrusted bodies of millions of grasshoppers, shoals of tiny fish bones, brine shrimps, larval fish like splinters of glass, colorless moths, seeds and stalks; grotesque bloated grunters, bony herrings, frogs, tadpoles and water birds that had perished in the increasingly saline waters, and been entombed when the water evaporated.

The girl dreamt of swans, chaotically misshapen creatures frozen in death that were forcing their spirits through films of salt to reach her during the night. Had they come searching for truth, but found encasement? She awoke from dreams where her fingers were red raw from trying to peel away the salt to straighten the pinion feathers of the swans and let them fly.

They passed through old times, coming through hillock after hillock covered in spinifex, of Country that had a serious Law story for every place, and of everything belonging to that place like family. The genies kept calling the names of these places which were thousands of years old, and which joined the Law stories of naming, titles of belonging, maps of exclusiveness that ran like this, throughout the continent. Oblivia kept quiet. Listened to the names. Tried not to think in case the spirits heard her and dragged her into their realm. She would not die on this country.

While the genies were drifting even further back into ancient times with their name calling, Warren Finch was making the equivalent leap into the future, and impatient to get a move on and back to his job of bloody well running the country, he told the genies to speed it up. They were getting out of here. Before the bloody country got fucked up good and proper by Horse. *That cunt of a man. Can't turn your back on him for a second.* The genies looked concerned, but not overly bothered, having seen it all before, on other occasions when they had to get him out of a jam. Tops! They might make him last another few days out in the bush. Yep! The boss! Too right! Power crawled like a pack of cut snakes through his body. He was an addict to it. Addiction? They knew he wouldn't last long. Couldn't. They had seen the man explode if he was not in control. They knew that what was left for him was time. But, like the man said, he had work to do, and everyone knew how nervous Warren could be if he didn't get a fix from being in charge, and feel the power surging through his blood. He would chase it down anywhere. Do anything to assert power. *Why couldn't he just chase that girl around a bit more? Crazy thing had his measure already.* Warren always thought it was a waste of time to hold up the entire country just for the sake of a few people getting in his way. Well! Bring it on. He knew it. They knew it. Impatience was a fact of life. Yep! Everything will be fine. *I will be fine. The girl will be fine.* He convinced himself of it. *She would grow up. Why wouldn't she? What else could she do?* He was bored of marriage already.

Doom, Mail and Hart understood the deal: they could only hold him up for as long as they could possibly get away with it. Already he had imbued every molecule of air with the stench of Horse Ryder. Rah! Rah! Rah! Can't keep still for a minute. *Can't stop talking about Horse Ryder.* But, even they thought he would maintain some interest in the girl he had taken. His keepsake. This little challenge he had set himself—a promise wife. They knew the threats on his life were real this time. *Why can't he take it seriously instead of worrying about what Horse is doing?* The girl saw an endless journey ahead in an unchanging landscape that they would continue walking forever. Just like ghosts! Perhaps they had already crossed over into that world. Would she escape? Do ghosts escape?

A day passed of counting the fluffy fledglings transforming into orange wash and white feathers that were hidden in the grasslands by the shores of salt pans while waiting to fly. The country was consuming the girl's memory. She could not carry the past and had to let some of it go. A few of her old messages to her swans had returned from places that no longer existed—address unknown. The Harbor Master had come along and saw the burden she was carrying, and for a while, he walked beside her while trying to persuade her to give up some of her treasured nightmares. He sat around in the salt sorting out which thoughts should stay, which should go, telling her off for sending away anything he thought was really valuable. He was the kingmaker of policy too. *You always need a few of those bad thoughts to chuck around.* He kept telling her how he could not stand the sight of Warren Finch. *Look at him. Stalking along. Planning and scheming some other stupid thing—probably how he is going to kill you off since he is sorry he bothered with someone like you in the first place?* And the genies? *Mate! I know a ghost from the Middle East when I see one.*

Maybe you are from the Middle East yourself, the girl growled and walked away from the Harbor Master who was piling up her thoughts into salt columns of what was to be kept, and what cut loose.

This is not all we do, Doom said, feeling that he ought to prepare the girl for their departure—once the owls left the desert after the rats perished in these hottest months.

There was a shop he owned, he said, in the city where she would live. She did not understand what he meant. *Cities are where people die.* That was what old Aunty always said about cities. *Illness places. You will be arrested for being a terrorist.* She wondered about what he said, and thought: *But I like it here now.* He looked at her sadly. *You could ask Warren about the city.* Could she ask him what would happen to her? Why would she do that? Speak! *To terrorists from the city?* The salt lands now became unreliable, temporary in her mind. *I specialize in many things. Birds. People. Books. I am not always there. Travel with the boss a lot. Love to spend time at the shop though,* Doom said.

He explained that he, Edgar and Snip were all involved in specialist trade and had the most beautiful shop in the city. It was the place where you could feel the country: *This place. I made a place in the city to hold my heart. Like this place.* He said that they sold birds, old butterflies from all over the world, exhibited rare eggs and feathers, bird books, snake books, musical instruments, traditional maps of routes and footpaths, maps for following foxes and bees, old instruments for finding dreams, stars, or fossils. This was the place to seek professional advice on cultural law, societies, myths and almost anything anyone needed to know of the human condition from Edgar, Snip or him—*the filler of ears, the purveyors of information.*

She was to learn that Snip loved nothing more than selling his customers gadgets to find stars, and that Edgar Mail specialized in selling old sheet music he had collected from elderly men and women in the inner laneways of ancient cities. He also recorded and spent tireless hours publishing the music from these works. His own music was printed on the old printing press in this shop. They believed in their enterprise. *Our customers are people seeking knowledge about the world. Mostly from the Middle East, Europe and Asia. Australians? Not too many. We are specialists you know. You will probably want to visit us from time to time.*

Oblivia tried to anchor these new pictures of the genies in her mind, but she had no idea of how to hold the details of what she had never seen. Their words died as soon as they were spoken and buried in her mind. She squinted in the sun, had to blink to see what lay ahead in the endless story of yellow lofty crags in salt lakes, owls, rats, snakes, when she saw a speck in the horizon of blue skies. Yellow! White! Blue! Black!

A LAKE OF WHITE WATER

A lake of white water, not a mirage, lay far ahead. This was where she saw the swans. Black wings swirled down from the clear blue skies to skid across the water. The girl thought it was her dreams catching up with her, coming back in the daytime. She needed to run to see if these were her swans but knew not to, to watch from a distance the swans gliding on the white water, *while I glide swanlike . . . I glide and glide*. From the sides of her eyes she saw the hurdles. Warren Finch would see she had not forgotten the swamp. She never knew how the genies would react.

Questions surfacing in her mind about leaving ran from the girl, and disappeared into the vista of the white sea. She felt homesick, a terrible yearning to go home. She ran towards the swamp that wasn't there. The swans saw her coming over the salt, and before she had a chance to come anywhere in reach, they snapped loose her spirit from theirs, and took to the air. She watched until they were out of sight, flying further ahead, in a southeasterly direction.

Warren watched her run. *Sure! Sure! I'll be there.* He spoke loudly into his mobile phone. *I am ready. Let's do it.* His words caught her, ran along the surface of her arms as she ran, and as though a net he threw had unfurled over her, she realized in this moment, that she was attached to him. She would never escape, even if she ran forever from a world that had fallen apart.

Doom tried to console the girl about the swans flying away. *They were not your swans. They are free birds.* They belong somewhere else. She felt residues of bad luck lurking inside of his voice. It was his bad luck that the swans had sensed, why they had flown. Around their feet, a little breeze picked up grains of salt with dead grass and carried these along, signaling the owls to start their retreat, back towards the east coast for the summer. *Most would not reach their destination,* Doom said sadly. *So much work done for nothing. Why breed?* He knew that they would all be gone that night.

Hare stew.

Meal fit for kings. And a queen. Eat before the lizards steal it.

The Milky Way lit the landscape, and Snip took the girl away from the campfire to give her a lesson about the night sky. *I think you will like it. There is something pretty special up there tonight.* She had learned a lot about the alignment of the planets from him. The genies often pointed to the path in the west where Venus would fall earlier each night, until in the winter nights it was Mars that was the first to fall. *Remember! Winter rains will fall on this land, and in the middle of the night, a cloud of mist will descend to touch the earth.*

Remember to come back here, Snip said, as they stood on a hill, staring at the sky.

The thought of returning seemed unlikely. She could not imagine how it would be possible.

These are the methods of positioning yourself for finding South, he said, explaining that they were in the galaxy of the Milky Way that rose like smoke from the horizon until its river of stars ran directly above them. Their light rebounded off the salt and it was this phenomenon that seemed to make the stars shine more brightly. He showed her how to position where she was by drawing a line through the Southern Cross and joining it to a line drawn to the halfway point from the Pointers. *This will form a V for you, and from there, if you draw a line down to the horizon, you will know where to find South.* Or another way, he explained, was by forming the same triangle by drawing an imaginary line down from the brightest star in the sky, *Canopus*, and across from the star *Achernar* which sits low in the southern sky.

However, this is not what I really want to show you, he said, taking her hand, and pointing her fingers along with his into the northern world of the sky, he drew along the stars the outline of a swan in full flight.

Do you see it?

She nodded, seeing the swan's long head arching down towards earth.

That is the constellation of Cygnus, the Swan. The star of its tail is a supergiant named Deneb. Look for it up along the Milky Way. If you can find it in the sky, you will be able to follow it north, until the weather becomes warm again.

She continued looking at the swan's changing position, wondering how she would remember to find it again.

Don't always look in the same place. He will move across the sky. Remember you will only see Cygnus at the onset of winter. Just like your swans I imagine.

In the darkness with a dying fire, they waited for the final moment when the earth opened the spinifex grassland abodes and the hands of the spiritual ancestors released the owls like pollen into the skies. The swooping waves of owls flew over their heads, the young traveling eastward with their parents in a colony of thousands.

Men may do the same one day if they fear too much. Imagine it. Imagine a dust cloud traveling right through this country, Snip's voice was almost a whisper, and in that moment, the clouds heralding the cool change appeared from the east, traveling in a westerly direction.

While the girl and Warren slept, the genies were searching for a few stray owlets in the spinifex. Doom said there had to be one or two that had not fledged. He promised one for Oblivia to keep as a pet. *In the morning I will have one for you,* he said. She thought of this owl while sleeping in a low-lying valley filled with white flowering lilies that shone in the starlight breaking through the clouds.

But the valley became a box when clouds settled on the hills, and very quickly it was filled with an overpowering perfume pouring into the air from thousands of flowers. Sometime during the night her lungs ached for fresh air, and this was when she heard Warren moving away. Very silently, he was slipping away into the night, but she thought it was already morning and they would be going back to join the others.

Shh! he said, and left. Her tongue failed to form words to ask him where he was going, and she watched him walking further away into the night. He did not return, and she was unable to prevent herself from falling back to sleep as the heavy putrefied air swallowed her into a nightmarish dream. Those boys from long ago emerged from the ground. It had happened suddenly with the ground swelling and growing around her until she was covered in total darkness, but she knew them instantly, knew what they were doing—she had not killed them in her memory. She remembered their closeness to each other, in touch, smell, and breathing. Of being joined together with them as firmly as a ball of animals rolling over wet ground. She saw through them as they were falling in, over, above, coming through her in sepia-colored waves of brown, gray and red. They rolled in desert wind over the surface of the land, and down the green and yellowing spinifex smothering the hillocks that rose and fell into valleys of lily-colored skin, and over the distances of salt marshes.

The landscape had closed over with mist, and the perfume of the lilies under the mist was suffocating even the flowers. Her arms and hands pushed at the fumes but she was unable to reach fresh air higher up, and succumbing to the intoxication, she crawled away towards her memory of the tree. She reaches the tree in this state, and falls back into the safe darkness to hide. From the shadows of her dream she sees the swans lifting off again from white water, pushed upwards by vaporized hands reaching out of the lake. They have been rejected, pushed away by the country from her outstretched arms.

She was coiled inside the tree in a dream, and when she woke, she could see the valley surrounded by hillocks decked by clouds.

Better get ready. We will be leaving soon. Warren spoke slowly but firmly, as if to a child, and the way he watched her, she thought he had been in her dream. She felt violated by the way he continued to stare at her with his eyes moving over her. Perhaps he had watched. It seemed that he knew what had happened. Perhaps it had not been a dream. *You better eat something first,* he said, handing her a piece of damper.

She ate the brown bread that was made from seeds and bulbs. It had a sour bitter taste under the salt that had been added to the dough before it went into the ashes. *Take your time,* he said, after noticing how she was struggling to swallow each piece. She washed the lumps down quickly with cold tea. She watched him doing the same. They left empty-handed. Whatever had been brought in with them, the pannikins, swags, simple things like the tin billy, were left behind.

Soft light filled the lily plains with William Blake hues in the first light, which was like looking at the living museum of another time surviving in the arid landscape. Warren told her that some people saw these flowers as a fragment of life from another era, when there might have been a different language that once described the wetlands and rain-forest in the heart of the country, before it disappeared. *This living fossil was all that was left of those times,* he explained. She knew it was a ghost place. Closer to the eye, groups of pale green, firm fluid-filled stemmed flowering plants luxuriating in their freshness opened their petals. Each stem had stormed through to the surface from a large swollen bulb that grew at least a meter deep in the red soil. This garden of lilies rose to the surface he explained, only if water lay long enough to soak through this dip in the landscape after heavy rain. The flowers open. She thinks the petals are like the wings of old Aunty's white swans. He asks her if she is all right. She nods. She can look after herself.

Warren Finch and the girl walked through hills, the ones that were called the great bodies of the spirit men moving through the land. *What about the others?* she tried but failed to ask Warren as she kept looking back to where the genies had been camping.

They have other things to do. We will see them later, he replied simply and to the point, no differently than how he normally spoke to her.

He looked as though he had aged, grown old on this trip. She kept thinking something was not right, that something had happened to them, and she kept looking back with growing concern as the distance grew greater. But only the old voices of Aunty talking to the Harbor Master could be heard coming from behind her, through the sound of the ground breathing, casually talking behind Warren Finch's back. The Harbor Master said he was pretty sure the genies never existed. He had never recognized them as real people. They had come out of a brass lantern from the Middle East as far as he was concerned. The old woman crowed on about the men on the boats she had seen murdering each other out of rivalry and jealousy over women. *Oh! Yes! I saw it all. All the time you know. Did you cause this?* The old woman was talking loudly, starting to accuse Warren of every travesty, until she got around to what she really wanted to say, *you killed those nice boys,* and the girl looked away from Warren who was telling her to keep moving, because she was thinking that he had murdered the genies too. The Harbor Master became silent because the old dead woman's ghost was putting things in the girl's mind about Warren Finch. *Girls were always thrown overboard—I told you about that. Girls were left to die in the bush. You know the public pay phone really only rang sometimes . . . Unwept girls, all killed by their husbands.*

The Harbor Master turned controversial, snubbing Bella Donna's ghost, which was raving on like a madwoman about how the Aboriginal killer husband Warren Finch would end up killing Oblivia too, *because he was already proving his true colors by killing the genies.* The Harbor Master swung away from the old woman's spirit every time she came close to him, calling her, *Liar. What you think all Aboriginal men are violent or something?* He poked his bony face in Oblivia's while walking backward in front of her as she walked ahead of Warren Finch. In the end, the Harbor Master spurted out everything in his head through hissy spit: *You know something? Warren Finch only saw Doom, Mail and Hart, dead on the ground. He didn't kill them.* He makes a fist with his hand and with the index finger pointing from it like a pistol, he waves his arm around in the air, while calling over his shoulder to the old woman raving behind him to shut the fuck up about Warren Finch and warning her to stay away from them, and walking backward quicker to stay in front of Oblivia's face he releases more spit-hissed words, and on he goes: *They were killed instantly—BANG! BANG! BANG! No muck-ing around. Just smack, smack, one shot each was enough. Knocked their lights straight out* (clicks fingers)—*knocks them flat in their sleep.* Oblivia was really frightened now. She stared ahead and walked even faster as though she thought the only way to stop hearing the Harbor Master was to walk through his frightening face, and all the while she was look-ing around for old Aunty and old Aunty was calling from somewhere behind, *Wait for me*, and all the while trying to convince herself to ignore the healing man's powers, for that's right, no man would take over her mind. But the old Harbor Master was relentless and was using his bony fingers to jab her in the chest, and on and on he went in his tirade about the deaths he witnessed—while telling the old woman to *git out of their country*, that nobody else saw what happened, not even that idiot-features Warren bloody Finch. *You want to know who did it? Not that gutless wonder Warren—he didn't do it—look at him? There's no way in the world that a slack-assed cunt like him could kill face-to-face. He gets other people to do his dirty work. You want to know what I saw? A mob of assassins who killed them! All of them came running, hooded, and disguised in Army fatigues through the scrub but I saw them.*

Oblivia looks side-on across the haze-covered spinifex as though she fully expected to see soldiers from the swamp following them, but all she sees through the *wiyarr* is Bella Donna's ghost straining to drag things out of the ground and calling for them to wait for her, and Oblivia thinks she must be digging up the genies, or she found some dead girls, and this makes her heart pound even harder and she walks faster and hears the old woman's voice reciting—*So mastered by the brute blood of the air. . . . Before the indifferent beak could let her drop?*—and she tries to walk through the Harbor Master who looks where she looks, and he walks backward quicker, but ignores what the old woman was doing and he continues talking right into Oblivia's face as though he is taunting her to use that half-dead tongue of hers to shout at him to get out of her way. *There must have been dozens of those blokes running amuck with their revolvers with silencers and whatnot, and sneaking through the spinifex with infra-red searchlights strapped onto their heads. Like combat soldiers. Yes, just like soldiers in some war zone, although who knows if they were soldiers or not—I just don't know for sure what they were, or if they were from the whiteman's hell. Could've been from the swamp. They could have been anyone, just like you or me, or more like me than you because you would be too gutless to kill anyone, just like you are too gutless to speak. Allright then! They didn't know "someone" was looking at them through the darkness with my own infra-red night-vision binoculars eyes.*

Oblivia thinks he is tricking her and tries not to look at his eyes and continues to look around for Army men, although she cannot hear the old woman anymore who she figures must be still trying to dig up bodies, but the Harbor Master goes on about how good his infrared-vision eyes were. *I saw the whole thing coming, just like silly Warren knew it was coming, only difference is a person like me can dream wherever I want to go, whereas Warren Finch, he's a dog! Well! Look at him. He has to call someone on that mobile of his to tell him what's going on and he hides somewhere else.* The Harbor Master paused to pay his respects to the genies, *I really and truly hope you good boys haunt the living daylights out of some of those buggers. Come back and haunt Warren Finch too if you like. Yea! That would be good.* And he continues berating Oblivia, *That's the reason why your-suppose-to-be-husband Warren bloody Finch was acting strange last night. I saw him sneaking around in the night too. He knew there were people wanting to assassinate him. He heard their vehicles. You better lay low, I am telling you girl, if you are going to keep hanging around with that idiot. He will get you killed before too long. You can bet on that. That's why you will never see those good fellas again. Really decent blokes too they were.* Oblivia was listening now and walking normally, so the Harbor Master slowed down, but continued talking, and whenever he spoke about Warren, pouted his lips in his direction. *The coward Warren disposes of the bodies quick smart. Buried his staff members in the bush. Hardly dug a hole deep enough for any of them. You would think he'd do something better for his mates. Shallow graves. Real shallow. Better get a rifle too if I were you. You are just another staff member. Remember that.* The Harbor Master blamed Bella Donna's ghost for killing the genies.

He really had it in for her. *You know how she needs to kill off any strong black people. It gives her strength,* he claimed. Yulurri! *Murderer!* Yulurri! *She led the assassins right up to them like a bloody big road train heading through the bush with an arrowhead marking the spot just in the front of where those three boys were sleeping. Didn't know what struck them, it was strange seeing it happen—real quick like that. You don't want to think about her any more if she is going to cause trouble like this. Get rid of her from your mind. You don't need her now.* The Harbor Master looks back, and although the old woman's ghost was nowhere in sight, he tells her to git away from them. *Get away from Australia. Yulurri! We don't want you overseas ghosts here.*

At the end of the day of walking and the Harbor Master's tirade to Oblivia, they reached a sandy river overgrown with the vines of paddy melons laden with fresh yellow balls of fruit. A flock of white corellas stared with black beady eyes as Warren Finch and the girl passed by, then continued gnawing with sharp pointy beaks on the paddy melons held in their claws. Families of bush ducks flew from out of the reeds on the side of a dry riverbed, where there were still ponds of water from the flood after the rains of months ago.

Across the river the next morning, Oblivia was alarmed to see that there was a small rural township of less then a dozen unkempt houses painted in every combination of bright primary colors, flash blue, red, green, and yellow. All was quiet, and it seemed as though these houses had been willed to appear like a playful whim in among the spinifex, and if you turned your back, would disappear. Oblivia saw that they were close to the roughly cut airstrip that ran through the thickets of saltbush where, the evening before, Warren had taken an interest in walking along its length and kicking the dirt runway with his feet. She noticed that he did not use his mobile phone now, and this made her feel even more vulnerable, unsure of what was going to happen to her, and of the possibility they would be seen by strangers in this town without his genies to guard them.

She could not help staring at the houses.

Just people, Warren snapped, as though he knew she was wondering about who lived there.

What kind of people? People. People, who are more interested in talking to their white daddy and granddaddy graves about selling cattle, horses, or people for that matter; they work at the petrol and diesel service station over there. Mostly used by cattle trucks. He spoke impatiently as though speaking to a child. She knew that he did not want to speak to her. Did not want to answer questions. The town was silent. It looked deserted.

In the distant mirage beyond the houses, Oblivia saw the green and white service station. The sight of the green roof became a thought to reach, not of running away, but taking back her life. He knew her thought as she looked off in the distance, and said: *It won't pay to go over there. You will find that this is a pretty rough joint. We will wait here. The plane won't be long.* His mobile phone rang once, twice, and three times before he answered it. *Yep! Right!* He seemed relieved to be leaving. She could hear him talking about the plane's arrival time and then the droning off in the distance. She listened to the sky too—for the heartbeat of swans flying, and for a few moments of panic, caused by the thought of being forcibly pushed onto the plane by Warren, she was again standing on the shores of the empty salt lake. Only the warmth of the swans remained where they had rested on the ground covered with low-growing tussock grass and saltbush.

Within moments of the blue airplane landing they were gone. Only the deafening howl of the engine could be heard as it flew above the saltbush landscape, over the salt lakes, and into another world. There was nothing but clouds, and the frightened girl thought how the clouds would look around the mountaintop of the old woman's homeland, and thought she should have asked the old woman a question about clouds, because she did not know: *Who spoke of great seas of clouds where wind was eddying under the crevices?*

THE CHRISTMAS HOUSE

After clouds, always mist, and another ghost story to tell.

Ah! Beautiful, isn't it. This is where we will be living from now on. Well! For you this will be your home for a little while at least. Look! Right down there, can you see it? Just there! That place! It will be your home from now on. Warren Finch sighed, his face marvelously at ease as he looked longingly through the small window of the plane. Below, the city she saw was a sea of stars twinkling from the base of mountains, and sprawling across flatlands to the ocean. The plane flew through dozens of searchlights splashing back and forth through the skies, and on to Warren's relaxed face while he was humming that old song "Sea of Heartbreak"—*sea of dungkumini, malu of heartbreak the lights in the harbor, don't shine for me,* and the relief was in his voice: *Yes! It is good to be home.*

There was no way Oblivia ever expected that she of all people would see the riches of paradise from a plane. *How come?* She thought about the Heaven people taken from the cities by the Army and dumped in the swamp. They prayed all the time for the chance to see their paradise again, *How did I lose you, where did I fail?* The lights he called home spun meaninglessly in her head. She searched for the distant light of the burial chamber he had pointed out, to show her where she would be living and from the sea of lights below, all she extracted was a single glow. She looked away to censure the old woman creeping from the clouds and into her head, forbidding her from asking the question about women and girls who have disappeared: *Can you see any left dead on the side of a road in that light?*

Ah! Don't worry, you are dead already, the Harbor Master answered on the girl's behalf. He was also somewhere on board the plane—said he was the bloody pilot. *That's right,* he laughed, *better remember to put the wheels down. Who was to know if she was dead or alive?* The plane bounced on the winds of *one pilot short,* in its descent to land.

Warren kept talking: *You are going to love it here. You'll see. It will take a little bit of time but it will be better for us if you give it a chance.* He spoke philosophically, *so it is equally important that you make an effort to do this for me and for yourself. You will find that life will be better if you see things like this.*

They stepped from the aircraft and into a world shrouded in fog and darkness. Warren Finch was immediately surrounded by a group of security people, and within moments, they were leaving in a shining black, chauffeur-driven limousine with a small Australian flag fluttering in the breeze. Several security cars, that had been discreetly parked, would also accompany them for the rest of their journey.

The limousine careered through a foggy maze of concrete industrial buildings, high-rise offices, factories and houses. In this closer glimpse of paradise, the girl could see that much of the city had cracked; the city was breaking up, as though the land beneath had collapsed under its weight. This had happened a long time ago and now, the natural landscape was quietly returning and reclaiming its original habitat. In its strange kind of way, the city was creating a garden. Through the cracks in the footpaths small trees had sprouted, and ferns and grasses became obstacles through which people were struggling to steer a clear path as they walked. She saw more mature trees with the orange fungi *Pycnoporus coccineus* growing from branches and tree trunks, while ferns and grasses that swayed from mossy walls and rooftops caught her attention with each gust of wind. There were places on the roads not hit by heavy traffic where long grasses grew.

She saw no camp dogs hanging about these streets. No birds. There were only crowds of people moving quickly past one another with blank faces, and many others living in footpath ghettos, like people were in the swamp. They were begging for food. She heard frogs croaking in the drains where the rainwater poured in such profusion it was hard not to imagine an underground river flowing beneath the city.

Warren continued a running commentary like a tour guide. He spoke about why people were running, what they were doing, whether they went into restaurants, grocers, supermarkets, fish shops, meat shops, women's clothing shops of every description, shoes, pets, computers, furnishing, delicatessens, banks, office buildings that stood side by side reaching for the skies, down and up through narrow streets and onward, while countless lights shone from the homes of families, single people, couples, and apartments where parties were held, and couples made homes, made love, grew children, cooked food or brought home takeaway, and new furniture, and spent all night discussing life or conspiring, or deceiving, or divorcing, or engaging in adultery, throwing out rubbish, playing computer games about war. He talked more or less about all of this while the girl was thinking about something else. She was trying to determine the natural sound of the wind through the distortion of sounds passing through the laneways between buildings.

The Christmas house of prehistoric green was lit up like the solar system. It stood in a garden of worse-for-wear Norwegian fairy tale forest firs covered in glowing balls of colored lights that swung madly on the wind-tossed branches. Owls were calling out to one another from the deep foliage like calls from the genies they had left on the salt lake. The girl looked at Warren but he was too occupied with the spectacle of Christmas lights, and what lay ahead. The journey they had taken was now clearly wiped clean from his mind. The first thing she noticed as they stepped from the car was the fragrance of the trees clutching the mist, and the house groaning in despair each time it was buffeted by winds coming in from the sea.

The Harbor Master and the old woman exiled among the clouds

were both awestruck with the glamour of it all. Could this be the home that Warren had been pointing to from the plane? *It's bloody marvelous* the Harbor Master claimed, but the old woman scoffed at its cheap imitations, and described how pretensions made her feel nauseous by pretending to vomit on the bonnet of the shiny car.

The driveway was lined on either side by a parade of adult-sized glowing snowmen. The people greeting them enthusiastically at the large door shone in the way that people usually greeted Warren Finch. He said they were his anonymous friends. This was a safe house, which immediately had the Harbor Master asking what he needed a safe house for. But before the girl could think of an answer, she became too wrapped up in being ashamed, and looked away. All she had seen looming at the doorway were giant-sized people with red hair blowing like fire in each gust of wind. They were not introduced. The man, the woman, and two children, one boy and one girl, became an avalanche of fiery white ghosts flying out of the house, and descended on Warren with nonstop pattering.

Don't tell me this is your E-thyl? Is this really her? The big woman squealed.

This was a safe house because it was typical, Warren had fore-warned Oblivia. *Typical of what? Australia! Paradise?* Even she could believe it was a place that nobody of right mind would want to come to and she had been nowhere. Old Aunty squealed like the big woman. The Harbor Master pushed his way in front of them and yelled to the girl to keep away from the bunch of rednecks. This had the old woman and the Harbor Master arguing about how you could identify a redneck. She insisted that they were only missionaries. *I know what a missionary looks like*, he claimed combatively. *How would you know anything? You think every white person is a missionary.* The girl wanted to disappear from hearing her name falling off everyone's lips. *Yes! It was true then?* They had been talking about her for days, practicing that name, because they did not want to offend Warren's lady. *Why, she will be the first Indigenous lady of the country soon.*

E-thyl was a very pretty name the lady claimed, and said she in-sisted on knowing how she had been given such a name. *You sure you got it right? You sure it is not Ethel? That's a girl's name. I don't know where you get a name like E-thyl. Was it Aboriginal?*

The girl was covered in goose bumps every time she heard the name. She hated the name. Wondered where it had come from too and would have preferred to be called nothing, like normal. The girl wore filthy clothes—the ones that she had on when they left the swamp. Warren laughed at everything the red-haired people said. He had not stopped laughing since he had arrived. Should she laugh too?

She felt thinner and darker than normal people while standing next to this strange family that she thought were the typical Australian family, because Warren said so. And beside their snowy whiteness, she felt an out-of-place darkness, much darker than Warren even whose golden skin glowed in the soft yellow lights of the house. The more she saw, the more in awe she was of how white Australians lived. Unconsciously, she edged herself up against the wall to keep out of the way of the endless movement of these big people scrambling and gushing with every footstep in welcoming Warren back into their home.

Hold on now! I have only been gone a few weeks, he joked and laughed loudly, and even the girl was surprised to see him competing to be more extraordinary in a plain, simple laugh. The din of laughter echoing throughout the house was deafening for someone who never laughed. She thought *Why laugh?* How do you laugh? To say continuously, *Ha! Ha!*

Oh! Boy! Our Warren, the woman and her husband beamed in satisfaction, and together they raced through the dark echoing wood-paneled house to see the Christmas decorations in the backyard, while calling back for the girl to follow.

Come on. You got to have a look, Eee-ah? Come on. It's better than last year even. Now Warren was speaking like these people, even forgetting how to pronounce her name. *What's wrong with you? Get going. You think that they are contagious or something? Might turn you white?* A voice that sounded like the Harbor Master echoed in her head.

The large garden was a forest of full-grown pine trees decorated with colored lights. It stretched all the way to the edge of a rocky cliff where waves crashed, but the red-haired lady said it was a good thing they had planted the trees to muffle the sound of the ocean, *because you get sick of it roaring day and night. It was enough to give you a headache.* Underneath the dripping canopies of the trees a single seagull was lost somewhere in the needles, singing its airs to the seagulls gliding far away, over the sea.

The family ran breathless along curving paths, brushed against the wet foliage of the trees, and deep in the forest were greeted with Christmas carols sung by a glowing meter-high smiling robot snowman with a red carrot nose, and black top hat. *It's an extravaganza—a miracle,* Warren exclaimed, saying that he had never seen anything like it in his life. *It was first prize mind you, in the whole of the city,* the children and their mother said proudly.

Warren looked on warmly, his face flushed and glowing as the soft lights touched his skin. He said it reminded him of how great Christmas was in this house. And there, in a corner of the yard, sat many more secondhand Christmas trees of all shapes, sizes and conditions in pots. The girl learnt that these were orphan trees. They had been dumped by people in the city, and were waiting to be planted one day—once space could be imagined for them. *Yea! We drove around and collected them all—couldn't bear to see them die senselessly,* the wife claimed. *It does not pay to take your eyes off them though,* the husband added with a wink, *otherwise their numbers would increase.* Then they ran from the mist in a jostling stampede back to the house just in time to experience a crinkling smell of smoke, as the electricity short-circuited the wet lights. *It was different in the old country, where you had to run around with a torch in the middle of the day to see where you were going.* The woman's voice filled the house.

Christmas! Christmas in the city was different now. The girl had to listen very hard, to keep up with the quick-speaking red-haired people racing through everything stockpiled in their heads for this moment, as if every precious second counted while Warren Finch was in their home. She watched words tumbling out of four mouths that never stopped moving—open and closed, up and down. Their voices shouted to be heard above each other to complain about power surges in the city, and the malfunctioning Christmas lights that were never like this before. They remembered a time when you could leave the lights burning all night without anyone batting an eyelid. *Bring back the good old days when we could even cover the whole yard, trees and all, with the snowflake machine.* The only good thing apparently, was that it had been another bumper season for the growth of the Christmas trees. The red-haired man was jubilant about this. Conifers loved the rain, and the perpetual mist, and did not seem to mind if the sun never shone.

Which is a good job with the way it has been raining all the time, the red-haired man said with a sigh.

That's right love, the wife replied with another happy peal of laughter.

All the trees must have grown approximately three meters, just since spring.

Whatever happened to the good, old, hot Australian Christmas, hey, Warren? It will be snowing next thing.

Warren said it was all to do with global warming and climate change, but his moving-mouth friends were more concerned with the failure of the electricity in the yard. Still there was great relief that they had been able to show him the lights, since the woman said, she could not remember when Warren had missed seeing the lights of Christmas in their house: not since he had been sent by his elders to the city as a young man to complete some of his education.

The refrigerator was worshipped. Glorified like the supreme spirit of the city. The huge blue fridge dominating the kitchen was like a house within the house—bigger than a humpy. Colored lights lit up the interior when you opened the door. Warren was told that it was a new fridge. That it had come from overseas. It had been the biggest in the shop, the biggest you could buy, and with Warren there for Christmas, they were pleased that they had gone ahead and bought it. Whenever they spoke now, it was about some item extracted from the fridge for consumption. Food had to be talked about while it was eaten like people do in Paris the lady said.

Warren Finch was in his element. He relished the conversation about food and talk of regional differences in dairy products, recipes and dishes he had tasted at various restaurants in countless countries he had visited since the last Christmas. Oblivia had only seen him eating with the genies, where he did not seem concerned about what he ate. He put anything in his mouth. She watched as they talked endlessly of things of no importance to anyone but themselves, and now about the brands of butter you could buy in places called the "new" supermarkets, which was not like the old days, they claimed, when they had no butter at all during the long drought. They said it was almost as bad as the place where the girl had come from—*God! Blessed girl.*

Isn't that right, E-thyl? The girl's failure to answer their questions stiffened the room. She did not know what these conversations were about. Warren, who had never stopped smiling, just shook his head in a familial gesture that the family understood, without wasting words, *don't bother, don't fuss, not worth the trouble.*

Well! Eee-thyl will have to know which butter to buy if she is going to be living in the big city now.

Why? The red-haired husband asked in mock astonishment. *E-thyl might not even like butter.*

Of course she likes butter. You like butter, don't you, Eee-thyl? The girl nodded, but she had never tasted butter.

A woman can be good for other things—not just being knowledgeable of which butter to buy.

Warren laughed. Mentally, the girl noted the joke, thinking it might be useful to know how to make him laugh one day.

In this introduction of what gave peace and pleasure to Warren Finch, the girl had found hell. She wanted to scream. She hated everything about these people. Her mind left the room to look for the genies' camp among the owls and rats, and somehow, in a slim crevice of nonstop talk bouncing off the wood paneling, she heard an owl outside calling from a Christmas tree. She wanted to leave. Go outside. Disappear. Crawl away from this dead wood house that Warren had claimed would be her home. Her mind walked through its wooden cocoon where geography was lost, and where momentarily, she saw the ghosts of trees with branches swinging in the wind, that swung out and would hit her.

Noticing her silence, the woman said, *E-thyl, you just make yourself at home, love. This is your home now too, you know.* The girl's fingers ran along the wood panels which she visualized as tree trunks in some dense forest in her head. *Why could he not have been like other men?* asked Aunty Bella Donna of the Champions. She was standing in the back of the room trying to pull the girl from the tree roots and telling her to start acting polite and grateful, and stop that chatting to herself like an idiot. Harbor Master stood in the doorway. He just yelled at the girl that they were a pack of racists. *Couldn't he just have been like the men who killed their wives in the bush? Not go around bringing them to places like this. You would be better off dead. Skeletons left propped up against a tree somewhere. Sun bleaching bones with pieces of skin hardened to leather, and pieces of rag from their dresses fluttering in the wind. A bird picking about on her bones! Things like that!*

The girl escaped. She left the table where the continuous sound of voices grated like gravel thrown across the floor of her brain. In the corridor of that vast house she felt lost, although relieved in being alone, and tried to remember the route of the journey with Warren. No plan of escape came easily to mind, so she explored the Christmas house.

The voices faded as she followed a corridor lovingly decorated with festoons of pine branches that were tied with red ribbons in big bows, and large silver bells tinkling automatically from an inbuilt sonar detection device. Otherwise, it was a quiet house with empty rooms where only the sound of clocks could be heard ticking from walls, mantelpieces and cupboards. She was guided by an orange, gray, black and white marbled cat that ran ahead and led her into its favorite room. On entering the room, she discovered it had been permanently divided into more rooms, and these smaller rooms had been partitioned within, into strange, little alcoves on the Christmas theme that replicated in miniature scale nostalgic wintertime memories of foreign countries.

She felt as though the meowing cat was sweeping her along, urging her not to linger too long—*Don't get sucked into other people's worlds. And don't knock anything over and spoil the dream.* They passed each elaborate world of dreams, where miniature winter people went about their business walking, stopping to talk to others, living lives among reindeer, tending baby deer, riding colorful sleighs, and looking at a cheerful Santa with elves, and grinning snowmen. There were carol singers that looked into rooms full of brightly wrapped presents, decorated Christmas trees, dinner tables laden with feasts, bowls of delicious apples and pears, and behind them, a countryside full of red robins singing in bare-branch trees, and miniaturized forests of pine trees laden with fake snow.

The girl examined each of the created worlds closely with a dark, morbid fascination, consciously searching for failure, proof of fault, in the perfect images of nostalgia. She heard herself saying: *Did not exist. Did not exist,* and drowned the old woman's delight in recognizing all the places she had known once upon a time, and the Harbor Master mumbling in her other ear about all the racists running around and ruining the country. The cat protested. *Meow! Meow!* Insisting it knew the consequences of falling in love with constructed fairylands, *so mind you don't break anything because the red-haired people really love their memories.* But the girl had already become lost in the theater of the remembered foreign lands. She did not want to be reminded of footsteps on gravel when Aunty Bella Donna of the Champions was already walking among Christmas valleys, and pulling the girl back to a day long ago when up in the mountains they searched the vista for a house in a village that no longer existed.

They traveled to fields in the miniaturized scenery where saintly looking people talked to birds, and small children lived in the care of swans while their fathers and mothers were away at war. These were lands where swans had been fed by a spring under a great ash tree where its three roots of fate kept spreading throughout the world to create the past, present and the future.

There, in another theater, the old woman pointed to swan gods singing to swallows, *where the neck of the long-lived swan is curving and winding;* and to the swan that swims on the river separating the living from the dead. She wanted to find a swan lifting off from a quiet lake and leading a people to their doom in the sea. Where had such a cruel swan come from? Was it living out Aristotle's death song of swans, and sung because it believed it was going to heaven, as Socrates assented, as it flew to sea to die? Heaven! The girl could hear an angel in the heavens above humming the swan waltz. Her swans might already be on their way back from heaven.

A globe contained disgruntled fishermen sitting around on the snow ice fishing in another winter, with lakes and seas frozen over, and birds in plight as snow fell. On icy waters, old Aunty showed the girl her cursed people who had been turned into swans. They dipped into freezing shallows to feed on the aquatic plants below. Some, the old woman said looking into the globe, were spirits condemned to live in the sea for centuries, while others would fly in a lonely sky forever. They were cursed like the children of Lir she said. They died because they were too old and decrepit when they had changed back to their human form, after living nine hundred years through an evil spell that had cast them as swans. Their fate twisted between Erin and Alba on the sea of Moyle.

The girl had spent hours searching for deception in these countless miniature scenes of Christmas, perhaps because she hoped that some tiny voice would reach up to her ear, but the more she leaned into the little scenes, only their happy faces returned her gaze. And the more she searched, the more she found old Aunty's stories of swans really existed in other people's memories too. She even found the sailors aboard the East India ship in the year of 1698, and watched as they watched a black swan off *Hollandia Nova.* Sailors ran on the beach as they chased swans over great sheets of shallow water. Then, on a wooden ship on a Christmas sea, she discovered two black swans in a cage heading to Djakarta in 1746. And black swans in the Europe of 1791, at Knowsley, in England, where they were bred in the Earl of Derby's menagerie, and also in France—in the Empress Josephine's ponds at Malmaison—and the waters of Paris at Villeneuve l'Étang. She saw small graves of black swans with people standing around the little brown plots of earth, including Sir Winston Churchill, mourning his war gift from Australia before World War II.

After exploring all of these little scenes that had been created by months of labor, she had found no eucalyptus tree trunk with strange writing in the dust, no swamp lined with people guarded by the Army. She could not understand why this history did not exist in this world of creation. It was incomplete. Wrong. This was the flaw that she had searched for and found. There was no miniature black girl such as herself in any of these depictions of humanity, no swamp world of people quarrelling over food, not even Warren Finch among the black shepherds, or a black Wise King.

What became of the time when a young Bella Donna of the Western world ran through the snow with her family and countless others as exiles? Where were they in the scenery of Christmas? Where were the escaping boat people who had placed their fate in a swan that led all the rickety boats that failed the decades adrift on the mercy of seas in that world of unwanted people? Where were the deserted boat people cities that had existed on the oceans of the world? She moved on with the knowledge that there was no link between her and Warren Finch's world.

CITY SWAN

The fiery woman worked her fingers to the bone to get into the girl's brain, as though this was where one removed grime, salt, vegetation, blood of dead animals, lice, and whatever thoughts about having different origins she had brought into the house. Big Red, that was her name the woman said, after she had found the girl asleep in the corridor. With her sleeves rolled up, the woman joyfully prepared a more proper wife for Warren than what he had arrived with.

The girl had slept against a wall with the cat, and dreamed of a river walled up with knotted debris composed of words describing tree trunks, branches and leaves that had been washed away by previous floods. She knew it was not a safe place to stand against the wall breaking up in the flooded backwaters where volumes of words kept spilling over her head. Submerged and struggling, she bobbed up to surface every now and again, while swimming through schools of coppery red fish that were larger than whales jammed right to the steep banks of the river.

It was midmorning when Big Red had transformed the girl with enough hot baths to convince herself that she had found the true color of the girl's skin. She styled the girl's hair, contouring her wild golden-tipped brown curls to remain close to her head, and coiled the rest into a bun at the base of her neck. She painted her fingernails cream. The wedding gown was next. The girl was thinner than expected and not as tall. She knew to expect her to be dark, not that dark, but the color was fine for the cream silk that had been ordered. Now the dress itself did not fit.

She hissed between teeth filled with pins, cursing Warren for having created a monumental problem by wanting so many things to be done like this. *A wedding gown from Italy! What next?* It was the bride's job to give her measurements. *How would he know?* And he should have given more warning if he wanted to leave it to somebody else to organize everything for him. *Hold still! Don't move an inch.* The girl dared not breathe. Yet! Yet! *My dear,* she sung finally, saying she would build Rome with her bare hands in a day if she had to. Why? *Because,* she explained, *Warren deserved to be happy for all he has to put up with.* And with a pin she would stab the girl if she did not make Warren a happy man.

You are a very lucky girl. This is going to be the happiest day in your life. I hope you know that. So, don't mind me. Who am I to complain over a simple little thing like not having the dress as perfect as it should be?

Finally, the dress clung to the girl's body and the cream silk with embroidered lilies fell down to her ankles, and Big Red who found it hard to believe in miracles, admitted Warren had chosen the right dress. *Unbelievable! Who would have thought you could put the bush where you come from into a frock.* The girl looked into an oval mirror and saw herself like golden syrup in a cream dress with the same color arum lilies of the land of the owls, and gloved hands. She looked grand, said the children applauding their mother who was gushing with pride. Red said Ethyl looked exactly like a fashion queen from a magazine. *A miracle,* she said to Warren. *And don't you do this to me again.* Warren looked at the girl. He looked relieved. He embraced the woman strongly. It was plain to see that she meant the world to him.

Oblivia felt like she had been turned into a dolled-up camp dog and vaguely nodded to the question of whether she took Warren Finch as her husband to love and obey etcetera—since what did it matter whether she said, *I do* to Warren Finch, or fuck you, arsehole if that was what she was supposed to think, and who was no less of a stranger in the room to her than anyone else there staring at her. Did it matter? Not the idea of marriage. This was the whole point with Oblivia, long after the house had filled with guests who greeted the redheaded dragon woman profusely as they entered. The man who officiated the marriage wore a tight black snake suit that could have been a boa constrictor strangling him. His face was sickly gray. He looked as though he had seen a ghost. Perhaps he was a ghost, Oblivia thought—she even thought it was funny, wondering whether she was really in some other reality, and if this was what the ghosts of white people did all the time, getting married, saying I do, promising the world and whatnot. She wasn't going to be anybody's slave. While the marriage celebration proceeded with color and glitz, the only strange person in the room was Oblivia with her girlish thoughts. *But, you have to understand,* said a woman expert on Indigenous affairs in a small gathering of like-minded among the guests, *this marriage will cement bonds with these people. It is their law. He will need to keep his principles on his road to ultimate power.*

You need to understand something about Warren, Big Red confided in the girl. *His friends are important business people. Born rich. Men of old traditions lodged in other parts of the world. They give money to his work. They want a separate voice to hold sway in this country. Do you understand?* Only her eyes in degrees of openness indicated which of the cleanly shaven men embracing Warren mattered, while his own cleanly shaven face touched their own. They were either like people cast out in the desert or close-knit, like blood brothers. The girl followed Big Red's eyes, like a ribbon from her hair that had caught the wind and flew along an invisible current through the house.

These are all very close friendships. Big Red smiled even more stiltedly and self-knowingly at the wives who politely kissed both Warren's cheeks, fingers lingering suggestively as they slid a gloved hand across his cheek. She said nothing about those close friendships. Red said they were rolling in money. *Most of which is the laundered profits of exploiting natural resources which has wound every cent of its way around the globe many times before it lands in this multicolored fashion parade, my dear.*

The girl watched the kissing, hugging and laughter to congratulate Warren for marrying *his beautiful promise.* They glanced over to her, smiled, gave a small wave. *You see how they love Warren? They are also very important benefactors who will see to it that Warren becomes the head of this country. Do you know what a benefactor is? I suppose you don't. They give your husband a lot of money to help him become the most powerful man in the country. Not that he isn't already. I am not saying that.* Red looked at the girl strangely, and saw there was nothing one way or another disturbing her, so taking a deep breath and with a sigh of relief, ended the commentary: *Well! Whatever!*

Warren smiled amicably, briefly, politely to hear snippets of important news among these high-profile advocates of worthy causes, human rights, moral judgment, espousing correct answers for saving the lives of Aborigines, displaced people, freedom of speech, endangered species, the environment. And in fact, Red said, *Between them all, all of them have enough causes to cover the entire planet. You think they could bloody well save it.*

He drifted easily into careful quotes that one would expect from a happy groom, and to the varied questions of friendly media profilers. They smiled with great appreciation each time he spoke. He locked eye contact. It was impossible for the women journalists to break from his gaze until he freed them. The politicians, old hands at the artistry of seduction, cautioned a compromising situation, by ushering Warren aside. They spoke in hushed tones to fill the moment by clinking glasses to honor his peculiarly bizarre but honorable marriage whether they thought it was exploitation or not, the thing was, it was a novel idea indeed.

The matron Red eyed her special guests sarcastically, and was scathing in telling Oblivia about how they all wanted to know about customary law practices now: *See how they are staring at you? Look at them biting at the bit to say that they have always acknowledged arranged marriages. See how they are pulling Warren aside? Read their lips: Oh! Warren, What does it mean? Will this work? Last week they all wanted to outlaw it. You watch: They will be racing and falling over themselves to get back to Canberra in the morning to dust the cobwebs off that old 1970s customary law report and scratching their heads to figure out how to be first to bring all your old laws and practices into legislation which they had pre-*

viously outlawed to death. That's what they are all whispering about over there. Trying to be honorable. Such hypocrites. All of them. Fancy trying to justify oblique practices from another culture they know nothing about and wanting to build it into the normal practice of Australian law. But what can you say? Men from the mountaintops will always come down to the molehill to conquer it. That will always be the vice of the conqueror.

The tables were festooned with red fish, octopus, squid, oysters and silver urns overflowing with prawns, crayfish, salmon and all other things cooked red from the sea. A line of waiters queued at the door with platters of teaming roasts and vegetables under shining silver lids. It was a banquet, more food than the girl had seen in her entire life, and the sight of so much food for one meal made her nauseous, and unable to eat. Inside her loneliness, she felt the pangs of hunger the night she had raided the fishing nets in the swamp, and had not found a single fish. Then, she lost track of the number of cattle, pigs, sheep, and poultry slaughtered, and vegetable fields that had been raided, the sea emptied, and all of this—deteriorating into the guts of seagulls eating the rubbish.

She had no guests of her own. Even old Aunty and the Harbor Master had boycotted the wedding. The girl stared blankly into a world where hungry swans flew around the house in a frenzied flight of destruction. In the melee of crashing and swans' hisses, the huge birds strike at food off dinner plates and attack the banquet. Strangely, other things fall apart in her mind too, because somewhere far off beyond the house and wedding music and guests milling in talk she could hear the single cry of a swan gliding down a lonely river calling for its mate. She turned pale. This was old Bella Donna's story of the swan flying with a piece of bone in its beak.

The neck of a motionless swan lay limp on the bank of the river so far away. Its mate flew on and on, and the girl could hear the swan's wedding song coming closer as other things began to take shape before her eyes, and Warren's guests became swans. Their clothes were transforming into swanskin with feathers of glitter and shine.

It was a funny old world the girl thought, seeing people too preoc-

cupied to notice their own metamorphosis. They were too busy thinking about the proper way to smile at a promised wife first lady who
stared back at a room full of swans. Oh! My God! She smiled at the
busy swans preening one another, and again, gliding across the glassy
room to the music of Johann Strauss. Oh! My God! The girl had been
captured in the blissfulness of being a bride. Look at her! She danced
towards the swans flying through the air—and then, crying as they
faded away, was unable to accept that they could have changed back
suddenly into Warren's guests.

But the room danced with French champagne, chatter and music,
and as guests were introduced to the girl, she found the sense of their
humanity enticing. Warren's guests had learnt about poverty from not
being poor themselves, in places where you did not hear the screams
and yelling of help. Their words could stay on a flat horizontal plane
from one end of the spectrum to the other in speaking about the emotions of the world. Well-fed speech was flexible, versatile, and heavily
pregnant with a choice of words that could be tilted with enough in-
flection to win hearts regardless, so when she listened to Red, she had
to remember they were actually oppressors, capable of slipping down
to the bottom of a fetid well to destroy whoever got in the way of their
success. She shook their hands just like they might have been swans.

In a room celebrating the glory of the country through political maneuvers, there were no genies. This thought had struck her like lightning,
and when Warren caught sight of her she froze. He patted the arm of
the person he was speaking to, excusing himself to collect her. His arm
guided her from one person to the next, circling the room in farewells,
while she wanted to walk away. *You are supposed to be a trophy wife,* Warren whispered into her ear and capped it with a light kiss. He was obviously thrilled by what he overheard from his guests.

   This is astonishing. He actually went ahead with it.
   Married his promise wife.
   Someone said he just went straight in and took her from a bush camp
where she was living in squalor with ducks and what have you, and she

had been raped and everything. *A really violent place where children were neglected.*

No!

Well! No one can be too surprised. That's the kind of thing Warren would do.

I agree. He has always been a man who will stand by a principle.

But she was half mad when he found her.

Was that when she was living in a tree or something?

They say she didn't even know her name.

Why? I never heard of someone not knowing their own name.

Well! It is true. Not all people are the same.

Bullshit! We are one country here. We are all Australians. All equal. No one is any different.

Well! If you don't believe it, go and ask her what her name is.

Oblivia overheard too. She felt strange, and could not understand why he had taken her away from her home either. *It is just games,* Warren said, squeezing her hand and smiling at his friends. *Why would people play these games?* Her head felt as though it was being whisked around inside a sphere tugged by swans circling the skies and narrowing in their search to find her.

Finally, they were back where they had begun, walking down through the pine trees where white mist rose through the foliage, and a violin was playing Edgar's grass owl rhapsody. She stopped to listen, and the music grew louder as it spread through all of the trees. Warren held her arm firmly. She pushed him away, trying to break free, she wanted to go back.

Where? Where do you want to go to, he said, while he maintained his grip on her arm.

Where is he? Edgar? she thought, trying to pull away.

Don't be stupid. Come on. Let's try to dignify the occasion. At least you should be capable of doing the few simple things you are supposed to do. Who put on that music? Listen! See! The music is being piped through the trees. That's all.

The girl struggled to look back, and strained to hear the music as it faded into the background of the farewells of guests crowding around them. Red's big lips smiled broadly. All eyes were on Warren as they wished him well, showering him with embraces in a wave that lifted the bride into the car while shadows flew overhead. But! Just when she thought the swans had arrived, the shadows disappeared from the curls in the mist, and then, it was sunshine. There was nothing but blue skies as the door closed, long before the violin finished playing its serenades.

Driving away, Warren happily chatted about the simply marvelous wedding to the driver he called mate, or to whoever else was on the other end of the mobile phone which was ringing constantly. *Wasn't it great, Ethyl?* Every call he included her, to back up what he thought about his marriage. *Yes, she loved it, didn't you, Ethyl?* Warren's voice went on squashing her thoughts of salt lakes, spinifex and owls. She had lost the battle to preserve Edgar's music in her head.

The phone rang like an alarm bell interrupting her thoughts, to dominate the past, to insist the future be heard. She felt that the voice on the phone belonged to a snake. The marriage belonged to his viperous world. Then he was arguing with the phone. *It means nothing . . . Something! Something? Believe me it means nothing.* He looked out the window as he spoke, and she wanted to scream at him to stop robbing people of their thoughts. She hated how he killed silence.

She was certain that he had intentionally stopped her from hearing the music, just as he made certain that she would never reach the point from where her emotions would overtake his plans, to leave him somehow, to return to the swans. He reached across and touched her arm and she flinched in that instant as his voice drew her back into his world.

Warren smiled and said he had a little present.

Don't you want to know what it is?

He waited until she looked at him before he handed her a small red coral box. It was carved with tiny birds with fat bellies that were larger than their wings, and each bird looked up with golden eyes.

Go on, open it. The slightest touch to the clasp on the side of the box released the lid which sprang open, and sounded a tune. *It is from Swan Lake the ballet. I thought you would like that.* Inside, on its bed of silk, lay a silver ring. She looked at her left hand with the gold wedding band that sat loosely on her finger.

Take it, he encouraged, and then put the ring on her finger.

This is for the right hand, he said, adding how he had had it made especially for this day. She looked at the design. Two thin bands were separated by crescent moons that encased a small silver brolga, and a swan.

Do you like it?

It is very nice. Thank you. She imagined that she had spoken politely, like Red, but said nothing. She wished the mobile phone would call so that the voice of the snake would sit between them.

I have another little present for you, he said. *In case you are thinking about where all of this is heading, you need to know one thing. You will never be going back to where you came from. I will tell you the reason why. It no longer exists.*

Oblivia looked straight at him.

His smile was victorious now, having conquered her indifference at last. *Simple! The place does not exist anymore. There is no time for places like that. So I did them a favor. I had the place closed down the day we left. Listen!*

He tapped the phone, held it to his ear, and spoke. *Is everything ready?* His voice was cold with authority. A shiver ran up her back. Then he placed the phone to her ear. She listened. The countdown finished, and then, a male voice said, *Do it: Now!* She heard the explosions whistling through the receiver and vibrating down her fingers. She had to hold the rattling phone away from her ear, but even over the noise of the moving car, could hear the piercing sounds of everything that had flown to the sky. Warren's face had hardened. She had only seen men around the swamp using their physical powers to destroy. How could this man destroy something so enormous that contained her world? All she saw was a very fine-looking man in the suit he had chosen for his wedding day. His thumb silenced the mobile and after taking a deep breath, he placed it back in the pocket of his jacket.

That was for you, he said at last.

What is for me? That? What do you mean? The words did not surface, but the sound of her voice rose through a bottleneck as though gasping for air.

They had not protected you. Nobody did. You know it is true or deep down in your heart you do, just like I know it. Their job was to protect you. That was the law. He took her hand with the ring, and twisted it around her finger, and she saw a third bird, an owl, and she could not understand how she had missed seeing it before, but instantly, she felt calmer, emptied, as though nothing remained of herself which had been scattered far away.

So it's very simple. Really. Anyone would understand why places like that cannot exist. It is what the whole country was thinking—even if the Government was never prepared to do anything about it.

What will happen to them—those people? He asked the question for her. She imagined the swans agitated and frightened by the panic of people being cleared out of their homes. Flying off. Their flight shifting in clear blue skies from the sound of the explosions, the black columns of smoke chasing them away. What would happen if they had continued swimming around the hull, confused, waiting for her to return? Did he destroy the swamp and the swamp people too?

They had two choices. Either being moved into the nearest town where they would have to learn to live just like everyone else. Or, being returned to homelands where their real laws and government exist. There will be no Army looking after anybody anymore. Stupid idea in the first place. Intervention! Safer futures! Can't for the life of me see why stupid thinking like that has lasted a century.

What if they don't like it there? What if they go back? Again, he felt the need to frame questions on her behalf, to explain his apocalyptic decision. She was still thinking about the swans and about what would happen to her, if she could go back, and if the swans were not living there anymore.

What if, what if? What does it matter to you, or us? They only have themselves to blame. But if you want to know: Everyone on earth is obliged to live a life without endangering somebody else's life. I work at trying to make people safe. Why do you think I went up there? I wanted to have a look. See what the place was like for myself. That was how I found out that

I was right all along from the time when the old people told me about you. I had already known that you were to become my wife when I saw what had happened to you. I knew about the arrangement our families had made from a long time ago when I was a boy. You know, I could have closed them down a while back, but I just wanted to make sure, and I needed to go and collect you, and in any case, it was better to do it this way. You have a future ahead of you now. They were doing nothing to change things by themselves for the future so they had given up the right of sovereignty over their lives.

She only half listened, without having any idea of what he was talking about. His boring words went in one ear and straight out the other. *Bloody sellout!* There were two others in the car. The old woman. Old Harbor Master. Both sitting in the front seat with the driver. They were discussing this matter too. *Who does he think he is? God! Where did he learn about bombing people's homes? Where does he think he is? A war zone. In Afghanistan? That old war! How long has that been going on for? Does he still think he is in Europe or America? Doesn't he know this is Australia? Who gives him the right to decide on other people's sovereignty?* The old woman was saying how her bones would be blown up now, and she would have to go and find them, *Let me get out of this car*, then she disappeared.

The girl looked at the passing buildings—the black and gray concrete statues lining the footpaths. She could feel the cold dampness coming off each building as they drove on. It was the same feeling of fear she had had from the abandoned dogs savagely sniffing through the sedge grasses while circling the swamp, huddling the black-feathered chaos until the water was red and putrid from the smell of rotting flesh and wet feathers. Inside a small pocket of bravery hiding in the crevices of her brain, she imagined herself being united with the swan ghosts flying away from the massacre. It was the only way she could wish herself out of this place. The brolgas would just leave naturally and rejoin the masses further east—back in Warren's country—and dust off their old rookeries.

What about the genies? Haphazardly, she held up three fingers to his face, and waved her other hand around, and blew mouthfuls of air.

There are no genies. Genies don't exist. The things you see here are what exist. Nothing else. Trust me and I will show you everything you need to know.

Oblivia winced at Warren's denial, and stared at her three fingers while slamming them into her other hand.

Where are they then?

I told you they have been moved to town.

The owls? All the eggs we counted? Those men?

Very casually he leant over and covered her face with his. The Harbor Master raised his eyebrows and spat in disgust, *A kiss to seal a dream with . . . Look! Girl! He's got lips like Nat King Cole.* She started to disbelieve herself. Her memory was unreliable. Why would she have traveled over salt lakes? She had beaten the odds. Had not been left to die in the bush. She lived in this city with a rich man. The wedding seemed like a daydream. The redheaded family were just ghosts of people from storybooks that she thought of meeting one day.

She remembered Aunty Bella Donna of the Champions once saying that no story was worth telling if no one could remember the lesson in it. These were stories that have made no difference to anyone. Old Aunty was fading away forever. But . . . even true stories have to be invented sometimes to be remembered. Ah! The truth was always forgotten. She was in a car with a stranger.

GYPSY SWANS

In among gray city buildings as solemn as each other, and at the end of silence, they reached a laneway of old and run-down buildings, to stop in front of what Warren Finch called his home.

He called it The People's Palace.

The first thing Oblivia noticed about the building was the iron bars lacing the windows and the single door of the shop front. The building was a cage. It reached up to the sky like a giant finger that had come out of the ground to orchestrate the heavens. Cold winds flew down the street with sheets of rain. The building frightened her. Would she be locked inside its guts? Like the women locked in the guts of Country?

In the grinding rain there were many poor people in shapeless brolga-gray coats milling around the laneway, who stared sideways through the limp wet hair falling down over their faces. Some held out their hands for money, but then withdrew them quickly, and passed by without raising their heads. Underneath their hair, some stared at her from the corner of their eyes. Theirs was a primeval kind of surveillance, like wild dogs. She pretended not to notice how wet the people were who slept against walls, some standing, and others lying under pieces of cardboard while Styrofoam and plastic rolled over them in the wind. They lay on the concrete sideways with an ear to the ground, as if trying to hear the stories that lay underneath. Oblivia did not understand then that what they were really listening for was the hint of another tidal surge flooding in the sewers below the city. Harbor Master looked around, then bent down and put his own ear to the concrete footpath and said Warren Finch's home was a piece of shit. These people threw venom from their souls at him. A woman walked by with a pink towel wrapped around her nostrils and mouth, and stared at the bride. *The air is bad here girlie,* she muffled.

They stood in the rain as Warren unlocked the cumbersome gate and the heavy green door with apparent ease, giving the impression that he knew the building well. *Welcome to my home,* he said.

Is this a shop? she thought, picking up the voice of Dean Martin singing along with the Harbor Master, *Well! It's lonesome in this old town . . . Goin' back to Houston, Houston, Houston.*

No, this is not a shop. It is a place. That was all he said.

They stepped inside a lantern-lit world of water gardens and concrete ponds from which rose enormous antique fountains, while overhead roaming in mist, were large and colorful puppets of birds, dragons and people with wings that swayed from long strings attached somewhere in the ceiling. In this idyll of constant movement, jets of water spouted in the air from wrought iron or brass horns carried by larger-than-life cupids, giant maidens and young men, or spurted out of the beaks of enormous swans and geese, and from lotus flowers, or from the mouths of frogs and dragons. Whenever the water reached its zenith, it loosely and noisily fell into a *Klangfarbenmelodie* of music, dropping into the multitude of shallow ponds, from where it was sucked into pipes, then spouted back up into the air again, taking with it Dean Martin's song of what it was like to be going home, to *Houston . . .*

In this crowded space, where eyes swung hocus-pocused through the kaleidoscopically fantastic creation, there was even more drama unfolding, with statues of ancient Greek men and women watching on with faces of wondrous serenity over ibis, eagles, the imagined animals of fairy tales, and giant lions with heavy manes that lay on the floor with heads upright, staring into the distance. Wherever there was space not taken up by the human ability to marvel in its imagination, ropey plants, palms, aloes drooping and stringy battled to survive in the atmosphere of wetness and dimness, by stretching half-starved stems towards whatever light came through the windows.

There were cats asleep on pedestals, mantelpieces, steps and shelves, and any place free from being sprayed by mist. The cats watched Warren Finch with yellow eyes as he led the way. A brighter light came on from somewhere above, and when the girl looked up, she saw a break in the clouds passing over the glass dome roof. He led her to a wire cage that belonged to another century. It surrounded the elevator that he explained was a masterpiece of engineering. *A bloody marvel that still works perfectly even after practically two and a half centuries,* he claimed. *It must have been the pride of the city when it was first built.* He pressed the dirt-and-grease-coated brass button that shone on the mark where fingers had been pressing it forever. *Bloody impressive!* She saw him quiver momentarily, while they waited for what did seem like forever, for the lift to come. It slowly descended, whining with pain, until suddenly falling the last meter with a thud. A manlike creature like those she had just seen on the street outside, pushed open the concertina door, and said very slowly: *Hello, Mr. Flinch. You're back.*

Hello Machine. How have you been? Pretty good? Meet the missus. He did not mention her name.

The man grunted and said that he had nothing to complain about. He looked at Oblivia with old dog-type eyes for a split second, and then continued looking at the floor. By the time the lift had struggled several floors up to the top of the building, he had managed to say *Hello, Mrs. Finch.* The fountain garden far below was bathed in yellow lights that reflected off the water, but looking down made her feel dizzy. Beside the lift were several flights of dimly lit steps. In the darkness, Warren placed a key into a door with the number 59 barely visible, screwed onto it. Inside, he switched on the lights and walked through the rooms.

Everything works, Warren said, while striding around the apartment that looked as though it was never used. She was given a quick demonstration of electric appliances: stove, fridge, jug, toaster, microwave, washing machine, television, radio. Rubbish: left nightly outside the door. Water: Hot and cold shower, bath, basin, kitchen sink. Toilet: how to flush. Cleaning: broom, mop, bucket, wipes. Cleaning liquids: kitchen, bathroom, toilet, laundry, floors. Clothes: there were some spare clothes left in the wardrobe. He slid a glass door open and she could see a line of clothes hanging for her. Shoes on the floor. Underwear in the drawers. He continued on, and quickly explained what she could and could not do in the apartment, which he said was *yours now.* Frequently, he called out lists of instructions with: *You must promise me that you will remember.* Then he emerged from the bedroom, bags packed, one in each hand. The mobile was calling but he did not answer.

Her eyes had been glued to the images changing on the television until it occurred to her that the mobile was still ringing.

I will call them back in a minute, he said, and looking at her for a moment as he tried to remember something he had to say, he continued: *I will try to get back on the weekend.*

Her eyes were now fixed on the bag in his hand. Warren could see her face locking into meltdown, another panic attack, and thought he better say something to her, before she destroyed the place, or stopped him from leaving. Yes, that would do it. He would explain his work to her—where he had to go.

Sometimes Canberra. That's the nation's capital. I am in government you know. Sometimes the world. Anywhere. My parish is the world. Wherever I am needed in the neighborhoods of power. That is where I work: where I do business. Your business is to stay here and be my wife. Machine will look after you.

It was his words that described hugeness that helped her to realize how powerful he was, and her lack of power, in a place that she did not know.

Just ring the lift if you need anything. You can trust him so don't worry about asking. You will be good company for Machine. He is a good man and he does a good job. He broke the slight awkwardness in his voice by looking at his watch to confirm his departure.

Look! He said impatiently, *I have got to go right now to catch the flight. This is something you will have to get used to I am afraid. I have to go tonight because I have been away too long and I have a lot of very, very urgent work to do, starting first thing in the morning. Look! I will call you.*

Then he left. She heard him talking to the man he called Machine on the other side of the closed door, and shortly afterwards, the slamming concertina gates, then the rumbling noise of the lift wobbling back down its own neck, and the whining sound of creaking ropes fading further away.

She now belonged in the menagerie of exhibits artificially created by the weirdo named Machine. That was how the Harbor Master described the situation.

From that moment of silence, Oblivia would be waiting for Warren to come back.

Countless times, the girl stood in front of the large glass windows of the apartment, as she would do numerous times in the future. What did she watch? Cold rain mostly, that fell on the sun-deprived walls of the buildings across the laneway while she daydreamed about how she would escape through the mazes stacked in her mind—thousands of unknown city streets and distances across the country too great to be imagined, to return to the swamp   imaginary flights that always fizzled into a haze-land between the here and then that stopped her every time. She followed the routes of rainwater pouring through the moss and black lichen that grew in profusion down the shady walls, or dripping melodically like piano notes onto the drooping foliage of fig trees, banana trees, tropical trees and ferns growing from cracks in these buildings. She watched dark-hooded people drifting into the lane to sleep. Those who formed a huddle for security at night, then left in the morning. Sometimes, she would be awakened in the middle of the night when she heard people screaming *King Billy*, and she rushed to the window to watch dark shadows scattering though the waters flooding in the laneway, the old drought-buster spirit when tidal surges flooded through the sewers into the lower, poorer, and central parts of the city, usually at times when violent hailstorms from cyclonic weather struck the coastline. She watched the people from the lane moving away, or sheltering from the rain and hailstones under pieces of cardboard and plastic, or standing around for hours in floodwater, holding their belongings to their chests, until the waters subsided.

Old Bella Donna's books about swans wrapped in fishing net were left on the table like a souvenir. Oblivia had found the package one night while roaming around the apartment after she had woken startled from a nightmare taking her to the brink of madness. Her common nightmare of being caught in the improbability of returning or leaving, of being locked in this moment forever, and there it was on the table. Had Warren come back? She froze, looked into the shadows, then started searching the place with the kitchen knife while the Harbor Master was winding her up so fast, urging her on to kill the useless prick if she found him, that she was racing around in a frenzy like a madwoman cut loose. The books could have been a wish come true. Washed up from the tracks of dry salt lakes. Hauled through the clouds outside the window. She had missed the genies tapping on the glass, to grant her wishes if she had any more to make.

The Harbor Master kept calling Warren Finch a fuckwit for leaving them all in this dump of a place. He was itching to leave. He said he had seen her bloody books in the vehicle where she had left them. *On the edge of the salt lakes.* The books smelled of the hull. If she touched one, or picked it up, images of being in the hull flashed through her mind.

Somehow, the books became good company. Pages were flicked over, and lines recited, and reflected upon: *The wild swan's death-hymn took the soul of that waste place with joy.* Was this wasteland the swamp? She left the books on the table, and touched them frequently as though they were her friends. She sang over and over, a chant, her lonely in- cantation to the swans flying over Country, *All the black swans sail to- gether.* She moves on, finds another thought—*He who becomes a swan, instructs the world!* This swan could spread his wings and fly where his spirit takes him, and Oblivia imagines the past disappearing in this flight to a frightening anticipated unknown future. Shakespeare's *Sweet Swan of Avon! What a sight it were . . .* where a Mute Swan, or Whooper

Swan, flying ten thousand leagues, had taken the old swan woman's people across the sea. But her mind turns away from that vision, and returns to anticipate how her own black swans from the swamp were moving over the country she had traveled, and listens to them singing their ceremonies in flight, and she holds this thought in her mind because it soothes her, instructs her in endurance and perseverance.

Days passed and weeks turned into months of not knowing how she could continue reminding herself of the home she had been taken from, a place that no longer existed in the way she remembered—*Now, when you awaken, remember the swan's last dance.* As quickly as she tried to reconstruct the swamp in her mind, the quicker the images of watery slicks consumed the hull, capturing *the earthed lightning of a flock of swans* . . . and the rotting abandoned hulls flew away in the wind from a world fallen apart. It was not safe to have thoughts that were now wavering into forgetfulness until all that remained were vague memories too hard to hold. She no longer felt safe thinking about the hull. Slowly but surely, her life had become anything Warren Finch wanted it to be, *the Swan I tempted with a sense of shame* . . . and he was already doing that by not coming back.

In the middle of the day Oblivia watched the liftman from her window, when he was down in the narrow lane, right where the water was gushing out of the pipes carrying the water flooding from the top of the building. His shoes are wet from the windswept rain, but he continues emptying the rainwater from their bowls and feeding his cats. They follow his every move despite not liking the rain falling on their fur, because they are hungry. They are mainly orange marmalade cats; black and gray brindle cats; black-and-white cats. Soon, they are just wet cats. He judiciously supervises the feeding ritual to ensure that each cat manages to grab a bit of food.

Machine reminds her of Warren. The dominant, stronger cats are often discouraged from being too greedy with a swift kick from the tip of his boot. Other times, when in a hurry, he does not bother emptying water from the bowls. On these occasions, he just throws scraps of meat all over the laneway and wherever a bit lands, the cats rush towards it, and it all ends up in catfights. He watches for a moment or two as though he finds pleasure out of the spectacle of fur and claws, then he turns his back and saunters off towards the street entrance to the building. Other times he seems to be sick, and just empties tins of congealed cat food onto the ground in the running water. Then afterwards, he picks up all of the tins and carts them away in his rubbish bag.

Over rooftops where the crows wait, she would often see right out to the gray bay where the clouds were chopped by wind. She listened to the sound of ferry boat engines whining in the rough, and the jets that flew continuously over the roof tops, and she wondered whether Warren might be on board, antlike, up in the sky. In the street below, in the constant sound of traffic, she saw delivery trucks traveling back and forth to feed the city, as if the entire population of the country existed only in this place.

Sometimes, when the weather eased, and if she looked closely, out into the shadows of the grayness, she would often find the dark form of a fisherman huddled in his secret fishing place among the rocks along the edge of the bay. She watched the small motorboats slowly churning over the choppy water, where hunchback fishermen went back and forth, then as night fell, the boats moving between lanes of flickering red, green and golden globes, and a seemingly never-ending trail of bats traveling from one abandoned park to another across the city. Then she moved away from the window. Her daily routine was completed.

Warren Finch still did not return, and she did not wish he would come back. She started to believe that one day the view from the window would change. A plane might fall from the skies, straight into the deepest part of the bay in front of her, with his body still strapped to its seat. She waited expectantly, anticipating the time when she would become one of the hunchbacked people on one of the little fishing boats, with eyes blinded by a stinging sea spray as they searched the crash site.

The rain never stopped falling. Sometimes it fell so hard it was impossible to see the bay. The telephone never rang. She had placed the receiver on the table and left it there.

• • • •

Oblivia avoided Machine like the plague. Never wanted to see him. She did not even watch him feed the cats anymore. She feared that one day he would knock on the door and she would have to answer it. Yet, the liftman did his job of looking after her. He regularly left groceries and money outside the door in a box along with the household and personal things she hardly used. She stacked the things left by Machine into a mountain as high as the ceiling until the construction tumbled. She restacked bath soap, tins of food, laundry detergent into a higher pile. Most of the perishable food she did not eat, she left in the rubbish bin outside the door, where more food was left for her.

One night she woke up thinking that Machine was searching through her rubbish somewhere in the building, some place where she imagined he lived in a den like an animal, and where occasionally she thought she heard a phone ring. She felt disgusted and threw her rubbish from the window into the lane, but always quickly afterwards, she would see him picking up every single thing she had dropped with a pointed stick, and dropping it piece by piece, after he inspected it, into a large, green rubbish bag. It was these little incidents that fed her loathing of the ugly man. Her mind grew fat on it. But she could not leave. She depended on him. And still she did not wish that Warren would come back.

Sometimes, in the middle of the night, she would suddenly wake up to the sound of the concertina door of the lift slamming repeatedly in her head. She would run to her door and listen. Always watching the brass, hook-shaped door handle, waiting for it to turn. She thought Warren had come back. He had changed his mind. Then she heard slow, labored breathing, and she wondered if each achievable breath would be the last. Instinctively, she knew it was the liftman on the other side with his ear to the door, listening to her—checking to see if she was still alive. She could hear Warren calling Machine on his mobile phone when the thought crossed his mind: *Keep checking just in case she tries to kill herself.* He could hear her heart pounding. The knife she slides across her hand is so sharp, that she often cuts herself. She tries not to breathe while waiting for the door handle to move. The blood falls from her hand. But he always leaves with his shoes dragging across the floor. The concertina doors open and slam shut. The lift begins whining back down to the lower floors.

It was only when the lift faded away that she would breathe normally again, but one night after he left she heard breathing coming back to her through the walls, in rhythm with her own breath. She now understood it was this sound that had brought Machine up to the top floor of the building. The sound flooded the apartment. She was too afraid to turn on a light, and went from room to room trying to find the sound, but it was coming from everywhere. It came from the air of her breath. The air was wrapping breath with breath.

Then she knew. She could feel the presence of their bodies, of beating wings from lean-chested birds, lightened from the long journey, with necks stretched in flight. The swans had arrived. Above the building they flew in a gyre that was lit intermittently by strobes of searchlights. All around, soft breast feathers fell lightly. The swans flew through the narrow lane outside the window, and upwards into the darkness, after their eyes had found hers. Their search had ended.

The swans flew around the building looking for a place to land. They tried to land on the roof then flew off towards the bay. Their numbers had grown. Along the way, the land had given up its swans from all the drying inland watercourses, swamps, man-made lakes and sewerage ponds, drains and cattle dams. The migration had assembled a black cloud that flew in the night on its long journey to find the girl.

But the swans were gone in the morning.

CITY OF REFUGEES

Late at night gangs of street children heard the swans singing and followed them into the lane. Their world was the deep night while the city was in blackout to conserve energy. The swans were driven by nervousness, but their bond with the girl was greater than fear and held them to the lane. Hundreds of swans circled the building every night, flying in lines, sometimes coming so close their wings clipped the buildings and triggered a chain reaction of downward spiraling. Again and again they returned, and flew through the narrow corridor with even greater compositions of desperation than the previous night.

These aerobatics were how the swans communicated. With all of the nervousness generated at night, the swans kept away from the busy city during the day. Instead, they waited in the polluted waters of the bay, and in ponds in the ruined botanical gardens of the city, and any other abandoned flatlands with a sprinkling of water.

They returned in the quietness of the night and flew continuously through the lane, the closest they could get to the girl staring at them from her window. It was the flight of the obsessed. The continuous trumpeting of great numbers of swans joined harmoniously with their soft whistling to twist a melody that was somber and grief-stricken, but this music was charming to the street kids. They barged into the lane and were ready to challenge any fear they had of being threatened by the roaming cardboard-box street dwellers that had claimed the lane as their own.

The life of the deepest part of the night in this pitch-black, power-starved city was always left to prowlers like the street kids looking for something to do. They roamed the shadows to feel alive. They were the sleepless of the world with no peace in their souls. They were the children of the homeless poor people of the city. Well! They were boys and girls of all ages and from all racial backgrounds mingling together like friends when they followed the swans through the city to the lane.

You know what they believed? That the lane was blessed. A filthy lane was the place to find heaven. So! The kids arrived in hordes, groups of seven or eight that soon became hundreds. All the leaders had a bony *Staffy*, the dog of choice, Staffordshire bull terriers, with thick necks adorned with studded collars and led on rusty chains. It was miracles these children were after. And they felt closer to a miracle just from looking up to the sky and seeing the swans as they swarmed through the lane. They started calling the very ordinary lane a sacred site—*The holy place.*

They developed war games, firing nonstop rap songs in quick succession. Soon, they could not stop themselves from challenging one another to jump from the edges of buildings they had broken into, hanging out of windows on the higher levels to be at the height of swans in flight. They played a sound game by toying with the rhythms from the swans' beating wings. Their chants dared one another to fight for territory, or *to fly off, take off, fall to death, never come back.* In this cacophony echoing through the lane, they spent hours learning to replicate the glory of the city's cathedrals, as they swung between buildings on ropes worsted from rags of old clothes, trying to touch the swans.

The melee of sounds bounced back and forth along the walls, and exploded in the lane below so loudly, it could have woken the dead. The only ones disturbed though were the sleeping bodies inside the platforms of flattened cardboard boxes; the nests constructed by slow hands. This invisible world of the city, a place where decades of dampness, flooding and rain had ridden the lane with slimy algae, was now the street kids' cathedral.

Those who slept there in rubbish-bag coffins stuffed with newspaper to keep warm, while water leaked continuously from the rooftops, were unable to get a decent night's sleep. Nor could they die in a sweet dream. So, they just lay there, and cursed the fact that they were still alive.

The river of swans continued on, they flew trancelike through the gaps between the buildings. They circled and spiraled towards the moon, and gathered something in the air that had been locked out by the walls of the city. They were capturing from the skies the small packages of memory of the girl who was thousands of miles from her home. Perhaps this was what they sprinkled in the lane with feathers dropping, sprinkling dust down like magic so that her mind ran straight back to the swamp's ancient eucalypt, tangled in vines from countless seasons of bush banana.

You know it doesn't work like that, the Harbor Master often claimed while standing beside the girl in her apartment to watch the spectacle in the lane. Even the Harbor Master's small monkey, who thought it was Giuseppe Verdi's Rigoletto, and was always dressed magnificently in brocaded silk jackets, confirmed this was not like the real world whenever it was asked to throw in a bit of good advice. What a disappointment. It had no intentions of becoming the fortune-telling monkey of the lane.

The Harbor Master had brought his monkey friend back from overseas, after he had gone on a cruise ship around the world in search of Bella Donna's homeland. *Had no luck,* he said, *in finding the descendants of her swan leader.* He spat in disgust about his adventure. It was only a love boat he said. The ship had no idea where it was heading. It was full of gypsies searching for something to happen in their lives, their world had been like that from the day their ancestors had been expelled from the Garden of Eden. So he got off the stupid boat with the pie in the sky people and hitchhiked the rest of the way like a real man, hopping along the floating islands of boat people until he found success.

What he found was that there were swans in most continents of the world and finally, he believed he had found the old woman's swans. There were not many left. The poor things had flown back to paradise, which was an oasis in the desert, just like *the Middle East*. He had watched these swans for a very long time while they stood around in dried-up marshland where decent people were reciting poetry, and for the hell of it, singing for rain, as though rain would open the gates of the most fantastic gardens of all times. All he learnt was that those swans were completely mad so he left them there. They were too blind to see that gardens were everywhere. The whole earth was paradise in the eyes of its custodians.

Whereas, look at the monkey, he said. This creature had no illusions about paradise. *He carried his paradise inside himself like a little holy man. Flocks of pigeons followed him wherever he walked though the seas of humanity.* The Harbor Master said the monkey was his guru. He was better fun than trying to bring a swan across the world that was overweight with its own dooming prophecies.

The monkey and I flew back to Australia on a Qantas flagship—full of choir singers singing old Mamas and the Papas songs over and over until you hated the sound, "each night you go to bed my baby, whisper a little prayer for me," etc., etc.

Once the Harbor Master returned to The People's Palace and saw the large crowds forming in the lane for the coming night, he said that he would be staying around for a while. *This looks interesting*, he claimed. The little monkey thought so too even though he was really a serious creature that looked as if he belonged in an office where a lot of money was being made.

It was not long before the world of the lane did not intrigue the monkey. It silently chewed reused PK gum with its big brown teeth, and looked as though it was reflecting on its life so far thinking that all up, it could have been better. Still, nobody could say the monkey had a victim mentality because he was now a drifter, or because the world of the lane had overnight turned its fur gray, and before too long, the gray had turned white like a snow creature from the arctic circle, far snowier even than a Japanese macaque.

The fact of the matter was that the snow monkey simply did not like Australia. It had turned ancient-looking with all of its yearning to go home, to go back to a city of millions, possibly a billion people, to some quiet little monkey house with a big rock in the front yard from where he could sit all day long and beg pistachio nuts from passing tourists. *Gee!* the creature said while shredding a lettuce into thousands of little pieces to resemble its own shattered mind, *the lane was not like the jungle—not a proper jungle.*

But that was not everything. There was much more to be said about what happened in the lane. Oblivia changed her mind about her nerves, and frequently, she left the building at night to rescue the fallen swans. Many fell in the *street kid* game. The rescuing maneuvers became a regular occurrence. Oblivia, the Harbor Master and the monkey would rush to the door as soon as they saw a swan falling.

In an instant they abandoned their fearfulness of the city, as well as the ongoing debates about whether they liked Australia or not, and stampeded into the crowded lane in the middle of the night. They would be off without a second thought, while hassling each other along the way to be the first one to open the door that kept out boogie men like Machine, so that they could *be bop a hula down* the gauntlet of at least a dozen flights of stairs—instead of taking the slower-than-death lift that still had an electricity supply attached to it, probably because only someone like Warren Finch could afford to pay the excessively expensive electricity charges in the city—then chase one another in circles to find the actual front door through the maze of fountains, cats and statues, while cold shivers rushed down their spines.

She knew Machine never slept and was always watching, but she did not hesitate in her hasty exit through the front door to the lane. Once outside, with the Harbor Master egging her to fight the people sleeping in the lane with her knife, and the monkey's little fingers raiding everyone's pockets for food, a Mars Bar or PK gum, she realized how easy it was to grab a swan under her arm and make a hasty retreat back to the building.

Whenever she found herself in the lane, Oblivia realized that she could move inconspicuously like any of the other darkened shapes covering the ground and no one would care less. This was so, even when the conglomerate of bodies huddled together under blankets, paper and cardboard frequently erupted and flew apart in waves of swearing and fights. They would settle again momentarily like a butterfly pausing to rest, when some old peacekeepers switched on the ghetto blasters roaring *Benedictus qui venit in nomine Domini*. She pushed and shoved people aside, all psyched to fight anybody that got in her way, but swans falling in the lane right on top of people did not exactly cause a world war. The multitudes sleeping in cardboard and newspaper bedding kept on snoring, having already anticipated a bit of night clubbing.

Before long, Warren Finch's apartment became a menagerie; a swannery for stunned, injured and recovering birds. Oblivia was a recluse but no Greta Garbo locking herself away and letting bygones be bygones forever. She could not get out of The People's Palace fast enough to save another swan.

Glass was a big problem. Swans in the swamps have no idea about glass. In each desperate attempt to reach the girl, some would crash headfirst into her window. Some would fall into the lane after being swiped by the street kids playing their game of hanging out the windows on the upper floors of the catastrophic city's abandoned apartments that smelled of decades of rose fragrance, impregnated aromas of herbs and spices—cumin, turmeric, cardamom, or of cat urine—and where old people lived in dank smelling rooms.

When absolute silence entered the lane during the early hours of the morning, and the swans began to disappear over the rooftops, the rain-soaked street kids with vacant eyes left too. They would come down from the buildings to wander off to crash on the busiest streets in the city where they slept. These bundles of rags were barely noticeable pushed up against shop windows, and were almost absorbed into the scenery of the most prestigious department stores. There they stayed, and you would never know if they were dead or alive. Their lullaby was the continuous sound of shoes clipping the pavement. The general public watched over them like guardian angels rushing by, while ignoring the dreams pervading the air, that sounded like trumpets from heaven calling for a shepherd to take the children home.

So far, Oblivia had avoided the police. While the sirens of police cars raced towards the lane, the door to The People's Palace would open immediately, and be slammed shut behind her after she returned with another rescued swan. The girl suspected Machine called the police. His turf war! Just as it was his door to open and close. His building. His dilemma of noticing that swans not only filled her apartment, but makeshift pens on the rooftop too, waiting to be returned to unknown places he had never set eyes on.

Oblivia could not understand how she kept seeing glimpses of herself on the television. The monkey had noticed her first because out of boredom it was flicking around with the control switch to find a nature documentary, preferably about monkey homelands or performing monkeys, and ended up watching an old sepia-colored Marlene Dietrich movie. Everything was going along fine until the monkey yelled out in a startled squeal, *Who is that?*

This was when the Harbor Master began watching the movie to see what the monkey had seen, and he saw the same thing too. The girl was changed almost beyond recognition, as though Marlene Dietrich's spirit had jumped out of the television and into the girl and then appeared in a news flash where she was standing right beside—of all the people on earth for goodness sake—Warren Finch. This person whoever she was only flashed across the television screen in a split second. But it was enough. Enough to see that the girl was dressed up like Marlene Dietrich in sepia and parading like the actress, and was actually beside Warren Finch. This same news flash was repeated many times through the Marlene Dietrich movie.

The Harbor Master was nursing a sick swan on his lap, and so was the monkey, and wondering why he was looking after these creatures in a squalid apartment. He asked Oblivia, *Where did you get clothes like that?* This was what the Harbor Master wanted to know, after seeing the pale sepia-colored satin dress most of all, as she and Warren Finch walked off in the distance, and noticing the matching high-heel shoes. He said she looked unbelievable. *At first,* he exclaimed, *I told myself no way—I really couldn't recognize it was you.*

After this happened, all the Harbor Master wanted to do all day long was sit around waiting for a chance to see Warren Finch on the television, just to criticize him. Any news about the Australian Government was just grand. The Harbor Master believed that because of bloody Warren Finch, he had become a specialist in Australian politics—not that this was difficult to do, he claimed. They were all gutless wonders. He grumbled continuously about not being able to stand the sight of the man, so whenever he saw the new president of the country on television—because this was what Warren Finch had finally and seamlessly become (through an inspired shove of the exceedingly long-serving and unpopular Horse Ryder from Government during the course of one stormy night when so many trumped up and legit charges of conspiracy against the machinery of the party flew like a flippen maelstrom through the corridors of power in the country)— the Harbor Master and the monkey yelled at him for the complete sell-out that he was; a complete reprobate of the first order who had dumped his wife and turned against his own people. *Ya moron,* they screamed at the television.

The acclaimed monkey genius Rigoletto had become so obsessed with watching the news, he started to make specialized comparisons with how politics worked in the monkey world. He claimed that Warren Finch had stepped out of line with his own society. That he had left his people for dead. They were now joined to the throngs of banished people wandering aimlessly around the world, always searching and always lost, and who created more banished people wherever they went.

You give people no choice, the Harbor Master, sick of sitting in swan shit, shouted at the television. *You want them to be like you—a lost man. Like you did to this girl here. What is she now? Hey? Tell me that? Come here now. I want to fight you.*

Now Oblivia was left to rescue the fallen swans herself, because the

Harbor Master and the monkey could not be bothered. They were too obsessed about having no real voice in the politics of Australia. Neither would leave the television for a minute. They were consumed in a running commentary about Warren Finch.

This massive consumption of electricity just for a television, and glut of injured or recuperating swans also consumed with television viewing, did not stop her from wanting to see herself on the television as well. Then finally—bingo! What a shock on the seven o'clock news. She quickly noticed the really small things that were totally opposed to how she thought about herself. Where were the downcast eyes for instance? Why the lack of self-consciousness? Where was the shame? How could she have agreed to allow people to stare at her like that? She had to adapt to the television picture of herself with fingernails painted red or pale pink, speaking through lipstick, looking from eyeliner and orderly designed hair, and how she moved with an air of confidence dressed in Marlene Dietrich clothes.

The Harbor Master said she looked beautiful but Warren Finch was an ugly man. These sightings of the president with his wife became more and more frequent the more that they watched the television together, so they had to surmise that Warren Finch was forcing the girl to go mad from seeing herself being paraded around as the wife he wanted her to learn to be. And equally alluring, they reasoned that these daily sightings of the Indigenous president of the newly created Australian Republic with his promise wife were intended to be very newsworthy to the viewing public that adored the country's first couple.

Yet there was more to think about. It had taken numerous glimpses of seeing herself masquerading around the place as Marlene Dietrich, for the girl to realize that Warren Finch was stealing parts of her life for his own purposes. *Yes, that was how he was covering up his mésalliance of a marriage with her.* She did not know how it happened, but somehow, a part of her life was being lived elsewhere with her husband. She came and went into a different life which Warren Finch returned through the television screen.

The Harbor Master and the monkey were deeply committed to their investigative arguments about this theft of her identity by an impostor—or not—and argued with Oblivia who believed it was her all right, and this gave them the excuse to be more or less glued to the television because why kill the dream, when otherwise they would have to be rescuing swans. They complained: *Wasn't the place crowded enough?* It was all they could think or speak about, including abusing that ugly man Warren Finch, saying *we are sick of you*, because they were stuck in an apartment with poultry swans. There were now so many of them nestled in the apartment it was hard to walk around the place without thinking you were in a stinking swannery. So the Harbor Master and Rigoletto, now covered in swan lice, sat tight in front of the television, unwilling to move unless it was absolutely necessary to feed themselves.

Oblivia had swans living on the rooftop where the cold wind whistled continuously, and now many needed to be released. She believed it was her job. It was the only reason why she was staying, and had not become a permanent television wife. Soon it would be the swan's breeding season and each swan would have to be reunited with the rest of the flock before their instincts to breed became too great, forcing them to panic on the rooftop and in the apartment, while attempting to escape.

Oblivia knew that she must take them to clear land, or to a large stretch of water so that they could have the space to run and take to the skies. She needed help to find this space in the city that sprawled like a maze in her mind, with neither the Harbor Master nor the monkey interested in helping her. They were more interested in Warren Finch than swans, or becoming lost in the city, and said if she wanted help: *Ask Warren Finch's Mr. Machine to take you to the genie shop.*

Machine was sitting in an armchair on the ground floor with his favorite white cat wrapped around his neck like a scarf; it chewed the man's hair as though it was feathers. When Machine saw Oblivia standing in front of him with a piece of paper signed by Warren Finch, saying he should help her relocate the swans, he shouted in shock. *Well! Well! Well!* He was surrounded by misted water spurting several meters high from a colossal fish mouth and falling, but that he was damp did not worry him. He just kept swinging along to the amplified sound coming through the loud speakers of Dean Martin singing *Houston,* while a pile of damp cats purring and snarling at the white cat tumbled all over him. *What's the matter? You want a tour of dilapidation? Want to see the ruined city or something?*

Machine said he would need some time to study the street guide—an old disused book he pointed to on the table beside him that was half a meter thick. He thought it would be very difficult to work out the easiest directions to reach the magic shop she was talking about. *Okay.* This was a skewed dream of a city, he explained, with tidal surges at any time, and in saying he never liked people much, asked whether she realized that there were millions of them rushing around right outside their door—people doing anything to save themselves in the day to day? Mostly he grumbled about how the city was stuffed and nobody cared what it looked like anymore. *Everything is falling down around you. Nothing is getting fixed up. Pigeons are flying everywhere. The sky is full of them. I have seen thousands of the things circling around this building alone. Their shit—falling everywhere. They call this globalized depression. I call it shit. Subsistence life. The trouble of being micro-managed by the government with intervention this, and intervention that, until passivity breeds the life out of you and you may as well be dead. You want to become like that? It was an absolute disgrace. You are better off staying where you are—inside.* But still, because Warren Finch's signature was on the note, he agreed to take her there, but only at night for these reasons: hatred of sunlight, and because he did not like walking around in the city during the day when it was crowded, although even the Harbor Master had told her that in reality, he had only seen dribs and drabs. It was a ghost city. Hardly anyone lived there any more after the thousands of unemployed people had moved away and disappeared into thin air apparently. Machine patted his knee cat and said: *Be ready when you hear a knock on the door.*

After several hours of waiting that night and being scared out of her wits, there was a scratching sound on the other side of the door. *Quando! Quando?* The Harbor Master interrupted what he called, *another bloody quandary to deal with,* and told her straight to *F–N straighten up*, and that she had better get used to answering the door. The lice-scratching monkey agreed, and claimed the Harbor Master was a natural mastermind at getting things done in a timely fashion.

So! Olé! She answered the door and found an owl sitting there. The little bird busy scratching with its beak was disturbed by the door opening and flew off in fright. It descended slowly down the atrium. Instinctively, the girl knew the owl wanted to be followed, and even more than this, she thought that Machine had become the owl—the one that had been promised to her by the genies. She quickly looked at all of the swans jumbled into the apartment honking over the top of the sound of the television: *Take/me! Take/me!* She quickly grabbed the swan with the strongest wings flapping in readiness for flight, and left dressed in her darkest clothes with the hood of her jacket pulled down over her head as she entered the lane outside.

Out into the rainy night, and walking quickly through street after street and lanes and darkened alleyways with the swan in Warren Finch's knapsack strapped over her back, with her mind swinging around in her head about why she had not been smart enough to see what was not visible to anyone else, such as the owl-like features in Machine's face, she followed the owl that could have been him.

The owl kept a hasty pace in its flight. There was no time for fainthearted indifference about whether she should follow it or not, though she was being taken far away from The People's Palace. Any idea of how to return had not dawned on her yet, although she was keen to return as quickly as possible in case she had to be transformed into Warren Finch's television wife again—because she was forced to go everywhere with him. *In your dreams*, the monkey claimed, *Let's escape. Why not kill Warren if we ever see him again? Then we can all go back to the swamp.* How? How played over in her mind a thousand times a day. What a word *how* was. It could drive anyone mad. The owl flew on oblivious to any quandary she was having about needing to be somewhere else. Even if she had changed her mind and wished she had never left, it was too late. The owl kept her alert to its sudden shifts in direction, and often flew high to cross buildings while she had to run down and around them while lugging the heavy swan, to find a way to keep following. She was convinced that the creature wanted to lose her in the labyrinth.

The air was like ice. Massive clouds soared across the skies of the city. A hard wind blew the owl along until finally it landed on a lamp post in front of a long-abandoned, boarded and nailed-up shop where, on the business sign, painted monkeys and owls danced across faded yellowish words that she was barely able to read, *The World of Magicians and Genies*. The owl shook itself to end its flight, and then suddenly flew straight through a crack in the deserted building.

This was how the world stood in the darkness, but whenever a rouge neon light flickered brightly, it lit up the street, and she could see behind the boards and inside the shop. But genies were oblivious of time. A rose fragrance that had been sprayed in the shop for decades by those who had worked there, was still in the air of this otherworldly, something not of this time, unbridled to time perhaps, magic shop that brought it back into existence.

The first thing she noticed as light flashed into the building was movement on the floor. It was alive with the city's lizards and skinks that had gathered in the warmth of the room. Perhaps, she thought, they were participating in a historical conference about old homelands when lizards lived in trees. The desks where the genies had sat looked as though they had been gathering work for hundreds of years, while the books that they had written in had grown into tall mountains. She could see the notes and drawings they had left behind, notes about the measurements they had been taking of grass owls, seashells, seeds, feathers and odd things like that.

There were elderly owls in the room. Not local. These came from other wild places in the world. The old owls sat very still and civilized on perches, so as not to waste their breath on life's flippancies. Only the younger owls did that—flying soundlessly to and fro across the room—leaving and returning from the city streets. The room's other large bird life consisted of several old rare and valuable parrots that preserved the entire history of their species inside their heads. Who knows why the genies wanted them saved? What could anyone do with information about what no longer existed?

The girl heard the parrots chatting about the ordeal of traveling across the world aboard bankrupt ships with the genies. These vessels were now rotting down in the harbor. Permanently anchored. Saved up for a rainy day. She thought the parrots looked lucky to be living in perpetuity in this ageless room. They would always remain perched on their ornate bird stands studded with pearls, but deep inside their little ticking hearts, she knew they looked around their diminished world, and pondered where they had ended up.

Sometimes the homesick parrots' thoughts caught them in a nostalgic moment, and they would suddenly utter words from ancient languages. The girl watched the parrots waste their knowledge; their rare and valuable words disappearing into thin air. Never to be spoken again when the lost languages faded away.

Well! Holy! Holy! The swan flew in the dead of the night. Its faith was in itself. The great black bird had struggled to be free from the girl's arms and like a racehorse, ran in the direction of the neon sun where three strange men had appeared. They may have only been drunks, or spies sent by Warren Finch to keep an eye on her, but slunk away when noticed, and disappeared in the fog.

The great swan was soon in the air, wings spread in slow flight, just above Oblivia who was running after it down the street. The swan was completely savvy about directions in the city and took shortcuts, for within minutes she was back inside the lane. *Where you been?* Odd Machine was waiting at the door, angry but relieved that she had come back. He complained about how lonely he was, but she sped past him and ran back up to her apartment. The healed swan joined others outside in flight paths leading to the eel pond in the botanical gardens in the center of the city where flocks of great numbers were assembled for the night.

Now swans were set free every night. Oblivia had faith in the owl with the Dean Martin *Houston* song stuck in its head, as it flew continually waving and gliding and twisting its body as it looked around, to suddenly change course over buildings. She followed its flight through the darkness on whatever route it took, keeping the bird in sight, and knew that the owl would always end up in front of the abandoned magic shop.

It did not matter that the owl's destination was just around the corner from The People's Palace and that she was pursuing the owl over vast distances for nothing. She told the Harbor Master and the monkey that an ordinary, logical route was not the point. If she had walked there herself in the most direct route possible, she would never have found the old genie's shop on the long-abandoned street where the city's ghosts came at night, and where it was best to release swans returning to flight. It was the desire she followed, of completing an arduous journey that allowed her to see the right perspective of the neon sun shining through cracks in the boarded-up frontage of the shop, and she grew stronger by imagining the genies still working in their workshop on the other side of the boards, and by believing that the spirits in this place—all of the ghosts that had never been taken home—also ran with the swan along the street, and helped it to fly. It was a ghost street. Very exciting: there were thousands of ghosts there. She had seen them herself, she claimed, although the Harbor Master and Rigoletto were not really convinced about her story. They knew a thing or two about ghosts.

Rigoletto sang his anthem, "Questa o Quella." Badly sung opera was enough for the street kids to stop using the lane. They left, while shouting that whoever was singing like a monkey should stop. The gangs found something new to do, and gathered on the street corners waiting, to follow the owl leading the darkly clothed and hooded girl with a swan under her arm, or sometimes slung over her back.

The street kids kept their distance from Oblivia staring at the boarded-up building. They punched each other in the head to stand back to pay a bit of respect for the traditional owner of the land. They wondered whether she was just mad, you know, having gone crazy in the city, and crept in closer to see over her shoulder. None had the girl's ability to visualize how the genie's shop had once been, of seeing the tiny birds buzzing inside an antique Chinese aviary constructed of wire that had once been forged into decorative swirls. She ignored their voices whispering in her ear, *What are you looken at, sis?*

Inside the aviary flew the smallest hummingbirds in the world— but only if you thought of them flying, flying from cone-like nests in which they slept. The more she stared at the stillness of the nests, the more the hummingbirds would become animated, and would begin darting around the fresh flowers inside the cage. The street children were oblivious to the ghosts of the street crowding around them to watch the hummingbirds, but they felt that there must be something special about the building, and were organizing a break-in.

Oblivia knows that her nights on the streets will not last long and she ignores the owl flitting around the light poles to catch insects, and the street children breaking into the building. She has too many other things to think about. For instance, she never knows when she will have to dress up again to appear on television—and what if Warren was already at the apartment waiting to pick her up? Already she feels that she will not be living in the apartment much longer. Feels it in her bones. Even the Harbor Master was packing his things.

Ships' bells can be heard far away in the harbor, and the black swan released from her arms stands alone and confused on the empty wet street. Each swan was the same; uncertain about its ability to fly again until the wind off the changing tide pushed it along, and its webbed feet would start running down the road with their heavy load. The wind gusting along this corridor grew in intensity, and soon picked up the running swan and pushed it into flight.

The neglected city had thousands of pigeons flying around the roof-tops of buildings, and trees sprouting out of the sides of cathedrals, chestnuts growing from the alcoves; fig tree roots clung to the walls, and almond and apple trees grew from seeds that flourished in the damp cracks. In these trees while pigeons and pet budgerigars slept, down below the troupe of owl, girl and swans traveled with a mul-titude of ghosts. Their parade implied a pilgrimage, a dedication to their never forgone longing for what was and had been, a prolonged hurting, like the Portuguese word *saudades*, describing the deep yearning of those left in limbo, and the melancholy dream passing through every quiet street in the city. Then Oblivia would again feel an excitable urge exploding in her stomach, to rush back to the apartment in double-quick time before dawn, for she was always hoping to become the television wife, to see herself as greatly loved, with the jubilant political husband—head-of-state world leader—to actually experience what it felt like to be beside someone like this, and which would prove once and for all it really was her in the picture, that she felt this love seen on television, and by establishing her authentically beyond any measure of doubt to the Harbor Master and the stupid monkey.

In those nightly pilgrimages they heard the *Monteverdi* vespers sung over the droning of ancestor country. The winds whistled through the buildings, and through the skies, she was able to see that many swans were gathering in each ancient breath, and their flight formed landscape through the perpetual rain.

Yes, the swans were multiplying, nesting among flooded trees, reeds and swan weed, and had already overfilled ponds in the abandoned botanical gardens and a small lake in the city's zoo, then the city's shallow lakes where they were breeding along the bays, gullies and inlets.

At night, squadrons of swans flew up and down the brown-colored river that cut through the city, and Oblivia sensed they were in training for something even they had not quite anticipated. She thought that they were trying to tell her something. The thought shifted around in her mind—floated here and there while it grew, and then she was tossing it around something big, throwing it about, slamming it against the wall of her brain, until it became something ugly and angry, too hot to hold, too tough to manipulate and examine, the thing that she was too afraid to recognize—that not only was there was a lack of communication in her so-called marriage, feelings of betrayal, manipulation, and abandonment were the goalposts where havoc scored inside her head.

The thought stuffing up her mind made her angry, and she tramped on in the nightly parade, unable to concentrate on the swans flying up and down the river. Well! What was the problem? Obsession. Television wife. She started to ask herself questions: Why was she always in a hurry for someone she only saw on television? Who she only knew through the television? Where each image was a portrait of a happy marriage? Even she believed it. And whenever she saw herself on television, she could only explain herself in sketches of what she appeared to be—the image presented, rather then remembering her actual presence as Warren Finch's wife, and always, forgetting the details of ever being with this man who was her husband. She could not remember him—had no idea, even what he looked like unless she saw him on the television. But none of these things mattered really. What really mattered was that she could not admit to herself that Warren was using an impostor. *Of course,* the Harbor Master kept explaining with the impact of discovering nuclear energy, *the big high-and-mighty Warren Finch doesn't want to be seen with some complete myall like you for a wife. She is the pretend wife. Not you at all.* But, Oblivia wouldn't believe it. Could feel it in her bones that she was the television wife. She promised herself, the Harbor Master and the monkey, she would prove it.

Of course they wanted to know how she was going to do that. But her mind slipped, went slack, played tricks on her and, without the steam to propel the thought, she again concentrated on the swans, following them with poetry running through her brain, *The swan has leaped into the desolate heaven: that image can bring wildness, bring a rage to end all things, to end* . . . The swans continued the circuit and she followed while she thought less about the apartment, and more about the need to keep up with flight. They were communicating with her about flight, long flight, not about Warren Finch who was living it up elsewhere—resuming life as usual as the head of state of a dilapidated country in a dilapidated world.

The monkey had changed too. It decided to move out of the apartment because it had become too dirty. He had heard the girl talk about seeing poor, neglected monkeys in the zoo. He became very excited and left quietly in the middle of the night when the Harbor Master was asleep in front of the television. He went to the zoo and unlocked the door to the monkey house. From then on, he was the head honcho of a dancing troupe of monkeys that went to live as fugitives in the cathedral in the city, among the almond and fig trees growing from crevices in its sandstone walls. Free at last, the monkeys were popular buskers in the city malls. Always cashed up to pay the street children for protection.

The Harbor Master stayed home sulking about the monkey becoming independent and the apartment being emptied of swans. He sat on the couch. He was in rough seas with the Panasonic television that blared old cricket games in the apartment night and day. Games that had been played years ago, and in between the news, where he could watch Warren Finch's face growing older every day. But there was no great satisfaction in watching someone grow older. Well! Not the face that never reached the destination of fulfillment, where Warren's continuing triumphs—each seemingly more glorious than any before— were always sensed as personal failure.

Yes, the Harbor Master still preferred to glare at the television. It was as though he was trying to steer the whole darn spectacular life of Warren Finch from the couch, propelling him along blasphemously, while hollering over some invisible howling rain, *You know, people can talk and talk about how they are going to save the Aboriginal, world, ditto people . . . it goes on all the time, always wanting to save people who would rather talk about how they want to save themselves. When are you going to start thinking straight about that, Mr. Warren Bloody Finch?*

Well! Let's end the bad vibes with the cricket bats and kneepads that were all flying about the room. Why be so unhappy? Any of Warren Finch's newest major concerns were challenging to the old Harbor Master. He always had to prove how he had seen better, or knew about something that was absolutely more amazing in some off-beaten track of the world to laugh about. Still! You could not avoid the fact that Warren's life was being lived at a higher percentage elsewhere with the glamorous "promise" wife, the First Lady of whatnot, than being wasted in hanging around, and minding reality in a swan-filthy apartment.

THE STREET SERPENT

This was not all you will see in the city, this junkyard from where swan flocks ascended into the heavens, and flew the brisk breeze among swallows and pigeons up where ghosts shouted down: *What a load of rubbish!* But the swans overcrowding in the botanical gardens were edgy with hunger. They searched for swampy waters and found nothing. These old luckless things could only return to the abandoned sprawl of overgrown gardens, to roam among the butterflies and insects. A place that served no purpose to city people who grew nothing, but ate their food from packets. They called this sprawling greenery *a flippen and friggen untidy mess!* And saw no point to having this old fashioned, overgrown park in a city where there were people starving—better off living off the Government, and safer on the streets, like those living in the lane.

You could watch people like that walking by the old city's botanical gardens that made them think of a nursery rhyme for children, of still believing the city's legendary story that this tangled mess of brambles was the home of an overgrown *Lepus europaeus* called the hare king, but otherwise ignoring the place, applying the same sense of invisibility usually given to anything useless, obscure and made redundant. This landscape was once prized throughout the world as having the richest library of the most precious, rare and extinct flora on Earth.

The people in this city did not regularly use words like *once upon a time* for being nostalgic and remembering things, but once, when it was hoped that the bad weather would change back to normal climatic patterns, the city had also hoped that the historical richness of the site would never be lost. Whatever was within man's power to save his environment was done for the rare old trees, flowers and shrubs, but in the end the struggle to save greenery seemed meaningless. The long drought killed kindness in hardened hearts. Then, when the drought was replaced by soddening rains, year in and year out, the canopy grew into an impenetrable wilderness too dangerous to people, and the precinct was just another place locked up forever.

Oblivia ignored the rusty old signs. What were signs to her? These ones were wired all along the fence of wrought iron. She did not bother reading the warning of the dangers of entering, or notice what the penalties were for trespassing in neglected areas such as these old botanical gardens. The signs that might have once stopped homeless people squatting, now robbed the city's memory of the gardens. Who in the street life of the city would guess why such a wasteland had ever been created? It was as though places of antiquity had lost their usefulness to those who lived for the moment, the here and now, and where the gates were forced shut by boa-constrictor thick renegade vines, wound like a monster's woven carpet throughout the wrought iron lacework.

The swans circling in the sky above the neglected gardens guarded the green leafiness of their island in the city, while people who had come from other parts watched the phenomenon like it was a thing of wonder. The Chinese people, who had long lived in the city, praised each sighting of swan flight for its momentary beauty, and called the swans *hong* in their own language. A story floated around the Greek side of the city, of likening the swans circling the island of wilderness to a long ago belief of a mystical island surrounded by white swans where Apollo was born. These were all poor people's stories. A good feeling was left in the air from seeing swans, they said. The air felt lucky. Even—prosperous. Safe. Warren Finch was in the city. Everyone felt in a blood-tingling way that something big was about to happen.

• • • •

All of the broken birds had been set free from the apartment in The People's Palace, and now, in the botanical gardens, Oblivia was watching the assembling swans swarm in numbers so vast they blocked the moonlight. But this freak of nature plagued her. When had her swans bred? Where had time gone? How many seasons of swans' breeding had passed by and she had not noticed? How long had she lived in the city?

This was the reason why she never went to the genies' magic shop anymore. It was not just that the owl never returned once all of the swans had been released, or even that the owl's memory had receded from her mind as silently as its flight. It was how she had been kept captive, while time had been stolen from her in those long nocturnal journeys following the owl around the streets with a swan under her arm. Now she knew there had been many seasons of swan-egg cradling and cygnets reared which signaled above all else, that she had spent more time in the city than she had ever expected.

The girl had not even thought about saying *goodbye* or *sayonara* to Machine, nor said *yunngu*, that she was going away for good, nor a simple *ciao* to the Harbor Master. Leaving was leaving. Nothing more than a curious unemotional response—a flatness of spirit for the flight inward when being removed from places, as it had from being pulled off the hull and before that, from the tree. She left Machine to piss around in his own fairy tale. Left him mooning over his cats. The Harbor Master? Left imagining why his monkey had just trucked off for nothing, and to blow his mind away with whatever took his fancy about Mr. Fat Cat, Indigenous leader of the country, Warren Finch on television.

She had just kept walking, barely noticing the network of overgrown hedges reaching for the sky inside the wrought iron fence surrounding the botanical garden. When she was far away into the park steaming with early-morning mist, she no longer heard the skin and bone dogs barking on the street outside. The street kids and their dogs still followed her from the lane as though she was some kind of reclusive ghost kid, just like an Aboriginal Tinker Bell fairy. Would she lead them somewhere? That was the thrill of it all.

But now, outside the botanical gardens, they held back and just hung about on the footpath, too augured in dusty city mythologies of what lay beyond the gates—where they heard thousands of noisy myna birds pealing hotly at one another from orange aloe flowers growing all over the place like weeds, and flying aggressively through the dense undergrowth. Their dogs panted for water beside the legs of their owners, while all the while the ghosts from the park were out there in the street in broad daylight, whispering scary stories close into the ears of the children about this and that, but mostly about the troubles of dark nights in this wilderness, and scaring the dogs stupid too.

Where was the guidance from elders? It was the cruelest fate for children of bad-weather times, whose brains had been clogged with mysteries of their own making, more than you could imagine—where would you believe? The skies were haunted with the ghosts of swallows and pigeons flying about. Among the throng of children out there on the footpath, their Mohawk-haired leaders of skin and bone were swearing black and blue at their mad dogs snapping at the air. These animals saw invisibility better than anything real, and everything untrustworthy, while all the while, they went on lurching madly about on their chains.

Well! What would you expect? This was not an ashram out on the street. Theirs was a city that bred the jumpiness of sissy-girl boys who normally saw ghosts flying about—right above the streets. They always pointed out the ghosts traveling through the mist and smoke rising over the city—and even traveling procession-like in the sky trains of diseased bats. Well! Lucky virus bats were asleep. They were dangling upside down through several groves of trees in the old botanical gardens.

And what of the Aboriginal girl they followed? That skinny thing in dark trackies, hoodie covering her face with the swans flying around her? Well! If you think like a sissy girl, then she was not real neither. They saw her as a spiritual ancestor because they knew what an Aboriginal looked like, since they were modeling their subsistence as it were, albeit only on junk food, on the country's original inhabitants. She was their backfill now.

possibly be? *Warren at last visiting . . .* The apartment felt as though it had become alive.

A sensation of phenomenal energy swishing around madly— horizontally bouncing from one wall to the other, and each time it passed, cold air slapped the Harbor Master across the face until he had been struck countless times.

It had to be Warren Finch who lay dying on a stretcher on television too lifeless to look at his watch or answer his mobile phone, but he had come back to the apartment like a crazy person with no time to spare, and acting like he could not find his favorite pair of socks. Well! He left everything in his path upturned and strewn, because sure enough, he would not be staying long. His voice was another matter: it was like a large ball at the end of a piece of rope being dragged into the ear of the Harbor Master, as well as Machine downstairs with his cats—*Where is she?*

Then the Harbor Master snapped. He felt very alone with the solemn television presenter who was trying to become his friend while he spoke intimately about the life of Warren Finch who lay covered in bloodied sheets on the stretcher, and as the journalist was trying to speak with the ambulance men frantically working with drips and life-saving equipment, they moved to take Finch to a hospital. But, the old man was no longer in the mood to know whether Warren Finch was dead or alive. He packed his bag in a jiffy, all his clothes (not much), found the monkey's exotic clothes of course, and after a quick, final glance around the apartment, he left very speedily, through the gushing fountains, and the mist settling on the mossy statues. He walked straight past the openly crying Machine who was hugging his wailing cats, and was all too occupied watching the television to notice the front door slamming and the Harbor Master screaming, *Where is the wife in grief?*

The swans have all gone to the sky, but the sound of their wings beating quickened every beat in the girl's heart. Swish! Swish! The sounds resonated, but she felt only the familiar claustrophobic sense of being trapped in a confined space, a place where her vision had been reduced to a keyhole view, of being slung back into the roots of the ancient eucalyptus tree. It was a view she had seen before, a blanket of swans forming into a giant bird in flight.

But this world was falling apart, and the girl's heart raced like a trapped animal looking for the fastest way out. There were voices everywhere now with the news spreading quicksilver through the dense population in the streets. Yes. The city itself was screaming for her, beckoning, beseeching, or if you like, crucially confronting her with its great pain by trying to pull her into its troubles. *Ahhh! Ahhh! NO! She's looking the other way. Is she actually doing that? Her husband is dying for pity's sake. Don't go. She is running away. Come quickly! Come back you somebody. Somebody! Stay!* The city people cried a million buckets of tears for their famous Warren Finch to live. But! But, this president's wife, she was a very good question indeed. What was she doing? Where was she? The problematic promise bride who had turned up from nowhere! Her name being just too plain forgettable and foreign—the real heart of the issue: Who would remember such a fictitious, ridiculous name? *Where are you, you person?*

She barely heard the quibbling of thousands of people calling for her around the city. It was really more the memory evoked from long ago, that warned her to keep running from painful voices falling over the reeds in the swampland to reach her—bowling over the beauty of wild flowers that were kind of special, and crackling branches of trees where dozy fruit bats had fallen flat on the ground.

Now she could be seen by the swans in the sky as she ran around the marshy lake in the botanical gardens, and through the hare king's bramble tunnels where she sees the gray hare run off in front of her, and heads after it loping through paths that the foxes had dug. All the while she is looking skyward—trying to keep up with her swans flying overhead in the cloud, and needing not to lose them, she must stay under their shadow. It is as though she is running in somebody else's dream, where someone like Warren Finch is calling—*fly me to the moon.* She sees the three genies too. They are like giants standing in passing clouds, talking to one another while they struggle to steer the swans flying wildly away from the city. *Listen! Can't you hear? She's making a wish. She wants to fly with the swans so that they do not leave her behind.*

Swans were not the answer in times like this. The big birds were struggling up there in the sky. A changed wind blowing in from the opposite direction was so strong that the wings of the swans were being buffeted. The wind circled like a cyclone and carried everything in its path towards the center of the city, including people hurtling through the streets who had wanted to see their visiting head of state. The swan wings became sails that were being blown backward in squalls moving towards the noise of thousands of screaming people caught in the storm in the streets where Warren Finch had just been assassinated.

Whether she ran or not in dreams of other things, nothing could change the fact about running against the wind, for she was back next to Warren Finch. Beside him, she felt strangely reunited to the moment when he had left the apartment on the day long ago when she had arrived in the city. She still feels the strength of his control even as he lies flat over her lap. She cannot move from his weight, but her mind switches uncontrollably in a futile struggle. She shivers with the shock of finding herself beside Warren, replacing the television wife, even though in her mind, she is still chasing after the hare king through raspberry brambles. Alone and exposed, she recognizes the faces of the street kids placed here and there among the crowds falling over her, hears the approaching sounds of sirens of police cars and ambulances speeding through the city. She feels terrified because they will think that she has killed him. She does not remember, does not know what has happened anymore. Was she just chasing the hare king? Everywhere the voices of police on loud speakers rip apart both reality and dreams, and she focuses on the helicopters hovering haphazardly low, with rotor blades whirling where the swans are flying above her.

The pains of distance roar through her like a flood emptying into insignificance, that leaves behind, as in dry plains, a surreal indifference in the midst of chanting crowds that have become hundreds of thousands deep, and still throng on the streets, as police desperately try to force through an ambulance. Hemmed in by the cries and screams, she is stuck, unable to leave, and cowers into Warren's limpness. There is no chance of escaping, except when she looks upwards to the swans correcting their flight above the narrow street with the sudden disappearance of the wind. He is going now.

The doors of the ambulance were quickly pushed closed, but nothing can move through the outpouring of grief from the surging crowds blocking the road. In this bedlam, where there is no control over what is happening, the security people manage to create a barrier and have the body loaded into a helicopter precariously hovering above the buildings. The girl-wife is left behind while the helicopter makes its way to the hospital, but the crowds break through the barrier in efforts to express their grief to her. She is enveloped in a sea of hands. Strangers one after the other shake her hand, tearfully hug her, and pass her on to the next person in grief, and the next, until she is lost and drowning in the crowds. She is pulled by this tide of grief through the city streets, packed with people crying and praying, people determined to express their gratitude to her, for the man who had watched over the global security of all peoples, whom they had known as Warren Finch.

The long day slipped into evening and by this time there were the hands of the monkeys, street children, the Harbor Master, security guards, police, the genie minders—strangers steering her into the night.

A mother of all storms could grieve too, along with all those sad old country and western songs piped through the flooding city streets that carried, among other drifting things, an abandoned Chinese dragon that only yesterday had played a bamboo flute sweetly from its mouth to evoke a desert homeland, when the mythical creature danced a thousand-year-old ceremony through this foreign and soulless city as a welcome to the new president. Well! Its festival was over. So were the drums, and the clanging cymbals, the big brass band, the Scots Highland bagpipes, and all the jazz and gospel choirs, as well as the spinifex dancers with clapping sticks in front of the swans dancing with wings spread wide. These people had welcomed the President of Humanity they treated like a living God with death. They were all probably sleeping now.

• • • •

Oblivia, the missing wife of the assassinated president, emerged through the large open mouth of the dragon. She looked around, still not knowing whether she had killed Warren Finch or not, and then stepped out into the ghost fog that rested its old body over the city. There had been another cyclone during the night and a tidal surge had flooded many of the city's streets. She held on to the golden tentacles that flowed along the side of the multicolored creature with mirrored scales, while it rocked and moved effortlessly through the darkness.

Only the monkey living in the main street's cathedral was up this early. It was listening to the silence of traditional Country—the only sound it believed belonged to this city. The monkey was way up high, sitting in a small fig tree that grew out of the steepled roof of the sandstone cathedral. He began saying his morning prayers to his distant monkey God, this God and that God, the God of the church where he lived. Prayers that took forever, until he could no longer concentrate on what he was praying for, or even believing which God loved him equally with other Gods. He started looking down through the lonely fog spirit traveling through the city, hoping nostalgically for a dawn chorus of songbirds that no longer existed. Then the monkey had to remind itself that some old habits died hard. The white furry creature sung a religious hymn of joyous awesomeness about how he too had become invisible like the gods, and how he actually felt magician-like. He could disappear then return to life again without even knowing it had happened.

It is only Rigoletto, a flock of common myna birds squawked as they flew out of the cathedral's nave, *that religious monkey from Asia*. The monkey ignored bird chatter, particularly that of starlings, crows and myna birds. He believed that he was too good for screechy types of birds. He preferred to think of himself as an old gentlemanly monkey that looked down at life, like he was now looking down at fog ghosts, but this time was different. He saw the Chinese dragon floating along the street with a cold-looking bony girl clinging to the side.

From so far above, he was not sure whether it was the girl he was supposed to be looking after or not. Rigoletto's eyes were not like they used to be, even if he could clearly remember a time in his life that was spent snatching fruit, and stuffing his mouth with a whole peeled mandarin while performing multiple somersaults on the top of a stick all day long for tourists. You need good eyes for that. He often reflected about this magnificent feat, and about how this so-called land of opportunity had robbed him of his spontaneity and each point-zero-zero-zero-one-half-of-a-percent of a dollar he could have earned from performing the trick right throughout Asia. He doubted whether he had the heart for showing off this kind of trick now. He felt that a big devil in this country had gutted him of every bit of spontaneous happiness he had in his body. Now he casually looked down with an accusing eye at the fog ghosts just to show—he knew it was her.

Rigoletto sprung from his perch in a heavy free-falling fashion that felt as though his body was full of lead, and in no time at all, he had scaled down the wall of the cathedral and half swam, half ran through the storm water, until he too was holding on to the dragon's golden tentacles to save himself. He worked his way along the dragon until he was behind Oblivia and peering over her shoulder and looking at her face, to make sure it was *her*. Lo and behold, it screeched. It was the Harbor Master's *gardée*.

This made the monkey very angry. He leapt in front of Oblivia, splashed about in what resembled a sort of dog paddle, and dealt with the crisis by thrusting himself as stiff as a board in and out of the water, and screamed his native language into her face to ask her what she was doing, which in Australian English meant: *You are crazy. What in the bloody hell's name are you thinking? Don't you know what you are doing? Haven't you got a clue in your head?* He swallowed a lot of water from screaming his lungs out for nothing in all forms of language. Swallowed language. Moral language. Peace and harmony language. Religious language. Angry language. Law language. Culture language. Political language. Enthusiastic language. Monkey language. The wings of language will never again fly so triumphantly in the soulless country. If the monkey wanted Oblivia to go back inside the dragon where she would be safe, she paid no attention to a single thing it said.

Instead, Oblivia looked straight through the monkey as though it never existed, and concentrated on the low fog shrouding the high-rise glass buildings on both sides of the street. Her eyes focused on the darkened haze of a cloud of flying swans with steam flowing out of their nostrils, their wings laboring in flight from pulling the strings attached to the dragon, pulling it ahead. She heard a voice coming from the water—coming all of this way from somebody's final resting place. Warren Finch's voice, teasing as he tried to hop on board the dragon of great hope and expectations, almost as mighty as the dawn swans flying Apollo's chariot while he pulled the sun across the sky. *Are you trying to escape?*

Then he was gone. Or it may have just been the monkey Rigoletto complaining as he swung himself behind her again, and when he had a good grip of some golden tentacles, he kicked her for all of his troubles, and as many times as he could to force her towards the dragon's mouth. But nobody feels the kicks of an invisible, oppressed, and foreign-to-boot monkey that did not like living in Australia. The defeated monkey ended up sitting on top of the dragon sulking, while nervously chewing bubble gum in its big teeth.

As he looked around the deserted and broken city, it was only a cheap form of advertising that managed to fly around his head. The flittering myna birds had spied an audience to spread their same old government propaganda about generous household assistance that they had been trained to sing for peanuts. Worthless incentives. The monkey had no need for a government. He stubbornly turned his flat face this way and that, looked into space, and was not buying any of it. He was more concerned about myna birds alerting the security people.

Rigoletto already knew that the flooded city was being scoured from top to bottom to find the girl-wife from a call he had received on his miniature mobile phone. The phone's ringtone went ding dong all night, until he answered it. It was the Harbor Master hollering into his ear that the girl was all there was left now for the people of the world that had gone into mourning after Warren Finch's assassination.

Listen! the absent Harbor Master chattered into the complaining monkey ear: *She was his wife so of course they want to find the only living thing that they think was close to their dead legend who they reckoned had championed peace for people across the world, even if he didn't, and was only a self-proclaimed Indigenous hero who had made it all the way to the top in a suit and haven't I told you before about the importance of looking well dressed in a suit, because it goes to show that even an Aboriginal man in Australia can get elected by the common Aboriginal-hating people to be the head of state of Australia, and that was a very good thing, even if it was the best thing that ever happened to the flippen what have you country, and now some mongrel moron still had to come along and murder him out of jealous racist spite. So, don't groan—of course she has to be found, even if you and I KNOW she was not close to him, and she can't save them from themselves, but she still belongs to these people because she is still the First Lady of whatnot.*

Any little monkey could rattle off a litany of worse things happening in his world, but Rigoletto sat with a steely red face on the dragon, and thought very seriously about prescribed responsibility as the worst kind of thing that could have happened to him. It was the only problem he had with being a pet monkey. He knew that he was supposed to step in like a man instead of just being a monkey and become the girl's guardian if the Harbor Master was not around, although very clearly, he recognized that the act of guardianship over others did not come naturally to him. He hated being trained to act responsibly. There was nothing in it. He was not the Harbor Master's pet monkey by any stretch of the imagination.

It was moments like these where a few guilty pangs forced Rigoletto to forget he was supposed to be a pet by acting like a wild animal. A wild animal was not supposed to look after people. It was supposed to be the other way around. Where was the beauty in a monkey worrying about people? His brain bolted from the reality of floating along a flooded city street on a magnificent but ruined dragon. His idea of beauty lay tens of thousands of kilometers away where long-necked swans foraged for insects in muddy rice fields with the swallows, in a world that enjoyed listening to exquisite plum-blossom music being played on a bamboo flute. He held this thought. He hummed through bubble gum sticking between his clicking teeth, and did not lose any sense of the flute's musicality in his own rendition of the plum- and cherry-blossom music that he had locked in his head.

These were only the delusional thoughts of a monkey that had enough troubles occupying his mind than to be bothered with fantasies being projected on him by the Harbor Master like, *You poor, old, good monkey.* He had the worries of a thousand monkeys. So *da, da, de, da, and la, la, la!* Presently, aloft on the dragon, his main worry was the soaking wet Rigoletto jacket. Would it shrink on his furry body and strangle him? A monkey sitting on a dragon in the middle of some common big-storms-of-climate-change-raising-sea-levels event was nothing to worry about. He hugged himself tight. Rigoletto had seen flooding on seaboard city streets all over the world. It was really just as natural as seeing water flooding in the lanes of Venice, Bangladesh or Pakistan.

Where are you Harbor Master? You got to come back. Rigoletto's experience of global warming was academic, not practical. He remained on guard while Oblivia continued to be dragged along with the dragon through the water, knowing that very soon she would be found. She was part of the most important story happening in the world right now. There could be no other way for the girl-wife. If she survived . . .

TRAVELING ROAD SHOW

I t was a terrific funeral. Everyone was saying just how marvelous it was. Best speeches. Good old-people's songs like: *Through the ages I will remember blue eyes crying in the rain.* Still the best bloke, that old Hank Williams, and others like him. But things took a turn for the worse after that.

The biggest cathedral in the country, where Warren Finch's body lay in state, kept overflowing with mourners. All sorts turned up to pay respects, including the everyday local mourners of the city. All those homeless people who would not go home. The poor from the streets and alleyway communes started elbowing for space with overseas dignitaries, heads of state of other countries—many with fragile diplomatic relationships with Australia. The earth's powerful demanded appeasement. They wanted their very own religious services. It all added up. No wonder the country was broke. Still, the country pulled together. It showed some respect and unity for the situation. Then other important people started filing through the door. World musicians wanted to play together for world peace. The world's most popular professional actors brought glitz and bling to mourning and paying respects to the big actor himself who had known them all. Even King

Billy kept calling into the city more and more tidal surges flooding through the streets, and up the steps of the cathedral.

All services for the dearly beloved, the mourning, the last respects, country and western music, hymns and special foreign music, were heard continuously, and on a daily basis. In actual fact, nobody thought a thing about the consequences of unabated mourning. Certainly, no one questioned the excessiveness of sorrow, and whether there was going to be an end point of mourning for Warren Finch. That was until finally, one day in the middle of a lot of smoke, what looked like most of the countryman's wildflowers and gum leaves arrived with scores of his ceremonial elders from his Aboriginal Government, and they sung his world. They said that they were smoking his spirit back to their own traditional country. *His spirit was no longer in this place.* This was when the sky practically fell down, when they—these people (his own people)—wanted to remove the coffin from the cathedral.

Total pandemonium broke out between all the different types of mourners until officials one, two and three, with more to follow, told these cheeky people from the bush of some far-flung part of the country with an unpronounceable name that nobody had ever heard of, that Warren Finch's importance as a man far outweighed any of their cultural considerations, *and hum! Peace, brother! Go in peace. Let that be the end of the matter.* Yet it was a stalemate! Stalemate! These people from the bush would not listen to anybody. They would not leave the coffin, and they just stood there among the choir singing, and made even greater smoke with their leaves, even though anyone could see that a long queue was forming behind them with urgent people becoming very irate.

The bush people wanted to talk about culture. No! Ears were only listening to the church choir. Everyone wanted to get firm now about this disturbance. These Aboriginal people were told to stop being un-Australian, and to leave—their time was up. Did they not understand that everyone had to take equal turns to stand next to the coffin? Move on! *Why?* the Aboriginal elders asked, *His spirit is gone now. Up in Country.* But their explanation would never do. Even if Warren Finch lay dead in his coffin, he was still head of state until someone else could take his place. *Was that possible? Yes.* He could still give advice and blessings to his government, just like he did when he was alive. And even though he was dead, he would always be one of the most loved world leaders that ever existed in the history of mankind. How could anyone argue about this? Who could replace him?

The more his Aboriginal people argued and argued, persisting it was their right to take his body home, as though his body was like that of a normal body of a kinsman and should be given a proper burial— the more they were treated like selfish people, and the more the idea of a final resting place became full of contention and attributed to the whole country's denial that Warren Finch was really dead, when they preferred to think of him as just sleeping like Sleeping Beauty.

Well! Grass grew. And the bush folk had made a permanent camp-site beside the coffin.

Finally, in a nasty episode of aghast, there was a string of official and much publicized questions raised about who these Aboriginal people were—who did they think themselves, and why had they turned up in the first place, and who had given them room to do native things without permission in the most important cathedral in the country, making everything feel tainted in their sorrow? Were they really Aboriginal? Did they really belong to Warren Finch's ancestral country? Anthropologists, lawyers and other experts like archaeologists, sociologists and historians were called to examine the genealogies of these people. An emergency legislation was bulldozed through parliament in the dead of night which claimed that Warren Finch was the blood relative of every Australian, which gave power to the government to decide where he was to be buried.

Ha! Ha! Ha! Roll in laughter, because it was funny, and thought inconceivable that Warren Finch could be buried in some wilderness place with no public access, where only a handful of Aboriginal people who knew the country would know how to get to his grave to say some prayers that they had made up themselves. There would be national prayers in time, legislated in a National Warren Finch Prayer Book. Would you trust Aboriginal people to stick to Australian law? The police were obliged under the regulations of emergency laws to intervene in the lives of all Aboriginal people, to throw the bush people out of the cathedral. Then, when there were no words left, and nowhere to live in a city that despised the presence of Aboriginal people, Warren Finch's clans-people went home.

The body remained in the cathedral, stuck there indefinitely in the smoky pall of burning coals—the incense of frankincense and myrrh, and emotional glue swelling in the brokenhearted city. The highly decorated coffin of the best black sassafras timber had been made by a master craftsman one hundred and fifty years before, who had willed the magnificent coffin to the nation for burying a great Australian man. This was the occasion, and the coffin was surrounded by burning candles, and adorned with the fresh bouquets of roses that kept arriving in the cathedral from rich people with enough money to keep sending roses grown on the plateaus of who knows where. The roses were piled into a mountain that mourners stumbled over, and spread like a range out into the frequently flooded streets.

There were no plans to bury the body. This was because no one in charge of the rare occasions of important world leader funerals seemed to consider it was necessary. It was not easy to make the final decision because as time kept passing with endless rows of grief callers parading by the coffin in the mass flowered cathedral, it was very easy to forget that the body had to be taken to a cemetery. Outside the cathedral, it was impossible to move through the city streets packed with fresh and decaying flowers and, every day, another round of mourners carrying *Farewell Warren* tributes on paper and cardboard signs held aloft on sticks.

And still more mourners came to see Warren Finch's coffin, pilgrim mourners weaving themselves through the country until they reached the country's most major cathedral, and kings and queens, counts and countesses, and other important overseas people who used up vast amounts of their country's wealth by emptying barrels of jet fuel to fly over vast distances and oceans to get to the cathedral. With the airport busy with flights, the tourist economy blossomed, so the Government kept welcoming visitors from the other side of the world. The mourners stood wherever they could in a slow line to the coffin.

As some more time passed, the infrastructure of the dilapidated city became an ever greater, uncontrollable mess. Rubbish everywhere. Power shortages. Infrastructure collapse. The sewerage system backing up and becoming clogged with nowhere to go. Stuff like that. Every foreign country dignitary expected to raise their own flag on the one flagpole outside the cathedral, have their own religious service, or the cathedral cleared of other nationals including Australians, or wanted a massive high-culture ceremony involving hundreds of their own nationals.

Whatever the homage, no one cared less if nobody else understood their foreign language, since the internal affairs of Australia figured way down the scale of worldly matters after Warren Finch's mysterious assassination which appeared more like stupidity, something that would have been easily avoided even in the tiniest and war-torn poorest countries of the world.

It was a form of greed really with everyone wanting a share of the grief, lingering and dilly-dallying in their worship around the city while negotiating greater opportunities for migration into the country to save it from this anarchy, and some settling in as immigrants and asylum seekers themselves, as though they wanted to become local, and not wanting to return home. Their airplanes parked all over the place stayed at the airport. There were highbrow questions raised about this: What was the role of a griever? It was not clear because no one had had to think about something like this before. Not in this city, state, or country.

The glut of reverence seemed as though nothing was good enough for Warren Finch after his death, a fact verified by the girl-wife who agreed to these proceedings. The Government people kept her whereabouts top secret, but she was just sitting around under lock and key in The People's Palace apartment. The redheaded family marched in and took over the executorial role of Warren Finch's immediate family. The pathetic, mourning Machine who was full of excuses for the girl escaping to the botanical gardens was ignored. He was told by Big Red to mind his own business, shut down his fountains spraying water all over the place, stop playing Dean Martin music, and to remove his cats. *And to do it pronto.*

Every day the security people in charge of *the widow* moved through the quieted building, to take her to the cathedral. The girl-wife widow, First Lady of whatnot, perhaps Presidential killer, became the object of consultation about the mourning business, where she was to shake hands and nod to whatever dignitary mourners were saying in their own languages. *I am looking for the swans, they are leaving,* she often told these people, mouthing the words soundlessly as usual, and gesturing with her hands. The diplomatic embassies looked puzzled as she tugged on their suit sleeves or ceremonial robes, yet they always followed her gaze around the nave in the cathedral, along the rafters, up in the hollow shell ceilings painted with frescos of angels with the wings of swans. *These are swans in a cage,* the French diplomat proclaimed to his people, and in the style of their old poet Baudelaire, they then murmured to each other, *And this swan, is castigating God.* The Harbor Master and the monkey Rigoletto always sat spellbound in a pew near the back of the cathedral. They were quite caught up with the razzmatazz surrounding the coffin, and the poetry the Frenchman recited, *A swan escaped its cage: and as its feet / With finny palms on the harsh pavement scraped, / Trailing white plumage on the stony street, / In the dry gutter for fresh water gaped . . .*

But, *here we are,* the whole country still cried and fretted for the loss of the irreplaceable Warren Finch, and asked: *Is this the best we can do?* Anyone would think that he had been the only Aboriginal person on the planet. The only one who had a voice, and could voice his opinion. He had become the only public Aboriginal voice of the era. The only one Australians would listen to, and reported in the newspapers, or had given their airways to whenever he spoke publicly. It certainly seemed as though there was national deafness to hearing what other Aboriginal people had to say of themselves. Perhaps it was the tone of voice? Or the message that could be heard, or could not be heard? Or the fact that the entire Aboriginal population bar this one individual did not have enough of the evangelical in their voices for proclaiming themselves sinners of their own race, like Warren Finch did on their behalf? Whatever the case, it seemed that the country was locked up inside a curse of national fever-pitch dimensions in its grief for this one

Aboriginal voice now dead, but still heard throughout the world. How can you describe such a tribute in sorrow? Imagine grief as art, where perfection above all else, was to be achieved. There was no doubt about it, that Warren Finch's life of striving for perfection had rubbed off on the nation that now emulated his life with perfect grief in pondering and procrastination, *How perfect could national grief be?*

A whole month more of silliness went by along with continual efforts to embalm the body to prevent decay, and then another month of flags continuing to fly at half-mast, until the major shock-jock news commentators took control. It was a field day of open slather about keeping an unburied body lying about in a public structure. In their broadcasting studios, they governed public opinion by plying paranoia into talk-back fever. The communication networks grasped the country in a teary anguished embrace of voices, crying for their opinions to be heard and listened to: *Why wasn't Warren Finch good enough to receive one last lap of honor? Wasn't an Aboriginal person good enough to be treated fairly and given the respect Australia gives to all of its other citizens?*

The city responded to its own questions by creating workplace strikes, protests, and rioting on the streets. The squatters burnt the abandoned buildings they had been living in. In the lanes of the city where the homeless lived, the grief found its own language. This nocturnal world destroyed everything that resembled its insular lifestyle by creating bonfires of every piece of cardboard shack they owned. Embracing grief escalated into a stranglehold of destruction and looting over the city. The streets overran with picketing mourners spurred on by a bellyful of Government conspiracies in their heads. The mouth-to-mouth talk rampaging through the streets was very simply this: *Warren Finch was not dead.* In the uprising that now demanded the government stand down, it was as though the protesting city thought Warren Finch could be found among the wanton destruction of public property, or under barricades of trashed cars and buses, or beyond the lines of soldiers that had been called in to deal with the troubles.

These were only normal people of the times. People who were struggling to keep up with what was happening around them, so hard to keep up with the memories—the missing, yearned-for things in life, which now included Warren Finch. They prayed for the people who had gone missing, those that had been snatched off the street, those that had had the life beaten out of them by thugs wearing balaclavas over their faces at the end of a lane, or those seen shot and fallen to the ground on a lonely wharf in the middle of the night, then disappearing without trace. In principle, it was normal to live in hope, to hope that loved ones would return to life in the lanes and squats of the abandoned buildings, or hope for luck through sprawling suburbs where fate was as slender as a spider's thread blowing in the breeze.

THE GHOST WALK

Fresh food and the body of Warren Finch traveled together. The important public officials, passionately depicting themselves as unified people, were obsessed with imagination, narrow though it was in their minds. Well! Aesthetics was all. They were pretty tricky to wipe their hands of the rioting city, by finally deciding to get rid of the coffin worshipping in the cathedral. It was a job that had to be done, and quite frankly, they finally agreed to be finished with hand wringing over rioters. They were over it. So, while standing around in the cathedral like a cohesive *think tank*, assembled to argue and shout each other down about what to do with the coffin, they reached a brilliant decision in total ignorance of the havoc on the streets, where the bishop of the cathedral was spending most of his time among the rioting picketers and youths breaking glass windows with rocks, trying single-handedly to calm everyone down. *You are in the Lord's presence would you believe?* He was just told to get out of the way.

It was not the Bishop's fault that he could not bring peace to the city, so with hands clasped behind his back, he strolled back inside his glorious cathedral. Then, with a quick glance around the building he had known for decades for peace and tranquility, he singled out the public servants amongst the people crowding through the roses to reach the coffin, and rightfully asked: *What brings you down here?* The most senior public servant, the director, drew the clergyman aside, where he spoke to him in the abstract logic of public official language about *Closing the Gap.* The bishop knew that this was the language of economic rationing but he could not reconcile it with the language of the church, of creating or closing a gap to catch the sinners. There was no gap between God and the church. Yet, all was not lost on him. He was able to surmise the Government had a strategy, and during the conversation of voices speaking hastily, he heard of an assembling plan that was frequently called, *Highway Dreaming Code.* Ah! It was high talk. Way above what a normal person could begin to understand. A hard-edged decision made on the spot.

The Bishop's question of *what are you going to do about this,* with hands gesturing at the enormity of the crisis, initiated a quicker decision than would have normally occurred in the realms of public sector abstract dialogue—as impersonal as can be expected when talking about a coffin rather than a dead person—and it rightly ended with the officials complimenting him for reaching this solution himself. *Dead right, Holiness. A last lap of honor. People need to see the coffin. This is exactly what the country has been calling out for. What could be more beneficial than respecting the voices of Australians right now? This would show all of those foreigners we are in charge in this city, and that is for sure. And they can all get their planes up in the skies and go home.*

Warren Finch would be taken on a final journey to farewell the nation, and the beauty of the thing was its giving the Government time to make a final decision about where to bury the coffin in the end. The lap of honor could take as long as needed, even forever, if the need arose.

Naturally, the widow had to be consulted first, and the decision was explained to her in simple terms to spellblind her with the obvious glamour in it all, flying up the highways in a magnificent hearse. She instantly agreed of course to have the coffin removed a-s-a-p, from the cathedral. *Okay.* She was more interested in the angel swans flying on the ceiling's frescoes, tethered with the ribbons of heaven, unable to fly off. She heard the angels breathing, their warm breath falling down onto her uplifted face, and she wondered if the angels would *fly the coffin home.*

. . . .

In the streets outside the cathedral, the rioters were sleeping in the pall of campfire smoke, low fog, or was it just the mist of sleeping gas, when the big Mack truck arrived. Perhaps rioting was exhausting work, or perhaps the city's angels had been rocking the night watchers' cradle, but no one stirred from the haze, lifted a head to see what was happening, stood up and yelled *daylight robbery* when the semitrailer hearse crawled in with the stealth of a sneaky fox. Even King Billy was asleep.

The huge vehicle slowly made its way through the snakelike barricades along each side of the road. The three-meter-high riot barriers had been set up before nightfall when riot police pushed and crushed people off the road. With the cordon up, a long chain of heavily armed soldiers in gas masks moved in, and were stationed on each side of the road.

The coffin was soon popped into the deep freezer of the *Fresh Food People* long-haul semitrailer attached to the Mack's cab—now painted up in blue, red and white, as though draped with the nation's flag. The semi was fully loaded and ready to hit the road at a quarter past three in the morning. *Soon,* the driver claimed through his gas mask to the sleeping widow accompanying him on this journey, *when we get the hell out of this,* he would soon be going somewhere else. This was the first and last thing he said to her. He was more interested in the road and the schedule. He normally traveled by himself and now it did not matter who was in his truck or how important they were, he still worked alone. This looming giant gripping the driver's wheel never slept. He stared ahead through black sun-reflecting sunglasses that rested on his white block-out covered nose. He wore his Aboriginal flag-colored cap down to his eyebrows to block out the sun that would stream in the driver's window, and to keep his personal world secret, beyond the reach of others.

The cab was overcrowded. Claustrophobic. As well as the driver with all the clothing he owned on earth shoved in a bag, his collection of holy beads hanging from the rearview mirror, and leprechaun good luck charms all over the place, he had to share the cabin with the security, all big sweaty units squashed up against each other, and the recently widowed First Lady thing—although what room did a mere slip of a thing like her need?

Even the Harbor Master, reunited with the recalcitrant Rigoletto sulking on his lap, had invited himself along for the ride. They were both squashed in a corner of the backseat next to Oblivia and were whispering to one another about having seen the security men before. It was hard to place where, the Harbor Master said, but he knew them. The girl thought the genies had come back into her life disguised as middle-aged men who now suspected her of killing her husband. These security men sat around in the cab of the truck and acted like Supreme Court judges. They whinged about dragging a coffin around the country, which they said was a stupid idea. Their power radiated through the driver's cab like hot air and the unmistakable, uncontrolled yearning of a courtroom that was seeking the truth about Warren Finch's killer. Unquenched, uncontrolled yearning that lasted thousands of kilometers with Oblivia tormenting herself with the question—did she, or did she not kill her husband, and was she just chasing the hare king that day? The driver pulled his cap further down onto his eyebrows. It was academic to him. He was not wishing for anything. Didn't care if she had an alibi or not, or whether it was easier to believe that she killed her husband than to believe she was chasing a hare king. He became lead-footed to cure any urge for wishing, thinking or yearning, pressing harder on the accelerator and sending the semi flying along the road. On and on they flew, hundred of kilometers of gum trees quivering in their wake, and flatlands of sheep and cattle-filled grasslands wondering what had just happened, while she tossed and turned over her alibi, whether she had one or not.

The road train carted the body everywhere—up the Hume Highway, down the Stuart Highway, around the Monaro—eleven highways in all. Twenty thousand kilometers of the nation's highways had been split down the middle to divide the country like two giant lungs.

The *See You Around* journey was for all people who bothered to stand out in a chilly night, or in the midday sun, if they cared enough to line the streets just to watch the *Spirit of the Nation* roaring by. The whole thing was a rhapsody in motion and could not have been more successful, as the road train roared down the highways of country and western music—mostly legend music by the country's great singers like Slim Dusty, Rick and Thel, a bit of Chad Morgan—Camooweal, Mt Isa, Cloncurry, The Barkley, Wagga Wagga, Charleville, Cunnamulla, Yarrawonga, Plains of Peppimenarti, and the Three Rivers Hotel. But mostly, the clockwork nature of the thing was to keep to the *Fresh Food People's* schedule of deliveries to its supermarket chain throughout the country, picking up and delivering crates of fruit and vegetables such as asparagus, mangoes, pawpaw, bananas and pineapples; or the oranges, apples, potatoes, strawberries and peas from the packing sheds and cool rooms of its northern or southern growers.

Along the way, the coffin was paraded and displayed for all to see in this festival of grieving. The black sassafras heritage coffin was wheeled out of the semitrailer on a trolley and set down in the middle of a dead-grass flat, banana plantation, or salt bush plain, where speeches were made in the slow drawl of the North, or a fiddle played through amplifiers at each tinker-tailor gathering, in fiddlestick towns, depressed cities, cutthroat roadhouses, or else, the coffin was rested on a bench in a mine's mess room, in machinery, produce, wool and cattle sheds, or laid on the best linen tablecloth over the dining table of a cattleman's station home.

It was a hard schedule, and the silent driver drove that little bit faster to keep on track when memorials could just as spontaneously spring up out of the blue when influential, backblocks politicians at the end of a dusty road demanded their impromptu *See You Around* event with the *Spirit of the Nation*. The driver did not complain. He did his job. Dragged out the coffin. Wore the consequences for making up time after listening to another dozen pipsqueak speeches for a half dozen people at another local church, football stadium, soccer oval, paddock, courtroom or meeting hall of the Country Women's Association, Boy Scout, or other local hall of fame.

The ghosts traveling in the road train were not complaining. The security guards enjoyed the view and started granting three wishes to whoever required them. Who were they to give two hoots if the coffin was continually being dragged out here or there in a journey that was endless? But the driver wished for nothing. He just kept growing older and driving on. He pushed the now less than splendid, soiled and chipped coffin out one more time, waited for the mourning to be done with and souvenir hacking to be completed, and pushed the defaced coffin back up the ramp and into the freezer. There was no time any more for deliveries. It saved time to cut the words *delivery* or *pickup* off the list. He kicked the security men out. Said that they were weighing him down. They were too congenial to their ever-increasing queues of wish seekers. He could not sit around all day for other purposes. Everything in the big freezer began to rot. The driver's eyes grew teary from being glued to the dusty road ahead, and he kept singing the same old song, *Yea! Keep your eyes on the road, and your hands on the wheel, we're having fun etcetera whatever.* But when he sang, he only heard the transport; the roaring road train's engine, wheels rolling over the highways. The widow never heard a thing said about Warren Finch in the endless parade of speeches. She had left before the journey began.

Goodness poor heart, the ghost walk. There are those who will warn anyone making this strange solitary journey, and will say: *You have got to take enough to make it through.*

This was what happened. Oblivia disappeared from the hearse's spectacular schedule after the wind dusted off an icy night. What was the reason? And what was it about those prevailing dreams children have about life, that make them to go ghost walking like this? Away! Anywhere! That's what happened to them. Was there ever a right way of leaving?

In a panicky night off she went, entangled in the vortex of a thunderstorm dizzily spinning over many kilometers in the higher strata of the atmosphere. She just walked away without any thought of where she was going. Death, dying, or living had nothing to do with it. The truth of it was that wars do this to children. War children, like the torn world of Aboriginal children. Where were the kind crickets singing? Or, the big leaf under which to hide? The country's hearth! Ah! She just walked around the smudged lines of the circles the giants had sketched in another of their hell maps.

She walked away from the semitrailer hearse, and listened for heartbeats: the silent chilled voicelessness of swans you hear in the weakened old and the very young tossed from the heavens, and those struggling to stay airborne with their wings stretched wide, locked against the force of the wind.

In a place where footsteps crackled on frost-hardened grass, her dreams were askew. Still! Quiet! Never mind! There were people approaching, shadows in the darkness that looked like old Aunty and the Harbor Master with the monkey twisting around on his hip. The old woman was talking to the Harbor Master but her voice broke with the chill in the air. *You'd be reaching for gold to find the place now.* You could hear her continuing to recite bits of her old poetry, although she and the Harbor Master had already disappeared, and were walking somewhere that was infinitely far away.

In the morning there were only blue skies where the girl widow had walked off to find a flock of swans. For her, the mad hearse journey had finished. Who cared? The driver shouted to the thin vapors of air rising from the cold earth all around him, when he discovered she had left. *You there? You there? Come back here.* But tell you what? What did he care about anyone disappearing from his cortege if they had no respect for the dead? He had not seen the said personage contributing much to the memorial anyway. There were appointments to keep. A heavy schedule raced through his mind. He had a stiff in the freezer to think about. The haul going overseas once they got through Australia. So, with his cap pulled down lower over his sunglasses—man, he was hitting the highway. The rubber burnt the bitumen. A trail of smoke was left behind. You would think he was raising Lazarus from the dead.

She watched the semitrailer roaring up the highway from the ghost town's park, among oak trees with exposed roots like the fingers of giants crossed for good luck. *There he goes,* she thought of Warren Finch, *he's still holding on to power, still searching for the ultimate paradise.* Yep!

The same stories you hear about power. A dead man was still making people run after him. It was the first time she had really thought about Warren Finch for a very long time.

Alone in this quiet forest where only a blackbird's song rung out while the last stars disappeared, and the scream of the schedule became a dot on the awakening horizon, she suspected he was not dead at all. But who knows what thoughts will come right out of the bushland when you are alone? She saw for herself how Warren Finch could loom monumentally in the atmosphere like a gift from God. He was so indestructibly alive, just like the sky. Even in the middle of nowhere, he was still around, just as he was when she had watched the coffin absentmindedly on the long journey, where he was being preserved as though he was some masterpiece in an art gallery. And just like famous paintings, he would never die as long as people looked at his dead body and appreciated the unique quality of his extraordinariness, and the propaganda of what he stood for in the world.

With leaves dropping from the oak trees at the slightest hint of a breeze, she thought about the frailty of perpetuity, and imagined she could still hear Warren talking on his mobile phone from the coffin in the semitrailer's freezer, where he was continuously calling the driver and complaining about her disappearance. His muffled voice now giving the orders and snapping at the driver, the mobile capped to his ear, *Where in the hell did she go?*

Yes, she knew something. Warren Finch's elaborate montage-self never intended to be buried. He was insisting that the glassy-eyed driver forget what he called the girl widow. She could look after herself. He was wondering why she was brought along in the first place. He yelled down his mobile from the sassafras coffin in the freezer. *Well! Let it roar. You are doing the right thing, driver. Keep going, man—you got no time to frig around.*

For what was death? It was just a matter of continuing on, keeping his ideas streaming out of center stage in perpetual memorials. The fact of the matter was that it was hard to kill off someone who had gotten as big as the United Nations itself. Naturally, the gift from God would have to go around the world after this. No drama. Death was not an excuse for burying a person, and a bit of good history along with it. No—no drama at all.

Somewhere in this landscape, swans were stirring. It was a bright starry night. As the entire flock awakened, great hordes wove in and out of the tight pack with necks stretched high. These birds anticipated the movement of wind in the higher atmosphere. They gauged the speed of northerly flowing breezes caught in their neck feathers and across their red beaks and legs. The swans made no sound, but stood still while the wind intensified through the ruffling feathers on their breasts. Then suddenly from somewhere a startled swan flies up, and is followed by the roar of the lift off, and the sky is blanketed by black swans in the cold night, and Oblivia recalls the old Chinese monk Ch'i-chi's poem of the flight of swans in the night, like *a lone boat chasing the moon*. She watched, and knew she had found her swans. They had found each other's heartbeat, the pulse humming through the land from one to the other, like the sound of distant clap sticks beating through ceremony, connecting together the spirits, people and place of all times into one. These were her swans from the swamp. There was no going back. She would follow them. They were heading north, on the way home.

On this night, she traveled over hills of heavily scented eucalypt forests, until she reached the shallow swamps of wintertime flowing through the scattered tea-tree country where most of the land was perpetually underwater. The swans rest, but there will be days of walking through water to follow them.

She was not the only one who kept away from the heavy migration of travelers—poor families on foot, and those able to afford to travel in a vehicle like Big Red's family—who had been forced to leave the ruined city. They were the people with passports and not a threat to the national security. They were not like potential terrorists: this colorful procession of licensed travelers—those who had passed the rigid nationality test for maintaining a high level of security in the country, and could pay the tax that allowed them to pass through the numerous security checkpoints on the highways.

Oblivia joined those who were traveling incognito on unofficial and illegal crossings through the swamps. There were so many people moving through the country, she was never alone. They were all searching for the same shallow pathways, and dazed like her, all following each other, while trying to take their life somewhere else. There were people dressed in dark clothes across the landscape, trying not to look conspicuous. Some were former street people. Others were the homeless people who had slept on the footpaths with cardboard blankets, or in empty buildings. Now in hordes and all traveling north, they crowded the swampy lanes on pitch-black nights and nestled close to one another for safety. Most had white hair, even the children, and similar stories of what happened, *it was those snakes. It was the last straw.* A moment was all it had taken, many had claimed, to turn anyone prematurely white; that night when the rain and wind hit the city like a brick wall had been thrown at it after Warren Finch was killed.

The navigators at the top of the line of the people traveling through the water were continually arguing among themselves about their weapons—if a bread knife was better than a sugarcane cutlass for cutting through, or whether the thickness of a long pole was better cut by an ax, but whether or not they were arguing, they had to decide which direction either left or right that any idiot would take through the shallows ahead. And then they continued yelping: Yep! *Good job I traded that bread knife.* Yep! *Good job I made that bamboo pole longer.*

These men claimed to be the policemen over this stretch of country, although in the real world, they were only a bunch of intergenerational environmentalists, turned greenies, turned *ferals*, turned strapped for cash to save a multitude of furry or feathered threatened species in international forums, or their favorite rare trees. They knew the swamps. Their families had grown up with rising waters. When the opportunity arose to make some money, who could blame them for becoming entrepreneurial? Human removalists, they called themselves. It sounded nice. Sure it was not legit or leftie, but what was? Their mantra while leading the incognitos was a list of challenging superiority-complex questions, such as, *what makes you people from southern cities think you can speak for us? What makes you think we can't speak for ourselves? What makes you think you are better than us?* Or, *How would you know this country better than us?*

They guided dirt-poor people through rough country, even though the plain and simple truth was that they were just people smugglers, not interested in public investment, or becoming security-conscious public servants. Whether they thought what had happened in the city was of any consequence, what did it matter? There were plenty of snakes around this neck of the woods too. *It was all of this mixed-up weather,* they claimed. Anything was possible, but that was not their problem. Their job was simple enough. Ask no questions, and get enough people through expansive low-lying flood water in the flat lands in a transaction that implied: *We can show you a thing or two about hardship if that's what you want.*

The job was simply this: keep the line from falling into deep flowing water: *Stop anyone from being washed away.* It was easy enough. The environmentalists and their families lived rough along the water's edges like nesting swans or a colony of egrets, in makeshift rafts, or roughly made reed huts. Even their babies knew how to cling to the watery nests, or the bosoms of their mothers. It helped to have lived numerous seasons with spreading water to remember how to stop being washed away. Still, it was always difficult to predict before a crossing began whether there was a likelihood of flash floods. The last-minute cancellation of a crossing was always imminent. Refugees would squat by the water's edge in the rain until conditions settled, while the water-navigators argued the toss in numerous committee meetings about whether the water's stability was a goer, so a journey could begin.

But it did not matter how adept these environmentalists were with the bush, or with travel through water, or whatever else they could do to save lives. They were not to be trusted in the least by the refugees of every nationality coalesced by flights from the ruined cities—young or old who were hardened fighters too. None of them wanted any extra favor for who they were or where they had originally come from, and being essentially numb about risk taking, they asked no questions, and just told the people-smugglers to get on with it: *All we want to do is head north. We don't care what happens. Just do your job. Anything will be worth it. Just show us where the Aborigine people live.* So for days, sometimes weeks, the lines of humanity walked knee-deep in yellow billowing water, and if the predictions were wrong, waist-deep or up to the neck of children, which left each person to figure out how to keep carrying the burden of treasured belongings. The leaders called, *Say c'est la vie, or drown. Chuck it all.* The trail was littered with submerged electronics, cartons of beer, some huge paintings that had become completely transformed by the mud, as did the books about birds or the high country, or any treasured books of philosophy, music, Shakespeare's sonnets.

Usually, the only treasures that survived were animals. Many had brought along the family watchdog, their old *daras*, and these were left to swim alongside their owners or were carried, like those tagging along with the dog boys, hungry puppies stuffed under their jackets, among hundreds of street kids on the run. Someone had brought along their cow, the old beloved black-and-white *bulaka*. It was not like traveling on an airplane, or a catering bus. Forget that. Nobody had any food. No airplane. *Budangku yalu julaki-yaa.* It was more like a self-serve journey, which meant everyone was constantly hungry, always too *balika*, looking for something to eat. The mortified travelers, who had not killed anything before, killed the cow finally. It was difficult to think of anything else. It was butchered in a frenzy in the water, and eaten raw, with no fire, *budangku yalu jangu-yaa.* Afterwards they had nothing. Not anything. *Budangku yalu jumbala-yaa.* Still, what was hunger to these people? They had always known hunger, and about this alone they cheerfully narrated their stories, rather optimistically, about how they were surviving on nothing: *Yea! Who cares about hardship? It is just being cold and wet, that's all, and being rained on, but was worth it.*

The more enterprising street people who had pillaged poultry before leaving the city, had a ten out of ten chance of feeding themselves on the journey. These fowl thieves carried bantam roosters and treasured, egg-laying white silky hens stuffed inside their clothes, or a half dozen ducks, close to their hearts, and secretly hoarded the eggs.

The buskers of the city sung through hunger, and kept singing through the night to keep warm as the weary line walked on, while more water seeping out of distant hills and creeping along the crevices joined the flow of the flood on the flats. You could say that the country was a drain that wanted to drown strangers singing up its landscape.

Oblivia walked with her head down, but she also watched elderly men and women, and children holding cats, *kinikini* stuffed inside their jackets, trying to shield their pets from the savage attacks of dogs sniffing out anything they could eat. The dogs were often attacked with bamboo poles, which quickly escalated into brawls with the dog owners. The water leaders often lost control of the line when tempers flared over dogs, and the fighting broke into splinter groups.

Whenever skirmishes broke out, the line needed to be brought down to earth. A meeting was held in the water to break people into groups that related to each other. But lawlessness was what it was. People walked wherever, fought whoever and however, and often ended by walking off in all directions. Of course, there were consequences for anyone who thought they could make the crossing by themselves. Many were forcibly returned to the line. For others, it was important that the people they had paid to take them across did not walk off the job, or get killed.

With the journey headed deeper into the swamps, Oblivia walked with dozens of people with cages of birds whose song was a reminder of their old lives while they traveled towards the uncertain future. Nanny goats. Billy goats. A sheep. Someone with about a dozen pussycats stuffed under his jacket. Oblivia thought of Machine. Perhaps he was somewhere, or still in the city. She carried in her arms a heavy fledging swan, having to *mulamula* it around all the time, inside her hoodie windcheater next to her knife. This was a half-grown cygnet that she called *Stranger*. The cygnet, like Rilke's swan laboring with what could not be undone, had refused its destiny. It had no interest in swimming away, or to fly with its flock. The great flock of swans, wary of the dogs, kept a safe distance from the travelers, but Oblivia watched them swimming in the distance, or sometimes flying overhead, as though reassuring herself that she would not be abandoned.

Darkness would fall and the trails of bats, thousands flying over-head, heralded the worst time for the disintegrating line of people, call-ing to one another throughout the night, straying out of hearing range and becoming lost forever. Very soon, the weariness of the line became total exhaustion. Many felt there was no end, or way out. They became increasingly disoriented in the sea of water and began to hallucinate, many rushing towards the mirage of the Aboriginal people's heaven they saw in the distance.

Only a few refugees from the city finally managed to reach the other side. The feral policemen leading the line, who abandoned the refugees that remained in their care, would eventually be arrested and placed on trial for people smuggling, but not for genocide, or mass murder, which were crimes thought to be so morally un-Australian, it was officially denied that anything like it ever happened, like in the rhetoric of the history wars era—genocide, a horrendous crime against humanity that was unheard of. It never happened. Not in this country.

The swan girl's worry for the cygnet now hidden inside her clothes, under Warren Finch's old windcheater, probably saved her. She walked with her head bent forward, trying to be unnoticeable amid the dwin-dling groups of people. The Harbor Master looked very fearful with the frightened Rigoletto on his hip. He always knew where she was and crept up beside her again, and again. *Get out*, he demanded. *You are First Lady, not bullock being led around.* The line was struggling to stay together after days and days of tiredness and hunger, many falling by the wayside, unable to go on, with no one to help them.

There were murmurings, whisperings, and she could feel the pri-meval fear closing in as the crossing verged on mutiny. Anyone hiding animals was attacked. Groups of bandits moved alongside, picking off people they suspected were hiding food. There were numerous beat-ings of people unwilling to hand over their pets. The dogs roamed freely, sniffing for food, attacking those carrying animals. The Harbor Master arrived wet and flustered with sheer frustration written all over his face. *Why won't you just go,* he sneered at Oblivia, while adding, *I am not staying.* He pushed her, and she swayed to and fro, but held her ground. *You are an idiot,* he snarled in her face. *Go now.*

Oblivia feared that the dogs would eventually find the cygnet. All around, she heard the savage packs attacking people and their screams in splashing water. Even the swans overhead were terrified, and lost momentum in their flight. They swooped lopsidedly in terror. She felt fear with each step, expecting something to happen at any moment. It was too terrifying to be discovered escaping, she had seen other people being cast aside for not being obedient to the discipline of the crossing. But, when it was time to go, she disappeared quietly, in the moments when the black swan cloud flew across the line of traveling people, covering the moonlit water. She closed her ears to the sounds of the collapsing world behind her, and kept walking under the cloud of swans moving slowly just above the water, their loud beating wings creating a mad turbulence in the water that kept her camouflaged. Never turning once, she would not look back.

The only person who lived on the water among the flooded trees where no one ever goes was an old Chinese hermit. He lived on an island of sticks that looked like an enormous swan's nest. His white hair and whiskers were filled with sticks too. As usual, he was hoping to catch a fish, singing that old 1960s song "Wishin' and Hopin'," just like he always did to paint the sky gold with the memory of Dusty Springfield's voice. He was thoroughly besotted with the singer, and his feeling had only grown stronger since the first time he had seen her singing the song illegally in a dream of long ago, which hum! made him run from China.

The fish were still not biting when the wing beats of swans flying low across the water through the dawn fog were so close to his ears that he could feel the spirit of Dusty Springfield singing her *wishin' and hopin'* in the breeze coming straight from their straining wings, and her trumpeter bugling in their calls, and the drums rolling in their heartbeats. It was just another amazing all-bells-ringing kind of day living with his idol and it was all too joyous, but then down in the fog something moved. He thought he had seen ghosts. These ghosts kept walking towards him through the fog and shaking up the water, so he waited, and kept on singing his *wishin' and hopin'* song. It was too late for obsessing, to make his cares fade away because these all jumped and rolled in his stomach. When he saw it was just an old man carrying a monkey he thought he was lucky, but when he saw a girl who was the First Lady of whatnot, and with a cygnet as well? Well! He thought he was just too plain luckless for words.

He called to the strangers, *This is where you must go to enter another country,* but they just kept walking with the ghost wind blowing them towards where he pointed. When he realized they were not going to stop to speak to him, he called after them about his secret love for Dusty Springfield and how he was remembering her voice forever out there on the water. He believed they were ghosts though, and watched them go on their way until they disappeared into the watery horizon.

Later when he caught a fairly medium-sized fish, unlike the tiddlers that he usually caught to feed himself, he believed that the only real ghosts he had ever seen in his life had brought him luck. So, he sent a bit of his luck their way too, wishing the ghosts heading into the desert reached wherever they were going, and hoping that the Harbor Master found a camel to ride on the long journey—*to show them that you care just for them, sing the songs they want to sing. . . .*

The old Chinese man's singing to his songstress in the sky must have been a lucky thing, the Harbor Master told the wet and sorry Rigoletto after they were saved by the weather. The group was still walking in floodwater when the skies turned black with heavy clouds, and very soon afterward they were walking through a mad storm. A torrential downpour flew like a wild river in the wind. The big cygnet refused to swim and Oblivia had to stuff it back under her shirt. She could feel its heart thumping with her heart, but kept walking as though nothing was unusual in calamity. Well! The monkey knew about monsoons, and clung to the neck of the Harbor Master who was salubriously humming the highs and lows, and speed and caution, of Weber's Op. 34 Clarinet Quintet in B flat—although he was packing it really. The wind and rain blew so hard onto their backs that they raced along in the direction the Chinese man had pointed to, and where, soon enough, they were thrown out of the water and at the two-toed feet of a big fat camel standing in mud.

Lo and behold! The Aboriginal man on the camel spoke wisely—because he was supposed to—as he welcomed the strangers to his country. His pet cicada chirruped a song from under the piece of canvas that covered its cage when the camel man asked his talking companion for long journeys, since the camel did not speak, *Will you carry the monkey man and his soggy looking pet, or will we let the old camel do the job?* The cicada did not appear to have a direct answer to such a stupid question, if you could interpret the melody that remained unchanged to an ordinary ear not trained in interpreting how insects speak.

The Harbor Master was very weak from his ordeal, but still protective of the girl, and being an important man of another place, he bluntly asked the camel man, *Which one are you mate? Gaspar, Balthazar or Melchior? And is this the gate of heaven or what?* Perhaps the camel man did look like one of the three wise men. He was dressed in a thick green cotton shirt and red trousers—clothes stained reddish brown from the bush, while over his shoulders fell a large animal-skin cloak that protected him from the rain. His eagle-feathered cap was also fashioned from animal skin but it was now soaked with the rain that washed down his face and through his black beard, and over the seed necklaces hanging over his shirt.

The camel man said he was neither wise man, nor in heaven. Introducing himself, he said the name that people usually called him was Half Life, and he offered no other explanation. *I'm from blackfella land. My kingdom is right where you lot are standing. You got anybody else coming behind you?* When Oblivia glared at him as though he must have been mad, he sat the camel down and quickly slid off. The Harbor Master was the one he helped first. *Old man you ride on top. No more walking for you now,* he said. *Girl, you get up there too with that goose.* He threw the animal-skin cloak over them, and handed over his flask, as well as a large piece of wattle-seed damper from a bag kept around his waist. The camel, unhappy with having to be sat down in the mud in the twenty-first century, was fidgeting with its mouth harness, spitting and oozing snot from its nostrils, and turning its long neck around to sniff and fuss about having mud in its fur, but with a quietly spoken word from Half Life, the animal quietly rose to its feet.

We follow the track the ancestors of mine made. Look who is here, he told his country. There was nothing more spoken in the rain journey ahead. Half Life needed to sing to his kin people their country's songs with his cicada brother, as much as to the camel that seemed to enjoy ancestor music while it went sauntering on its way.

All journeys on the ghost walk are hard and long. There was no way around it. One can travel forty days and forty nights across deserts in bloom or drought, or a month of Sundays of eating nothing else but hares and rabbits roasted over a fire at night, but it was all the same.

Just be careful with my people though, or they will spook the bloody wind out of you. My theory about surviving a day with them is always take short breaths so you don't miss it if they try to floor the life out of you. This was how Half Life introduced his people. *You have to be related to people like this to love them.*

This is a real sacred place here, Half Life said as they came into view of their destination—a camp of his kin people living in the ruins of concrete-block buildings and rusted car bodies that were half buried with red desert soil, and from which grew clumps of spinifex, salt bush, native herb bushes, or the odd bare bush tomato and leaf-eaten bush banana, and the scrappy coolibah tree here and there—nothing to build a door with. Burrs and prickles covered the ground like a dense lawn, as well as chewed-up pigweed and twiglike arid country plants for the bull ants to trail through. Only salt soakages lay beyond to every horizon.

This is big Law here. We always come back. Spirits of our people live here. Ghosts living in abandoned car bodies. Some of them inside those old crap houses. Built by that top of the country's last government of self-serving politicians before it chucked the dummy and went bust when nobody bothered voting for them anymore. Nah! You wouldn't be bothered voting for people like that. They were like a bloody soap opera. Well! It's entr'acte times now. Better enjoy it before the next comedy of errors, another era with another round of tragedians and thespians mouthing off, and traipsing around on our block again, dragging us backward through another bloody century of destruction. Our elders bring everyone here so that we can hear the Law of our people from the country itself telling us a strong story about what happened to them. What they do. Oh! Sad all right, some of those stories. But good ones there too. You can hear children dancing in the moonlight, rock 'n' roll and shake a leg. Laughing. Those were the days. Make you want to cry how memories come looking for you. We move on again in a few days time. Palace next time maybe.

What was the point of complaining about how life had become? If all that was left of your traditional lands were tailing dams and polluted pond life, and the place looking like a camel's cemetery? *Still! No need to go around complaining because there is nothing left running in your brains except your bare-ass country and a pack of scrub donkeys,* said Half Life. *This is how we see life. Look around. Those donkeys follow us wherever we go.* The ground looked as though it was crawling, but it wasn't a miracle. It was a catastrophe. These were cursed people. Their worldly companions were a plague of *Rattus villosissimus*—the long-haired ugly rat—crawling grasshoppers, *Locusta migratoria*, and the flying ants swarming in the soup.

Oblivia looked at the ground-crawling camp and saw it was nothing special to freak out about, if that was what you thought about rat- and insect-swatting nomads looking as weather-beaten and windblown as she was herself. All of them living with sandy-blight eyes among thousands of wild camels and feral donkeys surrounding the camp, which Half Life explained, just kept following them through life.

We are Aboriginal herdspeople with bloodlines in us from all over the world, he added, and dreamily listed all the world's continents that he could remember being related to these days, *Arabian, African, Asian, Indian, European all sorts, pure Pacific Islander—anywhere else I didn't mention? Well! That as well! Whereever! Even if I haven't heard of it! No matter—we got 'em right here inside my blood. I am thick with the spirits from all over the world that I know nothing about. Nah! Man! We don't live on their tucker though. Here it's bush tucker all the way if we can yank it out of the mouths of these ferals running around and breeding up like plagues of rats, flies, insects whatever; no matter we got 'em, and that's why we are trying to eradicate all these mongrel hares and English rabbits from being one less of a plague on the face of the country by eating every chemically deranged single bugger of them. It's like their spirit will not go away unless we eat 'em. Of course that's some other country mob business but what can we do! What Law? Nothing! We are retarded people now because of the history of retardation policy mucking everyone up. Leaking radioactivity. Crap politics from long ago. Must have been a madhouse then. Glad to be rid of them. That we survive at all is just a bloody fluke of human nature. Got the picture, if so, then you are welcome, if not, I reckon you got no alternative really out here and whatnot for understanding surviving.*

Anyone could see that the community was one big, buzzing hive of activity where busy Aboriginal tribespeople never stopped working. They were as driven as the millions of flies that infested the camp, and you could *betcha* one thing: these people would strike an accord with the ghosts of a century or more worth of politicians and policy makers of Australian governments. It had been bigot country then. They would be smiling on these camel entrepreneurial people, and saying success at last. For here, every individual seemed totally obsessed with being some kind of economic independence human success story in an Australian-made hell. There were people bumping into each other all day long to discuss or argue about the plagues of feral animals. Who was looking after the barn owls? How the camels were penned or not penned, watered and fed, who could use which one or that one, or why one camel was more worthy or trustworthy than another. In short—worrying about every aspect of domesticating the animals once imported into the country by other people, that they were not eating.

Rigoletto hid under an iron bed and stayed well and truly out of the way while the mostly leather-skin-clothed women and children that looked more like animals to the monkey were endlessly chasing donkeys in the rain, or wrestling them like wet squawking sponges to the ground, or whipping them senseless to make them move away from the camp. Why these donkeys wanted to hang around these people was a complete mystery to the Harbor Master and he yelled out in vain, *Why don't you let the baby Jesus' donkeys alone?* So he was told to shut the fuck up. What tradition, the Harbor Master wanted to know, talked like that to old men? He ended up arguing constantly with the women who had been looking after him but now treated him like a donkey too.

The camp itself was strewn with carcasses of hares and rabbits or any other feral creatures thrown on the woodpile. It was hard to establish if there were enough people who would be able to eat all this food before the camp moved on. Then there were the pelts in various stages of being tanned or turned into items of clothing—cloaks and caps like Half Life wore, as well as shoes, saddles and ropes. At night it was no different, for no one slept a wink in the bevy of ceremonial singing and hunting, or packing up and moving camp. Why waste time sleeping when far into a wet rainy night, all the able-bodied huntsmen and women rode off on their camels, with each person carrying a pet owl as their night hunter, and only returning hours later loaded with a hundred and fifty or more rabbits and hares strung over the camels' backs? This was why the one big overworked feral shebang was monotonously the same, routine and endless.

At least you got somewhere, and all we have to do is keep going, that's all, the Harbor Master explained to the emaciated girl, although he could see the bony thing was not listening to him. He felt she was dying, and admitted that she had been too high maintenance for him as he sang to the country's spirits, long, long songs, that went across the country to her homeland. There was nothing more he could do. She lived in her own world with the cygnet that had now grown into a swan. There was too much noise in the camel community, and it made it harder for her to hold her thoughts together before they were forgotten. She could hardly remember what happened on the day that Warren Finch was assassinated. The images were like those recalled from a dream that flashed in her mind and were instantly forgotten. Her life in the city seemed to have coalesced into a stream of forgetting, of what happened so far away, and of memories that seemed implausible, or too hideous, and almost irreverent to be thought about in this place.

So Oblivia and the swan sat in their own little corner of this shifting world, out of the way of being trampled by the industrious people and their animals. The camel people were pursuing their own course, in its own order of mayhem and hassle, which was oblivious to having her, or any outsider in its midst.

Oblivia turned her head away when the groups of children came by all day long to touch the swan and to throw it some food, the bits of damper and grass seeds still attached to stems they had collected for it. They were full of questions, asking why she was looking after the swan, where she came from, what she was doing just sitting by herself for? *Why are you mental?* Irritably, she quickly shooed each group off one by one, with the language of a stick angrily prodded at them, only to end up with even larger groups of children whiling away the time by sitting in front of her and copying her every move, the hostile way she stared at them, and teasingly throwing stones over her head—giggling for the stick to be chucked around, until their parents called them off for more chores—*to hurry up and get going*, while leaving her to make her own decisions about life. It was up to her. Entirely. Everyone was free to have their own thoughts about where they belonged or what they needed to do. There were only two options: live or die. Make your own decision. They knew the girl's heart was far away from them, and assumed she was thinking about her own country.

Whenever Half Life walked by, he glanced at the huddle on the ground, noticed she was still there, and thought that perhaps he should see what was happening to her—whether her spirits were up or down. He thought she was crying. What would she cry about? Was she crying about that prick Warren Finch? Half Life had heard on the radio that the beloved missing First Lady, now hailed as the heart of the nation, had joined the *illegals* traveling through the country, and thought it could have been her, but he said nothing. Who needed the fuss? He thought that he could have done with a wife himself, but he was far too occupied with the work that needed to be done. They all were. He had no time for standing around talking about life, marriage, raising a family. This was sorry business. They were mourning here. And tomorrow, they would mourn somewhere else. No! He did not want any children.

Would he have to guard them with his life on his own country, lest the government took them away from him?

All she did, other than burying her head inside her jacket under her arms folded around her knees, was to look at the skies becoming clearer, as though it was there where she had to search for a road out, the road that emerged halfheartedly before disappearing again, that would only become fully visible when the swans arrived. She had become more eager to leave, to continue the journey before it was too late. She grew impatient and weaker. Conjuring her journey back to the swamp was hard work. It exhausted her. She hardly ate, and could only think of herself as one of the swans flying towards her, while niggling voices in her mind kept reminding her the time had come if she and the swans were to make the journey north to the swamp before summer set in, otherwise they would all die on the way. *You want to die out here? Like all those other women?*

She thought about death. Visualized the journey towards dying, and thought this was how Warren had planned to abandon her after all—just like other men who had dumped their disappointing wives in the bush. Left them to die. Only their bones were leaning against a tree somewhere, and those poor things still waving towards home for an eternity. At this point, she thought Bella Donna's story must really be about the last swan arriving back at the swamp with one of her bones in its beak, bringing it home. If this was so, so be it. She would be dead, that would be the end of her grand old love story, a fable of what happened after Warren Finch was killed, when his "promise wife" was so heartbroken, she ran off and died in the desert. The missing First Lady. The enigma. Her body never found. She would be like Lasseter's Reef. Adventurers would just about kill themselves in the desert while trekking around the place searching for her. She would become a legend in the bastions of Australian civil society interested in the anthropological studies of Aboriginal people, just as long as it appeased the dark theories of a discipline that kept on describing the social norms of Aboriginal men as dangerous and violent. They would speculate about her bones in absentia, and wonder whether she really was a child bride—just a little girl—so they could experience the sensation of charging Warren Finch posthumously with incest, pornography and raping a child; or whether or not the bones were of an ancient woman, or of an assimilated woman; or of somebody with sapwood-imbued bones who really could have slept for a very long time in a tree—just like that Rip Van Winkle fellow—yes, the bones of a girl who had never really matured, never fully grown. Well! How could you tell? It was hard to imagine. Why wouldn't she show Warren Finch who was the greatest? Yes, it was easy to think about dying. Would you call just lying down in the grass to die revenge, payback, or a suicidal act?

So she waited more and more impatiently for the swans to arrive, becoming more fearful, and feeling more dependent on them to guide her safely through the laws of the country, the spirits who were the country itself—if they were still alive, and flying towards this isolated camel people's camp, a speck in the vastness of an undetermined landscape for those unable to read it, frightened at the prospect of having to attempt the journey alone through unknown territories without a guide to clear the path to her country. Then one day, when the caravan of people, camels and donkeys finally realized its intention of leaving when the soakages dried out and actually left during a surprise rain shower and followed the rainbow, nobody noticed she had been left behind.

The Harbor Master was the first one you could blame for negligence when he left with the camel people. He was a ghost of a man too preoccupied with losing the magic of lightning-speed travel. He was old-fashioned. One of those types too overcome with disappointment for this new world. He had to reach his destination in God speed. How could he think of traveling an eternity with camels and donkeys for God knows how many days, months, or *friggen* years? Sweet Dreams Baby! His destination was what? thousands of kilometers away—think of heaven. And heaven was not the next waterhole up the road, which dying camels and old nomads thought was good enough to call it a day after walking all day long in the sun. His spiritual resting place was his own chosen place, where huge angels that were called something good like *Prosperity* and *Eternity* watched over monkey country. His eternal resting place was not going to be in any barren wasteland that kept being killed off by political stupidity.

Anyhow, you only had to take a look at little Rigoletto in the pelting rain for pity's sake. He was too wound up and frightened about being trampled by wet, frisky camels running about, to come out from his hidey-hole under the iron-frame bed. The little monkey sat motionless with his arms tightly folded around himself. He looked like a rock. He clutched his possessions to his chest. What? The stories? Worried in case a camel or donkey would try to eat his stories?

Yes! The Harbor Master could only dream of getting away from the spinifex shrubbery, the claustrophobic way this landscape can close in, surround, ensnarl. He clung to the monkey hope of living the high life on the balconies of the eternal white marble palace. On the Taj Mahal, Rigoletto would move gracefully through time, shaking the hands of passing tourists with his lips stretched back and through baring teeth, telling a good story. This dream of escaping was worth . . . millions! *Can you imagine, Rigoletto?* Millions of people handing over peanuts, bananas, pomegranates, oranges and the whole apple cart to hear a little monkey snarling through one of his favorite stories about living a thousand and one nights of hell with the Harbor Master. *We will never go hungry if we live in a palace, would we, Rigoletto?* But to get there, they would have to survive the journey through a lot of country with the camels Half Life described were destined for the ships exporting them to foreign markets. It seemed like a bit of a plan.

MARSH LAKE SWANS

So holy and beautiful to behold this country where the swans flew hillock over hillock as far as the eye could see along a rolling landscape of saltbush, stubby plants, pittosporum, emu bush and flowering *eremophilas*.

Their flight having begun at the old abandoned botanical gardens in the city so long ago, it was a journey foretold, clear in the oldest swan to the youngest cygnet—the flight through thousands of kilometers from the southern coast to a northern swamp.

Bushfires came in walls across their path. As the grasslands burned, the swans flew high, sailing through winds gusting above the smoke in a journey a thousand meters up in their dreaming of home. Each kilometer was achieved by wing flapping and slow glide through floating ashes that flickered with fire and dazzle-danced the sky in the full-throated blizzard of heat flying over the hills, before falling on the country beneath. The swans, their strength crippled, breathed hot smoke-filled air, and the smell of their own singed feathers crawled into their lungs. Wrapped in fear, they whistle up the dead to see how they are going, before surrendering to the air, plummeting thousands of meters down into the fire. It tested the will of their wings flapping slower, almost unconsciously, instinctively remaining airborne.

It happened this way, until the remaining bony creatures find they are descending into the stagnant, blue-green algae blooms of a flooded plain where the trunks of dead trees are a reminder of what was once a forest. Then they continue, the swans flying through seasons and changes in the weather, and over traveling refugees, and the fence posts of flooded and then bone-dry lands. It was as if the ancestors had pulled the swans across the skies, passing them on to the spirits of gibber plains, ironstone flats, claypans, salt lakes and drifts, towards a sacred rendezvous—a tabula rasa place—where all of the world's winds come eventually and curl in ceremony, and where Oblivia waited at the camel camp amid the drying soakages, to be cleansed for entering another country.

She whistled to them; tried to blow music from the flute, a swan tune that dances around the hills. It was old Bella Donna's swan-bone flute she had always worn around her neck just like the old woman did before she died. The flute was made from the wing bone of a Mute Swan and had been in Bella Donna's overseas family for generations. It could have been a thousand years old. Only the cygnet the girl had carried in the crossing had gently played with the bone in its beak, otherwise these days, the girl treated the small wing bone like a necklace, a *walku-walku* hanging over her clothes or over her back—the only belonging left from her home on the hull. She knew the sound was known to be sacred to swans. *You can't use something like this for fun.* Her music danced on among the din of winds rustling through the grass and ruby saltbush; and the swans flew down to rest among the arum lilies on an insect-infested marsh lake.

Miracles are funny things. The Harbor Master looked around for his miracles every day, but only saw the reality of living rough as guts with the herdspeople sipping tea in the rain with all those camels moving about them with a plague of stink beetles, and women and children slinging stones at the donkeys they said were *feraling* up the place. He said that those favorites of his the *Prosperity* and *Eternity* angels had lost their minds if they thought this was it. But what was life if you could not have hope? Maybe the angels had forgotten to bring his miracles in the way of first-class airline tickets so he and Rigoletto could fly off to the heavenly marble palace. Maybe they had lazed about and dropped the *bloomin'* requested miracles off at the wrong place. He blamed history for making him think these mongrelized depressing thoughts.

The swans welcomed into the country's song now spent days in the swamp while it never stopped raining. They danced the water, stirring it up, even at night with wings spread wide, lifting and dropping as they ran along the surface of the water, as though dancing in wing-exercising movements. In this way they communicate with each other—while the girl watches, knowing how she must read the country now as they do to follow them home. Then once more, the swans fly, and dance the rainy skies above the swampland, and return, skimming across the water to land.

This ceremony of swans continued, where together in mass blackness, they swam in circles. Reeds and water lilies become trampled. The swans pause, then lift themselves out of the water to stretch the white tipped wings that beat quicker, faster, as more circles are made with wings and tails splashing, and synchronizing heads dipping underwater, webbed feet kicking up water as they move, then the pulse is broken, and the huge body of swans breaks up and reforms.

Wings beat the water on one side, but when they switch sides, the beat of the other wing changes the tone of the music. They are almost prepared for flight. Oblivia follows them into the water and the swans observe her as though she is a newly hatched cygnet. Hour by hour, after dipping deep in the water to forage for weeds, they glide towards her to drop their offerings with little bugling sounds, until they can see that she is surrounded by floating weeds. She sleeps on the wetland among the grass at night, while the majority of swans continue the unbroken ceremony, but there are always swans resting beside her, necks curled over their backs and asleep, raindrops falling over feathers, heads nestled under wings.

. . . .

It was at night, after an icy wind had descended from out of nowhere in the middle of the day to push the temperature down to zero, and the ground had become frozen, that finally with the wind running along the ground like a spirit, the swans flew away from the leaf-littered water.

The night was alive with the sound of thousands of wings and noisy bugling when the swans were ready to go. From up high flying slowly, they were buffeted in the wind, looking down to the land stretched before them. Circling in the sky, the black cloud began diving, and swooping low over Oblivia, they pushed her to go.

Again the Gypsy Swans moved to be gone, but only if she was following them. There could be no going back through the face of a gale. No more circling in wind. It had to be now. Oblivia thought that she was in the sky, flying, and could not remember the journey. She and the swans were caught in the winds of a ghost net dragged forward by the spirits of the country. The long strands of hair flying among the swans, holding them together, and those long strands capturing her, made her fly too, close to the ground, across the country.

When dawn broke, the winds had disappeared, and the swans and the girl had arrived at another water-laden swamp land of water lilies and ant-covered grasses spilling in the air with a million flies and moths, and where only bird-infested coolibah trees dotted the landscape. It was land screaming with all of its life to the swans, *Welcome to our world.* All the spirits yelled to the girl to *eat the water lilies.* It was land where the swans would rest, then dance this country too, where the same frosty evening would take hold, before bringing the old wind people up, and again, the swans would have to leave, lifting off, circling and pulling the girl along, before the wind set the pace and blew them forward. The journey could only continue this way for the months it would take before the winds stopped coming at night.

Then the winds grow warmer and disappear in the atmosphere laden with dust. Without a breeze, the land becomes so still and lonely in the silence, you know that the spirits have left the skies. It does not rain anymore. The land dries. Every living thing leaves in the seemingly never-ending journeys that migrating creatures take, just like those herds of deer that Bella Donna remembered for marching flat out across vast deserts and forsaken tundra, to where the swamp had perished.

All now shared the spirit of the drought, like the skin-and-bone swans still trying to fly until all that was left were the empty bags of feathers that fall from the sky. Most did not fly again. Oblivia thought she could call the swans away and continue on. Her thoughts were full of their stories. She stood in the mirage and recited the poets' lines to the swans' beauty—Keats, Baudelaire, Neruda, Heaney—but their poetry stayed in the stillness where she stood, recalling McAuley's swan flying to quit the shore . . . *That headed its desire no more.*

There were stranded swans scattered all over the open bush, among the spinifex, caught on power lines, on the edges of dried-up soaks and inland lakes. If you were there you would have seen them everywhere. But the main flock struggled on, continued flying during the night.

In hotter skies, their wings beat faster in desperation until finally, they become completely disoriented. They lose faith in their journey. They lose each other. The remaining swans fly in every direction in search of the last drying waterholes. They stand on baked earth and hiss at the sky they cannot reach, then the time arrives when no more sound comes from their open beaks. The weak, feather-torn necks drop to the ground, and eventually, with wings spread they wait for the spirit flight.

EPILOGUE: THE SWAN COUNTRY

All the raspy-voice myna birds have come here, to this old swamp, where the ghost swans now dance the yellow dust song cycles of drought. Around and around the dry swamp they go with their webbed feet stomping up the earth in a cloud of dust, and all the bits and pieces of the past unraveled from parched soil.

A crew of myna birds foraging the waste toss useless trinkets this way and that. The prickly pear trees that had grown up, and all the rusted junk scattered across the bone-dry swamp, were the sort of places where only the myna birds lived.

From a safe distance, you could hear these birds swearing at the grass in throwback words of the traditional language for the country that was no longer spoken by any living human being on the Earth. While crowding the stillness the little linguists with yellow beaks sang songs about salvaging and saving things, rearranging sound in a jibber-jabbering loudness. All the old sounds were like machinery that rattled and shook while continuously being reworked into a junket of new pickings. In this mood—Well! You had to hear these soothsaying creatures creating glimpses of a new internationally dimensional language about global warming and changing climates for this land. Really listen hard to what they were saying.

One day, all that will be left of old languages will be what has been vaulted up in the brainwashed minds of myna birds. They listen to every single sound, but all that they will remember of the English language of these times, will be the most commonly used words you would have heard to try to defeat lies in this part of the world. Just short words like *Not true.*

Oblivia sat on the hull with her old Stranger swan dozing on her lap, and through the reddened haze of midday she gazed across the ravaged landscape that had once been a swamp. Trees that were long dead creaked sometimes, but after a while, only the dust-stained First Lady of whatnot spoke to the drought.

She was not surprised when the drought echoed her words in the North country's open space. Why wouldn't it speak back to her? It was a close relative who had always lived in the same house. They echoed each other: *Listen, Hard Up! No-hearted cruel thing! Lucky for me with no words left to come into my mouth that I got back.*

Having lived in the dry country for several thousands of years, the ghost of the drought woman had seen as many generations born and die and when those beautiful swans rose up one day to the skies and disappeared, it broke the water lilies and weed-covered lagoon, pulled itself out of its resting place, and filled the atmosphere from coastline to coastline of rotted tree stumps, flat plains, or solemn river bends across the country. Then it continued in the southerly direction that the birds had flown.

In its far-flung search for the swans, the slow-moving drought left behind smoldering ashes and soil baked by the dryness, and the whole country looking as though it had been turned over with a pick and flattened with a shovel. When the swans were found, the drought turned around on its hot heels and howling winds, while fires blew smoke across the lands on fast moving currents, and came back to the swamp.

Oblivia claimed that party time was over at dustbowl, and told the drought she was jack sick of it.

You got your old job back. I am giving this last black swan back to you, and to tell you the truth of the matter, I am done with carrying it around with me. You look after this swan, she ordered. *His name is Stranger.*

Thinks he doesn't belong in drought country. See if you can make more swans from this old pensioner.

The drought woman seared the atmosphere like ancient chastising aunties anywhere across the world from the back of beyond, and screeched: *Don't drop the swan.*

A *jamuka* whirlwind jumped in Oblivia's face from out of nowhere, swung through the door of the abandoned hull of the warship still sitting in the dry clay, and stood in front of the First Lady thing nursing that black swan on her lap. Oblivia always sensed the way old fingers work, that were now invisibly examining the swan she was holding next to her chest.

Feathers ruffle across the bird's back, on its breast, along its neck— in a manner suggesting all was not well, of things not being done good enough, of things not being taken care of properly. A pondering turbulence circled in the hull, where pots and pans were slammed, creating an impression of foul nature for as long as it went on being a din, while another sound coming up from underneath, a jarring song, was being sung with words that were vaguely familiar to her. Strange melodies abruptly begin and end, as heavier things of her old abandoned home are slammed on the floor.

A creepy voice full of dust said exactly what Oblivia already thought about the old wreckage of scraps: *There and there for one thing! Feathers properly wind damaged, frayed, singed and all that—can't walk.* The drought woman told her of all people, *You have to carry the swan.* Oblivia thought she was being put upon by some proper big dependency that was now far too much for her, and she snapped at the swan, *That was the big problem about being a survivor swan—outliving your lifespan, getting too fond of gobbling up the muck in the sewerage ponds of life, and not laying down and dying like the others!*

The old swan leader kept throwing back his head over his wing, and his long neck flowed like a snake resting over his black plumed body. His eye canvassing the landscape like a stranger trying to find the quickest way out of the place. The huge bird was never the same after losing his flock. It found being alone unbearable. It never stopped looking for the other swans. It was the kind of creature that belonged in old Banjo Paterson's poem about black swans, perpetually straining for the sound of wings beating, of *lagging mates in the rearward flying*. The old swan's red beak clicked twice, then as time passed, as it does but not for nothing, it clicked three times, or perhaps, twice again. The swan had some strange equation going on in its head. This continuous clicking of his beak exaggerated even greater numbers of swans he anticipated would return in his ghostly rendition of what life once was.

Oblivia sensed that he was waiting for the equivalent of one thousand years of swans, an immense flock, one that was capable of overcoming all adversity, but she told him straight in the eye to give up. *They have all gone now and finished up, and none are coming back.* Talk like this grieved the swan. It swooned and dropped its neck to the ground. To see the swan like this made the girl feel sick of the virus thing talking in her head, and telling her that she and the swan were joined as companions, of being both caught up in a *mal de mer* from the yellow waves of dust spreading over the land. The old swan would have to fight to win back control, to settle the dust, and return the rain. He was old now, but the girl tells him: *If I could fly high up in the atmosphere like you instead of swilling around in dust storms, I'd make it rain.*

But how in the hell would I know? Its belligerence was unbelievable. It was not interested in saving the world. Defying everything. How would she keep telling the swan another million times that the lake was gone, having to hold its beating heart closer to prevent its wings from spreading in a swim through the dust, treading it like water, and whispering the truth: *Deader than a doornail! Drier than Mars! Don't you see that it is all bulldust out there?*

Her mind was only a lonely mansion for the stories of extinction.

They say that the gift from God kept getting out of his grave after Warren Finch was finally buried in his country, beside the river of that time long ago when he first saw a swan. The story goes, *He wanted to give his promised wife some gift. Oh! Yes! He still had power of eating the brains of politicians. That was why there were no smart politicians in the country anymore. It was really true.*

It was just fate that brought him back. On the face of it, his body could have been anywhere else on the planet by now, if the semi-trailer's axle hadn't broken down on a bad day in the North, and the mad driver hadn't called it a day by dragging the heavy sassafras coffin out into the boiling heat that one last time, and telling Warren Finch, *I am going to bury you here you bastard, and be done with it, then I am going home.*

This might be the same story about some important person carrying a swan centuries ago, and it might be the same story in centuries to come when someone will carry a swan back to this ground where its story once lived. Well! Talk about acts of love. A place where white whirlwinds full of bits of dry grass and leaves blew in ashes from a tinder dry giant eucalypt, where a swan once flew in clouds of smoke from fire spreading through the bush land, with a small slither of bone in its beak.

It has been said by the few heartbroken-homes people, *mungkuji* left for that *kala* country, who come back from time to time to visit the swamp after Warren Finch had the place destroyed, and they had seen the girl-wife, First Lady of whatnot, Oblivion Ethyl(ene), that she always stayed like a *wulumbarra*, teenage girl. Well! She walks around the old dry swamp pretty regularly they say, and having seen her where there is a light moving over the marshes in the middle of the night, like a will-o'-the-wisp, they thought that they had heard her screaming, *kayi, kayi kala-wurru nganyi, your country is calling out for you,* which they described was just like listening to a sigh of a moth extending out over the landscape, or a whisper from the scrub ancestor catching a little stick falling from a dead tree, although nothing that could truly be heard—just a sensation of straining to hear something, which understandably, was how anyone should whisper on this spirit-broken place, from seeing their old homes scattered to kingdom come, of being where the Army owned everything, every centimeter of their traditional land, every line of buried song, stories, feelings, the sound of their voices, and every word spoken loudly on this place now.

There is a really big story of that ghost place: a really deadly love story about a girl who has a virus lover living in some lolly-pink prairie house in her brain—that made the world seem too large and jittery for her, and it stuffed up her relationships with her own people, and made her unsociable, but they say that she loved swans all the same. Poor old swanee. You can see swans sometimes, but not around this place. It is a bit too hot and dry here. *Jungku ngamba, burrangkunu-barri. We're sitting down in the heat now.* It's really just sand-mountain country. Like desert! Maybe *Bujimala*, the Rainbow Serpent, will start bringing in those cyclones and funneling sand mountains into the place. Swans might come back. Who knows what madness will be calling them in the end?

A NOTE ON SOURCES

Quotations embedded in the text of *The Swan Book* are from the following sources: Robert Adamson, "After William Blake" (page vii); A. B. Paterson, "Black Swans" (page 5); Bari Karoly, "Winter Diary," in *Leopard V: An Island of Sound*, London, Harvill, 2004 (page 22); W. B. Yeats, "The Wild Swans at Coole" (page 25); Richard Wagner, *Lohengrin*, Act 1 (page 25); John Shaw Neilson, "The Poor, Poor Country" (page 46); Seamus Heaney, "Postscript," in *The Spirit Level*, London, Faber, 1996 (page 68); James McAuley, "Canticle" in *Collected Poems 1936–1970*, Sydney, Angus & Robertson, 1971 (page 98); "Song (March 1936)," in *Tell Me the Truth About Love: Fifteen Poems by W. H. Auden*, London, Faber, 1994 (page 122); Paterson, "Black Swans" (page 142); David Hollands, *Owls, Frogmouths and Nightjars of Australia*, Melbourne, Bloomings Books, 2008 (page 149); *The Kalevala*, translated by John Martin Crawford, Cincinnati, The Robert Blake Company, 1910 (page 152); William Wordsworth, "An Evening Walk" (page 158); E. B. White, *The Trumpet of the Swan*, New York, HarperCollins, 1970 (page 177); W. B. Yeats, "Leda and the Swan" (page 183); Walt Whitman, "Song of Myself, 33" in *Leaves of Grass*, Book III (pages 196–197); Alfred Lord Tennyson, "The Dying Swan" (page 216); Douglas Stewart, from *Images from the Monaro: For David Campbell*, in *Letters Lifted into Poetry—Selected correspondence between*

David Campbell and Douglas Stewart 1946–1979, edited by Jonathan Persse, Canberra, National Library of Australia, 2006, page 226 (page 216); Shivananda Goswami, Baul song, in Mimlu Sen, *The Honey Gatherers*, London, Rider Books, 2010 (page 216); Mahmoud Darwish, "Now, When You Awaken, Remember," in *The Butterfly's Burden*, translated by Fady Joudah, Washington, Copper Canyon Press, 2007 (page 217); Heaney, "Postscript" (page 217); Leonard Cohen, "The Traitor" from *Recent Songs*, Columbia, 1979 (page 217); W. B. Yeats, "Nineteen Hundred and Nineteen" (page 238); Hank Williams, "Blue Eyes Crying in the Rain," song by Fred Rose, recorded 1951 (page 257); Charles Baudelaire, "The Swan, to Victor Hugo," translated by Roy Campbell, in *Poems of Baudelaire*, New York, Pantheon, 1952 (page 262); Ch'i-chi, "Stopping at Night at Hsiang-Yin," translated by Burton Watson, in *The Clouds Should Know Me By Now—Buddhist Poet Monks of China*, edited by Red Pine and Mike O'Connor, Boston, Wisdom Publications, 1990 (page 273); James McAuley, "Nocturnal," in *Collected Poems 1936–1970*, Sydney, Angus & Robertson, 1971 (page 295).

ACKNOWLEDGMENTS

I would like to express my gratitude and respect to my countryman Kevin Cairns, Chairman, and the Board of the Waanyi Nation Aboriginal Corporation, for your kind permission to use the *Waanyi Language Dictionary*.

Thank you to Aboriginal traditional landowners and elders of the Coorong, Ellen and Tom Trevorrow, for your generosity, friendship and guidance.

My gratitude to Professor Raoul Mulder, Department of Zoology, University of Melbourne, for research material on the behavior and ecology of black swans; Ray Chatto, Parks, Wildlife and Conservation, Northern Territory, for invaluable information about brolgas in Northern Australia; Bernard Blood, Curator of Lake Wendouree in Ballarat, for your wonderful story of swans returning to the lake after the drought.

I have watched swans in many places, and learnt the best place to see swans on the Liffy in Dublin from a truly amused interviewer at RTÉ Raidió na Gaeltachta. I learnt from Seamus Heaney's poem "Postscript," displayed at Dublin Airport, that if I wanted to see swans, I should look on the Flaggy Shore in County Clare. Many friends, colleagues, and family members very kindly and thoughtfully told stories, sent information, and swan presents, including music inspired by swans, or poetry, photos, pictures, objects, books, and life size statues of swans. Thank you Hal Wolton, Sudha Ray, Forrest Holder, Jeff Hulcombe, Ann Davis, Murrandoo Yanner, Evelyn Juers, Andreas Campomar, Benoit and Christine Gruter, Steve Morwell, Kevin Rowley, Pip McManas, my sister Robyn and brother-in-law Bill, sister-in-law Larissa, brother- and sister-in-law George and Barbara Sawenko, Francis Bray, Kim Scott, Terry Whitebeach, Stewart Blackhall, Robert Adamson, Dimitris Vardoulakis, Steve Morwell and Karina Menkhorst. Thank you to Nicholas Jose for showing me the nesting swans along the Torrens River, and Bruce Sims who went on visits with me to the Melbourne Zoo.

My daughter Tate traveled with me on a special trip to the Coorong, and also came on many walks along the Torrens River to see nesting swans and find the man who nurses a wild swan on his lap. My daughter Lily enthusiastically found images of swans that she sent to my computer in the middle of the night, and we had several special trips to the Melbourne Zoo where we visited a lone Mute Swan befriended by goldfish. Thank you to my stepson, Andre, for telling me the story about the swan that lost its way on a busy highway in Melbourne.

I am indebted to many people who offered encouragement and support, including my former colleagues at RMIT, and especially Antoni Jach. Thank you most sincerely to Evelyn Juers and Alice Grundy for reading the final manuscript and offering invaluable feedback.

I am very grateful for the support of Professor Wayne McKenna, the University of Western Sydney, and Professor Anthony Uhlmann and all of my colleagues in the Writing and Society Research Centre at the university.

Ivor Indyk, my publisher, editor and critic knows the work that went into this book. Thank you.

Thank you to my husband, Toly, for our trips to Lake Wendouree, and for many thoughtful references you found from the beginning of a journey that continued through many parts of the world.

Of course, all of those swans, and also our kelpies, Jessie then Ruby, and our cats, Pushkin then Luna, for the company.

This project has been assisted by the Australian Government through the Australia Council, its arts funding and advisory body.

ABOUT THE AUTHOR

Alexis Wright is a member of the Waanyi nation of the southern highlands of the Gulf of Carpentaria. Her books include *Grog War*, a study of alcohol abuse in Tennant Creek, and the novels *Plains of Promise* and *Carpentaria*, which won the Miles Franklin Literary Award, the Victorian and Queensland Premiers' Awards and the Australian Literature Society Gold Medal, and was published in the United States, UK, China, Italy, France, Spain and Poland. She is a distinguished fellow in the University of Western Sydney's Writing and Society Research Centre.